THE WORKER PRINCE

BRYAN THOMAS SCHMIDT

BOOK ONE IN THE DAVI RHII SAGA

Diminished Media group

John 3:30

PITTSFORD, MI

THE WORKER PRINCE

Copyright © 2011 by Bryan Thomas Schmidt.

All Rights Reserved.

Editing: Randy Streu, Jen Ambrose, Julie Maurer
Additional Editing: Paul Conant, Darlene Oakley
Proofing/Interior Layout: Bryan Thomas Schmidt, Jen Ambrose
Cover Art: Mitchell Bentley

Published by
Diminished Media Group
P.O. Box 52
Pittsford, MI 49271

www. diminishedmediagroup.com
www.bryanthomasschmidt.net

ISBN: 978-0-9840209-0-4

Printed in the United States of America

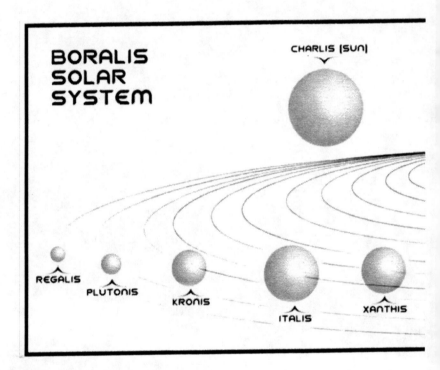

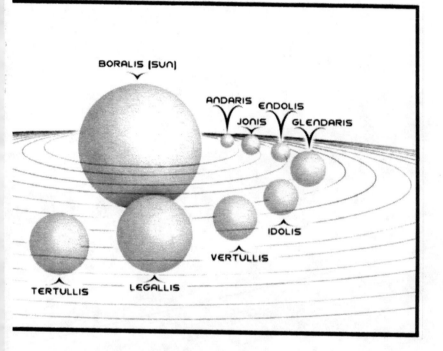

BORALIS (SUN)

ANDARIS   ENDOLIS

JONIS   GLENDARIS

IDOLIS

VERTULLIS

TERTULLIS   LEGALLIS

DEDICATION

For my parents

Who allowed me the freedom to dream

For Grandma Marie and Grandma Ethel

Whose support and gifts, along with their love,

made dreams possible

And For Lucy

ACKNOWLEDGEMENTS

The idea for this story came to me when I was a young, fifteen-year-old science fiction fan living in a small Kansas town where it sometimes felt like dreaming was the only way out. Over the years, I lost my original notes, but the idea in my head and the names Xalivar and Sol stayed with me.

It took me twenty-five years to start writing it and I wrote daily through some of the toughest trials I've experienced in my life. So this book you hold in your hand is a victory in many ways, and I'm very excited and proud of it and hope you'll enjoy it and share it with others.

Thanks go first to Lost Genre Guild for inspiring me to try writing for *Digital Dragon* and to T.W. Ambrose for encouraging me to write more space opera stories, and then agreeing to publish them. An abridged version of the prologue to this novel first appeared in *Digital Dragon*'s May 2010 issue.

Secondly, thanks go to fellow authors like Blake Charlton, Ken Scholes, Jay Lake, Mike Resnick, Leon Metz, Jason Sanford, Moses Siregar and Grace Bridges who have supported, encouraged and advised me time and time again, no matter how silly my questions were or how many times they'd heard them before. Special thanks to Blake and Grace for taking time to read and offer more specific advice to help me grow as a writer and to Mike Resnick for advice in figuring out this crazy business.

Thirdly, thanks to first readers and friends like Larry Thomson, Tim Pearse, Jeff Vaughn, David Melson, Todd Ward, Mike Wallace, Andrew Reeves, Chris Zylo Owens, and the members of the FCW-Basic Critique Group for actually seeming to enjoy my writing even in its roughest form and for giving me feedback which helped me to improve it greatly.

Fourthly, thanks to friends like Charlie Davidson, Aaron Zapata, Mark Dalbey, Nelson Jennings, and Greg Baerg, who, along with some of the guys above, have helped me escape from behind the desk and keyboard and laugh a little bit when I needed it.

Fifthly, thanks to Mitch Bentley for actually reading the book before creating the awesome cover art. And thanks to Randy Streu, Jen Ambrose, Paul Conant and Darlene Oakley for their editing and advice, the El Paso Writer's League for encouragement and fellowship, and Mike Wallace for the science of the Boralis solar system. Thanks also to Jeana Clark for the solar system map which brought it to life for me.

Thanks to you, the reader, for taking a chance on a new, unknown writer. I hope you like it enough to come back for more.

Thanks to God for making me in His image and giving me the talent and inspiration to do this and continually opening the doors. I look forward to seeing what's behind the next ones.

PROLOGUE

Sol climbed to the top of the rise and stared up at the twin suns as they climbed into the sky. Yellows and oranges faded under the increasing blue of oncoming daylight, leaving a red glow on the horizon.

For as long as he could remember, he'd started each day with an escape from the heavy, polluted air and the noise of people, factories and traffic. He'd hoped the peaceful, quiet sunrises would calm him as usual to face the day ahead, but today he had no sense of peace, and the silence of the city's edge drowned beneath the clamor within him.

My precious son! My God, don't forsake us now!

The wait had been interminable, punctured by endless prayers to God for a precious gift. Now they had to send him away—their Davi! Was there no justice in this universe?

He glanced at his chrono and sighed. *Wouldn't want to be late to serve the Borali Alliance!* After one last look at the twin suns, he turned and hurried back along the path toward Iraja and the starport stretched out on the horizon near the city's edge.

He labored more with each breath as heavy air filled his lungs. The depot occupied a strategic site at the center of the planet ensuring easy access from all regions. Ignoring the droning soundtrack of the city awakening, Sol timed in on the chrono and greeted Aron, his co-worker and lifelong friend.

"Regallis," Aron said, smiling.

"Regallis?" Sol asked. It seemed so far away—one of the outer planets in the system.

Aron nodded. "It's perfect. Good population, frequent tourists, fertile plants, peaceful, no pollution. Best of all, no slavery. Davi should find a very happy life there." Sol smiled at the thought. "I plotted coordinates for the capital. Figured it would give him the best chance."

Sol clapped Aron on the shoulder, as the idea blossomed. "Thank you, Aron. We knew we could count on you."

Aron, short and bulky, filled out the blue-green uniform jumpsuit, leather boots and tool belt both wore more fully than the thinner, taller Sol. They moved across a hangar toward their workstation, despite the deafening racket closing in around them—the constant hum of machinery, men raising their voices to be heard over it, the roaring of engines, and the staccato hammering of tools. The sounds, the chaos of starships in all states of repair and the smell of fuel and sweat combined to make the hangar a place most visitors preferred to avoid. Sol didn't even notice.

"What do you have left to do?" Aron asked as their eyes scanned the daily work assignments on their terminals.

"Test the seals and navigation system, replace injector. Then I need fuel." Sol sighed, ticking the tasks off on his fingers like always. There would be no time to work on the courier today.

"My friend at the fuel depot has left over military fuel cells. They almost never ask for them back. He volunteered some for the courier."

Sol beamed. If he'd ever had a brother, he hoped it would have been someone like Aron. "What did I do to deserve a friend like you?"

Aron shrugged. "Some people are luckier than others." Sol laughed at Aron's silly grin as they set to work on their assigned tasks.

As they commenced with their work, Sol stared through the hangar's transparent roof at the clear blue sky overhead. Through a break in the gray, polluted clouds, the clean purity of a blue sky contrasted with his daily existence. He and Lura had adored every moment since the birth of their son. Every giggle, smile, or sign of personality sent waves of warm amazement coursing through him. There was not any more precious gift than that of this little creature who'd come from their love.

Lord Xalivar's decree had taken the planet by storm. All first-born worker sons would be slaughtered for the gods. There were rumors that the crisis resulted from one of the High Lord Councilor's nightmares, but no one knew for sure. Xalivar didn't need a reason. Concerning the slaves, his word was law.

The gods! Gods our people don't even believe in would dare to take away our Davi! Sol and Lura desperately wondered what they could do to save their precious boy. After hours of discussion, they'd found a single choice.

The next morning, Sol had begun modifying the round, silver craft designed to carry supplies and papers between planets in the solar system. Being a mechanic at the depot put him in the perfect position. He installed a vacuum sealer and oxygen vents and hollowed out the carrier cavity to hold the cushion on which he would place their tiny son for the journey.

Sol enlisted Aron, who had access to navigation charts for the entire system, knowing together they could find a place where Davi would be found and cared for. The courier's sub-light drive would cut travel time to no more than a day to anywhere in the solar system.

Lura wouldn't eat and barely slept, sitting with Davi and refusing to leave him. At least Sol's work kept him occupied. He couldn't bear watching her suffer, and if he didn't act, Davi would be sacrificed with the others. Healing would come when they knew he was safe. Sol was, even now, working on a tracking device, which would send back a signal to the depot when the craft landed. They might never see Davi again, but at least they would know he'd escaped to a new life.

As the suns' rays warmed the space where he stood, it comforted Sol to know their baby boy would see the same suns wherever he wound up. Shadows crept away like their quat, Luci, who loved to sneak around feeling invisible with her arched back and long tail. Luci would miss the precious little one, too. Sol offered a silent prayer of thanks for the time they'd had with their precious son then turned back to his tasks.

✹✹✹

"LSP Squads are landing and moving toward our neighborhoods." A co-worker appeared beside Sol's worktable, his fearful eyes darting around like flies hovering over a corpse.

"We don't have much time," Sol said to Aron as the co-worker hurried off, and they abandoned the hulking barge to finish the courier.

Aron tested the navigation system, while Sol checked the seals. Less than thirty minutes later, the first reports of methodical killings came in— first-born males of all ages slaughtered by LSP squads moving from home to home.

"I hope Lura heard the news." Sol couldn't stand still.

"I'm sure everyone on the planet knows about it by now," Aron replied as both did their best to hurry without making any mistakes. "She's probably on her way here already."

Sol nodded, fighting the tension rising within. She would follow their plan and head for the depot with Davi. With his supervisors watching, he couldn't run home and warn her. He'd risk encountering the LSP squads, who tended to shoot first and ask questions later of citizens who interrupted them in action.

The supervisor was upon them within the hour. "There's no courier on your worksheets."

His gray jumpsuit bore not a blemish or wrinkle, unlike theirs which were covered with grease and grit. The stare from the green-scaled supervisor's disproportionally large orange eyes might have been intimidating if Sol hadn't already grown used to it. Tran hurried over waving the two lower arms extending from either side of his rounded, voluminous stomach. Two parallel arms extended out of his shoulders above them, one holding an electronic translator, which translated his words from his native Lhamor—a series of clicks and clacks—into the common used "Standard," the official language of the Alliance.

Sol's throat tightened, but Aron remained calm. "It's the courier for Estrela Industries, Tran," Aron said as he typed calculations into the navigation system's computer. "We got notification they've moved up the testing. It's for a top-secret program authorized by Lord Xalivar himself."

Sol and Aron had long ago devised the story about the courier belonging to an important defense contractor. They'd seen too many other workers killed just for failing to meet their quotas. Since couriers were a part of their regular routine, it was easy enough to excuse their working on it from time to time if anyone asked. Before now, no one had.

Tran mulled this over, staring at them as if he could read their minds. "It's almost done—a few minor adjustments." Sol used a wrench to finish checking bolts on the courier's hatch.

"Well, you can't leave today without finishing your assignments." Tran's eyes reddened with suspicion before he whirled and marched away.

At least they'd bought themselves time.

"If he goes to the manager—" Sol shuddered at the memory of past tortures for disobedience.

"He won't. He flinches at the mention of Xalivar's name," Aron reminded him, as they hurried back to work on the courier. Sol's breathing normalized again, and he hoped Lura was on her way there.

A clerk in a red jumpsuit appeared, handing Aron some parts for another project. As Aron signed the laser pad to acknowledge receipt, the co-worker looked at Sol. "They've started in your neighborhood. We just heard."

Sol and Aron exchanged a frightened glance as the co-worker slipped away. Sol's muscles tightened as his heartbeat climbed. He jumped at the communicator's beep, and then double clicked the talk button. "Station sixty-five."

"Your wife is in the lobby," the auto-bot receptionist responded. The line went dead.

Sol's shoulders descended as he turned to Aron. "Get the pod to Test Pad Seventeen-A. We'll meet you there." Aron nodded as Sol hurried toward the lobby.

Lura waited with Davi wrapped in a blanket, rocking him in her arms. She wore a simple white jumpsuit and tan leather shoes, her long brown hair flowing down her back. As it had for fifteen years, her beauty took his breath away. The most perfect human he'd ever met had chosen him. He felt like a leprechaun from an Old Earth fairy tale grasping a pot of gold.

Sol hugged Lura, seeing the fear in her eyes. "Come with me." Grabbing her arm, he steered her away from the four-armed auto-bot, which sat permanently affixed before a huge communications console. He tried to relax, knowing it was a mech but as they neared the door, Davi began crying.

"Is that a baby?" Tran's voice came from behind them, and they turned to see him frowning as he approached.

"It's our son," Lura commented, then put a hand over her mouth as Tran reached for a communicator on the wall.

The clerk who'd delivered supplies to Sol and Aron earlier entered at a run. "Tran, Station Thirty-Four has no fuel."

Tran stopped reaching for the communicator and turned to face him. "What do you mean they have no fuel?"

As Sol pushed Lura through the door, Tran whirled back around, scowling before the door slammed shut behind them.

Lura's tears flowed as they zigzagged through the chaotic hangar toward the test pads. They almost couldn't hear Davi crying above the din.

"I'm sorry..." Lura's hand shook as she clung to his arm.

"Let's hope Aron's got the courier ready." Sol tapped three numbers into a security door and it rose into a ceiling cavity with a loud, whooshing sound. He ushered her down a dimly lit corridor.

"I don't know if I can let him go," Lura said, as she had over and over since the decree's release.

"If we want our son to grow old, we have no choice, love." Sol's practiced emotional burying failed and his voice cracked as they moved past numbered doors toward Test Pad Seventeen-A.

The dark walls and floor of the narrow corridor absorbed what little light the reflector pads overhead provided. If Sol hadn't known the way, they would have progressed more slowly. They stopped before a gray door marked seventeen-A as Sol entered another key code into the security pad.

The door swung up and Sol rushed Lura and Davi onto the test pad, where Aron was busy double-checking the courier's navigation system.

Mounted on the launcher, the courier appeared bigger and taller than it actually was. Upon seeing it, Lura clutched Davi tightly to her chest.

"Lura, we must hurry!" Tiny daggers danced and sliced at the surface of Sol's pounding heart.

"I've got the coordinates programmed. And I borrowed fuel for the sub-light drive from Station Thirty-Four," Aron said and Sol winced. "It should take them a while before they miss it."

Sol climbed a small ladder and examined the courier one final time. "Tran's already been alerted. Why'd you do that?"

"There was no time to go anywhere else," Aron said, his face registering alarm.

Sol motioned to the courier. "Let's get the engines prepped. They don't know where we've gone."

Aron and Sol hurried about the final launch preparations as Lura held Davi and cried. After a few moments, Sol stepped down from the ladder to join her.

"He's going to Regallis, Lura. Aron checked it out himself. He'll be in the capital. Someone will give him a life we never could." Tears flowed as his hands caressed the feathery down atop his son's head.

"How can this be happening?" Lura said through her sobs. "We've waited so long for a child!"

Sol's arms wrapped around her, holding his family for the last time. "We have to have faith, Lura. God will protect him. It's time for him to go." He reached for Davi. Lura resisted a moment, then kissed Davi's forehead and surrendered.

His infant son lay so light in his arms—soft and warm. The eyes looked to him with total trust, but instead of cuddling with him as he wanted, Sol hugged the tiny boy to his chest and hurried up the ladder to the courier. Placing Davi in the molded cushion, he wrapped the safety straps around him, put the life support pad in place and turned it on. Its

LEDs lit up bright green. The note he'd written for whoever found Davi rested secure in the info pouch on the side wall. Everything was good to go.

Lura rushed up the ladder beside him. She removed her necklace his mother had given her before their joining ceremony and set it beside their son. Since the ceremony, Sol had never seen her without it. Tucking the family crest emblem inside the blanket where it couldn't float free and scratch their son, he reached for the hatch, bending down as he did to kiss Davi's head.

"Always remember we love you," he said, the last words his baby son heard before the hatch closed over him.

Sol clasped Lura's hand and led her down the steps. He nodded as Aron entered the launch code in the computer, and they all moved out of range to watch.

The courier's engines ignited, humming as they rose to full power in preparation for launch. The room vibrated around them as the courier's engines shot out twin columns of orange-red flame, rocking the pedestal upon which it rested, before launching into the sky on its journey to the edge of the solar system. Sol wrapped his arms around Lura as she collapsed against him, sobbing. Security forces arrived, surrounding them, and Sol glimpsed Tran's orange eyes peering in from the doorway.

CHAPTER ONE

"**W**hy do they keep staring at us?"

Farien nodded toward the dance floor and Davi realized all eyes in the Bar Electric were focused on them.

Sweet, fruity perfumes contrasted with stale sweat from gyrating bodies and afflicted Davi's nose. "I told you we looked good in our uniforms," he joked as his eyes turned back to his friends. After twenty-one years, he'd never gotten used to it.

Farien stood shorter by almost a foot than his friends, but made up for it in a bulk which filled out his gray uniform. The shiny gold buttons and shoulder insignia appeared ready to pop loose at any moment. Yao was the tallest, thinner than the others. A humanoid from the planet Tertullis, he could pass for human if it weren't for his dark orange tinted skin and purple eyes.

"I think they're staring at you, Prince Rhii," Yao said.

Like an old habit, Davi forced a grin and waved casually as the crowd watched his every move. "And to think I felt like just another cadet at the Academy." He looked around. "Serve-bot!"

Metal feet pounding on the floor mixed with flashing lights and the electronic tones of a recent pop hit blasting through speakers overhead. The automated robot waiter waded through the crowd toward their table. Other cadets, a few officers, and regular citizens were scattered between the dance floor and tables as identical serve-bots worked the room with drinks and food.

The serve-bot stopped at their table on one corner of the dance floor. "How may I serve you, sir?"

"A round of drinks for everyone, on me," Davi instructed.

"On you, sir?"

Davi chuckled. Bots' vocabularies were simple, practical, devoid of any colloquialisms or idioms. "Bill it to the Royal Palace, please."

"I'd need authorization—"

Davi sighed, holding up his ID. The serve-bot scanned it, its facial LEDs lighting up with recognition. "Right away, Prince Rhii."

Yao and Farien chuckled as the serve-bot hurried off.

"Come on, Davi, when are you going to drop the childhood nickname and use your real name, like a man. Xander sounds much more mature than Davi." Farien's face was serious, yet Davi couldn't help but laugh.

"It may be a nickname, but it's one I like."

Farien rolled his eyes. "Haven't you been teased enough over it? Don't you want to be taken seriously as an officer? We're not kids anymore. We're going into the world as adults."

"Let the man choose his own name, Farien. No one's asking you to change yours even though it sounds a little feminine." Yao and Davi exchanged a look and laughed.

Farien scowled. "It's not feminine! It's a family name!"

Davi and Yao just laughed harder as Farien took a huge gulp of his beer. After a moment, Yao turned serious again. "Now that you've made the public happy, how are you going to deal with the other crisis?"

"What other?" Farien asked.

Davi and his friends came to the bar to celebrate after graduating from the Military Academy. After receiving congratulations and hugs from their friends and family, the three headed off to Bar Electric to discuss their assignments and dream about the future awaiting them—which meant Davi had skipped out on the celebratory dinner planned in his honor at the Palace.

"They'll get over it." Davi dismissed it with a wave.

"When have they ever gotten over it?" Yao asked with a knowing look.

Davi sighed. "Yeah, they'll make me pay, won't they?" They both laughed. "Let's make it worth it then!"

"Vertullis," Farien muttered as he took another sip of his favorite off-world beer. "Babysitting slaves, great."

Davi chuckled and sipped his own beer. "What did you expect—some grand adventure?"

"No, but maybe at least an assignment on one of the distant planets with breathing apparatuses, aliens to encounter..."

"We can make our own excitement, as usual." Davi pointed at Farien and grinned. Farien rolled his eyes and they gave each other a high five.

"You'll be there supervising work crew guards. I get to be supervised by some newbie fresh out of the Academy like you," Farien complained, a glint in his eye. "Funny how your Uncle couldn't pull strings to get you a cushier assignment."

"You're a newbie fresh out of the Academy," Yao reminded him, shaking his head as Farien grinned.

"You can shut up, mister star-student-professor," Farien answered. Yao had received the most prestigious assignment of all.

His uncle's explanation was that Davi needed to earn the people's respect, not just count on it because of his uncle's favor or position. But Davi did sometimes wish his uncle would relax a bit and use his influence on his nephew's behalf. Xalivar was High Lord Counselor after all.

Seeing his friends staring, he brushed it off and reached over to squeeze Yao's shoulder. "Yes, congratulations, Yao, it's well deserved. The Presimion Academy is a fantastic school," Davi said, proud of his friend. The ceremony had consisted of the usual speeches, and faculty aggrandizing, but Yao had won recognition for his skills with math and sciences, and Davi had received the leadership medal.

"Instead of serving alongside newbies fresh out of the Academy, he gets to prepare pre-Academy newbies." Farien downed the last of his beer in one long sip and wiped his mouth on his sleeve. "Anyone else want another round?"

Davi and Yao shook their heads as Farien rambled toward the bar. "We'd better slow him down or there'll be trouble," Yao commented.

Davi motioned to the door as three girls they'd seen on the front row at the graduation ceremony entered. "I think the diversion we need just walked in." Yao turned toward the doorway as Davi stood, making his way toward the three beauties.

He approached their table and smiled. "You all look even better than you looked at the graduation."

"You remember us?" the dark-skinned one asked as the girls exchanged shy looks.

Davi laughed. "Of course. Who wouldn't notice you three?"

The music swelled as Davi asked their names and chatted with them a moment. Then he offered them his arms. They giggled as they stood, two of them looping their arms under his as he led them back toward the table.

"You know who I am, right?" he asked as they neared his table.

The girls all nodded. "Of course, Prince," the dark-skinned girl said.

Davi preferred the rare woman who didn't, but he nodded and bent to kiss her hand as they stopped at the table where Yao and Farien waited.

"Yao, these beautiful ladies are Bela, Jaqi, and Vivi," Davi said, helping the girls with their chairs. They smiled at Yao, ogling his uniform as Bela and Jaqi sat on either side of him. *What was it about Tertullians that seemed so irresistible to women?* Davi took the seat next to Jaqi. The sweet scents of the girls' perfumes teased his nose and made him smile. Vivi sat down on his left.

"We saw you at the graduation," Yao said, smiling awkwardly as Jaqi slid her arm into his.

"Congratulations on your awards," Jaqi said. "You must be very smart."

Yao blushed. Despite the fact they seemed drawn to him, he'd never been as comfortable around females as his two friends. "Well, I studied hard."

"Yao's being modest. He's been appointed a professor at Presimion Academy," Davi interjected.

The girls exchanged a look, then Jaqi scooted closer to Yao, resting her head on his shoulder. They'd worn beautiful gowns at the ceremony, but now their form-fitting pants and low cut blouses flattered their impressive figures. The most exotic of the three, Vivi's dark skin hinted at mixed racial blood, but Davi couldn't guess which.

Farien returned with another beer and smiled at Davi. "I see you two didn't waste any time."

"Meet Bela, Jaqi and Vivi," Davi said as Farien took a seat between Bela and Jaqi.

"So pleased to make your acquaintance," Farien said, as he put his arm around Bela. She smiled, snuggling up to him.

"Are you going to be a professor, too?" Bela asked.

Farien grimaced as Davi and Yao stifled laughs. "I'll be serving on Vertullis, making sure our worker population continues to produce at proper capacity." It came out with such bravado that Davi and Yao couldn't hold back.

"Oh, Vertullis. I always wanted to visit another planet," Bela said, looking impressed as Farien shot his guffawing friends an annoyed look.

"What about you, Prince Rhii?" Vivi smiled at Davi. Her accent was Southern with slow and precise words. He wondered why her family hadn't moved to another system with the others.

"Call him 'Davi.' He doesn't like formality." Ignoring sharp looks from Yao and Davi, he pressed on: "Our fearless leader will be leading the workers as well," Farien said, ignoring the fact that Davi would be his supervisor.

"Oh," Vivi said, her eyes sparkling. "I always wondered what the workers are like. I've never met one."

"Me neither," Davi chuckled. "We failed to offer you ladies libations. What can we get for you?"

As Davi turned to search for the nearest serve-bot, a group appeared in the doorway—Bordox and three of his cronies. A huge, hulking cadet with light yellow skin and a dark beard, he sneered as he spotted them, then led the way to a corner table across the dance floor. Davi frowned. He hadn't seen Bordox at Bar Electric in months. *Why today?*

His mind flashed back to an incident at the Academy after he'd beaten Bordox on the flight simulators. Bordox let slip about a rumor claiming the "royal prince's blood wasn't so royal"—an attempt to rile Davi up and create a distraction.

Davi and his friends had demanded to know what Bordox meant.

"Who'd have known you're so fond of folk stories, Bordox."

"If it's a folk tale, I guess you're the folk lore prince," Bordox cracked. "A starport rumor about a baby who arrived in a courier craft from the stars and landed near the palace, adopted by a lonely princess with no offspring." Then he and his friends had laughed loudly.

Farien had wanted to tackle him, but Yao and Davi managed to hold him off. It took their professor threatening to charge Bordox with impugning the reputation of another cadet without cause to end the incident, but Bordox had never really let it go. From that day forward, he and Davi became fierce rivals at everything. Bordox was not as smart or coordinated, and far less likable than Davi, but they each had their crowd and were very competitive. Since the incident, each set his goals of achievement at a level designed to ensure he could better himself over the other.

Davi sipped his beer and reached down to finger the necklace he'd worn around his neck since childhood. His mother had given it to him, insisting he never take it off, even though the symbolism of it was lost on him. He'd never gotten around to asking her about it, but he'd never seen another like it, and he knew many regarded it as a symbol of his Royal heritage.

"Would you like to dance?" Vivi's question broke him out of his reverie. He spotted Farien and Bela out on the dance floor, and Yao had taken Jaqi's hand and was leading her there.

Davi stood and extended his hand to Vivi. "Absolutely. I thought you'd never ask!" Vivi laughed and took his hand as he led her to an open spot on the floor.

Davi hadn't danced long when Bordox and his friends came onto the dance floor. Not finding immediate partners of their own, they began tapping the shoulders of other men, looking menacing if they showed any reluctance. Then, paired with the former partners of the frightened men, they maneuvered themselves to the area surrounding Davi, Farien and Yao.

Davi and his friends danced as if nothing mattered until the song ended, then Bordox smiled and leaned close to Davi. "So, folkloric prince, what assignment did you draw?"

"It's nothing as glamorous as yours," Davi replied, doing his best to ignore him. The music started again and Davi and Vivi resumed dancing.

"Lieutenant of the Lord's Special Police," Bordox responded with pride. The LSP was indeed a respectable assignment. Only the cadets deemed most loyal and sure to serve with lifelong honor at the High Lord's beck and call would ever be chosen. It didn't hurt that Bordox's father, Lord Obed, ran the LSP.

"We're going to Vertullis to keep the workers in line," Farien said, breaking the lull.

"Glorified babysitters. I wondered if they'd let you three do any real work," Bordox replied as he swung his reluctant partner around them. The girl seemed too afraid to do anything but try and keep up.

"Yao will be teaching math and sciences at Presimion Academy," Davi responded.

Bordox's smugness faded a moment, before he recovered. "Presimion, well, at least one of you was smart enough to draw a real assignment."

Davi wanted to reply but Yao and Farien maneuvered their dates in between him and Bordox. He did his best to maintain his composure, but Bordox had gotten him fired up.

"Are you hungry?" Vivi asked as the song ended.

Davi smiled. Not many girls would be so direct knowing who he was. He liked this girl. "Yes, I am, as a matter of fact. Would you like to order something?" She smiled, then nodded and he led her back to their table. Farien and Yao followed with the others.

As he helped Jaqi into her chair, Yao leaned toward him. "Don't let him get to you. It's all petty jealousy. You've always bested him at every challenge."

Yao's eyes met Davi's as Yao slid into the opposite seat. Davi smiled, calming the raging storm within. It was true. Despite the constant challenges, Davi had always come out ahead. Bordox was still looking for an opportunity to prove himself better. Davi sighed, as he glanced over the menu. Perhaps Bordox's LSP assignment would keep him off their backs. At least Bordox could feel superior for the moment, if he wanted. He didn't have to know that Davi would have turned down the LSP if he'd been asked. It held little interest for him.

Davi saw Bordox motion for a serve-bot, as he and his friends requisitioned a nearby table. They threatened the occupants, who stood and hurried for the door, while Bordox and his friends helped themselves to the food and drinks the party left behind.

Davi glanced over to where the bar manager and Bouncer-bot stood watching the events unfold. "Aren't they going to do anything about it?"

"His father's head of the LSP, remember?" Yao said. "They can pull bar licenses whenever they want."

Davi started to stand but Farien reached over and pulled him back down into his seat. Both of his friends shot him warning looks.

"Maybe you ladies would like to find somewhere more romantic to dine?" Davi suggested.

Their dates smiled. "That would be nice," Vivi said.

Davi and his friends stood, taking the ladies by the elbows and leading them toward the exit.

As they waited beside the air taxi post outside, Davi glanced through the Bar's window and realized that Bordox and his friends had abandoned the requisitioned table. The blue air taxi arrived and Davi's group climbed onto the two benches behind the cab-bot driver. As the door shut, Bordox and his friends appeared at the taxi stand, waiting impatiently for another taxi.

"He never gives up, does he?" Farien asked.

"Let's make ourselves hard to follow," Davi replied. "Taxi, take us to the starport please."

"Of course, sir," the cab-bot whirled around and steered the auto taxi into the flow of traffic.

Their dates' faces lit up. "The starport, really?" Jaqi said.

"We're gonna take a little tour before we head to the restaurant," Yao said.

The cab-bot consisted of a torso with two arms and a head, on which lights lit up when it talked, attached to a seat facing the control panel at the front of the air taxi. Created to take over simple tasks like answering phones or loading cargo, newer bots now performed even more complicated tasks, including some trusted with the safety of humans.

Davi relaxed as the air taxi turned between a row of buildings and rose up onto the main artery running through Legon, the capital city. While Davi and the others enjoyed the ride, chatting with their dates, the auto taxi executed a few more twists and turns on the transportation corridor before turning onto an off ramp marked with signs for the starport.

"You're not gonna fly us to some remote star restaurant, are you?" Bela asked.

"Not really. We're just trying to lose our friends," Davi answered as the air taxi threw him forward against the safety bar. There was another bump as something hit them from behind.

They all whirled around to see another air taxi with the cab-bot disabled. Bordox was at the wheel.

"You've got to be kidding me," Yao muttered.

Davi turned to the cab-bot. "Please outrun that taxi and take us to the north shore."

The cab-bot's facial LEDs lit up in the shape of a smile. "I am attempting to adjust our velocity, sir."

The taxi jerked as Bordox rammed them again. Davi leapt over the safety bar and pulled the manual override lever, pushing the cab-bot to one side and placing himself at the controls.

"Do you know how to drive this?" Vivi said, alarmed.

"Davi's the top pilot in our class," Farien said and smiled.

"Let's see what this thing is made of." Davi began pushing buttons, bringing the air taxi to a much faster speed.

Bordox launched another run at them, but Davi braked, and then slid in behind him, taking an onramp back up onto the air highway overhead. As he turned onto the onramp, Bordox's frustrated face appeared in the rearview mirror. Bordox's bulky body looked ridiculous behind the wheel of the air taxi. His dark beard couldn't hide his aggravation as he struggled to turn the air taxi around.

As they merged into traffic, Davi couldn't see Bordox behind them.

"Maybe we lost him," Bela said.

"I doubt it," Yao said as he and Davi exchanged looks.

In a moment, Davi saw another taxi racing up from behind. "Here he comes."

Davi weaved their taxi in and out traffic, trying to keep Bordox at a distance, but the other air taxi continued to close on them.

"What's his problem anyway? Why won't he leave us alone?" Vivi said, her voice shaking.

"It's a long story," Davi replied, braking and bringing their taxi in behind the other. "Who'd have thought he'd fall for that twice?"

Yao and Farien laughed as Bordox hit the brakes, forcing Davi to dodge and bringing them side by side.

Bordox looked over—-his face a mask of bitter resentment. His friends stared at them with sneers of contempt. Bordox and Davi wove their air taxis through traffic, each trying to keep the other at bay.

"We've gotta get away from this traffic before someone gets hurt—" Davi was silenced by a jolt as Bordox slid his air taxi in behind theirs and slammed into them again. The windows around them cracked loudly as veins creeped out in all directions covering the panes.

"Better get us down to the lower airways," Yao suggested, "before the windows disintegrate."

Davi nodded and dove onto the nearest off ramp. Bordox followed. Now, buildings surrounded them, but the traffic had thinned. A group of barges plodded along ahead of them. He aimed the air taxi straight at the rear of one of them and accelerated.

"Do you know what you're doing?" Yao inquired as he leaned over the safety bar close to Davi's ear.

"Just secure everybody back there, okay? I have an idea." Davi said.

"May the gods help us," Yao answered, shaking his head. "You ladies might want to get into those safety harnesses now," he said, motioning to the girls, as he and Farien began strapping themselves in. As the girls grabbed for their harnesses, and Yao and Farien turned to help secure and adjust them, Bordox rammed them again from behind.

The windows in both vehicles shattered, glass exploding around them with a deafening crash. The girls screamed. The wind blew against their faces, strengthened by their airspeed and pressing them back against the seats.

"Hold on," Davi said. Slowing a bit as they approached the rear barge, he suddenly accelerated and pulled the air taxi up over the top of the barge.

Alarms blared from the speakers overhead. "Warning. Violation!" a computer voice screamed.

"Is this even safe?" Jaqi screeched.

"He knows what he's doing," Farien assured her.

Bordox's air taxi cut across the incoming traffic lanes, zipping around the barge as Davi slipped between the two barges. In seconds, Bordox had squeezed in behind them again.

"I thought Bordox sucked at flying?"

"I guess he's been practicing," Farien said with a shrug.

Davi saw the first barge enter an intersection as Bordox accelerated toward them, and smiled. He had a plan. When the air taxi's front passed the corner, Davi made a sharp turn, whipping everyone to one side and landed safely on a corridor to the side.

Bordox's air taxi accelerated straight into the back of the second barge. Bordox and his friends looked shaken and confused, covered with blue Daken feathers from the barge's shipment of the frightened, squawking birds.

Davi and his friends exchanged high fives, laughing. "That ought to hold him for a while."

They watched as Bordox struggled to stand despite the slippery feathers all around him. His eyes met Davi's in a hateful stare barely visible amidst the feathers dangling from the sweat on his face.

"He doesn't look much different than he did before," Farien joked. Yao and Davi laughed.

"Can we please get out now?" Vivi asked, trembling.

"Just a few more minutes. We know a great place on the north shore you ladies will love," Davi said, relieved as he accelerated again and turned onto another corridor.

❋❋❋

The High Lord Councilor's Palace stood atop a rise at the center of Legon. An imposing complex of white buildings of various shapes and sizes, it offered an unobstructed view of the entire city. When Davi arrived, he headed straight for his suite.

"Your uncle is not very happy with you for skipping your celebratory dinner." His mother's voice stopped him outside the lift. He turned as Miri approached him. She wore a beautiful evening gown, with light skin and light blue eyes which radiated warmth. Davi saw the disappointment in her frown.

Raised by his Uncle Xalivar to act like an officer, Davi had been told time and again he'd command great armies. Like all sons of High Lords, he'd followed the prescribed course of schooling and training, excelling in almost all of it. He'd risen to and stayed at the top of his class in every subject and every training regimen, such that any failure in discipline had become unacceptable to his mother and uncle.

"I'm sorry, mother. Yao, Farien and I wanted to celebrate in our own way." Davi wondered what it was like to be an ordinary citizen of the Borali Alliance. Did they have more fun than he did? It's not that Davi didn't appreciate all the advantages his life had brought him, but always having to meet others' constant demands wearied him.

"The Vertullian ambassador was anxious to meet you. She might be very helpful to you in your new assignment," Miri responded, her voice softening from the previous scolding tone. He knew she adored him too much to stay mad at him for long, and the adoration was mutual.

"Is she staying at the palace? Perhaps I could meet her over breakfast," Davi said, as he leaned in and kissed her cheek.

"If you survive your uncle's wrath," she said, smiling.

Davi shot her a sheepish grin. "Maybe that can wait until morning, too."

"I hardly think so," said Xalivar's top aide, Manaen, from behind them. "Your uncle is requesting your presence in the throne room."

Davi and Miri turned to see Manaen standing in a nearby doorway. A member of Idolis' second most popular race, the Andorians, Manaen was tall and thin with blue skin and red eyes. "Of course," Miri said, motioning to Davi to go with Manaen. Davi turned with a sigh and followed Manaen back through the door. Miri followed close behind.

They stopped in a corridor. Each wall bore the shield of the Borali Alliance in embossed gold, a large door rose before them. They stepped inside the throne room. The throne stood centered on a raised dais set a few feet out from the far wall. A series of support pillars lined the sides of the long room with space in between for seating guests. The throne and the floor featured the same seal they'd seen in the corridor outside. As many times as he'd been here, Davi still found it impressive.

The High Lord Councilor waited beside a large window, staring out at the city, dressed in a gold robe with a white collar and cuffs. In the center by his neck lay the jewel known as the Lord's eye. Shorter than Davi but taller than Miri, he had a dark beard. Manaen stopped in the doorway, awaiting instructions as Miri and Davi moved into the room, a long, red carpet cushioning their steps. The carpet ran in a rectangular line to each corner then continued around pillars lining each side and ended behind the throne—creating a complete square frame around the room.

Xalivar turned to face them. Instead of angry, he looked tired. He motioned to Manaen. "That will be all, Manaen."

Manaen offered the expected salute with crossed fingers over a fist, then turned and exited, the door sliding shut behind him.

"The Vertullian ambassador was most disappointed she didn't get to meet you."

"So mother explained. I'm sorry uncle. Perhaps over breakfast—"

"I decide the agenda in my palace, Xander. Not your mother, or you," Xalivar responded. The anger in his tone surprised Davi.

Davi's given name was Xander Rhii, son of Princess Miri Rhii, sister to Lord Xalivar, the High Lord Councilor of the Borali Alliance, but, for some reason, his mother had always called him Davi. He'd grown quite fond of the nickname himself. All the men in the line had names beginning with X—Xander, Xalivar, Xerses, Xonas—but Davi stood apart, making him unique. Davi had never been one to follow the crowd. In the court of the High Lords, it was hard to be unique.

While Lord Xalivar was a revered figure, both loved and feared by many throughout the Alliance, to Davi he had always been his kind, but sometimes stern uncle. It wasn't often their conversations reached the present intensity.

"You would do well to show proper respect to those who can help your advancement."

"Why is he being sent to oversee workers anyway?" Miri interjected. "It's a waste of his skills." She surprised Davi with the anger on her face. He hadn't realized she was against his assignment.

"I cannot afford to play favorites. He has to work his way up like everyone else, if we want to take him seriously and accord him the proper respect," Xalivar replied, softening somewhat.

"He is not like everyone else," Miri said.

"He is not yet a Lord, sister. Don't forget it."

"He will be," Miri held firm.

Xalivar looked at her as if trying to understand her concern. "You've never been to Vertullis. Service there is a respected part of officer training. Most graduates spend some of their career there," he said. "Why are you so fearful of it?"

Davi chuckled as he watched them. No matter what, they would always be brother and sister. His mother had always been gentle and soft with him, while Xalivar had been tougher and more serious, although he'd never lived up to his reputation among the other cadets as ruthless and cold. At least not with Davi. Many rumors continued to float around about his uncle, but Davi had always found them hard to believe.

"I welcome the assignment, mother," he said, hoping to put her at ease.

"You see? The boy knows something about honor and responsibility," Xalivar said with pride.

"He is no longer a boy," Miri said.

"All the more reason to not treat him as such," Xalivar chastised her. Miri wilted. They all knew it was an argument she could not win.

"I will do my best to serve with distinction befitting our family," Davi said, hoping he could meet their expectations.

"We have no doubt you will. Perhaps you will also remember that gallivanting with your young friends—and using auto taxis for playthings; that—is not the proper behavior of an officer, especially a prince." Davi looked down, embarrassed. Somehow his uncle always seemed to know everything. "You are quite lucky no citizens were hurt."

"Bordox was provoking us," Davi said.

"There are better ways to deal with your petty rivalries," Xalivar said, shooting Davi a stern look which stopped him from responding further.

"What happened?" Miri asked.

"Nothing to concern yourself with. Two auto taxis needing repair. A few soiled uniforms," Xalivar explained.

"None of them ours," Davi added with a smile. Xalivar's eyes narrowed as he frowned at Davi.

"You'll be having breakfast with the ambassador at nine sharp. Don't be late," Xalivar said.

Davi suppressed a smile at the concession. "Yes, High Lord

Councilor." He formed a fist and placed his other hand with crossed fingers on top. Xalivar gave a slight nod at the salute as Davi turned and marched toward the door.

"Congratulations on your awards today, Xander. We are very pleased," Xalivar said as Davi waited for the door to open.

"Thank you," he responded as the door slid into the ceiling. Davi turned back to the corridor, his face beaming with pride, and marched out of the room.

***

Xalivar watched his nephew go, pride swelling within. His sister's son was the closest thing he had to a son of his own, his only heir. Up until the day's events, everything had been proceeding according to his plans. Xalivar had long known he would train Davi as his successor, but the rebellious streak Davi had demonstrated today concerned him. He would have to keep a closer eye on things to ensure that kind of behavior didn't continue.

Miri kept watching him as the door slid shut behind Davi. "I need him near me," she said.

"I can arrange accommodations for you on Vertullis if you wish," Xalivar said. Miri frowned. "It's the planet nearest to us. He will be well protected by my officers. If he is to be my heir, he must know about all aspects of the Alliance. And he must be able to gain respect on his own, not by relying on my power."

"He has a kind spirit," Miri said.

"Kindness is not a luxury rulers can easily afford," Xalivar said. Miri was too soft. "Perhaps this experience will disavow him of his fantasies. He could use a dose of reality."

Miri blanched, turning defensive. "He's not like you," Miri said. "He will never delight in their oppression."

Xalivar shrugged with disinterest. His failure to mold Davi into his own image was something she treasured rubbing in Xalivar's face. Miri was one of the few he would ever allow to be so direct with him. "Delight is not required, only recognition of the way things need to be."

Miri sighed and walked toward the door. Xalivar suspected his sister hoped her son would never be the kind of emperor he was. There had been many conquerors in the line preceding him, but Xalivar took special pride in his reputation as ruthless and arrogant. Except for Miri and Davi, no one dared question him on even the most routine of matters, and Xalivar liked it that way.

There would be no place for weakness in running an Alliance. One had to be firm and decisive, and given time, it would come as easily to Davi as it had to him. With the endorsement of the Council of Lords, Xalivar's family had led the Borali Alliance for generations. It ran in their blood.

Xalivar turned back toward his private suite, ready for some rest after a trying day. Davi would have to get used to that too. The days of a ruler were full and demanding. Perhaps the assignment he was about to undertake would serve Davi well. He'd never understood his sister's insistence on using the nickname which even Davi himself seemed to prefer. The men in his line all had honorable names and Xander was quite respectable. He sighed. That too would have to change.

✳✳✳

At breakfast the following morning, Davi joined Miri, Xalivar, and other distinguished guests. He sat next to Sinaia Quall, the Borali Alliance's Ambassador to Vertullis—who was less of a diplomat and more of an overseer in this case. A short, dark woman with her black hair in a bun, she chatted with him about the situation there, filling him in on the background and details about the planet he didn't already know. In the end, Davi found her charming and informative and appreciated the opportunity to get to know an important official on whom he could call if the need arose. Sinaia in turn assured him she would look after his well-being during his assignment there.

After he excused himself, Miri took him aside. His shuttle would depart in a few hours and he knew she wanted some mother-son time before he left. As they arrived in her chambers, she seemed overwhelmed with sadness.

"Mother, I'm worried about you," he said, noticing for the first time new lines around her eyes.

"You're worried about me? I think I'm the one who should be worried," Miri said, refusing to meet his gaze.

"Why? I graduated near the top of my class. I have been through years of training preparing for this. Uncle has a lot of people looking out for me. I know I will make you proud."

Miri smiled. "You've never done anything but make me proud, Davi. You know I adore you."

Davi put his arm around her shoulders and pulled her close. "And I you."

She tousled his hair. "I wish your assignment wasn't so far away. I like you close by."

"It's one planet away. Come and visit any time."

"Of course, I will." She smiled. "Do you have it?"

Davi gave her an inquisitive look. "What, mother? The necklace?" She nodded as he pulled the chain over his collar and let it dangle on his chest. The necklace was round and silver colored with a blue-green crest at its center. The four sections of the crest bore distinct images: laborers, soldiers, farmers and priests.

"Perhaps you could leave it with me for safe keeping—a remembrance of my son to comfort me in your absence," she said, stroking it.

"You know how much it's always meant to me. It's one of the first gifts you ever gave me."

"I know, son, but so many things can happen out in the field. If you lost it..."

"I won't lose it, mother." She'd always been very protective of the neck-lace, but she'd never before asked him to give it up. Davi was puzzled by the sudden change, increasing his worry.

"I would feel better if I had it with me," she said.

"But you've always insisted I wear it. I don't understand. Are you so worried I won't come back?" Davi looked into her eyes, wishing he could find the words to ease her worry.

Miri rushed into his arms, embracing him. "Never say that! I can't bear it!" She seemed close to tears.

"I'm sorry, mother. It was supposed to be a joke!" Davi held her, trying to reassure her.

"Never joke about such things," she said with tenderness. "I love you, son."

"I love you, too, mother." He would miss these times with her when they were apart. Tears flowed from her eyes. Davi stood there and held her a while, the necklace pressed against his chest by her embrace.

✷✷✷

Davi and Farien arrived at the starport a few hours later, their gray uniforms neatly pressed, and shook hands with Yao. He'd shared so many fun times with his friends. He'd miss having them around. After a few moments, he pulled Yao aside. "I need you to look after mother for me."

"Of course. Anything I can do? Is she upset because you're leaving?"

Davi sighed, raising his hands in the air. "Yes. More than I expected. She seems as weak and frail as I've ever seen her. I'm not sure why."

"She's always adored you and kept you close. I'm sure this is hard for her," Yao said.

"It's hard for me as well, but she's really broken up about it. She even asked me to leave the necklace with her for safe keeping."

Yao's eyes widened. "The one she's always been after you to wear? Did she have a bad dream about something happening to you?"

"I don't know. She wouldn't say. Just check on her for me, will you?" Their eyes met and Davi saw recognition of his depth of concern. His hand reached down to touch the crest where it rested beneath his uniform.

"Every day, if you want," Yao replied.

Davi clapped him on the shoulder. "I don't think it's necessary, but I trust your judgment." Yao smiled and they embraced.

"You take care out there, okay? I want to hear all about your adventures," Yao teased.

"Oh yeah, and you make sure those future cadets are up to standards, all right?"

Yao laughed. "I'll be as hard on them as I was on you two." He twisted his face into a fierce expression.

"Do us a favor and be harder on them, okay?" Davi said with a laugh. He glanced over at Farien, who waited impatiently by the shuttle ramp. They both laughed and shook hands one last time.

"Let's get this show rolling," Farien said, glancing at his watch. "Let the adventure begin!" He clapped them both on the back. Yao shook Farien's hand before he and Davi boarded the shuttle.

As the shuttle pilots prepared for launch, the engines hummed and ignited. Contrasting with the shuttle's white exterior, the interior was light gray. The cockpit held two black chairs facing a transparent blast shield, surrounded by controls. It was separated by a bulkhead from the passenger compartment which contained four rows of seats—two lining each exterior wall and two back to back down the center. Each had its own safety harness. The sole decoration was a large Borali Alliance emblem centered above the seats on the ceiling.

Davi strapped on his safety harness and began mentally reviewing what he knew about Vertullis and his new assignment. From what he'd been told the planet's capital city, Iraja was far from impressive when compared with Legon, but Iraja was also one of the Borali Alliance's major starports and the key shipping and receiving point for agricultural products in the solar system. His heart raced in his chest. He'd never been off planet before.

The thirteen planets in the star system all varied in size and shape, the outermost and innermost planets being the smallest. Three of the larger planets had several moons. Vertullis had two. While Vertullis, Tertullis and Legallis alone had atmospheres suitable for human life, due to Borali scientists' determination and skill with terraforming, all but one of the system's planets had been inhabited, though some with populations consisting only of a few workers and military personnel. The planets revolved around the two suns, Boralis and Charlis, in an unusual orbital pattern due to the effect of the twin gravities. Because of the limitations in terraforming science, the four planets nearest to the suns had been surrendered as viable habitats for humans. Of the thirteen planets, Vertullis was the sole planet which had a surface containing fifty percent forest, and it had one other distinction. It remained the only planet in the solar system whose native citizens weren't free.

Slavery was a subject on which he'd never formed much of an opinion. He valued his own freedom, and human beings, to him, had always seemed deserving of such freedom. But he had never met a

Vertullian. He had no idea what they would be like. Perhaps after spending time there, he would understand better. They might be great troublemakers, lazy, even subhuman as he'd been told. Throughout history, they'd been the enemies of his people, but beyond that he decided it would be best to wait and see. Regardless of what he thought of them, Davi determined to treat them with fairness and dignity. He had read stories of abuse by past supervisors and guards, and he would not allow such things on his watch.

The shuttle accelerated, forcing him back against his seat. He hadn't been on a shuttle since his early days at the Academy, and even though he'd flown VS28 starfighters in training, he'd never been out of Legallis' planetspace. Whatever else happened, he figured it would be an interesting challenge.

As twinkling stars filled the windows and the shuttle settled into its flight path, Farien snored beside him. Chuckling to himself, Davi leaned back and relaxed, glancing out at the black void of space. The blue tinged globe he'd always consider home receded rapidly as the shuttle broke orbit and arced off away from its surface. He'd never seen the planet from space before. It was far more spectacular than any of the pictures he'd seen. A new phase of life was beginning. He'd been dreaming of this for a very long time.

CHAPTER TWO

*T*here *has to be something better than this! Two weeks behind a desk shuffling papers is not what I had in mind!*

Since arriving on Vertullis, Davi's only excuse to get out of his office had been occasional forays to check on operations. His days consisted of report after report from subordinates and superiors: requests for upped production times, write-ups on incidents involving workers or fellow soldiers, etc. Despite his responsibility for numerous squads of men supervising farm workers in the region south of Iraja, his big adventure turned out to be anything but.

Never had Davi so wanted to blast off and e-post to his Uncle begging him to pull strings and get him out of there! He cringed at the thought of how his uncle might respond. Xalivar never responded well to any sign of weakness. Davi's head hurt from thinking about it all. *Either my head's going to explode or I'm going crazy.* The communicator beeped. A major from Administration invited him on a tour to show him around. *Finally, a chance to get out of this office!*

He met Major Isak Zylo at the shuttle port near the administrative offices
around nine the next morning. As Davi appeared, Zylo smiled and extended his hand.

"Pleasure to see you again, Captain." Short like with broad shoulders, Zylo's light skin seemed bright against the grayness of his uniform. His black hair and beard were both sleek and well groomed.

"Please, call me Davi. I think there's no need for such formalities among officers when they're alone," Davi said.

"Indeed. Call me Isak. Shall we be off?" Zylo led him aboard the shuttle. Davi nodded as the doors closed.

Unlike the shuttles Davi had flown in, this shuttle had been designed for in-atmosphere tours like theirs. Except for the thin framework, its top half consisted of transparent materials several inches thick, enabling passengers to enjoy an almost three-hundred-and-sixty degree view of the world around them. Davi and Zylo sat on swiveling chairs atop a raised dais in the center of the shuttle, enabling them to turn in any direction at a moment's notice with just the flick of a foot. The Ensign piloting followed a major artery out of the city and headed toward the agricultural fields to the south.

Downtown high-rises slid past as they left the starport then disappeared once they entered residential neighborhoods. The constant chattering of people mixed with music blasting from the electronic billboards floating overhead. Moments later, they reached the outskirts of the city and the landscape changed. His ears filled with the sound of his and Zylo's breathing, the shuttle's flight computer, red Zinga birds' gentle singing and eight-legged insectoid Amblygids' chirping, forming a pleasant drone.

They entered the agricultural regions where buildings stood further apart amidst great stretches of farm and grazing land. Transportation corridors ran throughout linking buildings to each other and to the capital. Workers tended herds of Gungor and Daken, while others ran harvesting machines.

From what he'd seen, the Vertullians lived up to none of his expectations. The workers didn't seem lazy or troublesome or at all subhuman. Instead, they performed their tasks as if they enjoyed themselves and required very little supervision. If there hadn't been soldiers guarding key points and supervising some of the work sites, he might not have even remembered the Vertullians were slaves.

As Davi watched the workers, Zylo smiled. "Have you had much experience with workers?"

"Not really," Davi said, turning back toward his companion. "Nothing beyond some reports."

"Ah, yes, the workers' reports," Zylo said, his voice rising in pitch as irritation flashed in his eyes. "'The quotas are unreasonable and unfair. The Alliance's demands are abusive.' You shouldn't give much credence to most of what they say. These people love to complain." He shook his head, his mouth crinkling with disdain at every word.

"You think there's nothing to them?"

"I think we should expect nothing less from a people like the Vertullians," Zylo said.

The Major's defensiveness puzzled Davi. He'd studied the history of animosity between the Vertullians and his own people, but from what he'd read, it seemed his people had often provoked the Vertullians. In any case, they'd never put up much of a fight. Conquered time and again throughout history, they'd fled the Earth and settled on Vertullis when their ship developed an engine problem. Upon discovering who their neighbors were, they tried to forget the past and sue for peace, but the Legallians conquered them again. They'd been slaves ever since.

The history books overflowed with stories about the laziness of the troublemaking workers, but Davi knew enough to suspect at least some of it was propaganda. He refused to form an opinion about them yet.

Desiring him to think for himself rather than simply conforming to society's views, Miri had arranged special tutors to expose her son to the writings of classic philosophers from Old Earth like Holmes, Locke, and John Stuart Mill. He'd read Martin Luther and Erasmus and many others. From these books, he'd come to believe in the inherent dignity of man and man's right to free will and self-determination. While he also believed in the superiority of the Borali Alliance—the greatest society in the history of humankind—his exposure to life on Vertullis had him wrestling all over again with issues he'd debated over and over in his youth.

It wasn't like he had anything personal at stake. He'd never known any workers, but they seemed as human as he was. According to his professors, their continual failure to defend themselves reflected on their validity and equality as men. Still, he found himself wondering how they'd come to lose the freedom he believed men deserved.

As they passed a clearing, he took in rows of workers assembled beside a barn to watch as soldiers administered punishment to another worker. The man had been strapped to some sort of electrical wires which disappeared into the barn. The soldier questioning him shocked him every time he gave a dissatisfactory answer. It disturbed Davi to see such a thing out in the open.

Zylo's hand on his shoulder drew Davi's focus away from the scene he'd been watching. "Sometimes we have to make examples of them so the others will learn."

"What could he have done to deserve that?" Davi wondered aloud, trying to conceal his horror.

"He was born a worker. They may be human but, trust me, they are not as evolved as our people. No sense of responsibility. They need to be motivated," Zylo said. Conviction dripped from him like sweat.

A group of soldiers leaned against the barn and laughed as they watched. To him, it seemed less about serious discipline and more about entertaining the soldiers at the workers' expense, but having heard Zylo's acceptance of it, he held his tongue.

"You know the history, of course. The Vertullians have long been the enemies of our people. Inferior thinkers—they have only one god, no respect for power, no ambition. The work gives their lives meaning. Left alone they'd all be aimless with no real purpose or direction," Zylo said. It was the standard justification his people gave.

Davi stared out the window as the shuttle flew past the clearing and into a small city called Araial, landing near the small downtown.

"I thought you'd like to see more than the agricultural areas," Zylo said as they stepped out onto the tarmac. "Workers are also employed in factories and maintenance in most of the cities."

The first thing Davi noticed was that the air seemed lighter, clean and refreshing, unlike in Iraja itself or in Legon where he'd grown up. Only the hiss of the wind blowing through the trees pierced the calm around him—a silence like he'd never experienced before.

They walked along between a row of buildings with eight or nine stories, instead of the minimum fifteen or twenty found in Iraja or on Legallis.

"Araial has a population around one hundred fifty thousand. It's small, but nice as outer cities go," Zylo said.

Davi followed Zylo around a corner and saw two soldiers with a worker backed against a wall between two buildings.

"For almost a week now you've failed to meet your quota," the taller soldier said.

"I try, sir, I do. The new quotas are impossible," the worker pleaded, his face filled with fear.

"The Alliance sets the quotas, not the workers," said the shorter soldier with a cocky grin.

"Your job is to meet them," the taller soldier added.

Davi watched the worker's eyes. He didn't appear to be making excuses. He appeared to be struggling to remain upright.

The shorter soldier poked him hard in the chest. "Did you think you could stop doing your work and keep making us look bad without any consequences?"

The worker shook his head, confused. "No, I—"

"Maybe we need to teach you a lesson." The taller soldier rolled his eyes as both soldiers grinned.

"No, please. I'll work harder," the worker said, backing away.

The taller soldier took a club from his belt and started banging it on the wall, inches from the worker's head. Wood splintered under the impact as nearby window panes rattled. The worker trembled in fear.

"You've said the same thing every day this week!" the taller soldier responded as he swung the club again and again.

Davi started toward them, preparing to interfere when Zylo grabbed his arm. "Let them handle this!"

Davi was shocked. "They're going to beat him!"

"He probably deserves it," Zylo said, unconcerned. "We get nothing but trouble from these workers."

"Nothing justifies cruel abuse of another human being," Davi said, yanking his arm free.

"These workers don't qualify for the term 'human,'" Zylo said with growing irritation. "You might want to know the situation before you decide to interfere with our soldiers doing their duty."

"Their duty is to make sure the workers stay on task, meet their quotas—"

"Their duty is to do whatever it takes to maintain the workers' production levels and focus," Zylo's cheeks reddened as he shot Davi a reproaching look. "Maybe someone who's been on the planet only a couple of weeks should observe first before rushing in. Lord Xalivar's order authorized whatever's necessary to keep the workers in line."

"He didn't mean *this*," Davi said, matching Zylo's accusing stare. He hadn't known about the order. Could his uncle have authorized such barbaric means? He wanted to respect his uncle's orders, yet what he had seen conflicted with what he knew in his soul to be right and just.

"Come on. There are other things I wanted to show you." Zylo grabbed Davi's arm and led him on past the soldiers across a well-groomed lawn. Soft grass bent with each step, cushioning his feet.

Over the next two hours, Zylo and Davi toured a few factories and then the city works warehouse where workers bore responsibility for keeping the city's parks and transportation corridors in top condition—picking up garbage, clearing debris, and tending landscaping and plants.

At his desk again, late that afternoon, Davi couldn't get his mind off what he'd witnessed. He stared at a plant on the windowsill next to his framed diploma from the military Academy. They amounted to the only decorating he'd had time for. Sparse light reflected off the standard gray paint common to government offices. His standard chair sat next to a standard desk buried under piles of files, in queue for the file cabinet behind him. Occupying space between stacks of papers were his computer terminal and communicator. The blandness of the room matched his mood, though he couldn't keep his eyes off the plant, a gift from the ambassador he'd met at the palace. It stood as the sole living object in the midst of dreary desolation.

His mother and teachers had taught him principles of law and ethics, intrinsic human rights, and the fundamental value of life. His uncle Xalivar seemed far from sympathetic, and they'd often had hearty debates during which he'd learned his uncle had a different perspective on the world than his. Even though their discussions had always ended with respect and under-standing, Davi couldn't bring himself to respect orders calling for such cruel abuse. Perhaps the rumors he'd heard from other cadets had some basis in fact. How could the uncle who'd been like a father to him have hidden such a dark side all these years?

He turned on his computer terminal and fired off an e-post to his mother. She would know the truth. It amazed him she'd never spoken about it before. Did she agree with what was happening?

✳✳✳

The next day, Davi travelled out to the farm where Farien oversaw a team of soldiers who supervised workers. The farm itself was larger than Davi had expected, giving Farien a great deal of responsibility, despite his disappointment at not being assigned to a higher position. Neither one of them seemed to be living a high adventure, but at least Farien got to work at the heart of things. Though they hadn't seen each other since their arrival on the planet, Davi hoped to keep their relationship friendly, despite the discomfort either might feel at Davi being Farien's supervisor.

As the fresh air filled his lungs, Davi found Farien leaning against a fence, watching as two soldiers loaded injured workers into a hospital shuttle. He took care to move up behind him unnoticed.

"Neglecting your duties, Lieutenant?" Davi said, smiling. The smell of bean plants and grain filled his nose.

Farien snapped to attention, expecting to be reprimanded. "We had an incident with some angry bulls today." Seeing it was Davi, he relaxed. Davi laughed. "Nothing which would keep them off task for more than a couple of days at best," Farien said. "Little more exciting than the paper cuts and headaches you supervisors are prone to, Captain."

"Stop rubbing it in, okay?" He would always consider them peers.

Farien shrugged, suppressing a smile. "What are you doing here?"

Davi motioned for Farien to walk with him. Farien turned to the soldiers by the shuttle. "I want an incident report by the end of the hour, okay? Get back to your duties." From the look on his face and tone of his voice, Farien enjoyed being in command. "What's up?" He turned back to Davi as they walked along the fence together.

Davi began filling him in on his conversation with Zylo the day before and the things he'd witnessed. "I'm wondering if you've witnessed any incidents of abuse," he said as he finished.

"Well, it would depend upon how you define abuse," Farien said. "These Vertullians seem very lazy to me. We have a number of them here who don't want to pull their own weight and meet quotas."

"New quotas demanded by the Alliance or the same quotas they've had?" Davi frowned at Farien's lack of concern.

"What's the difference? We're here to follow the Alliance's orders, aren't we?"

Davi had spent the afternoon before reviewing files on the administrative computer bank. The complaints and issues in the reports almost all related to workers who had failed to meet their quotas or filed complaints about mistreatment by soldiers. Davi had looked into several and found most of the quota problems related to increased demands by the Alliance, and, in some cases, the health of workers. He knew men could be pushed so far, and some-times what the Alliance asked from them seemed far from realistic. That didn't stop the soldiers from employing any means necessary to coerce the workers into producing higher and higher results. And the result was abuse.

"Some of the quota increases I've seen seem unrealistic to me. A man can only do so much labor," Davi said.

They moved past the fence toward a large barn. As they entered, a worker approached with a datapad, handing it to Farien. He read it over, then used the laser stylus to approve it and handed it back as it beeped to acknowledge his signature.

"Have you been out here to see the operation before?" Farien asked as the worker scurried away. Davi shook his head.

Davi watched workers loading grain and cut stalks into various machines which processed them and sealed them into shipping containers on the other end. He stood there a moment admiring the compactness of the machines.

"The machines do a lot of the work. They're all run by computers. All the workers have to do is supply the raw materials. The machines always seem to spend more time than they should every day waiting on the workers," Farien continued.

"Is it because they can't get the raw materials here fast enough from the field?" Davi asked.

"Not from what I've seen. Some of the workers just aren't hustling," Farien said.

"Switch their assignments then and get workers who are," Davi said. It seemed an obvious solution.

Farien lifted his hand in a lazy attempt at a salute. "Yes, Mr. Supervisor."

"Oh, come on. You know I didn't mean it like that!"

"Look, if you're asking me if I've seen soldiers get a little aggressive from time to time, yeah, I have. I've even been tempted to myself," Farien said. "But nothing out of hand."

"You'd tell me if it was, right?"

"Come on, you know me better than that!" Farien sounded a little hurt.

"Sorry. You don't seem to think much of the workers," Davi said, inwardly hoping he'd read his friend all wrong.

"That doesn't mean I don't know what's right," Farien answered.

Davi put a hand on his shoulder. "Sorry, I should have remembered who I was talking to." He trusted Farien, but Farien saw the world through a different lens, tending to be less focused on issues of right and wrong or justice than Davi. The average soldier didn't have to think about such things. He simply had to follow orders. But Davi wasn't the average soldier. Royals had much different expectations upon them.

"Yeah, don't let your higher position go to your head, Captain." Stung by the remark, Davi removed his hand from Farien's shoulder, then Farien broke into a wide grin. "Wanna see more?"

"Aren't I supposed to be the one giving instructions here?" Davi asked, chuckling as Farien led him back out toward the landing pad.

✹✹✹

Farien took Davi on a tour of the facilities in a Floater, which hovered above the ground by using the planet's gravity to manipulate the air. The setup was impressive and they witnessed no incidents of abuse. In fact, everything seemed to be running quite smoothly.

Afterwards, they ate in the soldier's mess at the back of the barn they'd visited earlier. They took seats across from each other at the end of a long table as workers served them plates of hot Gungor meat and Vertullian white bean salad. The presentation was professional, and the service as well handled as any restaurant. One worker delivered their plates as another provided cutlery and poured them drinks; each moving off in turn to wait on other soldiers.

"Well?" Farien stared across the table at him, anxious for his response.

"It's quite the operation out here," Davi said, munching on delicious bread made from fruit and nuts. "Very well organized!"

"Like I told you, nothing out of hand." Farien replied as Davi glanced down the table to where a worker was pouring drinks for some soldiers. A soldier stuck his foot out as the worker backed up. The worker tripped, struggling to keep his balance as the pitcher flew, spilling its contents on the floor and the uniform of another soldier.

"Hey! You watch it, slave!" The angry soldier said, shoving the worker as he stood and wiped at his soiled uniform with a napkin.

"I'm sorry, sir. It was an accident," the frightened worker said, bowing his head.

"Looked to me like he did it on purpose," said the soldier who had tripped him.

The angry soldier began shoving the frightened worker. "It's the truth, right? You think you can ruin my uniform without being reprimanded?"

"Of course not. I tripped. I'm very sorry," the worker said.

"You don't seem sincere to me," the angry soldier said, grabbing the worker by his collar and pulling him close so their faces almost touched.

The worker trembled, eyes frozen wide. Davi stood up, trying to control his anger. "Soldier, he already said it was an accident and apologized." The soldiers turned, reacting to Davi's uniform insignia as he hurried over, Farien close behind.

"These slaves show no respect," said the soldier who had tripped the worker.

"Perhaps you should have a medical officer check your leg to see if it suffered any damage when you tripped him," Davi answered, shooting him a stern look.

The soldier reacted with surprise at being caught. "Can I help it if he's not watching where he steps?" the tripper responded, still trying to pretend it was accidental.

"No, you can't control that. What you can control is how you treat workers. Any soldier who treats workers without dignity and respect can expect to be reprimanded," Davi said.

"Ah, come on, Captain. It's a little harmless fun," said the soldier whose uniform was soiled.

"Go get these soldiers something so they can clean up the mess." Davi motioned to the worker, who nodded and hurried off, suppressing a smile.

"That's a worker's job!" The angry soldier objected.

"Not today it isn't. You made the mess. You clean it up," Davi said as they both scowled. "If you want, I am sure I can arrange to make cleanup a regular part of your duties." He glanced at Farien.

Their faces became apologetic and they shook their heads. Davi returned to his seat at the end of the table.

As Farien took his seat across from Davi, he glanced back down at the shocked soldiers. "Don't you think you were a little harsh?"

"Don't you think that's unprofessional?" Davi said right away.

"A few men trying to have a little fun?" Farien crinkled his mouth as he finished.

"At the worker's expense! It's cruel and unnecessary. It's your job to ensure it doesn't happen again," Davi said. Farien bristled at the tone as the worker returned with cleaning materials. He offered them to the soldiers, who stood there in disbelief. Seeing Davi and Farien watching them, their attitudes changed and they set to work on the mess.

The worker started to leave but Davi motioned for him to stay and watch a moment as the soldiers knelt on the floor and used rags to soak up the liquid, then twist it out into a bucket. One of them glanced up at the worker with murderous intent. Davi stood and stared the soldier down as the timid worker slipped away.

On the way out to the landing pad, Farien remained silent and distant. As they arrived and stepped off the Floater, their eyes met.

"Am I supposed to protect that worker from those soldiers now?" Farien asked.

"If any harm comes to him, I want them brought up on charges. Warn them personally."

Farien frowned at the commanding tone in Davi's voice. "Soldiers deserve more respect than workers," Farien said.

"Workers are human beings, too," Davi said.

"They're not like us," Farien responded.

Davi stopped walking and turned to Farien in disbelief. "Tell me you're joking!"

"Come on, Davi, you know what I mean."

"Yes, I do believe my ears are working perfectly. Being our subjects doesn't negate their worth as human beings," Davi said, angry at Farien for having such a narrow mind.

"Soldiers and workers have different places in society," Farien said, irritated.

"All the more reasons why soldiers should be more dignified, above reproach. How can we ask more of our subjects than we ask of ourselves?"

Farien shook his head. "I guess we just don't see things the same, Davi."

"I guess we don't." Davi said.

"Maybe if you were out here in the field instead of being stuck in some administrative office, you'd understand better what we have to deal with," Farien snapped.

Davi shot him a look. "You have your orders, and I know you'll follow them."

"What're you gonna do? Take on the whole army over this?"

"If need be, yes," Davi said.

Farien shook his head. "Maybe Bordox is right and your royal upbringing is going to your head!"

Davi fought to control his emotions. Coming from Farien, the comment really stung. "Make sure it doesn't happen again!" He turned and marched toward his shuttle, feeling Farien's gaze boring a hole in his back.

✱✱✱

On the shuttle, as his pilot flew them back to Iraja, he sat in silence, replaying it over and over in his mind. Why had he gotten so angry? Farien and Yao were his best friends. They'd grown up together. Sure, he and Farien had different views on how the world should work, but it had never led to angry discussions like this. Besides, Davi was a royal, born of privilege. Why was he so concerned about the lives of the lower class? Justice and fairness aside, he had never known any workers before. It wasn't like he'd given it a whole lot of thought before his arrival on Vertullis. It seemed obvious his anger had taken Farien by surprise as well. He'd have to apologize as soon as he could arrange another visit.

After the shuttle landed, he spent the rest of the afternoon handling paperwork in his office, wishing he could forget what he'd discovered that day. His computer terminal beeped, notifying him of an e-post. He clicked on his inbox to find an e-post from his mother:

To: AgriCptSouth@Federal.emp
From: HRHMRhii@Federal.emp
Subject: Your concerns

My dear son:

Your e-post brings me to a day I knew would come but had long dreaded. I raised you to be an independent thinker, not dependent on the Alliance or your family for forming opinions. I wanted this for you despite the fact so many in our Alliance have never been afforded it, and I offered it knowing that someday it might lead you to some conclusions about our Alliance which might cause you pain or discomfort. If this is the case, please believe I am full of regret, for you know I would never do anything to cause you harm. But you were born for leadership and raised to lead, and good leaders must be able to make hard decisions, which cannot be done in an intellectual box. This day has come faster than I had hoped, but here we find it upon us, and so, as I have always done, I will respond with honesty to your questions.

Your uncle doesn't see the world through the same eyes we do. This is the result of both his years of isolation as the leader of the Alliance and the natural development of his personality and knowledge through various experiences. Our father was a very difficult man; though please don't hear this as making excuses. He tolerated no failure from his children or anyone else, and I am afraid the harshness he passed down has manifested itself in your uncle even more than it existed in himself. Whatever the case, I fear as time passes and various events come to light from which you have in the past been shielded— for your own good, I might add, out of a mother's deep love—you will more and more find yourself coming into conflict with both the ideas and ethics by which your uncle guides himself.

I beg you to be very careful in how you respond to these revelations. He is, after all, the High Lord Councilor, leader of the Borali Alliance. Our armies, Lord's Council and population are sworn by oath of loyalty to serve him. Any criticisms you may have must be handled with great discretion. You can feel free to discuss them with me through our encrypted e-posts, but be very careful. Your uncle has many friends and spies. If you express yourself too directly, I fear how he might respond. You are like the son he never had, and I know he loves you dearly. This doesn't negate his lesser qualities, by any means, but please keep it in mind before passing judgment upon him. I too have long been disappointed by the Alliance's handling of the Vertullis situation, but I beg you to understand there is not much we can do to interfere. This pattern was established long before us and has the backing of the highest reaches of government. I long for a day soon when we can discuss these things with more freedom in person. In the meantime, know you forever have my adoration and love. I miss you dearly, my son.

> Love,
> Your adoring mother

Davi sat at his desk stunned. His mother had always been candid, but the content of her missive left him at a loss. He'd expected her to remind him of his uncle's love and urge him to not be hasty in rushing to judgment, but he'd also expected her to tell him he did not yet have the full picture to understand the reasons behind the decisions his uncle had made in regard to Vertullis. Instead, she confirmed everything he had discovered and been wrestling with. What now?

He would have to be careful. Xalivar would indeed have spies and most people in the Alliance were loyal to him. Davi needed to control his feelings and consider each move. Would he take on the whole Borali Alliance as Farien had said? Not even his status as a member of the Royal Family ensured success. He would be fighting an entire system and way of life for his people, and he knew few would support him.

Slow down, Davi, and remember your place.

Needing to get out of this office and distract himself, he decided to explore areas of the capital he had yet to see. After all, for the time being, this would be home. It might be a good idea to get to know his environment. He deleted his mother's e-post from the server and shut his terminal, returned the paperwork he'd been reviewing to his inbox and headed out the door.

Outside the noise of the city assaulted his ears. As the twin suns sank toward the horizon, the late afternoon light began to fade, dressing the transportation corridors around him in a mix of light and shadows. Past the end of a long block of administrative offices, he entered the narrower corridors of a residential district. The area surrounding the Borali Alliance's offices had become prime real estate and contained some of the largest houses in the city, most occupied by off-world government employees.

A few corridors over, a tall security fence sectioned off that neighborhood from the adjacent one. On the far side, the houses changed noticeably, three story apartment buildings mixed with small dwellings, the landscaping sparser, the corridors narrower. He heard even more noise here than in the area around the government center. People bustled around the corridors past shopkeepers on sidewalks drumming up business. It almost seemed like earlier in the day, rather than early evening. In such worker neighborhoods, life began when the people came home.

He wandered, pondering the juxtaposition between houses which seemed run down, set between pristine, newer dwellings on either side. In other places, a thatch-roofed house would have added plants or laser displays on the sides, its small yard kept tidy and fresh, while vines ascended the walls of sleek modern transparent aluminum dwellings with overgrown yards. Finally, he reached a point where the corridor made a sharp turn.

Turning the bend, he found himself in the market with rows of stalls and tents of all shapes and sizes, bustling workers and vendors. A few saw his uniform and looked at him with wary glances but most went about their business as if he weren't even there. The smell of various perspirations mixed with manure and fresh meats and fruits assaulting his nose.

Vendors offered everything from standard vegetables like green heads of lettuce, orange carrots, and shiny red tomatoes to more exotic ones like Feruca, Gixi, and Jax—fruits from other parts of the solar system. Feruca was black with a thin skin and soft pulp and was often served with various sauces. Gixi, a round, purple fruit grown in orchards on Vertullis and Italis had a delicious, tender pulp and sweet juice. Jax were blue and oblong with crispy pulp and a taste, which went from bitter to sweet during boiling. All had been discovered when colonists first emigrated here centuries ago and now were regular staples of their diets.

Other vendors offered livestock for sale, everything from blue Daken and goats to Quats and Qiwi, a long antlered creature from icy Plutonis. Dark brown with white spots lining either side of their spines, Qiwi stood waste high on Davi and had four long legs ending in black hooves. Their antlers grew up to forty centimeters out of their skulls. He also spotted Gungors, the six-legged brown animals with yellow manes raised for their tasty meat. Davi moved on past as vendors hollered prices and argued with customers, while the various animals brayed and moaned around them.

As he neared a tent, someone grabbed his arm—a smiling vendor who looked half-human and half-Lhamor, gesturing with his bottom two arms when he spoke, his forked tongue giving him a strong lisp.

"'ello, Capt'in, my frien', wha'ever you nee', I can ge' for you," he said with the accent of Italis and patted Davi's back like they had been lifelong pals.

There's a reason others of your race use translators. "No thank you, just passing through," Davi said, moving on.

The market fascinated him. He saw many species and products he'd never seen before, realizing how big the Alliance really was. He hoped someday he might have time to explore it. When he was younger, he'd dreamed of going on a starship to see the planets in the outer solar system—alien species, plants, animals, alien languages. He'd spent so much time in the office, he hadn't even bothered to discover what awaited him on Vertullis. He dodged another eager vendor and ducked into an alleyway. Quats moaned and darted out of his path, scattering the trash crowding the walls as they ran.

Might as well see what the neighborhoods are like on the other side.

Entering a corridor so narrow it was restricted to pedestrian traffic, he set about exploring. The corridor and buildings curved, making it impossible to see one end from the other. He walked past doors and windows of one dwelling after another. Separate units shared outside walls like one long building. The area appeared deserted. *Everyone must be at the market or already inside.*

A woman screamed around the bend ahead.

He quickened his pace, rounding the corner to see an Alliance Captain the size of an air taxi with a worker girl backed into a corner. His gray uniform was dirty and wrinkled, his hair graying around the edges. The girl looked to be upper teens, almost a woman, her face full of fear and apprehension. The Captain struck her across the face with the back of his hand and was preparing to do it again.

"Please," the girl pleaded, "let me go."

"You'll go, when I say you can go," the Captain responded, his voice like poison.

Neither had noticed Davi creeping toward them along a wall behind them. As he drew near, his nose crinkled at the overpowering smell of the Captain. He reeked of sweat and alcohol. Not even the girl's sweet, flowery perfume could overcome it.

"What do you want from me?" The girl demanded.

"I want you to show me the proper respect." The Captain swung his arm, but instead of hitting her face, which she turned away, he grabbed the collar of her blouse and ripped it open.

She slid along the wall, trying to get away. "I'm sorry, sir. I didn't mean to be disrespectful."

"Workers like you are always disrespectful," the Captain said. "Stop moving and come closer." She shook her head as he grabbed her and pulled her to him, trying to press his lips against hers. She kept wiggling and pushing, making it difficult.

"I'm gonna teach you what it means to obey now, slut," he said. Buttons popped as he ripped her blouse again and threw her to the ground, climbing on top of her and trying to force her legs apart.

Davi rushed up behind him, grabbing the Captain by the shoulders and pulling him off. "Enough, Captain," Davi said.

The Captain swung to his feet and whirled around, pulling free with a power that sent Davi stepping back. The sobbing girl picked herself up and cowered against the wall behind him. "Who do you think you are?" the Captain sneered.

"A fellow officer concerned with a peer's professional conduct," Davi said.

"I'm off duty," the Captain said.

"You're in uniform," Davi said.

"I guess this worker slut's not the only one who needs a lesson in respect," the Captain said, looking Davi over. He towered over Davi, muscles bulging from his jacket.

Davi stepped back. *Maybe he has slow reflexes.*

The Captain swung at him and Davi ducked, throwing a fist into the man's gut. His fist throbbed like it had hit an iron wall.

The Captain laughed. "Is that the best you can do?"

"Run," Davi said, his eyes meeting the worker girl's. "Get away now!"

The Captain swung at him again as the girl backed away. "Where you going?" The soldier asked, missing Davi as he whirled and reached for her. Her blouse pulled loose into his hands.

Davi glimpsed a necklace around her neck with a blue-green crest at its center. The Captain knocked him to his knees with a blow he hadn't seen coming.

Where are my friends when I need them? He struggled back to his feet.

The Captain swung again, and Davi dodged to one side. "You need to learn to mind your own business!" Keeping ahold of the girl with one hand, he swung again at Davi's midsection.

Davi ducked to one side as the girl tried to pull free. His adversary found himself pulled in two directions but managed to grab Davi's collar and jerk him roughly off his feet.

As the Captain pulled Davi closer and closer, the girl bit the Captain, who yelled and flinched, letting her go. Davi tried to use the moment to pull himself free, but the Captain pulled the collar tighter and cause Davi to slip and fall away from him and into wooden double doors which cracked loudly as they splintered from the force.

Seeing the girl slipping away, the Captain chased after her, turning his back on Davi.

Davi needed some kind of weapon. He thought for a moment of his blaster, but the Alliance had laws and he could think of none which would justify shooting a soldier, especially not to save a worker. Besides, the Captain had a blaster hanging on his hip.

As he climbed to his feet and stepped away from the door, part of it slipped back inside the house behind him. He looked at the splintered wood and began pulling free a section he could use as a club. Wood creaked and snapped as he pulled.

"Why are you doing this to me?" the girl screamed, as she continued dodging the Captain.

"Because you're a worker," the Captain said, grabbing her again as he looked around for something to tie her with.

Davi ran up behind him with the board. Seeing him out of the corner of his eye, the Captain turned, raising an arm, as Davi swung the board down hard atop his head.

The Captain's arm deflected the board, sending it hard against the side of his head. He froze and emitted a loud gurgling sound, releasing the girl and falling to his knees as blood poured from his ears.

Davi pulled the board away and saw that a large spike had entered the man's head at the temple. The Captain fell over face down and lay still as the salty smell of warm blood rose into the air from a widening pool around the Captain's head. *Oh my gods! I killed him!*

"Is he dead?" the girl asked, petrified.

Davi knelt beside him, feeling for breath. The strengthened stench almost made him gag but he swallowed hard. "I think so. I don't know." The Captain's chest wasn't moving.

The girl gasped. Davi saw her pointing at his chest where his ripped uniform revealed his own necklace—an exact duplicate of the one she wore around her neck.

"Where'd you get it?" the girl asked.

"I've had it since I was a baby," Davi responded.

The girl's eyes widened as she turned and ran back up the corridor.

"Wait! Come back here a moment!"

But her footsteps faded into the night.

Davi glimpsed faces peering at him from nearby windows and heard footsteps behind him.

A worker stood in the splintered doorway as it finally sunk in—he'd killed an Alliance soldier.

Davi took dark side corridors all the way back to his quarters, ducking into alleyways every time anyone approached. Gasping for breath until his lungs were about to explode, he ran as fast as his feet would take him, his soaked clothes sticking to his skin. *I hope no one got a good look at my face. How am I going to explain this?!*

CHAPTER THREE

When Aron had informed her that the courier craft malfunctioned, Luna feared the worst. Perhaps it had burned more fuel than Sol and Aron's calculations anticipated, running out and leaving her only son to die in orbit or forever drift in space. They had no way to know if it had landed, because its tracking device failed to maintain contact with the computer at the depot. Sol had been working on the device the day they rushed to launch the courier. Her only son was gone forever!

Worse, Sol had been arrested for treason and taken away. She'd heard rumors he'd been sent to a science planet somewhere, but she had also heard talk of his execution. She never really knew for sure. Just like that, she was alone.

Aron took care of her, taking her into his home to live with his family and treating her like a sister. His children even called her "auntie." But when the attention of government spies on his own activities made it impossible for him to remain, Aron and his family had gone into hiding, leaving Lura alone again.

After her brother-in-law's death in a tragic incident with soldiers, her sister came from the countryside with her children to live with Lura. She welcomed them. After five years of loneliness, she loved having a family again, and it seemed as fine a life as a Vertullian could expect.

The whoosh of the opening door drew her attention. It slammed into the wall as Nila stumbled through the opening, her clothes torn, her face bruised. Blood dripped from a cut on her forehead.

"Nila! Are you okay?" Lura rushed to help her.

It took her niece a few moments to catch her breath but then she nodded. "Two Captains. One tried to rape me. The other helped. Had a necklace. Like mine." Nila reached through her torn blouse and pulled out the family crest just like one she'd placed in the courier beside her baby son before it launched, taking him away.

"A Borali Captain with our family crest?"

Nila's eyes widened and she smiled with glee. "It's him, Aunt Lura! Your Davi!"

Lura stepped back, stunned. *Could it be, after all this time, God's finally chosen to answer my prayers?*

After she'd cleaned Nila up and put her to bed, Lura collapsed into a chair, feeling like she'd lost the power to stand. She couldn't believe it! She'd long ago given up the dream of ever seeing him again, and yet, according to her niece, the son she'd lost so long ago lived across the city?! *My Davi!* She thought. *Could it really be you?* She tipped her head back against the back of the chair and screamed.

Her first instinct was to run and embrace him but it might not be well received. The last thing she wanted was to scare him off. *He has the necklace, sure, but does he know who he is?*

She managed to kneel on the floor beside the table in prayer, seeking God's guidance about what to do next.

* * *

The knock on the door of his quarters almost sent him into a panic. *Could they be after him already?* Davi tried to calm himself. It had been two days and no one had come. *You're just being paranoid.* He opened the door to find a humanoid smiling at him.

"What are you doing here?" Davi asked with surprise.

"Is that any way to great your best friend?" Yao said with a laugh. "Can I come in?"

Davi chuckled, stepping aside and motioning for him to enter. "Of course. I'm sorry. I wasn't expecting you. School on a holiday?"

Yao stepped inside and the door slid shut behind him. "In a manner of speaking. Your mother sent me." *My gods! Word had gotten to her already?* "About your e-post."

"Oh," Davi said, trying to hide his relief. "Of course."

"She told me you're finding things here harder than you'd expected," Yao said, looking concerned.

"Yeah, well, it's not the glorified adventure we all talked about," Davi said. "You want a beer?"

"Sure," Yao said as he settled onto a couch. "She filled me in a little. You want to tell me more?"

"Okay, but first, how's Presimion?" Davi asked as he opened the cooling unit.

"It's pretty terrific, actually. I wasn't going to bring it up. Didn't want to rub in my good fortune in light of —"

"It's not like it's the end of the world," Davi said, closing the cooling unit and returning with two beer bottles. He handed one to Yao. "Let's call it a rude awakening to the real world."

"Ah, I see. Like a rite of passage sort of thing?" Yao took the beer and opened it, savoring its scent. His face lit up with delight. "Mmmm.

Been too long since I had one of these. Teachers aren't allowed to drink on Academy grounds." His eyes closed and he smiled as he enjoyed a long first sip.

"Maybe you should get out more."

"Maybe I should," Yao laughed. "I've missed you."

"I've missed you, too," Davi said, smiling and sipping his own beer, as he settled into a lounge chair across from him.

"How's Farien?"

"Oh, you know Farien. Give him a few men to boss around and a little freedom, and he's on top of the world," Davi said. They both laughed.

"The worker-soldier thing has been going on for generations, Davi," Yao said, cutting to the chase. "It didn't develop overnight, and it won't change that fast either."

"Have you ever met a worker?" Davi asked. Yao shook his head. "I know the history. But book learning and reality are not the same when you're staring a fellow human being in the face and one of you is supposed to be superior over the other by birth."

Yao nodded. "You don't think a Tertullian can relate? Your ancestors wrestled with this issue eons ago on Earth."

"Oh yeah? What did they do about it?"

"Well, much of the world outlawed it in the nineteenth century, but reports continued of slavery in various places almost until the colonists began departing for other systems," Yao said. Always a history buff, he read voraciously in his spare time—anything he could get his hands on from history to the sciences.

"Sounds like they never really found a solution," Davi said.

Yao shrugged. "Not totally, no. You realize you'd have to take on the whole Alliance?"

Davi smiled. "Farien said the same thing."

"How'd that conversation go?"

"Not well." Their eyes met and Davi saw Yao already knew what was coming. "He didn't seem to understand my feelings. To him, it's like a natural course of events. He's too busy seeing the workers' faults to see their humanity. He's bought the Alliance's party line one hundred percent."

"Well, we both know Farien's no great thinker. He's got a lot of qualities which make him an ideal soldier, but intellect is not at the top of the list. He probably hasn't given it much thought. Most soldiers never do. They train us to obey, remember?" Yao looked at him as Davi nodded. "On the other hand, I do see his point. You're treading a dangerous line here. You could lose everything if you fight this."

Davi stood and paced, his body stiff with tension. "So you think I should just ignore what's happening, get on with my life?"

"I can't tell you what to do, Davi, but it's a big risk."

"Now you sound just like Farien!"

"Hey, I'm on your side here, okay? One man can't change an entire culture!"

"This man has to try."

Yao sighed. "Why?"

Davi stared angrily at him a moment. *You've got to tell him.* Instead, he shrugged.

"Have you spoken to Farien since?"

"No. There hasn't been an occasion."

"Maybe we could pay him a visit," Yao said. "Be good to have the three musketeers back together again." Yao loved references to the classics. Along with history, he'd read many novels.

"Sure. Of course." Davi looked away, lost in thought. *Should I tell him?* He needed to confide in someone before he burst.

Yao looked concerned. "You look as if you haven't slept. Your eyes seem as if they're carrying the weight of the world. What haven't you told me?"

He's one of the only people you can trust, Davi thought. If nothing else, he needed to talk through his options. After all, there had been a few witnesses, and sooner or later somebody would talk. *But he's a loyal officer of the Borali* Alliance, he reminded himself.

"Come on, Davi. It's me," Yao said.

Davi could hold it in no longer. He recounted for Yao the events of the night before with the worker girl and the Captain.

When he'd finished, Yao looked stunned. "My gods! You're sure he was dead?" Davi looked at the floor. "They saw your face?"

"I don't know. It was getting dark, lots of shadows. But what if they did?" Panic set in again as Davi thought about it.

"It was self-defense," Yao said as he deliberated. "Given your status and reputation, I think they'd have to take that into account."

"You know the law. I was defending a worker."

"I thought you said you weren't having much of an adventure here," Yao said, trying to lighten the mood.

"What I said was not the glorified adventure we'd all talked about," Davi reminded him. They both laughed as they flashed back to the naïve daydreams of their Academy days.

"Amazing how grown up you can feel a few months after graduation," Yao said. Davi nodded. "We've got to ask your mother for help. She has the power to protect you."

"I don't trust the communications channels. The government has spies everywhere," Davi said.

"Sounding pretty paranoid for an officer of the Alliance," Yao said, but from the look in his purple eyes, Davi knew he understood. "Come on, let's fire off an e-post to Farien. Maybe he can come here and meet us. He might enjoy a night away from the field."

Davi chuckled, stood and led him to a nearby desk, where he sat again and turned on his terminal. "There'd sure be a lot more to do here than where he's stationed." He began typing an e-post as Yao looked on.

***

Lura and Nila wound through the worker neighborhoods past the security fence and into the free neighborhoods of the city. They hung to the shadows as the twin suns peaked over the purplish horizon to the west, hoping no one would try and stop them. Wearing the best clothes they owned, so they wouldn't look like workers, they carried fruit as a gift for the barracks and hoped to catch a glimpse of Davi. Lura couldn't resist. She had to try. She'd waited so long, almost given up hope. Nila insisted on coming along.

As they crossed the corridor from the residential district, the government area looked deserted. It seemed they'd chosen a good time to come and not be noticed. Lura had no idea how they would get the fruit to the soldiers without drawing attention, or even how she might be sure Davi would receive some fruit. As they walked the long block alongside the Alliance offices, she saw a small side gate up ahead. An air taxi pulled to a stop nearby and three officers stepped out onto the sidewalk. Two were human, the third a dark humanoid with purple eyes.

Lura's heart began racing as she saw their faces. *It's him! My God! He looks like his father!*

He wasn't the tallest of the three, but the middle one, tall and thin, so dashing in his uniform, with neatly combed light brown hair, and tanned skin. She fought the tears which welled up in her eyes. *Maybe we can talk to him.* The urge was so compelling.

She started rushing toward them, but Nila reached out and caught her arm. "Auntie, wait!"

The three officers stepped through the gate as Lura and Nila approached. Two guards intercepted them, bur Lura pushed forward against them, straining for another glimpse. *They're walking away from us. What can I do?* She thought.

"What's your business here?" the taller of the two guards asked, shoving Lura back.

"We brought some fruit for the soldiers," Nila said, her voice wobbling in fear. She extended the basket she carried toward him.

Take it, Lura urged him with all her heart.

"Soldiers can't accept gifts here," the other guard said, looking them over with suspicion.

"We're sorry. It's some fruit from the market. To thank them," Nila said. Neither of them knew what else to say. Lura's eyes stayed locked on Davi as he receded further into the barracks.

The guard knocked the basket from Nila's hands, spilling the contents. "No gifts! Go away!"

Davi stopped and whirled around, drawn by the commotion. His eyes fixed upon Nila, recognizing her.

He's coming back!

Davi's companions reacted with surprise as he hurried toward them. "Hold it there," Davi called out as he approached.

"You know these women?" the taller guard asked.

"I know her," David said, indicating Nila. He stepped back through the gate and stood face to face with them. Lura's heart pounded in her chest.

"They were trying to bring gifts here, Captain. You know our policies," the other guard began explaining.

Davi smiled, hoping to reassure him. "I'm sure they meant no harm.

Please allow us a moment." The two guards shrugged and turned back to their post as Davi pulled Nila and Lura off to the side.

"You remember me?" Nila said, fearful.

"We remember each other," Davi said as she nodded. "You ran away so fast the other night, I never got to ask you about this." He reached under his uniform collar and pulled a chain hanging around his neck. "It's just like yours."

Lura's eyes widened as the blue-green crest appeared, and she thought her heart might explode. All four were there—the laborers, the soldiers, the farmers and the priests. She couldn't help but reach out and stroke it gently with her hand.

"I know. I saw." Nila said, seeing Davi's surprise at Lura's forward behavior.

"I wanted to ask you about the symbol on it," Davi said.

Speak to him. He's your son. Lura kept telling herself, but words wouldn't come. She'd waited so long, dreamed of this moment, but now she couldn't formulate the words.

"It's our family crest," Nila said. "Where did you get it?"

"My mother gave it to me when I was a baby. I've always worn it," Davi said.

Behind them, a police cruiser dropped down from overhead and parked nearby, lights flashing. As two officers climbed out, one of the guards motioned toward the women. "It's those women there."

Davi's face turned red with anger as he turned to the guards. "There's been a big misunderstanding. They've done no harm."

Nila grabbed Lura's arm and pulled her back they way they'd come. "Run, Auntie! Run!"

Police! We're going to be arrested! Lura snapped out of it, realizing what was happening. Nila dragged her, picking up pace as she went, while Davi stepped between them and the police.

"Auntie Lura! Hurry!

Lura forced her eyes away from Davi and turned back around, running as fast as she could. Voices rose as men argued behind them, but no one seemed to be chasing them.

✳✳✳

Davi followed Yao and Farien to his quarters and the door slid shut behind them. They both shot hum puzzled looks. "What was that all about?" Yao asked.

"It was the girl from two nights ago," Davi said. Yao squinted with understanding.

"What happened two nights ago?" Farien asked. Davi and Yao had already decided Farien wasn't ready to know about the attempted rape and its consequences.

"Why'd she come here?" Yao asked, puzzled.

"I don't know, but the necklace she wears is identical to mine," Davi said, pointing to the chain around his neck.

"I've seen you wearing that. Where'd you get it?" Farien asked, forgetting his earlier question.

"My mother gave it to me when I was young," Davi said.

"I've never seen you without it. What does the symbol mean?" Farien asked.

"The girl said it's her family crest," Davi answered, watching them both for a reaction.

"Why would your mother have you wear the crest of a worker family?" Farien said, more puzzled than ever.

Davi turned to Yao, who seemed lost in thought. "Do you remember that rumor Bordox brought up at the Academy about me?"

"The starport's full of rumors," Yao said, writing it off.

"What if it was more than just a rumor?" Davi knew how farfetched it sounded.

"Are you saying you're the child of workers?" Farien said with disbelief.

"It seems rather odd for it to be pure coincidence," Davi said, still unsure what to believe himself. "But I've never known my mother to lie to me."

"Yet given who your uncle is, she would want to protect you," Yao replied. Davi nodded.

"You two can't be serious? He's a member of the Royal family," Farien said.

"An only child of a mother who never married," Yao said. Farien kept looking back and forth between them in disbelief.

"I have to find out for sure," Davi said. "They ran off. I don't know where they live."

"If they came on foot, it must not be far," Yao said.

"This is insane," Farien said, shaking his head as he turned away.

"I have to know the truth, Farien," Davi said. He had to find those women again, somehow. Then he remembered the security camera. Maybe he could get prints of their faces off the databanks and ask around. Someone had to know them—maybe someone at the market. But then who would want to talk to an Alliance Captain? He had to try. He had to know or it would always haunt him.

"Farien, not a word of this goes outside this room," Yao said. "When Davi finds out the truth, he'll let us know. It would be very dangerous for him if certain people found out about this."

Farien nodded. "Come on. I've been his friend all my life. You can trust me." Yao and Davi exchanged uncertain looks. Can we trust him?

Farien started to frown until Davi put his hand on his arm, squeezing firmly. "I know I can."

He hoped he was right.

✷✷✷

Getting images of the two women off the security tapes proved relatively simple. Tracking them down proved hard. Davi's first two trips to the market produced no leads. As he'd feared, few people there wanted to talk to an Alliance officer. On his third attempt, he went out of uniform. A couple of vendors recognized the women from the vidprints, but only knew the approximate area where they might live; nothing definite.

Davi wandered through worker residential zones, hoping for another chance encounter with them. His feet moved in time with the droning noise of the city around him. Since Yao and Farien had returned to their duties, he conducted his search alone, on foot, using air taxis a few times to get from his office to the areas he wanted to search. Though the civilian clothes helped a bit, his military haircut and accent still raised suspicion. He made no progress even with those who thought they recognized the women.

Because the workers' diets consisted of different foods than he'd grown up with, he discovered new smells as he passed by their houses. Some delighted his nose, while others caused him to cringe. After a week, he'd covered most of the areas mentioned by those who'd recognized the women at the market. Almost ready to quit in frustration, he decided to check one last neighborhood. Because he had a meeting at a nearby factory, he stopped there during work hours, in uniform. He knew it might hinder him a bit, but at this point it didn't seem to matter.

He wandered through one corridor after another, enduring the suspicious glances of the workers he passed. He'd about given up, when he realized he'd been so preoccupied with his thoughts that he'd failed to keep track of the twists and turns he'd taken through the neighborhoods. He knew he'd crossed the corridor parallel to the one he was on, so, seeing a walkway cut between two buildings, he decided to see where it led.

Entering a courtyard between two buildings, he passed a cart stacked with crates of groceries as a few chickens squawked and scattered at his feet. Then he saw her. At the end of the courtyard, sweeping outside a door stood the woman who'd come to the barracks with the rape victim.

Davi stopped, staring. She hadn't seen him yet. He didn't know either of the women's names. *What can I say? Come on, think of something!* Then she turned, saw him and stopped sweeping.

At first, he detected fear on her face at the sight of his uniform, but then, recognizing him, she broke into a smile. She mumbled something, raising her palm to the sky as if offering some kind of prayer, then set the broom aside and moved toward him.

"I was hoping you'd come," she said, motioning toward the door in front of which she'd been sweeping. "Please. Come into my home so we can talk."

Davi smiled and moved toward her. "Thank you."

The dwelling was small and intimate, permeated by the smell of candles mixed with dust. Wooden beams from the frame shown through the white stucco walls at the ceiling and corners. A simple table and chairs sat at one end of the room next to a cooking area with a hotpad and microwave. At the far end, a small entertainment console hung on the wall with a couch and chairs arranged around it. Everything looked much more primitive than Davi was used to. In fact, the building itself looked as if it might have been built in the earliest days of the planet's colonization. A few pictures hung on the cooling unit with magnets and one solitary painting decorated the wall opposite the door. Light came from a single reflector pad in the center of the ceiling, with more leaking through the door and a window along the wall near the table. A single candle at the center of the table flickered from air slipping in through a crack in the door.

The woman motioned him toward a chair by the table, smiling. "Welcome to our home."

Davi nodded, as he took it all in, and forced a smile. "Thank you. My name is Captain Xander Rhii. I'm the officer in charge of the Southwest farming district. My friends call me Davi."

The woman seemed to get excited at hearing his nickname. "It's so good to see you again Davi. My name is Lura. Can I offer you any refreshment?"

"Thank you, yes. I am thirsty."

She opened the cooling unit. "I'm afraid our options are quite limited. I do have some tea and juices."

"Anything would be fine, Lura. Surprise me," Davi said, smiling again. She returned with a can of Gixi juice and handed it to him. As she sat across from him, he popped the lid open and took in the sweet scent. "Mmmm. One of my favorites. It's been a while, too. Thank you."

Lura seemed delighted. "I'm so glad we found something you like. What brings an Alliance officer to our humble courtyard?"

"I came to find you—either you or the girl who was with you at the barracks," Davi said as he savored the sweet, smooth taste of the Gixi juice.

"Ah yes, my niece, Nila. Thank you for saving her from that soldier," Lura said, placing her soft hand over his atop the table. "Why us?"

Davi hesitated a moment, surprised by her forwardness. "Well, I wanted to be sure you were okay after what happened at the barracks. And I wanted to know more about this," Davi said. Removing his hand from Lura's, he pulled out his necklace and let it hang down the front of his uniform. "What can you tell me about it? Before the police chased you off, Nila mentioned a family crest?"

Lura pulled her hand back, staring at the necklace. "There are only a few like it in existence."

Davi nodded. "How would my mother have come to have one?"

"Who's your mother?" Lura asked with curiosity.

"I was raised by Princess Miri Rhii, sister to Lord Xalivar," Davi said.

At the mention of his uncle's name, her face turned white. "Legallis? The Royal Family?"

"Yes," Davi said as he nodded. He wondered if all workers had the same reaction to the High Lord Councilor's name. He sipped his juice again as she considered what he'd said.

"My God, I never imagined," she said, almost as if talking to herself. "When we sent you away, it was supposed to be Regallis." Her voice faded as she realized she was speaking her thoughts out loud.

"Sent me away? What do you mean?"

Lura stood and walked over to one of the pictures hanging on the cooling unit. She removed the magnet with great care and carried the picture back to the table like a precious treasure, setting it before him. "This is a picture of my husband Sol."

Davi looked at the picture. The man staring back at him had similar light brown hair and tanned skin similar to his own. Then he recognized the same nose and green eyes that looked back at him in the mirror. *My gods! The resemblance is startling. Could this really be?*

Seeing the look on his face, Lura's eyes showed her concern. "I'm sorry. I know this must be shocking for you to hear."

"No, please. Tell me everything," Davi said, doing his best to relax his face and sound reassuring.

"Twenty-one years ago, there was a decree ordering all first-born sons to be killed. The High Lord Councilor had a dream a worker child would arise to overthrow him," Lura explained. "The Death Squads began killing all first-born males among our people, on every planet of the solar system."

Davi searched his mind. His recollection of the history of the Borali Alliance brought back no recollection of such an incident.

"My husband and I only had one child, a baby boy born right before the decree. We couldn't bear the thought of losing him, after so many years of waiting and hoping," Lura continued. "My husband worked at the depot, repairing starcraft. He was able to modify a small courier to transport our child to another planet in the solar system. We hoped he would be found by someone who would raise him as their own and give him a good life."

Courier craft. A child sent to the stars. My gods!

"The courier malfunctioned sometime soon after its launch. Its tracking device failed, so we had no idea where it ended up or if it even finished the journey," Lura said.

"So you think I'm the son you sent to the stars?" Davi asked.

Mistaking his question for total disbelief, Lura shrugged, smiling. "I know it must sound crazy to you."

"My mother is a good woman. I've never known her to lie to me," Davi said, thinking out loud.

"I'm sure she's a wonderful woman, and I'm so glad to hear it. May I ask you how you came to be called Davi?" she said.

"I don't really know. It's like a nickname my mother gave me at birth. Everyone except for my Uncle and a few instructors has always called me by it," Davi said.

Lura looked away, deliberating a moment, before her eyes found his again. "My husband placed a letter to whoever might find our child. It contained his name and a note asking them to take care of him and raise him as their own. Our child's name was Davi," she said.

My gods! It has to be true! He didn't see how there could be any more doubt. *But why would mother have lied to me?* "How would my mother have come by the necklace?"

"Moments before the courier launched, I placed my necklace next to our child, hoping whoever found him would give it to him," she said.

"I don't know what to say," Davi responded, his mind racing. He had to talk to his mother about this! He dreaded hurting her, but it couldn't be a mere coincidence. What motive would Lura have for making up such a story? She'd had no idea he was a Royal before he told her—it seemed obvious from her reaction when she learned his identity. "Do you live here with your husband?" Lura's face turned sad and she looked at the photograph. "The Special Police took him away after we launched the courier. I don't know what happened to him."

No wonder she reacted that way to Xalivar's name! Could my uncle really be so different from the man I thought I knew? "I'm so sorry for your loss," Davi said, placing his hands atop hers on the table again.

She smiled. "You are such a kind soul. We're not used to finding such kindness in Boralian officers."

"I'm not like most Alliance officers," Davi said.

"No, you're not," she said with a laugh. "You're special!"

Davi pulled his hand away, finishing off the Gixi juice. "Please don't be offended if I take some time to think about all this."

"I'm just happy to have had the chance to meet you," Lura said, with a reassuring smile as he scooted the chair back and stood. "I hope I'll see you again."

"I'm sure you will," Davi said. He moved around the table, standing next to her, then took her hand in his and kissed it. "Thank you for your generous hospitality."

"Thank you for your kindness to Nila," Lura said as she stood.

Davi bowed slightly and walked to the door. "I'd appreciate it if my visit here stayed between us for now," he said, turning back toward her.

"Of course," Lura smiled again. Her face lit up every time she did. She was a striking woman with long, flowing brown hair. Feeling sorry for the hardness her life must have been, he returned the smile then turned walked out the door.

As Davi crossed the courtyard and entered the tunnel, he struggled to keep his pace steady while his mind raced. This was almost beyond belief! His whole life had unraveled before his eyes—everything he thought he knew about the world, about his family, about who he was.

His mind filled with question after question. Why didn't his mother ever tell him? Protecting him as a child was one thing, but he was far from a child now. She must have expected him to wonder about the necklace and his nickname. He'd always been one to ask a lot of questions. How much did his uncle know? Would the High Lord Councilor actually accept a worker child as his heir apparent? Based on what he'd been learning about his uncle, he doubted it. How would his friends and colleagues react if they found out? Certain his whole life would change, he wasn't sure he was ready for it.

He meandered through the neighborhoods for a while before realizing he needed to get back to the office. He was already late. Stopping on a main artery, he looked around for a familiar landmark. He spotted the market ahead through some arches. It would be easy to find his way back from there.

He headed in that direction; ignoring the stares of the people he passed. *Can they know by looking at me that I'm one of them?* He shook off the idea. The stares had been because of his uniform, as always. *Boy, I really am getting paranoid!*

He walked beneath an arch onto another corridor and glimpsed the tents and booths of the market up ahead. *Thank the gods, I know where I am.*

He quickened his pace as he entered the market and the familiar smells and sounds assaulted his senses. The market seemed less crowded. It was mid-afternoon, and most of the workers would be at their jobs. Raised voices came from up ahead. He rounded a corner between rows of booths to find the humanoid vendor he'd asked about Lura and Nila, arguing with two workers.

"It's a fair price!" The vendor's purple eyes glowed with rage.

"This fruit is not even ripe," said one worker, tossing two Gixis back at him.

"I provide the highest quality," the vendor insisted.

"You should be ashamed ripping off people!" The other worker said with disgust. "Give us back our money!"

The vendor spotted Davi passing and motioned to him. "Captain, please. You've been here before. You know my product."

Davi sighed. *Don't get me involved in this.* He turned to the vendor and smiled. He had bought some fruit there two days before and it was fine. "I didn't have any complaints."

"Well, he's an off-worlder. How would he know when Gixi are at their ripest?" the first worker said.

"Don't you men have jobs to attend to?" Davi asked. They showed no fear, despite his uniform.

"Our supervisor won't pay us if the Gixi isn't ripe," the second worker said. His face formed a question. He examined Davi like he knew him from somewhere.

The first worker angrily grabbed the vendor by the collar, his eyes still locked on Davi. "Stay out of this. It's a dispute between us. We want our money back!"

Davi stepped forward and put his hand on the first worker's muscular arm. He could feel the man's strength through his sleeve. "Let him go."

The second worker's eyes went wide with recognition. Davi couldn't imagine how they knew each other.

"What are you going to do? Kill us like you killed that Captain last week?" the second worker said loudly.

The words hit Davi like a rocket. *My gods, how did he know?*

"I saw you on my corridor, Captain. I saw you real good," the second worker said staring at him. The vendor and the other worker eyed Davi with worried looks.

Davi recognized the second worker as the man who'd stood in the doorway as he fled the corridor where the Captain lay dead. Davi pulled his hand off the first worker, turned and ran as fast as he could. *People are talking about it now. It's only a matter of time before the police come for me!*

He passed the end of the row of stalls, making his way along the transportation corridor ringing the market toward a nearby residential corridor. He ran as fast as he could, drawing even more stares from the people he passed. Dwellings flew by in a flash as he wondered if the stares had been about more than his uniform. He tried to remember how many workers he'd seen peering out at him in the alley. The gasps of his breathing echoed loudly off the walls around him as his eyes stung from perspiration falling off his forehead.

Passing through the security gate separating the worker districts from the finer homes, he continued around a corner as his eyes locked on the outline of the government buildings ahead of him. The intersection separating the government sector from the residential areas was quiet, so he hurried across and up the transportation corridor toward the barracks gate where he'd encountered Lura and Nila.

Activity near the gate ahead drew his attention. Lord's Security Police officers were talking with the guards. Two police vehicles sat nearby with lights flashing. Then he saw a face he recognized—Bordox in full LSP uniform.

Bordox spotted him too, and raised his arm to point. "There he is!"

The Security Police and barracks guards all turned to stare at him. Bordox and the LSP officers began rushing toward him, pulling their blasters from their holsters.

Davi turned and ran back the way he'd come. *Where can I go? Quick! Think!* As he passed the end of the block, the sirens of LSP cruisers drew nearer. Spotting an air taxi at the curb, he hurried over and jumped inside.

"Residential Sector Four, fast, please."

The cab-bot beeped, as the door slid shut. "Of course, sir." The air taxi accelerated.

Catching his own scent for the first time, he felt relieved the cab-bot had no sensory abilities. "Turn here," Davi insisted.

The cab-bot complied, making a sharp turn into the finer residential area. The transportation corridors became narrower. The air taxi would soon run out of room.

"My computer maps show limited access to Residential Sector Four from this corridor, sir," the cab-bot informed him.

"Can't you just fly over the buildings until we're closer?"

"It's against regulations, sir. Emergency vehicles only per ordinance-"

"I can get out and walk. Please get me as close as you can," Davi said, not waiting for the cab-bot to finish. Hearing sirens behind him, he glanced back. The LSP vehicles had not turned. He wasn't even sure if they could fit.

"Of course, sir," the cab-bot responded.

Davi saw LSP men exiting a vehicle at the entrance to the corridor and chasing after the air taxi.

The cab-bot turned a corner, winding the taxi through the narrow corridors. At the security gates leading to the worker residential areas, the air taxi pulled to a stop. "This is it, sir."

Davi slid his cab card through the slot near the door as it slid open. "Thank you. Please move on right away."

He rushed from the cab and out into the worker district again, hoping to lose himself in the numerous narrow corridors surrounding the market.

The air taxi departed behind him. *Did the LSP men see where the taxi stopped?* He hoped they hadn't.

Quats hissed and scattered as he ducked onto a side corridor. He continued, unsure where he was going, knowing he had to get away. He heard sirens as the LSP vehicles raced around the edges of the district looking for another entrance.

He ducked through an archway like the ones leading to the market, running as fast as he could, until his uniform dripped. His feet pounded the pavement like beating drums. Then someone called his name.

"Davi!"

Since when can Bordox run that fast? His mind registered the voice was female as he stopped and turned around.

Lura motioned to him from a nearby doorway. "Come this way!" She smiled reassuringly. *Where did she come from?*

He didn't hesitate, hurrying inside as she shut the door behind them. It was a small interior corridor with dwelling doors scattered on each side. He started to apologize for his appearance and smell but Lura motioned for him to be quiet.

Outside feet shuffled as someone ran past. *They're going to find me.* And then it was silent again until the sirens began moving away. No more commotion came from outside. Could he really have escaped?

Lura took his hand, leading him further down the corridor. "Were the Police chasing you?"

He nodded, out of breath. "Word has spread about Nila and the Captain."

Lura reacted with fear. "Oh, no!" She pulled him behind her. "Follow me. We can get back to my house through the tunnels."

"How?" He hadn't heard of any tunnels.

She nodded, pulling open a small wooden door on the corner of a building. Stairs descended.

Tunnels under the city?

"They run underground throughout the worker areas. Officers aren't supposed to know about them."

As soon as they entered, she closed the door behind them. It was dark and damp as they headed down. Every footstep echoed like thunder interrupting the droning rasp of his breathing and the thumping of his heart. He had no idea where they'd wind up, but he followed as fast as he could.

CHAPTER FOUR

Manaen's red eyes moved back and forth as he finished reading the report aloud off the datapad.

"If he wants our help, why is he running away?" Xalivar asked, his anger growing.

"Bordox is his rival from the Academy. They have a long history. Maybe if someone else had come after him—"

Xalivar cut Miri off. "I can't control which LSP officers answer such warrants. I didn't even know about it until this morning. How can we help him if we don't know where he is?"

Xalivar fumed when he learned his own nephew was assisting workers, no matter what the circumstances. They were the Lord's ancient enemies and deserved no mercy. He cursed Miri for making Davi soft. Xalivar had done his best to harden the boy, but there hadn't been enough time. Besides, it had been clear to Xalivar his nephew was far too sensitive to handle the reality of certain types of situations and decisions. He had always protected the boy from exposure, hoping he would come around in time. Now he wondered if Miri had succeeded in ruining her son for the throne.

"I'm sure he's looking for a way to get in touch with us," Miri said, pacing anxiously. "He knows we'll help him."

"What business does he have involving himself with helping workers? The workers are our enemies!"

Miri recoiled at Xalivar's anger. She had always been too soft. "Is it wrong to show compassion to fellow human beings?" Miri asked.

"The term only applies to them by natural default. They are not our equals," Xalivar said, annoyed at having to remind her of it after so many years. "Manaen, get me Major Zylo and Lieutenant Bordox. I want to see them as soon as possible. In the meantime, any further reports on this come to me right away."

Manaen nodded, hurrying for the door. "Yes, my Lord!"

Xalivar waited until the door slid shut behind his aide. "He was raised to lead and you made him soft, Miri. Leaders must be hard. They cannot afford to be blinded by compassion."

"Human beings cannot afford to be totally blinded to concern for others as you are, brother," Miri said, anger rising.

Xalivar rolled his eyes. *Not this conversation again!* He and his sister had always been different. Miri had protected Davi just as their own father had protected her, and now neither Davi nor Miri understood the harsh realities of leadership.

"If he is to rule one day, he will have to learn to make difficult decisions," Xalivar responded.

"You think he killed an Alliance soldier in haste? Perhaps he had no other choice! Perhaps it was an accident!" Miri threw her hands in the air.

"Whatever the circumstances," Xalivar said, softening his tone, "we both know the law. He will have to answer to the Tribunal of Lords. We will do all we can to help him, of course. If there is a good explanation, they will show him mercy. Have you had any contact with him since he's been on Vertullis?"

"One e-post to let me know he had arrived," Miri replied.

Her eyes caused him to doubt her. They always darkened when she felt uncertainty. She and Davi had always been close. Why would they not continue to be? The distance would slow them down, but electronic communications between Legallis and Vertullis were fast, especially for officers like Davi with access to Borali Alliance channels.

"Nothing else?"

"I already told you," she said, still angry.

"You will, of course, let me know if you hear from him?"

"Of course," she said.

Xalivar made a mental note to have her e-posts monitored. He hated to resort to spying on his own family. In the past, Miri's correspondence had been of no relevance, but this was different. Davi was Xalivar's known heir and he had to stay informed about all developments. He moved to the window behind the throne and stared out at the starport, hoping Zylo and Bordox would have good news for him.

✳✳✳

Davi sat in Lura's kitchen, lost in thought, as life spun on around him. He'd run fearing how Bordox might treat him, but he knew he would have return to Legon and face this. He'd been over and over it in his mind and decided turning himself in to the LSP would create all sorts of problems. The best route would be to contact his mother and go straight to his family first. They could determine together what to do next. Beyond the issues of the Captain's death, he needed to resolve the issues of his heritage or it would eat away at him. He had to know who he was.

At Lura's, he reconnected with Nila again and met Lura's sister, Rena.

They were all very kind to him, convinced he was their long-lost relative. He couldn't choose to know how to respond until he'd cleared it all up with Miri. When he'd attempted to sneak back to the barracks and send an e-post, the LSP had been there waiting for him. Instead, he sent a message at a kiosk on the sidewalk.

Afterwards, he proceeded across a public park to a ritzy neighborhood he hadn't visited since his second week on the planet. The home of Sinaia Quall, the Borali Alliance's Ambassador to Vertullis, stood in a cul de sac at the end of a palm-tree-lined corridor—the black iron fence declaring its separation from the world outside.

After the guard admitted him, the Ambassador's major domo escorted him to her office. The opulence still impressed him despite the fact he'd been there once before—the red curtains, gold-embossed furniture and fixtures, the fine Regallian carpets and paintings from artists around the solar system. The smell of papers from her crowded desk mixed with incense and her flowery perfume.

She smiled and stood behind her desk as he entered. Despite the height of the dark hair she kept permanently affixed in a bun atop her head, most people towered over her, but she compensated for it with intense self-confidence. She wore a blue suit, neatly pressed, as if appearance counted even when she was alone in her home. Her grip was firm as she shook his hand.

"Captain Rhii," she said with a warm smile, "I've been meaning to have you over again since the dinner right after you arrived, but I'm afraid the diplomats have kept me rather busy."

Davi smiled. "I'm sorry I haven't managed to drop by either. I've appreciated your kindness to me."

She shrugged as if it were nothing. "Your uncle has been a good friend. What brings you here today?"

After Davi explained what had happened with the Captain and the

LSP soldiers, she agreed that going to his family first was the wisest course.

"I don't like to take advantage of my status as a Royal," Davi said, starting to apologize.

"Nonsense!" the ambassador said. "Imprisoning a Royal would be as bad for the Alliance itself as it would be for your family, and my job is to serve the Alliance. I'm pleased you came to me."

After ordering supper and drinks from her servants, she excused herself and headed to the communications room down the hall.

An hour later, a shuttle picked him up in the park down the corridor. Once they'd cleared the planet, the pilot slipped into sub-light taking them to Legallis in just under ten hours' time. Upon landing, he headed straight to his mother's chambers at the Palace, and she accompanied him to see Xalivar.

"You seem to have made a name for yourself in the most undesirable ways," Xalivar said, stepping down from the throne as the door shut behind them.

"It was not intentional," Davi said.

"Of course not!" Miri said, but stopped as her face reverted to a worried expression. She looked at Davi, anxious for answers.

"Murder they're saying." Xalivar's look also urged him to explain.

Dave hesitated. He'd known the moment was here from the time he boarded the shuttle, yet standing before them, his throat grew heavy, and he found it challenging to formulate the words to explain. After a moment, he forced the words out.

"I came upon the Captain as he was about to commit a violation against a female. When I interfered, he turned on me. In trying to subdue him, I inadvertently killed him." He offered a silent prayer to the gods, hoping they'd understand.

Xalivar almost spat the words out: "Why are you helping workers? They are ancient enemies of our people."

Davi was shocked by the fierceness of his uncle's tone. "Alliance soldiers raping helpless young girls does not qualify to me as subduing our subjects."

"You think they deserve better?" Xalivar asked, irritated.

"They don't deserve to be treated worse than animals," Davi said. If his uncle didn't understand, he hoped his mother would.

"We do what we must," Xalivar said.

"Then we act dishonorably," Davi replied.

Xalivar's look warned him to mind his words. "One day, if you lead the Alliance, you'll understand the hard decisions which have to be made."

"I don't know if I could ever understand this!" Davi said.

Miri shot a look at Xalivar, which showed she agreed.

Xalivar stared at them a moment as if collecting his words and thoughts. When he spoke, his tone became softer again. "Inadvertently?" Xalivar raised an eyebrow.

"He was very strong. I tried to use a board to knock him unconscious, but a spike entered his brain and killed him," Davi explained. "His death was an accident."

"What an unfortunate thing," Miri said, her voice full of concern.

"You know the law?" Xalivar asked.

"I would hope the law would account for accidents," Davi replied, beginning to doubt he could count on his uncle for help.

"There were witnesses?" Xalivar asked.

"A few workers, yes," Davi said.

"You will, of course, write up a full report, Captain?"

Davi nodded. "Of course."

"Good. As soon as possible. Then I can go to the Council and get the arrest warrant revoked before real harm is done."

"You believe they will show mercy?" Miri said, hopeful.

"I believe they will consider the circumstances. I make no promises, but he is a Royal, and he has come himself to face it," Xalivar said.

"You are the High Lord Councilor," Miri said.

"I know who I am. But I am not a dictator," Xalivar said. "This is a matter for the Council." Davi and Miri exchanged a look. They both knew Xalivar had heavy influence with the Council.

"The Council on which you serve," Miri said.

"As one of twelve members, and I must recuse myself from this," Xalivar said. "The Council will be fair."

Davi's heart sunk. He'd hoped his uncle's influence might serve to keep the matter private. Xalivar's look told him the discussion was over.

"You dislike your duty assignment."

It was more of a statement than a question. "I have learned many things I did not know," Davi said.

Xalivar smiled. "Ah, I see you do indeed still have the heart of a diplomat, Xander." He laughed. "You will find life is full of hard choices."

"He has known this for a long time," Miri said.

Xalivar sigh loudly and shot her a stern look. "The choices faced by a leader are different." He smiled. "We have much to talk about. Your education has barely begun." He reached over and pressed a button on a pillar to his right.

Davi did his best to hide his disappointment. "I understand."

The door slid open behind Davi and Miri as Manaen entered and stood at attention.

"Go with your mother. I believe she has missed you. I have some things to attend to, but I'll join you when I can," Xalivar said.

Miri smiled warmly at Davi as he saluted his uncle. "Yes, High Lord

Councilor." Then they turned and walked out together.

***

Miri's suite was a section of rooms smaller than Xalivar's on the opposite wing of the Palace. The main room resembled the throne room with pillars lining the two long walls. A raised dais ran around the room with the largest section of the floor in the center, set down by several inches. Two couches sat angled around an entertainment center with a vidscreen. There was a desk in the corner with a terminal. Four rooms led off the main at each corner—a bedroom, closet, kitchen and dining area, and cleansing room.

As soon as they arrived, Miri embraced him like she had at the landing pad. For a moment, she held him like she'd never let go.

"When Yao told me what happened, I was so afraid for you," Miri said, still reeling from her brother's refusal to protect her son.

"I'm sorry to worry you," Davi said, stepping off the dais onto the center floor.

"When you had expressed your concerns by e-post, I should have arranged time for us to talk sooner. I'm sorry," Miri said, following him.

"It's not right, mother. If the general public knew about this—" Davi said as Miri put her fingers over his lips.

"Keep your voice down."

"We're in the Royal Palace, in your private quarters," Davi said.

"Which doesn't mean we can't be overheard," Miri said, knowing her brother spied on friends as well as enemies.

"When I was younger, he was always there for me. I never would have imagined he'd sanction such—"

Miri shushed him again. "We always did our best to protect you."

"From what? Reality?"

She winced at the intensity of his tone. "From things which might hurt you," Miri said, her eyes pleading. *Please don't ask for details.*

"I'm not the one who's being hurt here," Davi said.

"Yes, you are. You're feeling disoriented, as if this isn't the world you thought you knew," Miri said. "That's much the same way I felt when I discovered it."

"You didn't know it either?"

"When I was younger, about your age, my father protected me, too," Miri said.

"What about uncle, was he also protected?" Davi asked.

"Your uncle was raised to lead. He didn't have to be protected," Miri said. Their father had been very hard with Xalivar.

"I'm his heir, yet I was protected," Davi said.

"You're not his son," Miri said.

"He acted as if I was," Davi said.

"He's very fond of you, but the role of an uncle is different," Miri said.

"He protected me because of you, didn't he?" She saw by his expression that her face had answered for her.

As Davi turned away, Miri stepped toward him. "It was for your own good. I didn't want you to be like him." She'd brought him up to be compassionate, like her.

"I'd like to think I would never be that cold." Davi grimaced as he said it.

"You believe what you're taught to believe," Miri said, hoping some justification might ease the pain of discovering his uncle's cruel nature.

Davi turned back to her, shaking his head. "Humans are capable of intelligence. They can think for themselves, make their own decisions. You ensured I would learn that."

"Yes, but your decisions are based on your sense of morality and justice. Xalivar believes slavery is the right thing for the workers," Miri said.

"Because he doesn't know any different?" Davi refused to accept it.

"Because it's the way it's always been," Miri said with a sigh. *Please, my son, no good can come of this attitude.*

"A few select history lessons of the evils of the Vertullians, skipping, of course, our own mistakes or abuses, and any human being can be trained not to think about it?" Davi remarked.

Miri saw Davi didn't like it one bit. "This occurs in any society," she said, sinking into one of the couches.

"Which makes it right?" Davi's voice was loud as he fought to control his anger. Miri looked toward the door. "What are you afraid he might hear, mother? About a baby sent from the stars perhaps? Events you raised your son to be ignorant of?"

Miri couldn't remember the last time she'd been this scared. *Please, gods, I don't want to lose him.* She paused a moment wondering how to disguise her fear when she spoke. "What are you talking about?" Her voice shook as she spoke.

"About this." He reached below his uniform collar and pulled out the necklace. "A baby who came from the stars, a courier craft which crashed—we both know the story," Davi said.

Miri's face fell as she saw he knew the truth. Tears flowed from her eyes like rain. *I should have known it would cost me and kept that damn necklace to myself! Why didn't I just take it before you left for Vertullis?!* She took a deep breath to quelch the swelling desperation and anger inside.

"Isn't that how it goes?"

"I'm sorry," was all she could say between sobs.

"Why didn't you ever tell me?"

"I didn't know how," Miri said. "I dreamed of a child of my own for so long, and there you were, a beautiful baby boy. The note asked whoever found you to raise you as their own—I love you." She wanted to throw herself at his feet, beg his forgiveness, hold him and never stop.

"I've never doubted it," he said. Collapsing onto the sofa, he put his face in his hands. "Everything I thought I knew about myself, about my world—it's changed now. Who am I?"

"I'm still your mother. I raised you," Miri said. She'd been so blessed when she found him and wanted to honor the gift of his birth parents' sacrifice, so she'd given him the necklace and nickname. She'd never imagined they would find each other one day. More than once she'd wanted to tell him, not wanting there to be any secrets between them, but each time, she couldn't bring herself to do it. If only she'd never seen the necklace or the note that told her his name.

"I met her," Davi said, and she knew he meant his birth mother. "The girl the Captain tried to rape is my cousin."

Miri collapsed on the sofa beside him, unable to control her tears. "I'm sorry you never had cousins or siblings..."

"I don't care. I had lots of friends," Davi said.

"Is she nice?" She wasn't sure she wanted to know.

"Yes. And beautiful!"

Miri smiled, wiping at her tears. "I always did what I did because I love you. I want what's best for you."

"We both do." Xalivar's voice startled them both as they turned toward the door.

He stepped out of the shadows. *How long has he been there?* Miri wondered. *How much did he hear? Why didn't we hear the door?*

"You come here to my quarters unannounced—" Miri said, standing to confront Xalivar. Despite knowing his penchant for spying on people, she felt betrayed, disrespected.

"It's my palace. I go where I please, when I please," Xalivar said. "A worker boy raised in my own house!" *He'd heard it all.* "You had no right to keep this from me. To make this decision—"

"It's the Borali Alliance's palace, and I am your sister, not your subject," Miri snapped.

"Stop acting as if you are the one who should feel betrayed," Xalivar said. "He does not belong here!" She saw his fists clench and unclench at his side, something he always did when he was angry. Davi winced at his uncle's every word.

"He's an outsider! In my palace, Miri! Have you no loyalty to your family?"

"Have you no loyalty to yours?" Miri demanded. "He's been like a son to you his whole life. You loved him, as I do!!"

"Based on your lies—"

"I never lied," Miri said. She'd never lied. She just hadn't told him everything. The distinction had allowed her to feel she'd never misled him.

"You never told the truth," Xalivar said, fists clenching again.

"And you never asked," she reminded him.

"Have I been such a terrible nephew?" Davi demanded. "For you to hate me so much..."

"You are an enemy of our people," Xalivar said, frowning as his eyes met Davi's.

"He is a human being!" Miri's voice grew getting louder, along with her desperation. How could Xalivar be so cold to his own nephew? She knew he loved him. Witnessing Xalivar with Davi over the years had been her only proof that her brother was even capable of love.

"He will never belong here!" Xalivar's voice boomed. He punched a button on a wall communicator near the door. "Manaen."

Miri ran to him and fell to her knees, grabbing his arm in desperation. "Please, Xalivar. He's my only son."

"He just told you about meeting his real mother," Xalivar said, emphasizing the last two words to make them sting.

Miri looked away, fighting tears again. "I need him!"

"Then pack your things!" Xalivar said, pushing her away. She collapsed into a ball on the floor at Xalivar's feet as his fists clenched again.

"Don't touch her!" Davi said, stepping forward. The door opened and Manaen appeared.

"He is to be reassigned to Alpha Base on Plutonis at once. Get him suitable clothes and notify the commander," Xalivar ordered as Manaen and Miri reacted, confused.

"He is wanted for murder," Manaen said.

"Let the Council go to him, if they wish," Xalivar said.

Miri screamed and grabbed Manaen by the leg. "No! He's my son! Don't send him away!"

"He's sworn to serve the Alliance," Xalivar said, "As are you," then turned and marched through the door.

Manaen motioned to Davi. "Come with me." Pulling free of Miri, he turned toward the door. Davi followed reluctantly. The door slammed shut behind them.

Miri collapsed on the sofa again, sobs bursting from her like gasps for breath. Everything that mattered had just been stolen from her.

✹✹✹

Plutonis? The ice planet? Things had not gone the way any of the possible scenarios had played in his mind. He was being banished, but not for the reasons he'd expected. Maybe he'd been wrong about Xalivar. By sending him away, Xalivar had protected him from discovery. It would be hard for Miri, sure, but at least he wasn't being thrown out of the Alliance.

He'd feared the worst once his heritage came out, wondered if his uncle loved him the way he'd always thought he did. Now Davi thought his fears had been misplaced. Maybe Xalivar would make the murder charges disappear, too. Despite his anger and disappointment, Xalivar was taking care of his family. And Davi hoped Alpha Base would be a better adventure than Vertullis had been.

He couldn't get the worker's situation out of his mind. He had to find a way to change things. If Xalivar cared about him despite the revelations of his heritage, maybe there was hope he'd be open to considering that, too. It would take time, and it wouldn't be easy, but Davi intended to e-post him about it as soon as he got settled on Plutonis. He was sure his mother would help, too. He reminded himself he had two mothers now. He would also have to let Lura know what had happened. She had been so worried when he returned to Legallis. He would e-post her, too.

He was still trying to wrap his mind around his new identity. It was a big change, and he had a lot to learn. He knew nothing of the workers' religious beliefs, history, etc. Outside of anything he'd studied about them in school—mostly negative due to the Alliance's slant—he knew very little about them, which needed to change. He would ask Lura for resources to begin his reeducation. It would be strange at first, but he had to start thinking of himself as a worker now. Everybody else would. That would be hard as well. At least, he didn't have to change his name.

✳✳✳

Xalivar had gone to Miri's quarters after going over some reports with Manaen. Instead of the corridors, he'd taken a private passage only Royals knew about. He entered Miri's main room through the back of her closet, slipping in unnoticed, to hear Miri and Davi's conversation. Their words took him by surprise. *My designated heir sympathetic to the Alliance's enemies! One of them!*

Xalivar raged at Miri for allowing such a betrayal. Lonely and barren or not, she had no right to make a decision which put the Royal family at risk without consulting him! If word got out, it could jeopardize everything the family had worked for since his grandfather's reign! He had to protect the family as well as the Alliance. So he'd isolate Davi in a remote part of the system until his true loyalty could be ascertained and full damage control achieved.

Damage control started with select, trusted operatives searching Davi's quarters and office on Vertullis, clearing them of all personal belongings and references to Davi and his interactions with others. They then set about trying to locate anyone who knew the truth about Davi's identity. It would take longer and be difficult, because interrogations would have to occur with neither the interrogator nor the subject knowing the full details. They couldn't know. He wanted to control damage, not spread it. Davi's worker family would have to be dealt with as well. He should have ordered Davi to tell him their names, but it could wait until his nephew settled in on Plutonis. He took care not to act in a way that might cause distrust. He needed Davi to trust him now more than ever.

He sat gathering his thoughts, when Miri burst through the Royal passage, unannounced, into his chambers. "How dare you send him away!"

"How dare you leave me no choice," Xalivar responded. She was far too emotional for her own good.

"Plutonis is the edge of the Alliance!" Miri said, shooting him a cold stare.

Xalivar was glad then that he'd never married. He'd spent little time with women outside of a few social interactions and found himself unburdened by the guilt men always associated with such female stares. "Which makes it all the more likely he'll be safer there," he said.

"Safe from whom? You? The Council?"

"Do you realize what would happen if his heritage became public knowledge?" Xalivar said. "We could lose the throne! It could undo everything our family has been working so hard for over the past five decades!"

"No one has to find out," Miri said.

"How long do you think we could keep a secret like this with Xander on Vertullis, interacting with his newfound family?" Her ignorance sometimes amazed him. "I did what's best for this family and the Alliance."

"He's my son. I should have a say," Miri said.

"You're not the High Lord Councilor. I am!" Xalivar turned away. "You'll never understand the difficult decisions I am forced to make on a daily basis." He cursed his father for allowing her to be soft.

"I understand the difficulty, just not the choices," Miri said, then whirled and disappeared back into the passageway. Xalivar sighed and hit the button on the communicator to page Manaen. It was time to find out if everything had been arranged per his instructions.

***

Alpha Base was the outermost post for the Borali Alliance in the solar system. Close enough to protect tourist haven Regallis with regular fighter patrols, Plutonis also had few inhabitants and even fewer visitors, thus fewer prying eyes to protect military secrets from. Even the base itself was hidden deep within a manmade cave created by terraform scientists whose technology wasn't up to the challenge Plutonis posed them.

Snow was everywhere, and a cold which was almost overbearing. It felt like being nowhere, because that's pretty where Plutonis was—in deep space far from anything important. Inside the base, Davi and his companions lived as they always had because the computers generated an atmosphere suitable for humans. But when they ventured outside, they had to strap on breathing apparatuses, not to mention an assortment of heavy, winter clothes. The air was cold and thick and hung heavy in their lungs.

Plutonis only had two native species. The antlered Qiwi it was well known for and the humanoid aliens calling themselves Plutonians. Their skin was bluish green, and they had three eyes and four arms. The Qiwi and the Plutonians were the two known species in the system that could live on the planet without breathing apparatuses.

The surprising thing about the antelope was their ability to adapt to other environments. They had long been loved for their meat, but merchants also transported live specimens for sale on other planets. If they were transported on a ship on which the air quality in the hold was adjusted gradually over the course of the voyage, they could adapt themselves to survive in the environment of any planet. Thus, Davi had seen them for sale at the market on Vertullis. He had heard of some on Legallis as well. The Plutonians were not so adaptable. Outside their home planet, they required space suits; because the heavier atmospheres wore them out so much that their hearts would sometimes give out.

While he found the planet itself unpleasant, his duties as a squadron leader thrilled him. The squadron of eight would break into pairs on patrols, spreading themselves out to cover the outer reaches of the system. While they never experienced much excitement, Davi enjoyed the exploration and the thrill of being in flight. It gave him lots of time to think and to continue to wrestling through all the revelations he'd been hit with in the weeks before his reassignment.

He e-posted Xalivar after his first two weeks on base to thank him for protecting him and to remind him to take care of Miri. He also suggested he would welcome more discussion on the worker problem, but Xalivar's reply had not mentioned it. His uncle simply said Miri was doing fine and he'd been glad to hear of Davi's taking to his assignment. Davi had not written his uncle since. Instead, he formulated a plan, hoping to offer Xalivar at least a starting point.

His correspondence with Miri occurred with more frequency. Yao continued to look in on her once a week as Davi had requested. Miri worried about Davi, sad to be so far apart, but seemed to be handling it well otherwise, much to Davi's relief. Davi also e-posted Lura to reassure her of his safety and let her know things had worked out well. He'd heard no more about the Captain's death, though he wasn't yet sure what his uncle's negotiations might have produced on that front. No LSP had come looking for him. He would have to inquire about that as well.

To his surprise, he encountered a small team of worker mechanics on Plutonis. He knew Vertullians had mechanical aptitude. Lura told him his own father had been a mechanic at the depot on Vertullis. But he hadn't realized the Alliance shipped worker mechanics to all major outposts and trusted them with responsibility for the maintenance of all starcraft. Unlike his squadron mates, Davi took time to engage the workers in conversation. For them, lives as slaves on an outpost were much better than lives on their home planet. Here, at least, while facing some restrictions and the usual discriminatory attitude from soldiers and pilots, they were pretty much left alone to do their work and lead their lives. Several of them said such assignments were very competitive.

Seeing the workers every time he entered the launch bay set him to thinking again about his own heritage. It had been unsettling at twenty years of age to realize he wasn't who he'd thought he was. He was thankful for the rest he'd gotten during the voyage to Plutonis. The voyage had taken four days, and instead of spending his time wrestling with his thoughts, Davi had slept. Like his uncle, Miri offered little comment on the new realities in her e-posts, instead reassuring him that

Xalivar had things under control and urging him to relax. As much as he enjoyed being a pilot again, it continued to weigh on him that his blood relatives still lived as slaves on another planet. He had to do something to help them. He just didn't know what.

After a long patrol, Davi sent another e-post to Xalivar and Miri reminding them he'd lost sleep worrying about Lura and other family members. The situation needed to be addressed. *I'd expect you of all people to understand the importance of family*, he wrote. Miri's reply startled him:

To: AgriCptSouth@Federal.emp
From: HRHMRhii@Federal.emp
Subject: Your concerns
My dear son:
While I fully respect your feelings toward these people, what I cannot understand, after all the love and support we have provided is why you think these people still have rights to your love and devotion. They launched you into unknown space on a dangerous, makeshift craft. I think they forfeited their parenting rights and any claim to you with such an act. We are the ones who have raised you, supported you, and helped you for twenty years. We are the ones you should be concerned about, not the worker family whose only tie to you is genetic.
Wanting always what's best for you,
                    Your loving mother

Xalivar's e-post was short and to the point, reading: "I concur with your mother."

Davi knew his mother to be a caring person. Although this must be hard for her, he couldn't simply ignore people who were his family. After all, they had not given him up out of a lack of desire. They had done it to save his life from Xalivar's decree. Davi realized he couldn't fight this battle from six planets away. He had to go back and confront things face to face.

Miri had taught him not to use his Royal status for special treatment, and Davi had done his best to avoid it. But when he filed a request with his commander for emergency family leave, and his commander grumbled a bit about granting a leave to someone who'd arrived only a few weeks before, Davi used his status as Royal. He was granted leave and passage on a transport two days later.

Not wanting to give them time to argue, Davi did not notify Miri and Xalivar. Xalivar might well get word of it through military channels anyhow. Besides, Davi had asked his commander for passage to Vertullis—something he didn't want to have to explain just yet.

A week later, he arrived at Lura's door. Once she overcame her shock at seeing him, she embraced him joyfully. "I've been so worried about you. Thank you for the kind e-posts. I cherished every one!"

Davi smiled. "I'm sorry to have caused you any worry."

"Well, you should know by now that mothers worry. We can't help it," she said with a laugh. Thinking of Miri, Davi realized mothers on every planet must be the same and laughed with her.

"How was Plutonis?"

Davi told her about the antelope, the Plutonians, the worker mechanics and life as a pilot. He spoke with great passion, and she seemed enraptured by his story. When he had finished, he apologized. "I know it must not be as exciting for you as I make it sound."

"Sounds like a fascinating adventure," Lura said, her face sincere. She patted his arm. "Are you hungry from your journey?"

"I spent most of the time asleep," Davi said. "But I wouldn't mind a good home-cooked meal."

"Didn't you go to Legallis first?" She asked as if she expected it.

"No. I came to see you."

She smiled, surprised. "I'm so honored." Then she moved to the kitchen, opened the cooling unit and began preparing a meal.

"I had something very important I needed to tell you," Davi said, choosing his words with care.

Seeing the look on his face, Lura stopped what she was doing and their eyes met. "What is it?"

"I know the truth now, mother. I'm sorry if I caused you pain taking so long to accept it."

Lura smiled bigger than he'd ever seen and rushed to embrace him. "The hardest part was over the day we met. Welcome home, Son!"

He hugged her back as their tears flowed. It felt so natural to be in her arms, as if they'd always known each other.

CHAPTER FIVE

Before he'd finished reading the report, Xalivar's head already throbbed. Manaen had tactfully disappeared. *The little rat reads my dispatches,* he noted with displeasure. *I should have known. Maybe it's time to find a new major domo.*

After all he had done for Davi, this is how his nephew repaid him—betrayal. It hadn't been easy to get the Council to ignore the murder of a soldier. Xalivar had explained the circumstances to the members a few at a time in private, and all agreed it was bad for both the Royal Family and the Alliance to proceed with the charges. The few who were reluctant had been convinced with careful reminders of their own families' secrets. Now, here Davi was, trying to undo everything with one fell swoop!

What is the boy thinking, taking a leave without my permission? I am not just his uncle! I am High Lord Councilor! I should have never allowed Miri to raise the boy herself. I should have stepped in the moment I settled on Davi as my heir. This would not be happening if the boy had a proper sense of his responsibility to the Alliance and his place in it.

To make matters worse, Davi hadn't gone to Legallis. Emergency family leave to Vertullis meant one thing—the boy was up to something with his worker family. Why couldn't he let it be? Didn't he know the risks? Didn't he know his uncle always did what was best for him? The younger generation these days was so frustrating! So rebellious and independent! Just like a worker!

Maybe he had been too harsh in what he'd said when he learned of Davi's heritage, but he'd been shocked and dismayed by the discovery. He'd done the right thing in the end, hadn't he?

Xalivar punched a communicator on the arm of the throne. Manaen's voice came back right away. "Yes, my Lord?"

"Find him this instant and get him here! I don't care what it takes!

"Yes, Lord," Manaen replied as the communicator went dead. The time had come for Xalivar to start playing hard ball.

✱✱✱

Davi sat at Lura's table as she set out the food she'd prepared. He'd had a few days of getting to know family members. They were all very nice people, but still, the place didn't feel like home.

"Have you spoken with your mother, since you came back?" Lura quietly asked. He looked at her, confused. "Princess Miri?"

"No. I need to. I wanted a few days with you here first," Davi said.

"I imagine she's worried about you. Don't wait too long," Lura said, sounding almost like Miri.

Davi laughed. "Hmmmm. Maybe this having two mothers thing isn't such a good idea after all!"

Lura laughed, then tousled his hair before going back to retrieve another serving dish. "We both worry."

Her concern for Miri touched him. It pleased him to know Lura was sensitive to the feelings of his other family. It meant she'd understand when he had to take time with sorting things out, and he felt a little less pressure as a result. "Maybe I should send her an e-post then after lunch," Davi said.

"Sounds good. There's a kiosk near the park a few blocks from here," Lura told him.

"Yes, mother," Davi said, with a wry grin. Lura laughed. He was enjoying this time with her. It already seemed like they'd known each other longer. She appeared to be enjoying the time with him, too.

Lura brought the last of the dishes to the table, and then sat down across from him. "Do you want to say grace?"

"I'm still not sure I know what to say," Davi said. The religious adjustment would be hard. He was not used to talking to one god or even saying prayers. Sacrifices were offered at official ceremonies. People did their own private worship services from time to time for one or another of the pantheon of gods, but the worker's personal religion was all new to him.

"It's easy," Lura said. "You talk to Father God like he's a person. I'll show you." She bowed her head and Davi did as well. "Father God, we thank you for the reunion with our long lost boy, Davi. We thank you for life and breath and the food on this table, all of which we know you've provided. Bless us now and lead us in your will. Amen." She smiled at him. "Is that so hard?"

"I don't know all the right phrases and words," Davi said.

"The good thing about prayer is there are no rules for how you say it. It's the attitude in your heart which matters to God," Lura said. Davi pondered her words, realizing he had a lot to learn. "Well, don't wait for it to get cold now." She began scooping servings onto his plate.

Later, at the kiosk near the park, he found a message waiting for him when he logged into his e-post account.

To: CptSQuad4Alpha@Federal.emp
From: HLC@Federal.emp
Subject: Where are you?
Nephew:
Your decision to go gallivanting about could cost this family and the Alliance dearly! You are to report to me at once upon reading this missive!
       Xalivar

Davi sighed. Time had run out. He had to go and talk with his Royal family, but he still had no idea what he was going to say. Regardless, they deserved an explanation.

You'd better find the words in a hurry, Davi.

He e-posted for a Royal shuttle to be sent then headed back to Lura's to tell her his plans.

✱✱✱

Manaen escorted Davi as far as the throne room, but let him enter alone. Xalivar stood beside a window, staring out at the city.

"I gave you your orders," Xalivar said, without turning to face him. Davi heard the anger in his voice.

"Can't we talk about this?"

"Soldiers obey orders or they are disciplined. Don't think because I'm your uncle, you'll be given special treatment."

"I've already been given special treatment," Davi said.

Xalivar whirled around, glaring at him as his fists clenched. "Do you know what I had to go through to get the Council not to pursue murder charges against you?"

"I appreciate everything you've done for me."

"And this is how you show your gratitude?" Xalivar turned away again.

"I serve you best by being honest with you, don't I?"

"You serve me best by doing as I instruct you without raising unnecessary questions," Xalivar said.

Davi flinched at his uncle's anger. What could he say to make him understand? "I've been reading history. I don't understand why things are the way they are," Davi said.

"Maybe it's not your job to understand."

"Before the colonists left Earth to settle on other planets, the Legallians and Vertullians were at peace for twelve years," Davi continued. "When the Vertullians discovered they'd settled the planet next door to us, they didn't fight, they sued for peace. Instead, we conquered them and turned them into slaves."

Xalivar turned back to him. Their eyes met. "They cannot be trusted."

"They sued for peace and we betrayed them, yet they can't be trusted?" Davi saw from his eyes that Xalivar really believed it.

"Twelve years of peace during a time when everyone was distracted by other concerns," Xalivar said. "After hundreds of years of wars."

"Extremists and terrorists brought us together. Why would we forget all that when we settled here?"

"Do you know how many of our people have died at their hands? How many communities they destroyed?" Xalivar demanded.

"How many of them have we killed? Can't the past ever be the past?" Davi asked. He'd begun to wonder. His uncle's anger seemed pretty intense over something that happened so long ago. "Twenty years ago, I was supposed to die because of your decree, yet here I am. You let it go and protected me, because I'm your nephew." Xalivar's face changed when Davi mentioned the decree. Had he forgotten? *Maybe he wishes I hadn't survived.*

"I protected you, yes, and here you are trying to undo everything I've done!" Xalivar threw up his hands in dismay as his pupils narrowed and his face turned gray with worry.

"How can I stand by when my own family is living in slavery?"

"Do you wish so badly to join them in their plight?" Xalivar said. "Everything I've worked for, everything my father and grandfather worked for could be undone by this, Xander! Do you not care about this family any longer since you've found a new one?" They both turned at the sound of the door opening behind them.

Miri's feet shuffled on the carpet as she rushed in. "Why didn't you tell me you were here?" she said, looking at Davi.

"I didn't have the chance yet, Mother," Davi said.

"He was too busy arguing the evils of our oppressive Alliance with his uncle," Xalivar said. "He won't let this go. I should have raised him myself, disavowed him of his moral illusions." He stared accusingly at Miri.

"I raised him to think for himself," Miri said.

"Well, he's decided this family is the enemy now," Xalivar said, fists clenching again.

"You're still my family. I care about you," Davi said with frustration. Did his uncle really believe that?

Xalivar waved dismissively to Miri. "I cannot do what he asks. You talk sense into him." He turned and stopped beside the door to his private chambers, punching a code. The door slid up and Xalivar disappeared inside, leaving them alone.

"You're trying to fight a system which has been in place for generations, Davi," Miri said.

"It's wrong, mother."

"It won't change overnight," Miri said.

Davi knew she was right but was convinced he had to try. "Someone has to speak for the workers. People know who I am; maybe I can make them listen."

"Or you will make more enemies than you ever imagined," Miri said.

"So you would have me stand by and do nothing?"

"No, but I would have you recognize there will be more to convince than just your uncle," Miri said, frustrated.

"I have to start somewhere." Davi turned away, knowing she was right. "I won't give up. I can't."

"Do you want to go to prison? Do you want to be killed?" Miri's voice was tinged with desperation; worry filled her eyes.

"I'm willing to do what it takes to change things for my people," Davi said as their eyes met.

"The Lords or the workers?"

"Both, Mother. I belong to both," he said with a sigh.

"I can't protect you." Her voice was pained.

"I know. I would never hurt you, mother; I hope you know that." He looked at her with love and smiled.

"I only want what's best for you. Your uncle, too," Miri pleaded.

"Can't you see I have to do this?" Davi said, as tears ran down her cheeks. He hurt for her. He raised his arms and she rushed into his embrace. He stayed there holding her awhile.

✳✳✳

Xalivar watched the Royal Shuttle depart with Davi aboard from his private quarters. How could he have been so blind? He'd forgotten all about the decree! He'd forgotten all about the nightmares which kept him awake, night after night. He'd never given much credence to dreams, but after his scientists had reported an increase in male births on Vertullis, Xalivar issued a decree and sent his Special Police squads to destroy all first-born males. They'd seemed so real to him then, but twenty-one years had passed. No one had arisen to challenge him in the decade that followed. He'd ultimately come to believe the dreams had been nonsense, but now...

How could he have been so wrong? He would do whatever it took to protect the Alliance. He loved the boy, but love wasn't enough sometimes. Davi would have to be watched, although he didn't want him harmed. Not yet. He hoped it wouldn't come to that, but he was prepared to do what was necessary. Miri would object, of course, but neither she nor her son really grasped what was at stake. Anyone was expendable if they rebelled. It couldn't be tolerated.

The Council was scheduled to meet that afternoon, and he knew what must be done. He had to keep Davi close, and he had the perfect means right under his nose. Funny, he'd almost failed to see that, too. He'd been all ready to order Davi back to Plutonis. *I must be growing weary. I need to get more rest. I have to stay on top of such things.* He smiled. Yes, it was the perfect plan. So perfect, it would almost seem like a natural course of events beyond even Xalivar's control.

✷✷✷

"Let me get this straight," Lord Tarkanius said, leaning forward in his chair at the head of the table. "You now support the Council in prosecuting your own nephew for murder?"

Xalivar and Tarkanius sat atop a large dais, as officiators of the meeting. The other Council members were seated at rows of tables facing them. All wore the embossed white robes customary for Council meetings. Located in the Council Building, across the government complex from the Palace, the chamber itself was modeled after the U.S. Senate back on old Earth but smaller.

"Having now learned other details of the incident, yes," Xalivar said, looking at Tarkanius.

He heard several Lords' grumbles from around the room. They were all surprised by his change of heart. "You are no longer concerned about the scandal this could cause?" Lord Hachim asked from halfway down the aisle on Xalivar's right.

"There will be talk, of course. But we believe we can contain it," Xalivar said.

"I hear rumors your nephew abandoned his post at Alpha Base and traveled back to Vertullis," Lord Niger said. He was seated near Hachim, his skin and hair dark, owing to his African ancestry. "Why would he do that?"

"His sympathy for the workers has driven him to unpredictable behavior," Xalivar said. "It is quite disturbing even to hear him discuss it."

"Yes, I can imagine it would be," Lord Obed said from Xalivar's left. His skin had a light yellowish brown hue, common to people of Hispanic backgrounds and his brown eyes were intense like his son's. The overseer of the Lord's Special Police, Obed's and Xalivar's families had been rivals since their grandfathers' days.

You'd love to see me go down, wouldn't you, Obed? Not today.

He smiled to himself. The special session was off limit to visitors. No one would witness Xalivar setting his plan in motion. He was free to manipulate the Council just as he'd planned.

Xalivar could see the questions in the Lords' eyes and feel their distrust. They feared betrayal; good! He liked keeping them off balance. It gave him more power.

"Given the circumstances, I have no choice but to support the Council in upholding the law. Our sense of justice must prevail."

"And how will your dear sister react to this?" Lord Tarkanius asked.

"Miri has always been far too weak to govern," Xalivar said, dismissing her.

"Will she hold her tongue?" Lord Niger asked.

"I will assist her, as required," Xalivar said. A couple of Lords frowned with distaste. "The younger generation is harder to bring into line these days. Many of you have first-hand knowledge of this from your own offspring." Several nodded and groaned.

"Well, with your support we cannot refuse," Hachim said.

"All right, let us take a vote then to reissue the arrest warrant," Tarkanius said. "All in favor, say aye."

When the votes were tallied, the decision was unanimous. Despite their reservations, none were willing to quarrel with the High Lord Councilor. Some, like Obed, couldn't resist the chance to do his reputation damage. Others feared his power. None of this bothered him. He had manipulated them as he'd planned, and he would deal with whatever came next.

"Lord Obed, send your Special Police again to locate and arrest the Prince," Tarkanius said with regret.

"I am reinstating the orders as we speak," Obed said, typing on the terminal in front of him. Xalivar suppressed a smile, amazed at how easy it was.

✳✳✳

Davi sat at Lura's table again and described his discussions with Xalivar and Miri. "Did you expect them to change their minds simply because you asked?" Lura asked, her brow furrowing at his frustration.

"I guess not," Davi said. "I expected them to listen at least."

"Xalivar's father was on the Council when they voted to enslave us," Lura said, "His grandfather started the war. And Xalivar himself has always been against us."

"I hoped it was different now," Davi said with growing sadness.

"It's hard for people to change," Lura said. "For the Council, the stakes are very high."

"Of course," Davi said, "But my mother raised me to believe in humanity's right to self-determination, and even she argued with me about it." He knew Miri worried, but he'd still expected more support from her.

"The Lords don't see workers as human," Lura said.

Davi turned away and shook his head. He couldn't bear to look at her when he acknowledged it. He didn't know how to help her. "I can't accept it," Davi said.

"None of us have any choice," Lura said, rubbing his back. "Don't be sad, my son. None of this is a surprise for me. I've lived with it all my life."

She had prepared another wonderful meal. They ate together in silence, as Davi struggled to come to terms with what had happened. Even the delicious dessert of fresh Gixi pie couldn't overcome his somber mood.

Afterwards, Davi helped Lura clear the table and wash the dishes. "Who'd have ever thought I'd have a Prince drying my dishes?" Lura teased.

Davi chuckled. "I've never done it before. Hope I'm doing it right." He kind of enjoyed the experience of feeling normal for once.

"You're doing just fine," she said.

When they'd finished, Lura took him out for a walk. "There's someone I think you should meet," she said as they wound their way through the residential corridors and across the park where Davi had used the kiosk.

On the other side, they entered a residential district with several corridors of nothing but apartments, then came to a cul-de-sac with houses which seemed larger than most worker houses he'd seen. Lura stopped at the door of a large blue house, designed in the nouveau deco style so popular a decade before and pushed the doorbell.

A gray-haired woman wearing a flowery apron wrinkled and stained from years of work answered the door and smiled when she saw Lura. "Lura! Welcome! It's been months!" The two women embraced and the woman waved them inside, letting the door shut behind them.

"Calla, I want you to meet my son, Davi," Lura said.

Emotion exploded off Calla's face. Her eyes lit up and her smile was blinding. She hugged Lura again and swung her around like they were dancing. "Davi? After all these years?"

Lura nodded as Davi extended his hand. Calla laughed and embraced him with passion. "If you think your Aunt Calla will settle for a handshake after twenty-one years, you are quite mistaken."

"Is Aron in?" Lura asked as she watched them, amused.

Calla released Davi and motioned with her head toward the corridor. "Of course. He's in the study. Come." She led them into the house and down a long corridor, which seemed endless—not at all what Davi had expected from a worker's home. Another corridor appeared, almost out of thin air, and they turned right and stopped beside a door, where Calla punched in a code. This was no ordinary worker's home.

The door opened, letting them into a large office. A gray-haired man sat behind a desk, reading something on his terminal. He looked up, smiling as he saw both Lura and Calla.

"You'll never guess who this is," Calla said, motioning to Davi. Joy radiated like a sun's rays from her face.

The man stood and moved around his desk. He was short and bulky, with hands that showed signs of years of manual labor. He moved toward them, looking Davi over. "He looks so much like his father."

As he drew closer, Davi saw a face more youthful than he'd expected from one with such gray hair.

Calla smiled, pleased. "Yes, he does."

Davi extended his hand as the man chuckled, looking pleased. "Nice to meet you."

"This is your father's oldest friend, Aron," Lura said. Lura had told him about Aron's help with the courier.

Aron shook his hand with a grip full of strength, his large hand surrounding Davi's like a glove. "After all these years to see you again...Sol would be so happy."

"Aron helped your father prepare the craft in which we sent you away," Lura reminded him. Davi nodded.

Aron frowned. "Only we made a mistake in preparing it." His face turned sad as he recalled it.

"He is safe and sound," Calla said, placing her arm around his shoulder.

"We never saw your father again after that day," Aron said, remaining dour. "Such dark times," Aron continued, lost in memories. He regained his composure and motioned toward two couches and chairs arranged in a square. "Please. Sit."

"Mother told me he disappeared, but does anyone know where?" Davi asked, as he sat in a chair, wondering if he'd ever get the chance to meet his father.

Aron sat in the other chair, while Calla and Lura sat together on a couch. "None of us knows. But when the LSP take people away, they are never heard from again," Aron said.

"Davi was raised on Legallis, in the Royal Palace," Lura said.

"The Royal Palace? I guess our little courier's malfunction was not so disastrous after all," Aron said, chuckling. They all laughed.

"He's a Captain in the military," Lura said with pride.

"I recognized his Alliance accent and wondered," Aron said. "Are you a pilot?"

"Top of his class," Lura said, smiling at him.

Davi blushed. "I am certified in flight, yes."

"Davi has been working hard to convince Lord Xalivar to free our people," Lura said.

"A Borali Alliance officer questioning the High Lord Councilor?" Aron laughed. "How's that gone?"

"Not as well as I'd hoped," Davi said, turning away. He'd never felt so useless.

"It's hard to reverse hundreds of years of oppression, as history has shown," Aron said. "You are not the first to try."

"I won't go back to my assignment until I find a way to make them listen," Davi said. "I can't accept it." He feared he had no choice. He was running out of options.

"Many in the Alliance won't appreciate your attitude," Aron said.

"I know. But I was raised to believe man has a right to be free," Davi said, knowing he'd had more privileges than any of them.

"Raised to believe this in the Royal Palace right under Xalivar's nose?" Aron laughed. Calla and Lura joined him. "He must be quite disturbed by that."

"Davi's mother is Princess Miri," Lura said.

Aron smiled. "Maybe I should take you with me to meet some friends of ours." Lura nodded in agreement. "You might like to hear their thoughts on the worker situation. And they yours."

"Anything I can do to help," Davi said, smiling.

Aron patted him on the arm, smiling back. "Your father would be proud to hear you talk this way."

✱✱✱

Xalivar waited with Zylo for Bordox to arrive. After the Council meeting he had summoned them, wanting men he could trust to lead the search for his fugitive nephew. Neither man had been told why he'd been called to the Palace, so Xalivar could evaluate them, in addition to their military records, by how they responded to the assignment.

The door slid open and Manaen entered, followed by Bordox, who seemed overwhelmed. He'd never been in the throne room before. He took it all in, and then turned back toward Xalivar, as if afraid to turn away. *Might as well enjoy this*, Xalivar thought, making his way back to the throne as the door slid closed behind Bordox. He sat down. He always looked more imposing sitting there.

"Lieutenant Bordox, welcome to the Royal Palace." Tall like his father, Lord Obed, Bordox towered over both Zylo and Manaen.

He'd tower over me, too, if I wasn't on this dais. He could see why Bordox inspired fear in some. *And yet you don't fear Davi, do you?* His nephew didn't seem the type to inspire much fear.

"Thank you, Lord," Bordox said with a slight bow as his index and middle and fourth and fifth fingers crossed in the salute. His gray uniform was pressed and neat, like he'd wanted to make the best impression.

"I have been admiring your work on behalf of the Alliance. A very impressive record," Xalivar said.

"It's an honor to serve, my Lord," Bordox said, his legs wobbling a bit from nerves as he stood at attention.

I see none of the cockiness I'd heard about. At least he knows how to show proper respect. Xalivar reminded himself this was the same cadet who had been Davi's rival at the Academy.

"This is Major Isak Zylo."

Zylo nodded to Bordox. "Pleasure to meet you, Lieutenant."

"You, too, sir," Bordox replied, continuing to wobble.

I just complimented your record. You'd think you'd relax. "I've called you both here for a special assignment. The Council has announced murder charges against Captain Xander Rhii, my nephew."

Bordox didn't react, but Zylo's face showed surprise. "Captain Rhii, sir? I served with him on Vertullis."

"He was involved in an altercation with a fellow Captain. That Captain was killed," Xalivar explained.

Ah, there it is, Bordox, in your eyes—is that excitement I see? Good. Perhaps your resentment will serve me well. "Major Zylo will head the intelligence gathering. Lieutenant Bordox will lead in the field."

Ah, yes, your eyes seem pleased, Lieutenant. I hope your personal feelings won't keep you from obeying orders.

"Yes, my Lord," Zylo said.

"I want him brought in unharmed. His last known whereabouts was Vertullis." Xalivar couldn't resist playing with Bordox a bit. "I'm assuming your competitive spirit won't interfere with your understanding of orders, Lieutenant?"

Bordox's brown eyes showed surprise and he shifted on his feet. "Innocent competition between classmates, my Lord."

His eyes revealed he was lying but Xalivar smiled, admiring his resolve. "Good, Lieutenant. We're already three weeks behind him. You should both get started at once."

Both officers saluted again then turned toward the door as Manaen opened it for them. As they exited, Manaen turned back to Xalivar, his red eyes attentive.

"I want constant reports of their progress, Manaen," Xalivar said.

"Yes, my Lord," Manaen nodded then turned and followed the others.

Xalivar stepped down from the throne and moved toward the

window, as the door closed behind Manaen. *Miri will have to be dealt with.* He dreaded it. *I wish it hadn't come to this, but she's left me no choice.* He wondered why he was so conflicted. Perhaps he, too, had gotten soft.

✹✹✹

A week after their first meeting, Aron invited Davi to accompany him to a gathering of friends. The meeting took place in a large square in one of the residential districts on the edge of Iraja. Hundreds of workers attended. Davi hadn't expected anything like this! They all seemed so relaxed given the fact that mass gatherings of workers were forbidden. No one there seemed concerned about possible repercussions.

A makeshift wooden platform stood in the center of the square, and the crowd had gathered in a large circle around it. Davi and Aron wound their way through the chattering crowd toward the platform. Davi overheard people wondering what this meeting was about. Others chatted about their work and lives. Still others complained about there being too many people for the space. Volunteers handed out buttons with the initials WFR on them.

As they drew near, a young woman standing on the platform waved at Aron and ran to the edge to meet them. She wore a colorful dress bearing a WFR pin like the ones being handed to the crowd. Offering her hand, she helped first Aron and then Davi onto the platform. Davi was surprised by her strength. *Perhaps years spent as manual laborers did have its benefits.*

Aron introduced the girl as Brie. They were soon joined by a young man named Dru and another woman named Tela. Brie and Dru seemed like they had to be in their teens. Tela was around Davi's age and quite pretty. She had long brown hair and an attractive curved figure, medium height with blue eyes which sparkled. He had to force himself to take his eyes off of her. She didn't seem to notice his stare and continued talking with Aron, reviewing the agenda.

Brie smiled, taking his arm and pointing him toward some chairs on the platform. "Let me show you to your seat, Mr. Rhii." Was she flirting with him?

"Please, call me Davi," he said, smiling back.

Brie seemed to blush a bit at his smile and looked away. "Okay, Davi. Such an exciting day for the Resistance!"

Yep, definitely flirting. He glanced back toward Tela, hoping she hadn't noticed. Tela took no note of them. "Which Resistance?"

She laughed as if he were teasing. "The Workers Freedom Resistance, of course." She pulled a button from her pocket and pinned it to his shirt, letting their eyes meet a moment. She was so close her breath warmed his cheek. Again he found himself glancing toward Tela. Again she took no notice. No woman had ever shown so little interest in him. He turned back as Brie smiled. She seemed plenty interested. In fact, for a moment, he actually thought she might kiss him. *Forget Tela. Brie's rather cute.* Then she stepped back and hurried off to return to other duties.

But as he watched her go, Tela cleared her throat into a microphone. "Hello, friends! Welcome to the first gathering of the Workers Freedom Resistance! It's an exciting day for workers all over the solar system!" The crowd quieted to hear what she was saying. Her enthusiasm was contagious, her lilting voice arrested everyone's attention. Davi couldn't take his eyes off her. "We have with us today a man whom many of you know and respect, a man who has provided leadership to us through difficult days. I give you Aron Tal!"

Brie, Dru and Tela applauded. A few in the crowd joined in as Aron took the microphone.

"My good people, it gives me great pleasure to see you here today. For many generations, we have lived at the mercy of our old enemy and rival, whose sole mission has been to control and oppress us. But an opportunity has presented itself to bring about changes. Many of you know me as a man of patience and reason, but I tell you today—my patience has run out! The time for reasoning is very short. We must become a people of action and demand what we deserve—our freedom, our dignity, our planet."

Shouts erupted from all around them—showing the crowd shared his sentiments, though the looks on their faces made it clear most doubted his veracity. They applauded and cheered a few moments before Aron continued.

"The Borali Alliance has refused to talk with us. The Lords deem us unworthy of their time and consideration. They treat us worse than they treat their animals, but I believe in part we are to blame for this." Mumbles of surprise issued from the crowd.

"It's easy for us to blame the Lords, while we continue to do nothing but complain. Over the years there have been many voices, but no action. The time has come for us to work together. Only united can we take action that will have true impact. By uniting together with the same focus we give to our jobs, we can force them to listen." This brought more cheers and applause.

A few men near the front began to chant. "Freedom! Freedom!" Others joined in the cry.

"Yes, my friends. Freedom can be ours!" Aron said, stirring the fervor among them.

Davi watched an older woman push her way to the front. "Freedom for what? To be crushed by the Alliance? To be beaten? To be debased? Humiliated as we have been so many times before? It will merely lead to greater oppression," she shouted.

"Which is why we must work together. We outnumber them here on our own planet. If we stand together, they cannot hope to defeat us,"

Aron assured her.

Davi saw more of the crowd was getting into the idea now. More joined the chant, crying: "Freedom! Freedom!"

Aron spoke for a few more minutes, followed by a speech from Dru aimed at the younger people in the crowd. Afterwards, Tela got up and invited them to sign a petition supporting the Resistance. As the crowd dispersed, volunteers stood with databoards awaiting signatures, but few agreed to sign. Several expressed doubts like those of the older woman and walked away. In the end, the WFR leaders looked discouraged.

"Change cannot happen overnight," Aron said, trying to reassure them. "We must remain firm in our resolve."

"How can they yell so much and yet walk away so indifferent?" Tela asked.

"We have to inspire them to hope again," Aron said. "Those impulses have been smashed for years by the Alliance. They need to believe again. And they will in time." He embraced them each in turn, and then started home with Davi.

"What did you think?"

"You're trying to start a movement?"

"We're trying to unite our people, and get the Alliance's attention," Aron said.

"Large gatherings of workers will no doubt get their attention, and they'll send soldiers to arrest and detain you," Davi said. He admired the man's resolve.

"They have to find us first," Aron said with confidence.

As they walked back toward Lura's house, Davi became quite disoriented. He couldn't have found his way back to the square, let alone anywhere else. The location had been well chosen. Its narrow corridors and arches were barely wide enough for pedestrian traffic. It would be hard for the Alliance to move troops and vehicles in and surround them. Nonetheless, he knew the Alliance would find a way, even if they had to drop troops in on top of them.

Over the next two weeks, Aron took him to meetings in other parts of the city. The crowds varied in size, but they gradually gathered signatures for their petition. Davi thought the speeches grew better and better each time. Brie, Dru and Tela seemed encouraged and started treating Davi like one of the gang. He even got a smile from Tela once or twice—moments he wished would last forever. He determined to do whatever he could to help them.

At the end of the month, they appeared on an underground comm-channel show to present their message, and Aron asked Davi to say a few words. He stumbled through them, but they seemed pleased with what he'd said.

"You came along at the right time, Davi," Aron said as they walked back to Lura's. "We needed to make the Resistance public, get people stirred up."

"I don't understand why the Alliance hasn't sent troops to arrest you or break up the gatherings," Davi said.

"We publicize by word of mouth," Aron said. "I've been using the underground comm-channel to spread our message a while now. It's enough to bring people out to hear what I have to say."

"Whatever you're doing it seems to be working," Davi said as they entered the courtyard near Lura's house.

They both stopped under the arch, staring at what was left of her front door. The wood had shattered into splinters. Fear spread through him, as Davi raced toward the house.

"Wait! We don't know what's happened," Aron called after him.

He burst inside to find Lura and Nila being nursed by Nila's mother, Rena. "What happened?"

Davi and Aron halted in the doorway. Both Lura and Nila had cuts and bruises. Their dresses were torn.

"Soldiers came," Rena said.

"Soldiers? What did they want?" Aron asked.

"They wanted Davi," Lura said, tears rolling down her cheeks.

I thought the warrant had been dismissed. "My gods, what did they do to you?" Davi rushed to her side, gently caressing her head.

She grasped his hand in hers, smiling. "It looks far worse than it is." He tried to act as if he believed her, but his face gave him away. "The Council reinstated murder charges against you. They had an arrest warrant for you," Lura said, her face full of fear.

"One of them said he knew you," Nila said. "His name was Bord-something."

Davi stood there, incredulous. *No, it couldn't be.*

"An LSP Lieutenant," Rena added.

"Bordox?" Davi asked as they both nodded. He turned away. Had his uncle changed his mind? He thought the matter was settled. "How did they find you?"

The moment he asked the question, Calla appeared at the door out of breath. "Death Squads are going house to house, searching for Davi. He's wanted for murder!"

"We've got to hide you," Lura said. "They could come back any moment!" Panic rose within Davi. Where could he hide?

Aron nodded. "We have the perfect place. Let me call Tela. He hurried to the communicator on the wall near the kitchen, dialed several numbers, and then clicked it off. "Now we wait, and pray."

Davi looked at Lura and Nila and was overcome with regret. He hated being the cause of more hurt for them. Bordox would never stop searching, and if Bordox found him, there was no telling what would happen. He couldn't call his mother for fear his uncle might hear and notify the LSP.

So much for special treatment, mother. He had nowhere to run. They would have notified the starport. For the first time in his life, Davi felt so helpless.

CHAPTER SIX

They waited what seemed like hours, but when the shuttle arrived, Davi looked at his chrono—ninety minutes had passed. When the shuttle door slid open, he couldn't believe his eyes. Tela stepped out onto the ramp and smiled at them.

She's a pilot? She'd handled the shuttle with smooth ease. There was a stirring in his stomach. *I have to get to know this girl!*

The shuttle was an older model Davi hadn't seen in years. It had a gray exterior, instead of the white of recent models. Its interior had the four rows of chairs and harnesses in the passenger cabin and two in the cockpit facing the blast shield and controls.

Tela flew them to the far side of Vertullis over thick and undeveloped forest. It appeared that both the Vertullians and the Alliances kept busy enough with the existing agricultural and urban areas. The forest appeared mostly undisturbed. Tall cedars stretched around them as far as the eye could see. Wood had low value in the system—used mostly for making old-style furniture. Still, when Tela swung the shuttle in amongst them for a landing, it surprised him. Even more so when a portion of a rock wall opened to reveal a large hangar, into which they dove to land.

Stepping off the shuttle, Davi stopped and stared at what lay before him—a genuine Vertullian underground military base. Shuttles and a few Skitters were scattered all around amidst the tool kits, instruments and personnel needed to keep them operational. Mech-bots of various colors and sizes rolled around performing tasks from delivering supplies to starcraft maintenance. Everyone went about their business with a precision and seriousness rivaling any post in the Borali Alliance. He had never imagined such a place could exist. As he took it all in, Tela turned to the group and smiled.

"Welcome to the Workers Freedom Resistance," Tela said.

"I had no idea you could fly," Davi said, smiling.

"Why? Women aren't up to the challenge?" Tela snapped.

"That's not what I meant at all—"

"You fighter jocks are all the same!" Irritated, Tela turned before he could say another word and headed off toward a group of mechanics working nearby. Heat rose inside him. Women had affected him before, but not like this.

"I think it's great," he called after her, but she was already busy chatting with the mechanics.

"I knew you'd been busy with the Resistance, Aron, but I had no idea..." Lura said.

Aron smiled. "It's a well-kept secret whose time has finally come. We've launched a campaign to gather support among our people, and we hope Davi can offer assistance in moving another aspect of the program forward."

What do they want me for? His mind filled with questions. "How can an operation like this remain undetected?" Davi asked.

"Radar coverage is difficult to deploy due to the density of the forest.

Plus, once they clear the forest, our shuttles blend into intraplanetary traffic, and the Alliance hardly expects workers to have starcraft," Aron said.

The Borali Alliance rarely monitored intraplanetary traffic. "It must have taken years to build this," Davi said, full of admiration. He knew the Alliance took for granted that the workers were no threat, but he'd never imagined this possibility. "How do you acquire starcraft?"

"Well, since we're the ones who repair them, when one gets written off as unworthy of repair, we find a use for it," Aron said.

Davi couldn't believe the Alliance would be so careless in disposing of starcraft. "How do you get it here without detection?"

"Our mechanics send it out for one final test flight to ensure its status," Aron said. "When old shuttles designated for destruction disappear, they aren't deemed worthy of much investigation."

They do seem to have figured out the loopholes. "You have an actual hidden starbase here."

Aron laughed. "This is only the beginning. Let's see to your mother and Nila first, and then I'll show you around."

"Of course," Davi said, excited about seeing more. Aron took Lura's arm and led them through the landing bay toward a corridor carved out of the rock at the far end.

✳✳✳

After taking Lura and Nila to a makeshift medical bay, Aron escorted Davi on a tour through corridors cut out of rock. The base had been built using existing caves. Corridors had been either dug out from scratch or expanded from existing tunnels between caves. Other than the hangar, dormitories, and the medical bay, a lot of the caves remained in various stages of development. Digging out the corridors and stringing the reflector pads to light everything alone had taken years.

Their tour ended in a large cavern containing the command center. It was as well developed as any area Davi had yet seen, including computer terminals, radar banks, various displays, a very large vidscreen, and consoles spread through the center in a U-shape. Everything centered around the vidscreen and a large radar monitor table in the center for monitoring battles.

"How did you get all this equipment?" Davi said, taking it all in with awe.

"It's taken us years," a man nearby said, turning at the sound of his voice and smiling when he saw Aron. "We salvaged things wherever we could from old parts, things which had been discarded. A few things, like the radar table, were built from scratch to our own specifications."

Aron nodded as the man extended his hand to Davi. "Davi, this is Joram, one of our military experts."

Davi shook Joram's hand. "I didn't expect there would be a lot of military experts among the workers."

Joram laughed. "We've had to keep our knowledge secret, for sure. I'm well versed in military and cultural history. I also come from a long line of former military men, so I've tried to stay up on the latest materials. Nothing top secret for the Alliance, of course, but the web does provide quite a lot if you have the time to search for it."

Davi nodded. "It's amazing what you've done here!" His friends at the Academy would never believe it.

"You can see why we've taken great lengths to conceal it," Aron said.

Another man joined them near the radar table, handing Aron a datapad. "Aron, we got those reports in on the repair depots."

"Wonderful," Aron said, turning to Davi. "We know the locations of all depots in the Borali Alliance where workers have been assigned."

"I guess some of the Alliance's secrets are easier to crack than others," Davi said.

The new man smiled. "Our intelligence network gets more and more advanced each day."

"Davi, meet Uzah, head of intelligence for the WFR," Aron said.

Davi shook Uzah's outstretched hand. Their organizational structure was as impressive as their facilities and equipment. "This is great, but what do you plan to do with it? A full-scale military?"

Uzah and Joram looked at Aron, appearing to ask if Davi could be trusted. Aron nodded.

"We plan to do whatever it takes to free our people," Joram said.

"We're hoping you'll be willing to assist us," Aron said.

"I don't know what I can do for you," Davi said, recalling his conversations with Xalivar. "I don't seem to have much influence."

"With the Alliance, perhaps not, but you do have something which we have great need of here," Aron said. Davi had no idea what he meant. "Flight training." Aron turned to the others as he continued: "Davi was a leading graduate of the Borali Alliance's military Academy."

Joram and Uzah's reactions told him right away what Aron had in mind. "I've never done much teaching," Davi said.

"I'm sure our pilot candidates will be eager to learn whatever information you can offer," Uzah said.

"You've already met several of them," Aron said. "Why don't we set up a class for you tomorrow so you can meet them?"

"I wouldn't know where to begin," Davi said, flustered. He had never imagined himself as a flight instructor.

"Begin where your instructors began at the Academy," Uzah said. "We can train them on shuttles, and we've rebuilt several old simulators and placed them in a classroom. We also have a number of Skitters, which can be used for training in the forest."

Shuttle training would only offer experience at flight. Shuttles and fighters were too dissimilar for it to be of much use in the long run. Skitters were one-man ground craft which operated on a system allowing them to fly above the planet's surface. They were sleek and fast and easy to maneuver through trees and other obstacles. They also had similar controls and handling to Alliance VS28 starfighters.

"Skitters and simulators are fine, but they can't replace actual flight time. If we have no fighters, how can we provide proper training?" Davi asked.

Uzah, Aron and Joram exchanged a look and smiled. "Don't worry. We have plans in place to acquire some," Joram said.

Aron slapped Davi on the back. "Let's take it a step at a time. They must first be ready for such training, yes?" Davi nodded, still wondering how they would ever get a fleet of fighters here. "Good. As you can see, we have anticipated all of our needs so far. Everything else will come together in time." Davi was starting to believe them. He decided to stop asking questions and see how things played out.

✳✳✳

Xalivar had so far managed to keep Miri in the dark about the hunt for Davi, but her persistent questions about his whereabouts were getting on his nerves. It had been a matter of time before someone let slip to her about the reinstated murder charges. Given Bordox and Zylo's failure to track his nephew down, he'd decided not to sit around waiting but to do some investigating himself. The communicator on the wall of his inner chamber beeped twice. Manaen was coming. Good. He would bring with him some visitors who might provide some answers.

When Xalivar stepped into the throne room, he found Manaen waiting with Farien and Yao. Both had put on their finest dress uniforms, as Bordox had done. They stood at attention. He smiled. They knew him, because of their long friendship with Davi; still, they'd never managed to feel at home around him—a fact which suited Xalivar just fine. He liked keeping people off guard, particularly when he wanted information from them.

Seeing Yao in his full dress uniform reminded him of his dislike for aliens, especially those who'd been accorded equal status with humans with the support of the Council. Yet another thing Xalivar would change if given a chance. Aliens were fine for subordinate positions like Manaen held, but they would never be humans' equals.

He managed to conceal his displeasure as he turned to Manaen. "Leave us." Manaen bowed and turned back toward the exit.

Xalivar waited until the door slid shut behind him. "I have been following reports of your diligent work on the Alliance's behalf with great satisfaction. You are serving with honor."

"Thank you, sir," they said in perfect unison.

Such good little soldier boys. Let's see how loyal to the Borali Alliance *you really are.* "Have you been pleased with your assignments?" Xalivar asked.

"Yes, sir," they said in unison again.

"Good. Davi also seems to have enjoyed his assignments. Have you kept in touch?"

"From time to time, Lord," Yao said.

"We saw each other a couple of times before he transferred to Alpha Base," Farien said.

Xalivar took note of the look they exchanged upon the mention of Davi's name. "Perhaps you hadn't heard, but my nephew has fallen into some difficulties. He's wanted for questioning in the death of a Captain on Vertullis. Did you hear anything about it?"

Farien shrugged. "A couple of rumors."

"I saw the warrant on the web, my Lord," Yao said. His purple eyes almost seemed to glow a moment.

One or both of you are lying. I can see it in your eyes. "If you hear from him, you will, of course, report it right away?"

Both nodded. "Yes, Lord."

Xalivar knew nothing would be gained from attempting to force information from them. He could wait until another time. For now, knowing he would be watching might be enough to make them think twice if Davi contacted them. His voice changed to a tone of concern. "If you think of anything, anything at all which I should know about, I am very concerned about him, of course. He is my only nephew and designated heir."

They both nodded. *It's still there in your eyes.* "We are, too, my Lord," Yao said.

"Yes, I imagine you are," Xalivar said, doing his best to sound sympathetic.

"We will help in any way we can," Farien said.

That's what I'm counting on, and why you'll be constantly watched. "Thank you for your service to the Alliance," Xalivar said.

They both knelt, offering him the expected salute.

"Be sure and take some time to visit your families while you're here. Family is important. Dismissed."

They nodded, and then turned for the door. Xalivar watched them go, hoping they would somehow lead him to Davi.

✱✱✱

Yao and Farien avoided discussing their meeting with Xalivar until they were alone at Yao's parents' house that evening. After some time with both sets of parents, who'd gathered there for a dinner together, they snuck away to the game room and turned the stereo up so they couldn't be overheard.

"Have you heard from him?" Yao asked as they played a game of virtual chess. He wondered why Farien always wanted to play. Yao beat him every time.

"Other than a couple of friendly e-posts, no," Farien said.

"Well, let's keep it that way as far as Xalivar is concerned, okay?" Yao said, capturing two of Farien's pawns.

"You expect me to hide information from the High Lord Councilor?" Farien asked as he deliberated over his next move.

"I didn't say to hide it," Yao said, "but don't volunteer it." He enjoyed watching Farien strain his brain for the right move.

Farien shook his head. "I don't know about this."

"I have my doubts, too, but he's our oldest friend." Yao couldn't believe Farien was even questioning it.

"And that means I should let my career go down the tubes for him?" Farien slid his bishop across the board, threatening Yao's knight.

"Xalivar didn't threaten us," Yao said, his eyes urging Farien to cooperate. Even as he did, he thought again about all they had to lose. He took the bishop with a rook Farien hadn't noticed, watching as Farien frowned in frustration.

"Oh sure, I totally bought all his friendly chit-chat," Farien said. "If he's allowing the Council to issue a warrant for Davi, he's not on Davi's side."

"I'm not saying he is," Yao said. "Don't you think we owe Davi the benefit of the doubt?"

"What I think is I don't want to get mixed up in this mess," Farien said. "I've worked too hard to get where I am, and this could really screw things up for me."

Yao shook his head. "It's sure screwing things up for our friend Davi." Despite his own doubts, he was disappointed Farien had such a narrow view of things. *Maybe I need to talk to Miri about this.* He'd send her an e-post as soon as they were finished.

"Maybe he brought this on himself by killing an Alliance Captain," Farien said.

Is he angry now too? "It was an accident. He told us the circumstances," Yao reminded him.

"If he wants to blow his whole career getting mixed up with workers, it's his problem. He can't expect me to blow mine!"

"Gods, Farien, no one's asking you to ruin your career, just to look out for a friend a little," Yao said, frowning as their eyes met.

"A friend who's wanted by the Council and the High Lord Councilor," Farien said. "I'm not making any promises, and if you ask me, I don't think Davi would expect me to."

"Fine. You keep looking out for yourself as usual." He turned and punched a code in the panel next to the door, waiting until it slid open with a whoosh. "You seem to be very good at it."

He left Farien standing there, staring after him.

✷✷✷

Not wanting to go near the Palace, Yao arranged to meet Miri at the city's largest public park. She came alone by air taxi, her face haggard with worry.

"Thank you so much for contacting me. I've been so worried about Davi," she said. "I haven't heard from him since right after he took emergency leave from Alpha Base, and Xalivar won't tell me anything."

"I'm afraid the Council has charged him with murder," Yao said.

"What?! Xalivar promised he would make sure that didn't happen!" Miri said, her blue eyes filling with anger.

"I don't want to speak ill of the High Lord Councilor, but he called Farien and I in and asked about Davi. I got the impression he wasn't going to interfere with the Council's decision," Yao said, filled with regret.

Miri's face registered a mix of shock and rage. "What is he thinking? My gods! Davi came to us and asked about the workers. I'm afraid a startling discovery about his past has upset him."

"What discovery?"

Miri hesitated a moment, as if she were unsure how Yao would react. "He discovered I adopted him years ago from a worker family."

"We heard a rumor about it two years ago at the Academy," Yao said, understanding her meaning now.

"A rumor? So long ago? It was supposed to be secret," Miri said with surprise.

"We heard it from a cadet who never liked Davi. We figured he was trying to make waves, but Davi told Farien and I two months ago on Vertullis that he suspected it might be more than a rumor," Yao said.

Miri looked at her feet. "It's true." Her eyes met his and she was pleading. "Please don't hate him for it. I know it's a shock to everyone, but it's not his fault. I raised him as my own, because it never mattered to me, and it shouldn't matter to you."

Yao smiled, putting a hand on her arm. "He's the best friend I've got. He can't get rid me so easily. Besides, I don't know any workers. I have nothing personal against them."

Miri looked relieved. "I wish more in the Alliance thought as you do." Tears rolled down her cheeks.

Yao pulled her to him in an embrace. "It's okay, Princess. I'd do anything I can to help him. I'll let you know as soon as I hear from him."

Yao meant it, although he wasn't sure what he'd do if the help asked involved things which might be deemed traitorous to the Alliance.

"Thank you. You know you're like family to me," Miri said, looking up at his face and smiling.

He dried her tears with his handkerchief. "You are to me, too," he said.

"Thank you for your support of Davi," she said, sniffling as she recovered her composure. "And me."

"If there's anything you need, don't hesitate to ask," Yao said. "But be careful about Farien. He fears his association with Davi could hurt his career." Yao's might as well, but Davi was more important.

"There'll be many others, I'm afraid. Even Xalivar is more concerned for himself than anyone else," she said, her face graying with sadness. They both stood there a moment, pondering the gravity of it all.

***

Aron had skipped the flight-training classroom on the tour. Located on the opposite side of the hangar from the command center, it was clearly intended to serve a dual purpose as a ready room for pilots once training was completed. A rather large chamber, it contained four simulators on one side and rows of chairs and desks on the other. A laser board and vidscreen hung side by side on the front wall, behind a plexiglass podium.

Davi arrived to find twenty eager trainees seated and waiting for him. He was surprised to see Tela, Nila, Brie and Dru among them. The moment he saw Tela, his heart accelerated in volume and pace. He feared the whole room could hear it. *I guess I should've guessed she'd sign up for this. Maybe I can make up for upsetting her the other day.*

He walked to the front of the room, taking a closer look at the students as he moved up the aisle. *They look like kids, all of them. Most can't even be my age yet.* Of course, he'd started flying at sixteen and graduated from the Academy at twenty-one. For some reason, he found himself feeling so much older now.

Stepping behind the podium, he turned and smiled. "Welcome class.

Good to see so many future pilots here!" He turned to Tela: "And one very talented pilot already. How many of you have ever done any flying, besides, of course, Tela?" Tela frowned as a few trainees in the back raised their hands, but none he knew by name.

As he glanced around, he spotted several others looking wary, even angry at him. "Okay, we have our work cut out for us. Without fighters to train in, we'll be doing a lot of training on the simulators and then using Skitters to get you used to the speed and feel as much as possible."

Brie raised her hand. "Yes, Brie?"

"Skitters don't fly," she said, a puzzled look on her face.

Davi nodded. "Well, yes, that's true, but they do handle similarly to fighters."

Dru raised his hand. Davi nodded at him. "What about laser target practice? They don't have lasers either."

"Alliance Skitters do," Tela interjected. Davi smiled at her in appreciation but she just looked away again.

"We'll have to do it all on the simulators for now," Davi said. Brie raised her hand again. "Yes?" Would they always be like this?

"When are we getting fighters?"

"I don't know." He was beginning to wonder if giving some of these people access to fighters would be a good idea. They seemed too eager. Brie and Dru looked disappointed at his answer. "There're going to be a lot of things we'll have to figure out as we go along."

Several of the trainees sighed, frustrated. "How do we know they'll ever allow us to fly them?" a dark-skinned cadet said from the back row.

"That's what I'm here for," Davi answered as everyone in the room waited with anticipation for his reaction.

"Yeah, right," the cadet next to the other said, smirking at their buddies. "A Borali Alliance officer training workers against his own people." A couple of other cadets chuckled in agreement.

"Not just a Borali Alliance officer! The Prince himself!" said the dark-skinned cadet.

"Jorek! Virun! Cut it out!" Nila scolded, frowning at them.

"Look," Davi said, "I'm on your side. Why would your leaders send me here, if they didn't trust me?"

"Did your Uncle order them to?" Virun said with a smirk as his friends laughed.

Davi sighed. For the first time, he found being known as a Royal made him very uncomfortable. He fought the urge to snap back, instead chuckling and smiling at Virun. "Without the resources of the Borali Alliance, we do face some challenges."

The cadets mumbled in acknowledgement, some still staring at him as if he were to blame. "However, when I was in flight school, we also didn't have experienced pilots in the class either, and you have the good fortune to have two."

He looked at Tela again, who shot him an annoyed look. *What did I do now?* Several of the others were looking at her now. She looked uncomfortable, shifting behind her desk.

"Okay, well, perhaps we should cover a few basics of flight first." *Going to leave her alone and hope she gets over it. For a pilot, she seems kind of sensitive. Hope she has the endurance to do this.* He made a note to keep the question to himself, flipped on the laser board and began lecturing.

An hour and a half later, he wrapped up what he thought was a pretty decent lecture on the basics of flight and the trainees dispersed. He found Tela waiting for him in the corridor, eyes fuming.

Might as well confront this head on. "Tela, I'm glad you're here. I wanted to apologize to you for offending you when we landed yesterday—"

She didn't even wait for him to finish. "Don't single me out in front of everyone! They're already intimidated enough and they're my friends!"

"Look, I'm sorry if I made you uncomfortable. I really meant it as a compliment. You're a very good pilot. You can help them learn." The heat rose in him just being near her.

"As what? Teacher's pet? They'll resent me for it!"

"Well, to be honest, if you were going for teacher's pet, you'd have to be nicer to me," he joked. She didn't even smile. *What is it with this girl?*

"You fighter jocks are all the same," she said. "Or maybe it's just you princes!" She stared at him, disgusted, then turned and marched up the corridor.

Davi had to run to keep up with her. "What's that supposed to mean?"

"Over-confident braggarts, who think all you have to do is come in the room and the women will start swooning," Tela said.

"Wait a minute! We don't really know each other. I'm not like that at all," Davi said, trying to hide his own growing irritation. She was making so many assumptions which just weren't true. Sure, women had been impressed by his Royal status, but he'd tried not to take advantage of it. Then he remembered the girls at Bar Electric. *Most of the time.*

"Yes, you are. I've been around your type my whole life!"

"Really? You know some other princes?"

She scowled and rolled her eyes, hurrying off again, but he grabbed her arm. "You really are something, aren't you? Judging people without even bothering to get to know them? It seems to me I'm not the one here who's full of himself!" He sighed, regretting the outburst, even though it was true.

"Oh stuff it up your flight suit, air jockey!" She turned and stormed off, leaving him disconcerted. He'd never problems talking to women before. Why this one? And why did it turn him on so much?

***

Bordox had searched the entire planet for Xander with little to show for it. He had no idea why Rhii was helping the workers. There'd been a rumor when they were at the Academy, but even Bordox doubted that. It was Xander Rhii after all. The little Prince had always been soft. What Bordox couldn't fathom was how he'd survived five years at the Academy. Bordox had what it took. Rhii didn't. Now, Rhii's actions proved his success at the Academy was a fluke. The Prince had sailed through on his family name, charming the faculty and administration, or, at least, revealing their hypocrisy. Bordox knew he was ten times the soldier Xander Rhii would ever hope to be, and on this mission, he would prove it!

He arrived early for his appointment with Zylo at the Regional Office of the LSP. They'd decided to put their heads together and regroup. But Bordox was wondering if a head butt might not be the best plan. Zylo's intelligence was worthless. Every lead he'd provided had turned up a dead end. Bordox was doing all the work, and he wasn't about to bust his butt to see Zylo get all the credit. It always worked that way with higher level officers. The lower level guys did the work, while the higher level guys got the glory. Not this time! This was his chance to show Xalivar, the High Lord Councilor himself, who the best soldier in the Alliance really was. At last, Bordox would get the recognition and status he deserved!

Zylo even seemed to feel sorry for Rhii. Bordox wanted to laugh when Zylo expressed sympathy for the little rat. *Pathetic loser.* Such softness would never get in Bordox's way. He made his way to the conference room where Zylo was already waiting for him. *Sigh.*

"We've generated a bunch of new leads for you," Zylo said, tossing a memory card across the table at him.

"I hope they're better than the previous garbage you guys sent me," Bordox said.

Zylo didn't bother to hide his annoyance. "Intelligence gathering is not an exact science, especially when it comes to workers. They have no reason to cooperate with us. We do our best to fill in as many of the pieces as we can before we send the data to you. Your tactics haven't helped the results."

Bordox stared at him, hiding his contempt. *Not more of this bleeding heart softie crap!* "We're trained to use whatever it takes to complete our mission," Bordox said.

"No wonder the citizens call you Death Squads instead of LSP," Zylo said.

Bordox fought to control his anger. That was a moniker used to cut down and disrespect men who served a higher cause in Borali society. Bordox hated that moniker. His anger won and he exploded: "If you don't want to work with me, feel free to request reassignment! I'm sure Lord Xalivar will be very sympathetic!"

"Watch your tone! I'm your superior officer!"

Not for long! "Are we done yet? I have work to attend to!" Bordox stood and moved to the window, looking out across the city at the great view. Someday maybe he'd be in charge of an entire planet, an assignment far worthier of his talents. He knew he deserved more than cowing down to idiots like this.

"Xalivar gave us the names of two officers he wants us to monitor," Zylo slid a photo pod across the table.

Bordox grabbed it and looked at the pictures. *Farien and Yao!* He hated them, too. "Nothing but low-talent hangers on who followed Xander Rhii like puppies at the Academy."

"One of them is an instructor at Presimion Academy," Zylo noted as Bordox turned back to the window. "I assigned top operatives to keep watch on the one stationed on Vertullis. The Legallis office will handle

Presimion."

Bordox made a silent note of the fact that Farien was still around. *I think I'd better go pay him a visit myself.* He didn't trust anyone else. None of them had the talent he had. Better to make sure what needed to be done got done right. "Shouldn't we question them?"

"The High Lord Councilor already did. He wants their activities monitored in case the subject makes contact," Zylo said. "I assigned our best operatives."

I'm your best operative, you fool! It's why the High Lord Councilor assigned me to find his nephew not sit on some inconsequential wannabes like them. How could Bordox continue to tolerate even weasels like Zylo failing to recognize his true abilities?

"He wants you to coordinate monitoring of all passenger traffic at the starport. Everyone who comes and goes from this planet is to be monitored, their records checked thoroughly. Someone's hiding him, and we need to find out whom."

This guy ought to be a worker, with a brain like that! "I'll take care of it. I'd also like to pay another visit to some of the workers we already interviewed. There's a woman and a girl who know more than they told me."

"You can do what you want with whatever time you have left after the starport's in order," Zylo said, standing. The meeting was over.

Thank the gods! Such a waste of time being here with this idiot! I have my destiny to fulfill! They both headed off in opposite directions.

***

The trio met Miri in the back room of a little-known restaurant on the outskirts of the city. Arriving separately to avoid drawing attention to themselves, each used separate entrances to ensure they wouldn't be seen together.

The restaurant staff escorted them to a private room in the back, where Miri sat waiting for them. They gathered around a long table, waiting for her to explain. Instead of the usual white robes they wore to official meetings, each wore comfortable cotton slacks and shirts. Miri had never seen Lord Hachim, who took particular pride in his official role, dressed like a civilian. He looked awkward. Tarkanius and Kray appeared more relaxed. All of them knew her, but Lord Kray, one of the few females on the Council, was Miri's childhood friend.

As waiters took their orders, Miri passed around memory cards. After the waiters had served their beverages, the door closed, and Miri stood, smiling.

"Thank you all for coming. I called you here because we're all loyal to the Alliance, and I have important information about recent events which should cause you concern."

"Why are we meeting all the way out here and not at the government center or in the Palace?" Lord Tarkanius asked.

"Because this involves highly confidential matters, and I ask you to keep it that way, until we've determined a course of action," Miri said.

They all exchanged looks wondering what she was about to say.

"You've all known my character and loyalty to my family. So you'll understand what I am about to say comes out of deep concern for both my family and the Alliance."

"Of course, Miri," Lord Kray said. "What's going on?" She sipped from her Talis, a warm beverage brewed from beans grown on Vertullis—somewhat like the old Earth beverage coffee.

"I don't know how aware you are of the situation on Vertullis," Miri said, "but events have taken place which, I believe, have created a crisis there. These events have occurred with the full support and consent of the High Lord Councilor and have resulted in treatment of the workers which I believe is unacceptable. These memory cards contain evidence I wish you to review relating to these events."

"Are you saying there has been mistreatment of workers?" Lord Hachim asked.

"Mistreatment, subhuman conditions, and abuses of power," Miri said, nodding. *Please gods let them believe me.*

The three Lords exchanged looks of both surprise and concern. "The workers are not like us. We all know the history of their attacks against our people," Lord Tarkanius said.

"Yet the Borali Alliance has always stood for fair treatment of those under our rule," Miri said. "We set certain standards, which are not being upheld now under my brother."

"How much does your bringing this to our attention have to do with the murder charges your brother asked us to reinstate against your own son?" Lord Hachim asked, leaning back in his chair and watching her for a reaction.

Xalivar asked them to charge Davi? It hit her hard hearing it, though she tried not to let it show. "My son was charged because he questioned the Borali Alliance's treatment of workers. He documented a long line of abuses, bringing the evidence to Xalivar, who was not receptive. Anyone who questions my brother is at risk. He refuses to respond to inquiries. He believes the workers are subhuman, lower than animals, unworthy of trust or respect." *And most other people too.*

"Many in the Alliance would agree with him," Lord Tarkanius said, sipping his Talis.

"Then how can we blame the workers for calling us tyrannical?" Lord Kray asked, her brow furrowed with concern.

"Xalivar is consolidating his own power, taking on more and more responsibilities himself and relying less and less on your counsel," Miri said, hoping they'd noticed.

"He appears before the Council to make regular reports," Lord Hachim said.

"The Council began meeting every two months instead of monthly at whose request?" Miri asked.

The Lords exchanged a look. "The High Lord Councilor requested it, due to increased obligations," Lord Kray said.

Miri nodded. "I believe Xalivar wants to make the High Lord Councilor more like a kingship and less dependent on the Council. He has become more and more powerful and makes more and more decisions alone. If the Council doesn't take action soon, it will be too late."

"He has done nothing the Council doesn't approve of," Lord Tarkanius said, leaning forward in his chair.

"You'll change your opinion after you've viewed these memory cards," Miri said with anticipation.

"What are you proposing?" Lord Hachim asked.

"I believe it may be time for a change of leadership...for the High Lord Councilor's office to be returned to someone who respects both its powers and its limits," Miri said.

As expected they looked shocked to hear this from her. They examined her as if trying to determine how serious she was, but Miri made sure her expression never wavered.

"We will, of course, consider the evidence on these memory cards with great care," Lord Tarkanius said, after taking a final sip of his Talis.

Miri smiled. "Thank you. Please keep this meeting confidential until we've had a chance to discuss your reactions."

They nodded. "Of course we will," Lord Kray said. "Thank you for bringing this to our attention, Miri."

"I love the Alliance and respect the Council," Miri said. "It is my duty."

"The Council has always appreciated your faithfulness," Lord Hachim said as they stood, placing the memory cards in their pockets.

Miri watched as they departed one at a time, leaving her alone. She knew the risks of revealing this to the Council, but she had grown increasingly concerned about Xalivar's activities after learning what Davi had uncovered on Vertullis. Xalivar's refusal to be questioned about it by her or anyone else had convinced her that someone had to step up and call him to account. She was in the best position to do so.

She'd chosen the members of the Council to which she gave the evidence with great care. She knew their influence on the Council would help her case. She would wait for their response, and continue gathering evidence. In the meantime, she had a plan that would bring the abuses to the attention of the public.

Xalivar had asked the Council to charge Davi with murder! My gods, how could he do that? His betrayal was the last straw. Any second thoughts she had, faded away. Fine. If Xalivar had no loyalty to her or his family, so be it. She would not feel it necessary to be loyal to him. The Borali Alliance itself was more important, and she knew in her heart even their father would disapprove of Xalivar's excesses.

CHAPTER SEVEN

Xalivar had always had a soft place in his heart for his sister, but lately she was driving him nuts—going on and on about Davi this, Davi that. Xalivar had a lot of responsibilities besides babying his worry-wart sister.

The nightmares had come again. A kind he hadn't had in twenty years—ones that continued to haunt him, even in daylight. Now, Miri had stormed into his private chamber like a charging bull, heading straight toward him. He sighed loudly, but she paid no attention.

"You asked the Council to reinstate murder charges against your own nephew?! I knew you could sink low, Xalivar, but—"

"Where did you hear that?" He asked, cutting her off.

"I have friends on the Council like you do," Miri said.

"Your son is determined to create problems for me where none existed. I did my best to reason with him, but he won't leave it alone!" Xalivar was not in the mood for her angry tone. He had responsibilities she would never understand.

"He's your nephew! You could have tried harder!"

"He's an officer in the army, sworn to serve me. He refuses to serve. He's also a subject of the Borali Alliance," Xalivar said. "He's always shied away from special treatment, so I'm treating him like anyone else."

"Don't give me more lies, Xalivar. I'm your sister. I've known you all my life," Miri said. "You're singling him out because he defied you." She turned away, close to tears, staring out the window at the stars.

"He needs to know his place," Xalivar said, unmoved by her tears. *Such a drama queen.*

"You need to know yours!" She whirled around, pointing her finger in his face.

Xalivar had never wanted to hit Miri before, but he had to restrain himself this time. "You'd prefer I let him create a huge public scandal and bring the wrath of the entire Alliance down on him? I'm bringing him in, so we can keep this situation from getting out of control."

"You're so sure everyone in the Alliance would agree with you, aren't you?" Miri said. "I know for a fact many do not!"

"General public opinion is not my concern. I answer to the Council," Xalivar said. *And I don't really care what you or they think either, sister.*

"And answer you shall if you turn your back on your family," Miri said. "You sent his archrival to hunt him down like some kind of outlaw! Do you care nothing about his reputation? His safety?"

Since when did Miri grow claws? Did she really have the nerve? "Don't threaten me!"

"Don't threaten my son!" Miri turned around and marched back to the door. After a moment, it slid shut behind her.

Xalivar cursed whoever had betrayed him. He wasn't sure who'd told Miri, but he would find out. He would not tolerate people playing politics with his family. Perhaps it had been a matter of time, but he didn't need her enflamed emotions leading her to interfere in his business. He had enough to worry about. *They will learn what it means to cross Xalivar.*

The nightmares had reminded him of something he'd written off as inconsequential. He was starting to worry. He wanted Davi back under his nose where he could keep an eye on him. He would instruct Zylo and Bordox to retrace their steps. The search was taking too long. They needed to find Davi—and now.

✱✱✱

A week after their argument in the corridor, Davi found Tela sitting at the controls of her shuttle, reading through maintenance charts. He took care to make noise as he entered the cockpit so as not to sneak up on her. She turned her head and frowned when she saw him.

"We seem to have gotten off on the wrong foot," Davi said, sitting in the copilot's seat. "I've been trying to figure out how it happened."

"Maybe your charms won't work on me," Tela said. "I'm pretty good at seeing through people. Especially men."

"Well, that's just it. You seem to have taken some of the things I've said the wrong way," Davi said, hoping she'd take another look.

"Like what?" Her eyes remained on the charts.

"I didn't bring up your name in class to isolate you from the other trainees," Davi said. "I was trying to pay you a compliment. I'm impressed with the way you flew the shuttle."

"Well, thank you," she said, still avoiding eye contact, focused on her charts. "But the last thing I need is people thinking you're showing me special treatment. I'm there to learn the same as them."

"And I'm there to teach you," Davi said, "but someone with your flight experience is an asset for the entire class. You can help me to help them learn what they need to know."

"I didn't sign on to be a tutor," Tela said.

"I won't ask you to be, if you don't want to," Davi said. "All I'm asking is if they don't understand something I'm trying to explain, maybe you can jump in and help me clarify it."

"See?" She said, looking up for a moment. "You're asking me to teach. No thanks." Her eyes turned back to the charts as Davi wondered why he always seemed to choose the wrong words when he talked to her. A familiar buzz filled his stomach as heat rose within.

"Whatever you feel comfortable with," Davi said. "The last thing I need is someone getting killed because they didn't understand."

"I wouldn't let that happen," Tela said.

"Good. I can use all the help I can get," Davi said. "I've never been an instructor before. And I've never been a worker before either. It's all new to me. I pretty much have to relearn who I am." *I wish someone would teach me how to talk to you!*

"You're doing fine. You explain things well," Tela said, her blue eyes meeting his for a moment.

"Was that a compliment?" Davi melted inside like icicles in a desert. He smiled. "I might have to write that down. It might be ages before I ever get another compliment from you."

She laughed, rolling her eyes. "Don't get too cocky, okay? There's always room for improvement."

"Okay, so don't get mad at me when I suggest areas you can improve," Davi said. "It's my job as your teacher."

"You can't improve on perfection," she said, smiling. Was she joking?

"Now who's cocky?" He teased as she laughed. "Some of the cadets seem to resent me because of my past. They don't seem to realize, I'm on your side."

"Can you really blame them? You're the Prince."

Davi sighed, disappointed. "No, I suppose not."

She slid back in the chair and her face softened a bit. "Give them time. They'll come around."

"I don't suppose you could put in a good word for me?"

Tela's face crinkled. "First I have to convince myself."

"But you saw me at the rallies! Do you really believe—"

He stopped as Tela broke into laughter. "You're giving me trouble?"

She smiled and nodded. "I couldn't resist."

"Well, I'd better let you get back to your work here. I wouldn't want anyone to know we actually had a civil conversation."

She smiled at him and his heart fluttered. "You like making jokes, don't you?"

"When it makes you smile like that," Davi said. Her eyes turned quickly back to her charts. "Okay, well, thanks for letting me explain."

She nodded. "See you in class, professor." It sounded so formal. He contorted his face, and she laughed again, twirling strands of her hair around her index finger. "I'm trying to work here."

He nodded, stood, and backed out of the cockpit. The conversation went better than he'd expected. She'd laughed and joked with him. It was a start. And she'd twirled her hair—was she flirting with him? Best not to make too much of it. For some reason, all the way back to the command center, he found himself whistling a happy song.

✱✱✱

"Retrace my steps and see if I missed anything?" Bordox groused as he sat in the military shuttle next to Corsi. "I'm sick of that miscreant always making me look bad! Not this time!"

They hadn't even covered a third of the worker community. Plenty of places to hide remained, yet his mission had already been deemed a failure. He cursed inside. He'd been given a chance to best his old rival, and he was determined to come out ahead. Revisiting areas they'd already covered would just slow him down. But after Zylo's in accurate reporting of Bordox's activities, it's exactly what Xalivar had ordered him to do.

On their previous visit to one worker neighborhood, he'd found a photo of a man who looked very much like Xander Rhii in one of the houses. He had no idea why workers would have such a photo, but then again, he'd learned from interrogating the neighbors that a man who looked like Xander had been seen there a number of times. The woman had told him the picture was her husband, who'd disappeared twenty years before. In spite of his interrogation techniques, the woman and girl gave him nothing. Still, he'd never been able to shake the feeling they knew more than they'd told him.

When Bordox reviewed security tapes from the officers' barracks, he'd spotted the woman and girl on it, chatting with Rhii. All three had a friendly demeanor throughout. This time Bordox wouldn't let them off so easily. They knew where to find Rhii, and he would find out everything they knew.

"Why would a Royal be so friendly with workers?" he asked aloud, forgetting Corsi was sitting beside him. "It makes no sense. Xalivar has always led the oppression of the workers. Of course that weak, overconfident Prince has never made sense. He's totally unfit for military service. Too nice. Too sympathetic. Too independent."

Ignoring Corsi's nod, Bordox turned toward the window, lost in thought. Xander had been given opportunities which should have gone to Bordox. Now Bordox had the opportunity to put an end to the undeserved favoritism.

He arrived with a squad of five men at the courtyard outside the house in question. Everything looked the same as it had the last time he'd been there. He approached the door to the house and waited while his sergeant knocked.

"LSP, open!" Sergeant Corsi shouted.

A frightened woman opened the door, two wide-eyed young children hiding amidst the folds of her skirt. Bordox and his men pushed their way inside, looking around. No one else was in the house except the woman and children, who not been there during his previous visit. The house had been arranged differently inside then—much of the furniture remained standard issue worker, but the pictures and personal knick-knacks had all changed—someone else lived there.

"Where are the people who lived here before?" Bordox demanded.

The woman shook with fear. Her children started crying. "I—I don't know," she said with great effort, so frightened she couldn't speak. *Good. Be afraid of me!*

Corsi and two soldiers returned from searching the back room. "No one's here, sir. And everything is different than the last time."

Bordox cursed. He had to find these people—more certain now than ever that they had the answers he needed. "That's it. I want all the neighbors in the square right now!"

He grabbed the woman and shoved her and the crying kids outside into the square as his men rushed to knock on the neighbors' doors.

In a few moments, eight others stood trembling in the yard. Bordox walked among them as his men searched their houses. They all looked as frightened as the first woman. "Some of you I recognize. You remember me from before." He glanced around at the fearful expressions. A few found the strength to nod. "Good, then maybe you'll tell me what I want to know!"

Corsi came back with reports from the men. "All clear, sir."

Bordox grabbed an old man from the line and pointed his blaster at the man's temple. "I want to know right now where the previous tenants of that house are!"

The workers looked at each other. From their faces, it appeared they didn't know what to say. Bordox didn't believe them. Someone had to know something. An older woman stepped forward. "They moved out right after you were here before. We don't know where they are."

"What do you know?" Bordox said, blaster still held to the man's temple. Fear had always been his favorite tactic.

"Please," another man said, "we do our work. We make no problems for the Alliance."

"You're making a problem for the Alliance right now! Tell me what I want to know." Bordox said.

"We don't know anything!" The first woman said, as her two kids cried and continued clinging to her skirt. "We have no reason not to tell you! I don't even know those people!"

"You might not, but these people were here before. They were your neighbors," Bordox said, ignoring the woman and looking at the others with no effort to hide his irritation.

"They never mentioned where they were going," the older woman said. "All I know is the woman who lived there worked at Celedine Technology near the starport."

Bordox released the old man, who collapsed to his knees. He walked up the line, stopping a few inches from each of them to stare into their eyes. *They really don't know.* He cursed inside. Xalivar had warned him about excessive killings of workers. It would draw too much negative attention. He had to be discreet—the only reason these people still lived.

"If any of you see or hear anything, you will contact the LSP right away. Don't make me have to come back here!"

They all nodded, fear evident on their faces.

"Squad, move out!"

Bordox led his men back through the corridors of the worker district. They would go to Celedine Technology. He knew where it was. The more trouble it became locating Xander, the more determined he became to win. He would not have his career ruined by that incompetent fool ever again. He would bring him in, no matter what it took. Too bad Xalivar wanted him alive. Bordox would relish ending Xander Rhii's miserable existence.

✶✶✶

When Miri arrived, the Legallis starport hummed with motion— bustling crowds, a buffet of noise, constant activity. The small diner lay out of the way on the end of one of the numerous corridors, which wound their way out from the landing platforms. It would be easy to go unnoticed there. Besides, this time it was just the two of them, and meetings between old friends were not so unusual.

Kray looked Miri over with concern as soon as she sat down across the table. "You've lost weight."

"I'm fine," Miri said. She hated lying to an old friend, but Kray couldn't do anything about her sleepless nights in the Palace; her mind working overtime.

"Don't lie to me, Miri. I'm your oldest friend," Kray said.

Miri smiled. She'd been so busy the past few weeks; she'd had almost no time to relax. Sitting here for a moment gave her a much-needed break. "The life of a Princess is always busy." Even more so with her determination to uncover the truth about what was going on with the workers on Vertullis.

"Yes, and you've never been one to stay bored long," Kray said, nodding. "Promise me it's not because of worrying."

"A mother always worries, as you know," Miri said. Kray had three children herself. "But since we last met, I've been so preoccupied with other things; I haven't had much time for that."

As the waitress arrived to bring them mugs of Talis, Miri realized it was true. She'd been so focused on saving Davi, she'd had little time to sit around and worry about his circumstances.

"The information you provided was quite startling, as you said," Kray said, sipping her Talis. "We have discussed it quite often since reviewing it."

"I appreciate your willingness to take the time," Miri said, hope rising within.

"You have our support," Kray said. "But it will require a lot more evidence to validate an impeachment."

Miri nodded. "Public opinion will soon be on our side."

Kray looked at her with concern. "You must be very careful, Miri. As the Princess, your movements do not go unnoticed, above all when you interact with members of the media. Xalivar has many friends."

"So do I, Kray," Miri said smiling. "It will be handled with the same discretion as our meeting, I promise." Miri had not involved anyone associated with the Palace. She wanted no chance of leaks, but she knew she would also need to take other precautions.

"I hope so. Don't let the fact that Xalivar is your brother blind you in regards to your safety," Kray said. "He's never been kind to those who betray him."

Miri had seen plenty of evidence of this in the past. She nodded, sipping her own Talis. "I'm taking extra care, Kray. Really."

Kray's eyes stayed locked on hers for a moment before Kray smiled, relaxing a bit. "Good. There are few females at our level of power, you know. I need someone around who understands what it's like." They both laughed.

"I have always cherished our friendship," Miri said, reaching out to put her hand atop Kray's on the table. "So tell me about the children. How are they, these days?"

They continued chatting at the table for close to an hour as people came and went around them—two old friends talking about life and family. It did them both good to escape like this from the concerns of their lives—Miri from her worries about Davi and Xalivar, and Kray from the weight of government decisions. Miri realized they had not done this enough. She vowed to try and correct that in the future.

***

After two weeks spent covering the basics of flight, Davi allowed the first of his students on the simulators. His class had doubled in size since it started, with Aron and the leaders adding more and more candidates with each new rally. Davi had done his best to keep the new students up to speed with the others. Some of them had the advantage of prior flight experience, while others had skill with Skitters. He still had neophytes to train, but at least some had a head start.

At the moment, Dru, Brie, Nila and another boy their age occupied the four simulators. Tela and the other students sat at desks behind Davi, observing as he took them through their first mock battle. Each student pilot sat in a mock cockpit, with controls similar to those of VS28 fighters—a screen where the blastshield would be simulated stars and incoming enemy fighter craft. The simulator itself moved as the trainees moved the joystick. Combined, the effect was a sensation reminiscent of being in an actual fighter during a battle.

"Keep your tails up there," Davi instructed. "Easy on the joystick, Brie. It's sensitive, designed to move as one with your body. Dru, you've got one on your tail. Evasive action!"

The trainees reacted to his instructions. Dru tried hard to stay out of the fire of the enemy on his tail as explosions flashed in front of him on the screen with each hit.

Brie steered her fighter toward the enemy behind Dru. "I got him!"

Davi realized that her excitement was distracting her. She was coming in at an odd angle and way too fast. "Slow down, Brie! You're going to hit him!" Too late.

Brie's screen erupted in flashes of yellow light and her console went dead. "What happened?" Brie asked, confused.

"You're dead," Tela said.

"You got him off my tail though. Thanks," Dru said, chuckling.

Brie stuck out her tongue at him. "You're welcome." She turned to Davi with a sheepish grin. "I'm not getting it, am I?"

Davi smiled. "It takes practice." *For some more than others.*

Brie cocked her head to one side in a flirty way. "Can you show me one more time please?"

Davi smiled. "Okay. Look." He leaned over her from behind, holding his hand around hers on the joystick. "Pull back a tiny bit, like this. Enough to make her go the direction you want to go. Not too hard though."

Brie smiled, looking up at him. "Oh, right. I gotta practice it." Davi let go and she tried what he'd showed her. "Like that?"

Davi nodded, ignoring her flirting. "Much better. Keep practicing."

He turned back to the other students and saw Tela shaking her head and heading out the door. Virun and a couple of others followed her.

"Wait a minute! Class isn't over. Where's everyone going?"

The others looked at him and shrugged.

What's wrong with her?

Brie and the others climbed out of the simulators as other trainees took their place.

"Okay," Davi said, "let's try this again."

The second group was better than the first. A third did better still. At the end of the session though, Davi walked away discouraged. Some of the students would improve with practice, but others had him wondering if they weren't wasting their time. He wished Tela had participated. She would have handled herself quite well, he imagined. Her performance would have at least been more encouraging.

He left the classroom confused and wondering why she'd disappeared.

✱✱✱

Tired of watching Brie throwing herself at Davi, Tela had stormed out of the training room. It was disgusting, shameless—totally inappropriate in the classroom. She'd grown more and more irritated, until deciding she needed a breath of fresh air.

As she wound her way through the corridors, she started feeling silly. Why did it bother her so much? *You don't like him, remember?* She'd known women who acted like Brie before. It wasn't like she had any claim to Davi. They were barely friends.

Sure, things between them had settled down since they'd talked in the shuttle. He'd asked Tela's opinion from time to time, and she'd done as he requested, helping him explain things when the trainees didn't understand. So what was the big deal? Brie had every right to flirt with him. She'd acted like a fool. Why did she have such a tendency to do that when Davi was around?

She spent a few moments calming down, then turned back toward the classroom. Rounding a corner near the classroom, she spotted Davi exiting and heading up the corridor away from her. He looked very discouraged. She hoped not because of her.

She followed him across the hangar and into a smaller cave on the far side, where the Skitters sat parked in several rows.

Long slender bodies topped with leather seats and two handlebars attached to a control panel, Skitters had been designed for recreational use, but were so fast and easy to handle, they'd been adapted for other uses. Borali Alliance ground patrols used them on a regular basis.

She stood in the shadows as he began looking them over. Two mech-bots entered through another tunnel and began working on some of the Skitters behind him. As she stepped out of the shadows into the cave, Davi looked up at her.

"Hey," she said, with a slight wave and a smile.

"Hey," he said, going back to examining the Skitters.

"How'd the rest of the session go?"

He shrugged. "We have a lot of work ahead of us."

Not even eye contact. So maybe he was upset with her. "Sorry I left. I needed some air."

"I was disappointed you didn't stay for your turn," Davi said as he examined another Skitter. "Seeing someone actually succeed on the simulators would have been encouraging. I sure could've used it." His voice sounded tired.

"Was it really so bad?"

"You tell me. You saw how some of the students did," Davi slid into the seat of a Skitter, fiddling with the controls.

"Some of them are a long way from being flight-worthy," Tela said, watching the mech-bots working behind him.

"Some make me wonder if they ever will be."

It saddened her to see him so discouraged. He had always been so positive and supportive of the students. She wanted to do something to cheer him up. She took a seat on another Skitter and turned it on, hearing the steady hum of the engine and feeling it rise up off the floor to float on the air as she adjusted the controls.

"Come with me."

"For a joy ride?"

Tela smiled. "Sure. There's something I want to show you." She waved toward the Skitter he'd been examining.

He shrugged, climbing onto the Skitter. The engine hummed as it rose into the air. "Okay. Lead the way."

She slid the Skitter into gear and drove it out of the cave into a small tunnel. Davi accelerated his own Skitter and followed along behind her.

They emerged into the dense forest along a path. Sunlight streamed through the tall cedars, creating a patchwork of dark and light areas on the ground. The chirping of birds and insects blended with the hum of the Skitters as a light breeze tousled their hair. The sweet smell of cedar filled her nose.

Tela sped up, forcing Davi to speed up behind her. She admired the fluidness with which he maneuvered the Skitter. She'd never seen him fly, of course, but it seemed to her he must be as skilled as the commanders said. She wondered if he'd had much time to explore the forest around the base yet. She hadn't seen him in the Skitter bay, but then she hadn't been there much until the past few days herself.

She led him through several twists and turns then around a bend into a clearing where she pulled to a stop and waited for him to come alongside.

Amid cedars at the edge of the course on both sides there were several wood pylons with various markings. As his Skitter pulled alongside hers and stopped, she smiled. "Well, here it is."

"What is it?" Davi said, trying to make sense of the pylons and markers.

"Our Skitter training course," Tela said. "Aron asked me to set one up." Why was she so anxious waiting for his response?

Davi's looked around and smiled. "You did all this yourself?"

"Well, I may have borrowed some from a schematic of one of the Alliance's training courses. With a few minor adjustments to compensate for ours being on land and not in outer space."

Davi nodded, looking pleased. "This is impressive. You amaze me!"

He's impressed! She almost blushed. Why did she care so much what he thought? She'd never had time for men, not since her father's disappearance. She'd been too busy for much of a social life.

"Thanks. Wanna give it a try?" She opened the side pocket on her Skitter and pulled out a helmet. "Gotta put on the helmet to see how it works."

She slid the helmet on as Davi opened the pocket on his own Skitter and retrieved the helmet. As he began to put it on, Tela flipped the switch to activate the weapons simulator on her Skitter.

After they'd both adjusted their helmets, Davi nodded. "Ready."

Tela accelerated and took off like a flash, zigzagging in and out between the pylons. Wind nipped at the skin of her face like tiny bugs. Trees passed almost as blur as she focused on the markers and pylons. She glanced down at her control panel, verifying the weapons simulator was fully charged. The visor of her helmet showed a targeting frame as she passed the next pylon. Everything seemed to be working right.

The next pylon she came to, she maneuvered the frame to aim at the pylon and then hit the fire button. The visor image flashed as she hit the target.

She flipped her communicator on and keyed the switch. "Flip the red switch on to activate the targeting simulator. The black button on the joystick is for firing."

She slowed down, allowing Davi to pull alongside as he fiddled with the controls. "Do you see it?"

"Yeah," his voice came in through the helmet. "You did all this?"

"Well, I had some help. Go for a run," Tela said, accelerating again and aiming as she came to each target.

Davi raced his Skitter alongside her, also aiming and firing. They raced in and out of the pylons, keeping pace with each other. The visor kept count in the bottom right corner of hits and misses. So far she had been dead on.

The total time for the course at full speed was less than four minutes. They reached the end in what seemed like a few seconds. She pulled to a stop as Davi stopped beside her.

"How'd you do?"

"Missed two."

She smiled. "I didn't miss any."

"Well, you designed it. It's my first time." He said with a shrug, but she saw disappointment in his green eyes.

With an exaggerated shrug, she laughed. "Excuses, excuses."

He scowled. "Wanna go again?"

Gotcha! She grinned and accelerated her Skitter like a rocket.

Davi raced to catch up with her.

They followed a curving path which took them back to the start of the course, and then both launched into it again. Davi gave it his best effort. She had to accelerate a few times to keep up with him.

As they neared the end of the course, he zipped in front of her. Her Skitter misfired. She groaned in frustration, pulling back alongside and getting back on course. He laughed as they raced onward, finishing the course in less than four minutes.

"Perfect score," he said with a smirk.

That's the Davi I know. She shook her head. "I missed because you distracted me." But she knew his move to cut her off hadn't been the only distraction. She had butterflies in her stomach.

"Oh right, like the enemy won't ever try that," he said, shooting her a look.

She laughed. He was right. They couldn't count on total focus in a real battle. Maybe there were some things he could teach her on her own course after all.

"Shall we go again?" he asked, shifting excitedly on his seat. His voice had regained its usual energy, and she noticed the usual sparkle had returned to his eyes. The smell of adrenaline mixed with sweat wafted to her nose.

"Wanna switch sides?"

He nodded. "Catch me if you can!" He took off like a rocket.

She raced to catch up, determined that this time she'd be ready for any distractions.

✷✷✷

Bordox arrived at the LSP office early the next morning, anxious to see the results of the e-post logs he'd asked Corsi to locate from public kiosks near the worker house they'd searched. He'd noticed a terminal nearby in a park both times they'd been there. Maybe something would turn up.

They'd gone to Celedine after searching the house and coming up empty. A woman from the address had worked there for a time, but disappeared after Bordox's first visit to the house. The owners, loyal to the Alliance, had no idea where to locate her. Bordox was sick of dead ends.

He entered the office to find Zylo and Corsi already there.

"I found some reports of suspicious activity in the forest on the far side of the planet," Zylo said.

"The forest? What kind of activity?" Bordox asked.

"A few farmers reported shuttle flights, voices in the trees from time to time," Zylo said.

"I thought the forest was undeveloped," Bordox said.

"It is. We haven't even deployed full radar there," Zylo said. "And gods know the farmers are always reporting unknown flying objects out there. It's low priority intel, but Xalivar insists we check all possible leads."

Bordox nodded. He expected it would be another dead end, but then they hadn't been that far south yet. He'd make a pass or two down there as soon as he'd finished retracing the areas they'd already visited.

He logged onto his terminal and found a folder with the log records waiting for him. He double clicked to open it and began scanning the lists. Xander's worker name popped up several times in the weeks before Bordox's team had first searched the house. What had he been doing in that neighborhood so much? Hiding out? Living there? How was he connected to those people? Someone had to know something. Who hadn't he talked to yet? His eyes continued searching the e-post list. *There!* Xander had sent an e-post to Presimion Academy. *Of course!* Xander was always in touch with those two.

Bordox turned to Corsi who sat at a terminal nearby. "Corsi, get me files on all duty assignments for officers overseeing guards in the agricultural districts."

"All of them?"

Bordox whirled around so fast his chair squeaked. "Stop asking questions and do it."

Corsi hurried back to the other terminal as Bordox turned back to his vidscreen. He didn't expect Farien to volunteer any information. Farien and Yao disliked him as much as their buddy Davi did. Nonetheless, Bordox had the authority to question anyone he deemed necessary. Yes, indeed, he would enjoy this, though he knew Farien wouldn't.

He smiled at the thought. "Look for the name of Lieutenant Farien," he said to Corsi.

***

Tela arrived at the command center conference room to find Aron, Joram, Uzah, and General Matheu waiting for her around the table. The head of the Workers' military, General Matheu's uniform breast bore medals and ribbons he'd earned over a career spanning back to the Delta V tragedy. His hair was dark with graying ends and his stomach had thickened in a way common for men of his age. But the eyes which met hers showed the same strength and focus she'd seen in him for years.

"Tela," Aron said with a smile, "so glad you could join us." He motioned to an empty seat at the table.

The others nodded as she moved toward the chair. Matheu stood and closed the door behind her before returning to his seat.

"How's the flight training going?" Joram asked.

Tela shrugged, searching their eyes for a clue as to why she'd been summoned. "It's proceeding slowly for sure, but we are making progress. Except, some of the students are questioning whether they can trust the instructor."

"They're not alone," Matheu groused in his scratchy baritone.

Uzah nodded. "We have doubts of our own."

"Not all of us," Aron corrected.

"He spoke passionately at several rallies," Tela said. "We didn't have any trouble."

"How do you know he wasn't just trying to earn your trust so he could gather information for the Alliance?" Matheu asked.

"If he was going to betray us," Joram said, "he would have done so already."

"I've told you time again," Aron added, "I've known his family for many years."

"His worker family or the Royals?" Matheu snapped.

Tela knew his years of military disappointments had left him skeptical and extremely cautious. She couldn't blame him.

"The longer he remains here, the more information he can gather," Uzah said.

"I vouch for him," Aron said. "That ought to mean something."

"It does, Aron," Uzah said, his voice softening. "No one here doubts your character, but we worry your love for his family may be blinding you where he's concerned."

"You trust him too much," Matheu added. "He already knows the location of our base, the numbers and make of our starcraft. How much more can we afford to let him see?"

"He's done nothing to cause suspicion," Aron argued. "Being adopted by the princess doesn't automatically make him a spy. He had no idea about his true heritage until recently."

"It does bring his loyalty into question," Uzah said.

"The Alliance's the only family he's ever known," Matheu said. "Why would he turn against them after twenty years?"

Tela found it hard to understand the vitriol she was hearing in Matheu and Uzah's voices. "He may be arrogant, but he made it obvious in his speeches at the rallies that he doesn't approve of how the Alliance has been treating workers. He's been teaching us a lot about Alliance tactics in class."

"How do you know it's accurate?" Matheu asked.

"Because a lot of it matches the information already programmed into the simulators," Tela said. "He's also given us information we didn't know."

"Simulators can be reprogrammed," Matheu said.

"We won't be able to confirm the information is accurate until the fighting begins," Uzah said. "Can we really afford to wait until then to determine if he can be trusted?"

"Do you really think he reprogrammed every simulator?" Tela asked, feeling her irritation growing.

"The Boralians' one goal is to keep us enslaved," Matheu said. "They'll do anything to make sure that happens."

"Have you spent any time with him, General?" Tela asked testily.

"I don't need time with him!" Matheu snapped.

"Oh? So you're like one of the Old Testament prophets then," Tela responded. "Sorry. I didn't know."

"I am your superior officer!" Matheu jumped up from the table.

"We're all on the same side here," Aron said gently, raising a hand to calm them.

"The General's right," Uzah said. "None of us know him well enough to risk so much!"

Tela lowered her eyes to the table and took a deep breath. Why was she defending him so strongly? Okay, so they'd been getting along, and his attitude did seem to be softening. *But why do I care so much?*

"This fighting solves nothing," Aron said, looking as frustrated as Tela felt. "I've staked my reputation on him, and I'm confident I'm right."

"What if you're not?" Uzah asked.

"What do you want to do?" Joram asked. "Send him back and risk him going to the Alliance with everything he knows? At least here we can keep an eye on him."

"We can test him," Tela suggested. "Feed him false information and see how the Alliance reacts."

"We don't have time for such games," Matheu said.

"Well, he's here, General," Tela said, as she stood from the table. "And without him, we'll never be ready to fly those starfighters into battle. Trust him or not, we need him."

"We monitor all communications in and out of the base," Joram said.

"We'll know if he makes contact with the enemy."

When no one responded, Tela nodded and headed for the door, wondering when Davi had managed to win her over.

***

Just as Miri had planned it, the package left the Palace with the Royal garbage, wrapped in a discarded towel inside a bag tied with a red ribbon. The garbage traveled on the garbage skiff to a central dump, where it was unloaded and sat, waiting to be sorted for either incineration or a launch into space.

The courier had no trouble getting access to the garbage dock. The end of the month was a busy time, and no one was around to intercept him. He saw the red ribbon right away, untied it and found the package. He removed it before slipping the ribbon back in place, then disappeared.

An hour later, the courier dropped the package at a newsstand in the starport, leaving it taped to the underside of one of the many news monitors before disappearing into the crowd.

The second courier came ten minutes later, reaching under the monitor to find the package and quickly removed it before also disappearing. He dropped it at a flower stand outside the offices of Media Corp., an independent national broadcasting company on Legallis.

The package sat under a vase at the flower stand marked with a small piece of red tape for five minutes before Orson Sterling arrived to claim it. A burly, slightly overweight man in his early forties with disheveled hair, he bought the vase, careful to place his hand flat on the bottom as he carried it back inside Media Corp's offices to his cubicle.

He eagerly opened the package at his desk and popped the memory card into his vidscreen. Reporters waited a lifetime for a story like this— and it had come to him signed, sealed, and delivered. He alone knew the source. He'd been contacted a few days before by coded e-post from a special communications' center, not the Royal Palace. Miri had been very careful. Orson Sterling would be forever grateful to her.

CHAPTER EIGHT

Xalivar shut off the vidscreen with his fist. After two weeks, it had gotten so he couldn't even watch the news any more. He cursed whoever had betrayed him by leaking these stories. At first, he'd pretended it didn't matter. One story on one network was nothing to worry about. Orson Sterling was an overinflated loudmouthed reporter. Media Corp. reporters always slammed the government. But then it spread to every channel except the Federal one. Citizen groups formed in protest—Worker Rights Party, Worker Freedom Party, Lords for Workers; it sickened him. Didn't these people know what was best for them? Didn't they know the government was making decisions with their needs in mind?

To make matters worse, there were rumors the Council was discussing a special hearing about atrocities against workers. Xalivar cursed the citizens and the Council. He cursed Orson Sterling, too. Bunch of idiots who didn't have a clue!

Bordox and Zylo continued to turn up nothing in their search. Xalivar couldn't remember encountering such incompetence since the

Delta V disaster twenty-five years earlier. He'd hand-chosen rising stars to head that one, too. Could he be losing his touch? He used to be able to predict military stars and exploit them through special opportunities which built their loyalty to him. But now, he couldn't seem to pick winners. He sighed, glancing at the chrono. Time for another daily report from Manaen.

At least no one would see the worst footage. Xalivar had hidden the tapes in the Royal archive and supervised the destruction of any copies himself. What had been released seemed like light bruises compared to what those tapes revealed. He knew he needed to go to the Royal archives and destroy the tapes. Just in case.

He stood, straightened his clothes and hit the button on the door. By now, Manaen would be waiting for him.

✱✱✱

On his way to a meeting at the command center conference room, Davi ran into Aron heading the same way. "Good morning."

Aron smiled. "Good morning indeed. How are our trainees doing?"

"They're working hard and they need it."

Aron laughed. "If anyone can whip them into shape, you can."

Davi smiled, wishing he had the same confidence. "Some of them may never be flight-worthy. I have to show them the same things over and over. Others resent me for my past. They don't want to learn from me." He wondered how honest he should be with Aron.

"Well, don't give up," Aron said. "They're all we've got."

"Maybe with several months' training I could bring them along," Davi said.

"We don't have several months. I wish we did." Aron said as they entered the command center and found the conference room already packed.

"I'm no miracle worker," Davi said as they reached the door.

"Become one. You don't have a choice," Aron said.

"The untrusting are among the most talented. I could really use their help with the others."

"It's hard for some here to trust you. Even some of the leaders have questioned me about it. But I believe in you. They'll come around." He smiled, putting a hand on Davi's arm.

Entering the conference room, they both found their way to empty chairs. *What is that supposed to mean?* If this were the Borali Alliance, the weight of his status as a Royal would have prevented his opinion from being so easily brushed aside, but he hadn't carried that weight amongst the WFR from day one, and he was convinced he never would. He didn't miss it most of the time. This was an exception. Before he had time to think about it, the meeting began.

"Thank you all for coming," Joram said from the head of the table. "As you may know, Vertullis has an energy shield designed to protect the entire planet. Like similar shields deployed around Legallis and Regallis, this protects the planet from incoming laser weapons and starcraft. To pass through, starcraft must first enter a clearance code to lower a portion of the shield along their flight path. The Alliance put it in place to protect the planet if the need arose, but because there has been no external threat, they've never deployed it. For months now, we have observed the control station where Vertullis' energy shield is operated. The plan we have devised involves a multi-front assault. General Matheu has the overview."

Joram stepped aside as General Matheu moved to the head of the table. Around Aron's age and in a full dress uniform—dark blue, unlike the Borali Alliance army's gray, his face was hard, expressionless; his eyes intense—like a man who had lived through many difficulties. Davi had heard rumors he'd been a hero of the Delta V revolt years before.

"Our flight team will be broken into two teams—one to assault the starport at Legallis, the other, the starport on Vertullis. Infantry assaults will occur simultaneously at multiple locations on Vertullis—the government complex, the starport, and the energy shield control center. At the same time, the mechanics core at all Boralian starports will disable any grounded Alliance ships, preventing their launch. Our goal will be to capture Alliance fighters and return them here, while taking control of the energy shield around Vertullis."

"If the shield has never been used," a woman near the far end of the table said, "how do we know it even works?"

"It has been tested every year since its inception," Joram said. "We have confirmed that it's been functional during those tests."

Davi hadn't known Vertullis even had a shield. Having never flown there himself, he'd never had to ask for clearance to land.

"What happens when the Alliance sends fighters from other bases to attack us?" the woman asked again.

"As long as the energy shield is activated, fighters will be ineffective," Joram said. "Any fighters we launch can be cleared through the shield to engage them."

"You expect to steal fighters from both Vertullis and Legallis? Do we have enough pilots?" asked a man seated across the table from Davi.

"We have forty trainees in Captain Rhii's flight training class at present," Aron said. "He can better inform you as to their status and capabilities."

All eyes turned to Davi. *What am I supposed to tell them—that their plan is a complete bust? There's no way my trainees can be ready any time soon! They'll probably think I'm stalling because of torn loyalties or something.*

He stood, smiling, and doing his best to hide his feelings. "It remains to be seen if all forty trainees can even qualify as flight-worthy," he said. "Some of them have little if any experience with land craft, let alone starcraft."

"But you must have seen some progress over the past two weeks," Uzah said.

"Some are progressing quite well, yes," Davi said. "But I have concerns about certifying all of them without months more of training."

"We don't have months," General Matheu said. "They'll have to do the best they can." Curt and direct. Of all the WFR leaders, Matheu was the one who'd distrusted Davi from the start. Every conversation they'd had since his arrival had dripped with tension.

"With all due respect, it won't do us any good to take fighters and have them crash on the way back or get lost out in space," Davi said.

"You'll have to double the training time and work harder to prepare them," General Matheu responded, his look making it clear he wouldn't accept excuses.

"Half the candidates had prior flight experience," Joram said. "Those should be able to defend the others. The rest merely need to be able to follow their leader back to this base."

"I'm doing the best I can, but I can't guarantee they will be ready," Davi said.

Aron put a hand on his arm. "Captain Rhii is one of the most qualified pilots to graduate from the Borali Alliance Military Academy in the past five years. I'm sure he'll find a way to bring them up to speed." He smiled at Davi, motioning with his head for Davi to sit down. Davi sighed and sat back down in the chair.

"Besides the pilot issue," the woman said again, "do we even have enough infantry for these coordinated assaults?"

Uzah stood, smiling. "Our recruiting efforts have been quite successful. We have five hundred men in various stages of training."

"Various stages don't guarantee they'll be ready." The woman's stream of questions reminded Davi of Brie.

"They'll be ready. I'm quite confident," Uzah said, his face confident, but Davi wondered how he felt inside. *It seems to me they're taking a very fly-by-the-seat-of-your-pants approach. Do they really expect to succeed?*

"Once we control the shield, the military outposts on Vertullis, and have VS28 fighters, we will be able to protect and defend the planet," General Matheu said.

"And what if we fail?" The man across from Davi wondered.

"We cannot fail. Our people's lives depend on it," General Matheu said. They didn't need the look he proffered to convince them he meant it.

After the meeting, Davi walked out with Aron. "Do any of you realize we're attempting the impossible?"

Aron smiled. "Our people have a saying: Nothing is impossible with God."

"We risk losing so many in the process," Davi said.

"How many of our people have already died at the hands of the Borali Alliance?" Aron asked. "It's a matter of time before we're discovered here. Word is spreading. They can die trying or wait for the Alliance to come here and destroy them. Either way, the risk is the same."

Davi couldn't argue. He knew the workers' future depended on their success.

Aron smiled, patting his arm. "Do the best you can. You've been well-trained. I have faith in you."

The trainees had progressed over the past month, but Davi didn't want the responsibility for qualifying anyone who wasn't ready. Flying came easy to him, but when it came to the safety of others, he was more cautious. Davi appreciated Aron's encouragement. He just wished he had the same faith in himself.

✳✳✳

A few minutes after Farien returned on a Floater from reviewing the activity in the fields, Bordox and his men entered his makeshift office in one of the barns.

The Floater was a blue floating platform with two seats facing a control panel at the front. The largest Floaters had benches which held as many as twenty troops—more if ten more stood in the middle. Smaller models, like this one, held four or five passengers. Floaters moved by manipulating the air underneath as they floated along above the ground.

Farien sat at his desk as Bordox stared down at him with a serious look on his face, saying nothing.

"Hello Bordox. How have you been?" Farien said after a moment.

Bordox nodded. "Have you heard anything new from our old friend Xander?"

Not wasting any time, are you? "Why do you want to know?"

Bordox frowned. "The High Lord Councilor wants to know."

"I'm sure the High Lord Councilor, being his uncle, knows where he is," Farien said, unimpressed by Bordox's angry expression and tone.

"Your friend is a criminal wanted by the Borali Alliance for murder. If the High Lord Councilor knew where to find him, he'd be under arrest," Bordox said.

"I know all about the murder charges. It was self-defense," Farien said. "I'm sure he's out gathering evidence before he turns himself in."

"When was the last contact you had with him?"

"Look, Bordox, you've been giving us trouble for years. Why in the world would I tell you anything?" Farien said, turning his attention to the reports on his vidscreen.

"Because it's your duty to the Alliance," Bordox said.

"Do the Alliance a favor and go back to whatever box you crawled out of and seal it," Farien said, turning away and punching a button on his datapad.

Bordox came around the desk so fast, Farien didn't have time to react. The brute dragged him from his chair, before his hand wrapped around Farien's neck. He fought for breath a moment before Bordox relaxed his grip.

"How about I let you live and you tell me everything you know?"

"You can't just go around killing people, no matter what authority you claim is behind you," Farien said; would he really do it?

"I can make you wish you were dead," Bordox said.

A sharp pain shot through Farien unlike anything he'd ever experienced. He wanted to cry out, but couldn't catch his breath. Tears welled in his eyes, as Bordox pulled the shock device away from the small of his back. Farien collapsed to his knees.

"When was the last contact you had with him?"

"I saw him during Yao's visit a month or so back," Farien said. The words slipped out against his will, almost as if someone else had spoken.

"Good. That's better. Now, tell me why your friend is spending so much time with workers?"

"Because he's assigned to Vertullis, genius," Farien said. Shock waves hit again, causing him to writhe with pain.

"Since I'm here with the full support of the High Lord Councilor, you might want to show me a modicum of respect, Lieutenant," Bordox said.

"Look, he's been investigating some incidents of abuse, trying to gather the facts," Farien said.

"We found evidence of him spending a lot of time in a particular worker's home. There was a photo there of a man to whom he bears a strong resemblance. What's his connection to those workers?"

"Why don't you ask him when you find him?" Farien said. "I don't know whom you're referring to." Bordox shocked him again and again.

"Gods! I told you I don't know, Bordox!"

"I don't believe you," Bordox said.

This time Farien cried out, but stopped when the pain became overwhelming.

"Answer the question."

"His mother and her sister's family," Farien finally said. He cursed himself for being weak, but he couldn't take more of the pain.

"His mother lives on Legallis in the Royal Palace." The shock waves coursed through him again.

He managed to scream. "For the love of the gods! Stop! Please! He was adopted by Miri. His real family were workers, like you said at the Academy."

Bordox cursed as his fist hit the desk inches from where Farien's head had fallen in exhaustion. "It's true?"

Humiliation washed over Farien like wave. He couldn't believe he'd betrayed his friend. Bordox hadn't known the truth. What would he say to Davi? What would Bordox do to him?

Bordox pulled the shock device away, fastening it to his belt. "The Alliance appreciates your cooperation." He turned with his men and disappeared as fast as he'd appeared.

My gods, the pain! He lay there beside his desk, trying to shake it off.

✳✳✳

After a month on the simulators, Davi decided to give the trainees time on the Skitters. When they'd gathered in the Skitter cave for class, he began reviewing the controls. "Any questions so far?" Davi asked.

Brie smiled at him, cocking her head to one side. "So the way you make it go is this button here?" She pointed to the joystick. Tela frowned, shifting weight to her left foot.

Davi did his best to keep his distance from Brie, nodding. "Yes, Brie. You'll need to get used to it. It's easy to push it too hard and accelerate out of control."

"Okay, I'll be careful then," she said, smiling at him again.

Davi nodded. "Okay, let's take them out for a trial run on the course Tela's set up for us. Keep your speed slow until you get used to the controls and the feel of the Skitters."

He watched as, one by one, the trainees started their Skitters and accelerated into the tunnel. Tela took off first, followed by several of the more experienced trainees. The rest followed. Only Dru, Brie, Nila and Davi remained.

Dru started out being cautious but seemed to feel comfortable by the time he entered the tunnel. Nila accelerated next, fumbling a bit, then recovered and disappeared into the tunnel.

"Well, here I go." Brie smiled sheepishly, starting to accelerate, wobbling a bit, slow then fast. After a few moments, she managed to steer the Skitter toward the tunnel. As she neared the tunnel entrance, it looked like she might miss the opening and hit the wall, but, at the last minute, she steered to the right and entered the tunnel. Davi breathed a sigh of relief and followed.

As he left the tunnel, the sweet smell of cedars filled his nose. Trees surrounded them now, filling every space around the Skitter course and trails. The sounds of insects and birds rose above the hum of the Skitters—a constant drone, which faded into the background after a few moments as their ears adjusted.

Davi pulled alongside her, smiling. "You did it. Good job."

"Thanks," she said, looking pleased with herself.

They rode past Tela who waited outside the tunnel entrance. She shot Davi a cold stare. *What did I do now?* "All right, Tela, please take us through the course."

She turned away, avoiding eye contact and headed toward the front of the group, who waited at the start of the course. One by one, they followed her. Some of them seemed quite confident and steady, others more cautious and uncertain. Dru had moved up a few places, feeling more confident. That left Davi, Nila and Brie.

"All right, Nila. Go ahead," Davi called to his cousin, who was reviewing her Skitter's control panel on the far side of the clearing.

Nila nodded. "Okay." She accelerated with more confidence this time, following the others.

Brie accelerated full force and shot toward Nila like a rocket, her face in a panic.

"Let go of the handle, Brie!" Davi called after her, and then realized she was trying but couldn't do it.

As she closed fast on the unsuspecting Nila, Davi accelerated his Skitter and chased after her. He pulled alongside, reached over and tried to pull her hand free. Her sleeve had gotten pinched in the small space between the joystick and the arm of the Skitter. As she panicked, her fists clenched, triggering the accelerator. Her face morphed into a grimace as her speed increased and the wind pricked her face.

Nila rode a few feet in front of them, so focused on controlling her Skitter she hadn't noticed the activity behind her. Brie looked at Davi, eyes full of panic. Davi pulled his Skitter closer to hers and reached past her, leaning way over to one side, controlling his Skitter with one hand as he did. His fingers touched the start pin on Brie's Skitter, but he couldn't quite grab it. He stretched further and popped it out.

Brie's Skitter stopped instantly, almost throwing her off. Davi skidded to a stop, dismounted and ran over to pull her sleeve free, then lifted the shaken Brie off the Skitter. For a moment, she lay in his arms staring up at him with relief.

He saw Tela pulling up. She'd come back to check on how things were going. Seeing Brie in his arms, she scowled, then turned and sped away again along the course with Nila following.

Davi started calling after her, then realized she couldn't hear him. He set Brie on the ground. "Are you okay?"

"Yes, thank you. My hero!" she said, smiling.

"Try and be more careful. Maybe roll up your sleeves," Davi instructed.

Brie nodded. "Okay, right." She rolled up her sleeves.

Davi reminded himself to inquire about the status of uniforms again. Brie and several other trainees had not yet received theirs, and he didn't want a repeat of this incident.

For the rest of the afternoon, they worked the course with no further problems. Some of class could already race through the course at a decent pace.

Soon Virun and his friends began fiddling around with the targeting system, although Davi hadn't demonstrated it yet. As he watched, he thought some of them might be ready now for the mission, if they could just learn to obey orders.

"Very good, you men," Davi said, after they'd finish the course for the fourth time. "Why don't you let me show you how that works?"

"I think we've got it," Jorek said as the rest of his friends ignored Davi.

"The course can only show you so much. In a combat situation—"

"In a combat situation, we may be on opposite sides," Virun snapped. With that, the group revved their Skitters and headed back to the course again.

Davi sighed. *How can I get through to them?* He had no idea. As he mulled it over, Brie and Nila arrived at the finish line. They seemed to grow more confident with each run. By the end of the class, they maneuvered their Skitters with much more ease. They didn't seem to have the aptitude. The learning curve was too high. How would he get them ready? It would be impossible in the next few weeks.

This would be so much easier, if I didn't care so much. Pilots die. It's part of the risk. But these weren't any pilots. He was responsible for them. He walked away discouraged again.

That night, as he had often the past two weeks, he spent time in the Library studying the history and beliefs of his new people.

The workers had descended from a sect of the Protestants on Old Earth called the Evangelicals. The group was composed of people of varying theological beliefs who had found enough in common to unite, when they became more and more the targets of persecution on Old Earth. It had started with Muslims but then spread to groups such as Atheists, Agnostics, and even Mainliners—fellow Christians who did not share their Evangelical beliefs.

As a result, when colonization became possible, the Evangelicals decided to find a new place to settle and start over. They found their way to Vertullis and began a colony, until their old enemies found them and forced them into slavery.

As he studied their beliefs, Davi found himself more and more in agreement with them. Though they had but one God, their God was a god of justice and mercy, who sought a relationship with His people; a god who grieved over them, longed for them, loved them. A personal relationship with God was such an appealing concept to Davi, especially one who was willing to die for His people.

Miri had raised him to believe service to the higher cause of helping others was more important than service to one's self. Though the workers' religious rites seemed strange to him, in reading about them, they seemed to make sense. He started feeling more and more comfortable praying to their God and participating in services. In fact, he had plans to attend with Lura the following morning.

The workers believed God was with them at all times and working His will in their lives daily; that He was involved in everything that happened to them and was always working for their good. They committed their plans to Him and sought His blessing on their actions. Davi couldn't help but be drawn to a god who got so involved. He found himself wanting to know more and more.

✷✷✷

Tela ordered a Tertullian Hammer and settled into a booth at the pub to wait for her drink. Through the dome over head, she watched the sky fade from purple to gray as the planet's two moons started their nightly climb. Sitting there, she reviewed the day's events.

Again, Brie had flirted with Davi. And again, it had really set her off. She couldn't understand why. She and Davi were just friends. She didn't have time for men right now. She had the coming battles to think about and, ever since her father had disappeared, she'd decided love was a waste of time. So why would her heart not get with the program?

She couldn't get Davi out of her mind—the way he smiled at her, when the other trainees were making progress, the way he laughed at his own silly jokes, the serious look his face took on when deep in thought or lecturing on something intense. Why did she pay so much attention anyway? She'd already decided he wasn't for her.

As the waiter arrived with her drink, she spotted Davi behind him, coming in the door. Handing the waiter a few credits, she watched Davi make his away across the room as the waiter disappeared. He hadn't seen her yet as he looked around, nodding at various acquaintances.

Why hadn't he seen her yet? She was right in front of him. *Oh great! That bothers me, too! What's wrong with me?!*

Then he saw her and smiled, waving. *He's coming over!* She tried to be nonchalant, relaxing in her seat as she sipped her drink. She savored the smooth, fruity liquid as it warmed her throat.

Davi came right to the table. "Imagine finding you here, Lieutenant."

There it came—his smile. She returned it. "Another long day." The butterflies danced in her stomach again.

He nodded. "For me, too. Are you alone?"

Say no! Say no! "Yes." *What's wrong with me?*

He sat across from her. "Hope you don't mind company."

She shook her head. "No."

"We had a real near miss today with Brie," Davi said.

Ah, there it is! He's going to go right to it! "Yes, it was a good thing you were prepared."

"I wasn't. I almost panicked," Davi said. "Then I remembered the start pin acts as a kill switch. I haven't been around Skitters much in a while."

She smiled. "Thank goodness you remembered."

The waiter returned, and she watched as Davi ordered a Regallian smoothie. She admired the way his chin curved down from his head, the smoothness of his skin, the way he looked with his late-day shadow of a beard. *Oh my God, stop!*

Davi turned to her as the waiter left. "I don't think we can get them all ready. There isn't time." He frowned, discouraged.

"We'll do our best," she said.

He looked so sad. *Why do I want so much to encourage him? I can't bear seeing him so sad.* She searched for words that would encourage him somehow. "Some of them only need to fly well enough to follow others back here. They should be able to learn enough for that."

"I'm not sure Brie can learn much of anything," Davi said. Tela laughed.

He covered his eyes with his hand, embarrassed. "I'm sorry. Terrible thing to say." Tela laughed again. He grinned. "She's so naïve." They both laughed.

"Yeah, very naïve," she agreed. *What's this? He's not attracted to her?*

"She's like a little kid sometimes, too. So young and innocent," Davi said. Tela did a cartwheel in her head. *Yes!* "Several of them are. It's hard to believe they're in flight training."

"It wasn't so many years ago, we were their age," Tela said, doing her best to hide her relief.

Davi laughed. "I guess you're right. I feel so much older after all that's happened."

The waiter returned with his smoothie. He sipped it for a bit, lost in thought. "I feel so responsible for them. If they go up there and become easy targets..."

The waiter disappeared again. "That's a risk for any one of us," Tela said. "In war, people die."

Davi nodded, his face taking on a somber expression as he sipped the smoothie. "I don't have to like it." Tela laughed. "What's so funny?"

You. You're adorable. "Nothing. I'm sorry. You're sipping a sweet drink looking like they're already dead. It's funny!"

Davi took another sip of his smoothie and shrugged. "Sometimes I let whatever's on my mind come out of my mouth."

Tela smiled. "It's okay. It's one of the things I actually like about you." *I can't believe I just said that.*

His eyes brightened as they met hers. "You mean there's actually something you like about me? Wow! Big progress!"

She sighed and turned away. "You cocky fighter jocks!" They both laughed again. "No one wants people to die, but we have to remember the loss will be worth the price of freedom. We have been slaves too long!"

Davi nodded. "I know. I've been spending time in the Library learning the history of our people. I really believe in what we're doing." Tela couldn't help being impressed by his effort. "That doesn't make it any easier to think about sending kids to their possible deaths."

"Some of them may surprise you," Tela said.

Davi nodded. "I hope all of them do." He took another sip, savoring the fruity taste a moment.

On impulse, she placed her hand on his atop the table. "Me, too." She fought the urge to yank it back when she realized what she'd done. Yet he hadn't tried to pull his hand away. Did he like this? She hated being so transparent, but then touching him like this felt so nice.

She slowly withdrew her hand. "We'll have to work harder with them."

Davi nodded. "I've been thinking the same thing." He took one last long sip of his smoothie, and then set the empty glass back on the table. "I guess I should head back and start working up a more intense lesson plan."

Tela joined him as he stood. "Do you want some help?"

Davi gave her a puzzled look. "Really?"

She shrugged. "Sure, why not? I can come up with some decent ideas."

"I didn't mean it like that."

She smiled. "I know."

He nodded and tossed some credits on the table. "Okay, let's go."

She had an impulse. "Wait."

"What?"

"One more thing."

Without thinking, she rushed around the table, and, before either understood what was happening, she kissed him.

After a moment, she pulled away, straightened her clothes and headed for the door. "Let's go."

Davi stood there stunned and watched her go.

She turned back in the doorway. "You coming?"

He nodded, moving toward her.

Oh my God! She fought to control her expression. *Why did I do that? This is just what I need.* But then she realized, she hadn't wanted to stop.

✹✹✹

The next morning, Davi and Lura attended a worship service in the base chapel led by the base chaplain, Pastor Timoteo. As Davi sat down, he noticed Tela across the aisle. She looked over and smiled. He smiled back. He'd thought she had no interest at all, but then she'd kissed him. He still couldn't believe it. Right before the service began, she slid across the aisle to sit beside him.

The service was simple, with less elaborate rituals and show than he'd seen at the temples on Legallis. It focused more on God than on anything the believers had done, and the sacrifice demanded was a willing heart and life, not some physical object.

The Lords' religion consisted of offering sacrifices to the various gods to obtain something the believer wanted—forgiveness for some wrong done, help for some impending action, revenge, love, health, strength, etc. It focused on what the gods could do for the believers, rather than what the believers could do for the gods.

The workers' religion required believers to offer the God worship for all He had already done for them, to embark on a personal journey of faith discovery. He'd never understand how gods so powerful existed to serve man's needs. This God knew His place in the universe. It made sense to Davi and appealed to him far more than the Lords' religion ever had.

The service concluded with a time of prayer. Davi thanked God for his family—two wonderful mothers and so many cousins, uncles, and aunts. He had more than he'd ever imagined he'd have and discovering they were all good people made it so much sweeter.

He thought about Miri and Xalivar and hoped they were well. He prayed they could forgive him for the betrayal they perceived. He prayed for his trainees, to teach and lead them well; for wisdom and for their safety. And he prayed for the battle, for God's blessings and guidance of the plans of His people. He'd read about Christians fighting with God on their side. He knew they would need God to achieve their goal.

He prayed for Farien and Yao, whom he hadn't seen in a while. He hoped they were well and would forgive his betrayal of the Alliance. He thanked God for Tela and their budding romance and asked blessings and protection on them through the fighting ahead.

In conclusion, he prayed for his father, wherever he was. Then he asked for forgiveness for the dead Captain and blessings on his family. Davi hoped the God of the Vertullians would forgive him for something he couldn't forgive of himself.

When he'd finished, Davi was amazed how peaceful he felt. A burden had been lifted from him, as if everything was under control—much different than he'd experienced after worshipping the Lords' gods. It was comforting to know a God who would make the sacrifices for His people so they didn't have to do anything but come as they are. The history of this God interwove with the history of his people, a history which, as he learned about it, made him feel proud.

✳✳✳

Miri had not been down to the Royal Archives in almost a year. Located deep beneath the planet's surface in one of several caves dug out with lasers to create secure storage for important government materials, the Archives had very limited access. Besides the archivist himself, Xalivar, Miri, and their two most trusted aides alone had access to it, and the aides had to come together.

The archivist showed no surprise when she stepped off the elevator. "Welcome to the Royal Archives, Princess Miri."

She returned his smile as she placed her palm on the sensor. It beeped and the gate clicked, allowing her to step inside. "Good afternoon."

"Was there anything I might help you with?" The archivist asked.

She shook her head. "No thank you. I'm going over some old family papers."

"All right. Let me know if there's anything I can do."

"Thank you, I will."

Miri moved around the desk and weaved down the aisles between white metal shelves, making her way to a vault in the very back of the cave. Here she stopped, pulling up information on her datapad. She had never used the combination before. She entered the combination on the keypad then waited until she heard several loud clicks and the door slid open. She pulled the thick door wider and stepped inside.

Since her father and Xalivar alone had used the vault, she had no idea what she'd find there. She saw more metal shelving, faded gray. There were rows of old Earth books, some computer tapes and memory cards, some older royal vestments from past special occasions, such as her father's coronation robe and crown, her mother's wedding gown, and other similar items.

The label on a box of memory cards caught her eye. It read: 'Vertullis Revolt.' She grabbed one of the boxes and popped the top open. Retrieving the first card, she inserted it into her datapad.

She heard the sounds first—people yelling and screaming, laser fire. After a moment, the video appeared. Alliance soldiers used laser weapons to mow down slaves lined up in front of large pits dug in the earth. As one row fell into the pit, the next row stepped forward to be mowed down; their bodies falling into the pit on top of the others. This happened again and again to seemingly endless numbers of slaves.

Miri looked away, grabbing the memory card and pulling it free. The next card showed more of the same at a different location. She'd known about revolts being put down, but never heard of massacres.

She found it difficult to accept what she'd seen—Xalivar, in full military uniform, directing the troops himself and firing his own laser weapon in unison with them. *Xalivar not only ordered the massacres, he participated in them. My gods!*

Grabbing the boxes of memory tapes off the shelf, she looked around for something to conceal them in. A couple of large hats on a nearby shelf caught her eye. She chose the most modern, a hat her mother had worn on a ceremonial tour of the star system, slid the memory card boxes inside, then grabbed a scarf from the clothing rack, and stuffed it in and around the boxes so the archivist wouldn't see them.

She stepped out of the vault, shut the door behind her and entered the code to trigger the lock. Hearing the clicks, she tugged on the door to be sure it had locked, then headed back through the aisles the way she'd come.

CHAPTER NINE

Xalivar's jaw dropped to the floor as he flicked on the sound with the remote control. It took a moment for his eyes to register what he was seeing.

"These images are of Alliance soldiers committing mass murder of workers during the worker revolt ten years ago," Orson Sterling was saying. Xalivar frowned as he watched himself on the screen, firing his weapon. "As you can see, the High Lord Councilor himself led the massacres."

How can this be? The Delta V footage was hidden in the private Royal vault! Copies were destroyed.

He punched a button on the remote and changed the vidscreen to a private channel then entered a password. He chose one of the dates shown at random and began fast forwarding through the footage. It showed an empty vault. Could one of his servants have betrayed him after all this time?

On the third day he selected, he saw her. Miri was in the vault, viewing one of the memory cards he'd hidden there. Seeing her reaction, he knew right away. *Miri removed the tapes! My gods!* Betrayed by his own sister!

An old proverb came to mind: **Gods defend me from my friends; from my enemies I can defend myself.**

He fought to control the rage rising inside him. Miri had been leaking footage to Media Corp.? No wonder she'd made herself so scarce the past few weeks. *What have you done to our family, sister?* He buzzed for Manaen.

The door slid open and Manaen hurried into his chamber. "Yes, my Lord?"

"Where is the Princess at the moment?" Xalivar asked, clenching his fists.

"She's gone into the city, my Lord." Manaen said, handing him a datapad full of reports.

"I need to see her as soon as she returns."

"Of course, my Lord."

"And what time is the Council meeting today?"

"Just past mid-day."

"Has the Council requested my attendance?"

"They have, my Lord."

Xalivar cursed to himself as Manaen saluted and walked out the door. It slid shut behind him.

Xalivar turned off the vidscreen and began reviewing the reports on the datapad Manaen had given him. One came from Bordox, going on and on about Davi being the child of workers. Xalivar cursed again. It would be impossible to keep the Council from seeing it. *I'm ruined! My gods! Is everyone turning against me now?*

He searched his mind for a way he could use this to his advantage. If he took the report to the Council first himself, perhaps he could lessen the damage. After all, hadn't he instigated the search for Davi himself? He'd protected the Alliance's best interests without favoritism for his nephew. And the Council needed to know more about their missing murder suspect, didn't they?

He smiled to himself. *Yes!* They needed to know Davi was not like them—a worker! *Yes!* Let Miri try and protect her son once the fact became public knowledge! Xalivar would present it as a surprise to himself. Miri had deceived all of them! She had betrayed the Alliance, acted alone. He found it unacceptable and he knew the Council would also. *Yes!* Let Miri's friends on the Council hear this.

For a moment, he wondered if they'd been involved with the news leaks, too. He doubted it. They would not want footage of the massacres getting out. The Council had been involved in ordering the suppression of the revolts. No. She must be negotiating with them for leniency for her son.

Yes, my sister! See how much support you get when I am through with the Council. No one will dare to support you after this. No, my sister, soon you and I can discuss your activities alone. He laughed, pleased with himself.

✹✹✹

Davi took the trainees out on Skitters for the third time in a week. He raced through the course to the halfway point, and then stopped to watch as the trainees passed by. They'd made marked improvement. All of them could at least navigate the course to the end now, most practicing with the targeting system. It was time to shake it up a bit and take them out on trails. He needed to see how they handled things outside of a course they'd almost memorized.

All the trainees looked slick in their new dark blue uniforms. It seemed to boost their confidence. Good! They would need all the confidence they could get in the fight ahead. He chuckled at the sight of the cloth protectors each wore dangling in front of their lower faces to protect from the bite of the wind. Practicality had overcome their initial resistance. He waited until the last trainee passed, then followed along through the blur of the trees.

The spicy odor of cedars filled his nose as the drone of insects and birds blended with the hum of the Skitter in his ears. He found his trainees waiting for him in the large clearing at the end of the course. They were all smiling as he pulled to a stop.

"Well done today. Definite improvements," Davi said, removing the cloth protector from his face so it wouldn't muffle his voice.

"Getting so we could do it blindfolded," Dru said, growing cocky.

Davi knew Dru was still struggling but smiled. "Good! Confidence is the right attitude. How about we shake it up a bit?"

"Try it backwards?" Nila asked.

Davi laughed. "No. Let's try some of the forest trails. It's important to learn how to handle your craft under a variety of circumstances. In battle, there is no preset course to follow."

"Can we have a mock battle?" Dru asked, hopeful.

"Let's try the forest trails first, okay? One step at a time." Davi smiled. "You wanna pick a trail?"

Dru smiled, pleased. "Sure. Can I lead the way?"

Davi nodded and Dru took off, struggling for balance a bit after accelerating too fast. One by one, the others followed him onto a trail through the forest. As usual, Brie and Nila brought up the rear.

Tela hung back to join Davi.

"Nice job on the course, Tela," Davi said. "It's making a world of difference." She'd become such an asset.

"Glad I could help," she said and smiled.

They'd been spending a lot of time together since their night at the bar, though Davi had done his best not to reveal it to the other students. Sometimes, he avoided looking at her for fear it would show on his face.

But more and more, he wanted to shout it for the whole world to hear.

✸✸✸

Bordox and Corsi rode together on Skitters through a forest clearing. So far their search of the forest hadn't turned up anything. Even the local farmers who'd reported seeing activity here wouldn't talk to them at the sight of LSP uniforms. Bordox had grown bored and frustrated. How could Xander Rhii be so hard to locate?

A couple of his men rode back toward them, pulling up alongside. "No activity in that direction, sir."

"How far did you go?"

"Twenty kilometers. The forest goes on forever," the soldier said over the hum of the Skitters and the chirping of the insects and birds.

The chirping annoyed him, even more than the smell of the cedar. Bordox frowned, irritated. "You'll search every centimeter of it, if I ask you to." How could someone as stupid as Rhii hide so well?

The soldier nodded, "Yes, sir."

"Try another direction for now," Bordox said.

The soldiers turned and rode off, disappearing into the cedars to the west.

"The trees are so dense, the scanner is having difficulty," Corsi said, tapping the device attached to his control panel.

"I'm getting the feeling Zylo sent us on another wild Gungor chase," Bordox said.

"Gungors would be easier to find," Corsi said.

Bordox nodded. Even his men knew it was a waste of time.

✸✸✸

As they followed the trail, Nila's Skitter sputtered, a big cloud of smoke emerging from its motivator and trailing along behind them.

Moments later, it stopped.

Davi pulled alongside her. "What happened?"

Nila shrugged. "No idea. It lost power and then stopped."

"Maybe the motivator is bad," Tela said as she stopped nearby, waving her arms to clear the smoke drifting toward her face.

"Can we fix it here?" Davi asked.

Tela shook her head. "I'd have to ride in for another one."

"Can we tow it?"

"You might be able to rig something up," Tela said with a shrug.

"You catch up with the others and let them know what's happened. Then ride back and see what you can find at the base," Davi said. "I'll stay with her and see what we can manage."

Tela nodded, looking around—just Nila and Davi. Brie had gone on ahead. She looked relieved. Davi chuckled to himself as she said: "You be careful, okay?"

"We can handle it," Davi said as she nodded and rode away. He began formulating a plan.

"How do you plan to tow it?" Nila asked.

Davi motioned to the nearby cedars. Thick vines wound their way through the canopy overhead. "Get your laser torch out and let's see if we can cut down some of those vines." He grabbed his own laser torch from a pocket on the Skitter and stepped down onto the forest floor.

✳✳✳

Bordox and Corsi followed a winding trail through the forest, until they saw flashes ahead.

"What was that?"

"Looked like lasers," Corsi said.

"It came from up ahead." Bordox accelerated his Skitter and sped around a bend in the trail. Corsi hurried to keep up with him.

❋❋❋

Davi and Nila finished tying the vines into longer ropes then began attaching the two Skitters together with Davi's in front.

"We won't be able to go very fast, but it'll get us there," Davi said as they finished. He stood admiring their work as Nila smiled. His Academy training had paid off.

"Where'd you learn how to do all this stuff?"

Davi laughed. "Military Academies teach all kinds of skills. You never know what you're going to need."

Nila laughed. "Bet you never thought you'd be towing a Skitter."

Davi smiled. "There are a lot of things I've done on this planet I never thought I'd be doing. Let's mount up and get going."

Nila climbed onto her Skitter as Davi settled back onto his. "Might be a bit rough at first so hang on." He took his time accelerating. Nila did her best to match his steering.

❋❋❋

Bordox stopped in a clearing as Corsi pulled up alongside. He couldn't believe what he saw.

On a trail to the west, Xander rode a Skitter and pulled a girl on another Skitter behind him.

My gods! I found him! He ducked down, motioning to Corsi. "Keep your head down!"

"Is it him?"

Bordox nodded. "Let's get in front of him and surprise him. Call in the men. Quietly!"

Corsi nodded, reaching for his communicator.

Bordox smiled as he activated his Skitter's weapons system. At last, he would get his revenge.

✳✳✳

Davi stopped a moment and adjusted the vines. He'd strung them too loose the first time, making the ride rougher for Nila than he wanted. He cut them in half and retied the ends so the Skitters would ride closer together. This time, he attached them with four lines instead of two, checking to be sure the knots were tight.

"That should be better." *I wish Tela would hurry back with that motivator.*

"I'm sure it's fine," Nila said. Her willingness to do whatever it took made up for the fact she sometimes took longer than the others to get up to speed during training.

Davi settled back onto his Skitter. "All right. Here we go again."

He accelerated again, looking back to check on Nila. She smiled at him, offering a thumbs up. *Good. Maybe this time we can make some progress.*

✳✳✳

Bordox divided his men into groups and sent them in various directions, while he and Corsi then continued on the same trail as Xander. He was so excited; he had to force himself not to move in before his men were ready. He couldn't risk allowing Davi to escape. This would be the highlight of his career to date. Not only could he take down his own rival but he'd also be ruining the reputation of his family's rival clan at the same time. He started humming a favorite song.

✳✳✳

Davi stopped a moment, scanning maps of the forest on his datapad. "This side trail should be a short cut," he said to Nila. "Shall we give it a try?"

She shrugged. "You're the officer."

He laughed, clipping the datapad back onto his belt before accelerating off the main trail onto the short cut. "I wish all soldiers were this easy to please," he joked.

"I'm saving my demands for when it matters," Nila answered. They both laughed.

✳✳✳

Bordox ordered his men to move in from all directions on the point where Rhii should be. Bordox grinned as he and Corsi accelerated around a bend in the trees. Verifying his weapons had fully charged, he spotted his men closing in ahead. But his heart sank. Davi wasn't there. Bordox cursed.

"Where could he have gone?" Corsi asked, looking puzzled.

"Search the whole area! Quickly!" Corsi winced at the yelling. "He can't be allowed to escape!" Bordox fumed as the men scattered. "You, too, Corsi! Go! Go!"

Corsi nodded, accelerating his Skitter up a side trail. Bordox cursed again and examined the ground. How could Xander keep slipping through his grasp? They'd tear every inch of this forest apart if that's what it took. He had to be out here somewhere. He would not let Xander Rhii humiliate him again.

"Not this time Rhii!" he shouted. "You're mine!"

✳✳✳

As Davi and Nila pulled their Skitters to a stop inside the cave, Tela rushed toward them. "Thank God you're back. We've had reports of LSP troops searching the forest."

As soon as Davi stepped off his Skitter, she embraced him.

"LSP troops here?" Davi couldn't believe it. "How'd they find us?"

"I don't know, but we'd better be careful on the trails from now on," Tela said.

Davi nodded. Tela was still holding onto him. He liked it. "So, does this mean we're going public then?"

Tela rolled her eyes, letting go and looking around. Nila had already disappeared. They were alone. "Is it that embarrassing?"

"No, of course not." She sighed. "It's complicated. We're about to start a war. And since my father disappeared, I haven't wanted to get involved."

"Your father disappeared?" Davi hadn't known.

"My father was a scientist. He made some discoveries the Alliance deemed threatening. They sent him to the top secret prison on Legallis," Tela said. "Another worker spy, they claimed."

"Top secret prison on Legallis? Must not be too secret if you know about it," Davi said with a smile.

"I have no idea where it's located, but it's known to exist. A secret prison there for workers declared a threat to the Borali Alliance," Tela said.

Davi's mind started racing. Could his father be there? He had to make some inquiries. Maybe Yao or Farien could find something out for him. "How long ago?"

Tela shrugged. "I was a little girl. Twelve years, I think."

"Your father is still alive?"

Tela nodded. "Before she died, my mother had contact with a man who'd been making deliveries on Legallis and encountered my father working at the dock. They sometimes use the prisoners for various projects, and then send them back to the prison."

Davi's mind raced with thoughts about his father. He promised himself not to say anything to Lura until he'd had the chance to get more information. He turned and started back toward his quarters.

"What's the matter? Did I say something wrong?" Tela called after him, but he didn't hear her.

✸✸✸

Xalivar timed his arrival at the Council chamber so he could make a grand entrance when the meeting was well underway. To increase the Council's anticipation, he'd had Manaen send a message to Lord Tarkanius about Xalivar receiving shocking news of great import to the Council, which he would deliver in person.

All eyes fixed on him when he entered the chamber, and the session ground to an immediate halt. Lord Niger had been addressing the Council, but seeing Xalivar, he stopped and returned to his seat.

Xalivar smiled inside, his exterior expression remaining very grave. "I apologize for my lateness to the proceedings," he said, making his way to the dais.

Tarkanius nodded. "Your aide notified us you would be late. You have important news for us?"

"Yes, I recently uncovered a shocking conspiracy against the Borali Alliance which has compromised the Royal Family," Xalivar said. He heard gasps and watched the shocked reactions from those present.

"The Royal Family has been implicated?" Lord Hachim asked.

Xalivar blanched internally at the choice of words but maintained his composure and nodded. "I'm afraid so. The conspiracy was led by my own sister, Princess Miri," Xalivar said. More gasps and shocked reactions.

"Princess Miri has been a loyal member of the Borali Alliance her whole life," Lord Kray said.

Xalivar fought the urge to scowl. Kray always sided with Miri. They were the oldest of friends. *Well, let's see her argue with this!*

"I have uncovered evidence that my own nephew, Prince Davi Rhii, was adopted by Miri from workers." He waited for the gasps and shocked reactions. "This illegal act occurred completely without my knowledge and remained hidden from me, until LSP forces, under my command, uncovered the plot during their search for the fugitive, Davi Rhii."

"Your own sister raised a worker child in your household, and you didn't know?" Lord Niger asked.

"Not until now. I was quite shocked and disturbed by the revelation," Xalivar said, ignoring Kray's icy stare.

"He's an officer in the Borali Alliance military, an Academy graduate...the entire Alliance may be compromised," Lord Obed said, fanning the flames. Since Obed's son had written the report, Xalivar wondered how much he already knew.

Xalivar looked at the floor, forcing as much sadness onto his face as he could muster. "I fear it is so. My own men have informed me they are closing in on him now."

"And what of the Princess? What does she have to say about this?" Tarkanius asked.

Xalivar knew Tarkanius was among those who had met with Miri in private, causing Xalivar to question his loyalty. *All will be brought to light soon enough, Tarkanius. And those who betrayed me will answer for it.*

"She's away from the Palace, but she will be found and brought to me. I rushed here to inform the Council as soon as the evidence came to light."

"Your aide managed to come and go over twenty-five minutes ago," Lord Obed interjected with an accusing tone.

"This is a very serious accusation you are making," Lord Simeon said, ignoring his colleague. "We will initiate a full investigation."

Another possible traitor heard from. "I will assist you in any way I can,"

Xalivar said.

"Thank you for bringing this matter to our attention, High Lord Councilor," Tarkanius said. "Your forthrightness before the Council exemplifies the honor with which you serve."

Too little, too late, Tarkanius, my old friend. You've already proven where your loyalties lie. Xalivar nodded. This was going far better than he'd imagined. "Thank you, Lord Tarkanius."

"As soon as the Princess and her son are found, they must be brought before the Council," Lord Obed said, his face a cold stare.

"Of course," Xalivar said. "Now, if you will excuse me, I have urgent matters to attend to."

Tarkanius nodded. "Please keep the Council informed."

Xalivar returned the nod and smiled as he turned and hurried down the aisle again. Several Lords nodded warmly as he passed them. When the door closed behind him, he heard the room explode in chatter.

Good. Let them discuss it. Let them become distracted from whatever plans Miri set afoot. None can dare trust her now! He smiled and quickened his pace. Despite Obed's attempts, it had gone so perfectly. He didn't even notice the bounce in his own step.

✳✳✳

From: DRhii@vertullisonline.com

To: HRHMRhii@Federal.emp; YBrahma@PresimionAcademy.edu

Dear Mother & Yao:

I hope this letter finds you well. I want you to know that I am fine, but I miss you both and long for the day when I can see you again. I have been very busy with many activities I am not at liberty to discuss at this time. But I assure you, all will be revealed in time, and I am working hard to make you proud of me.

In the meantime, it was brought to my attention that many worker prisoners are being kept in a secret government prison somewhere on Legallis. I have reason to believe my biological father, Sol, is among those prisoners. There is also a man called Telamon, who would be there. I know the prison is top-secret, but perhaps you can make inquiries through channels for me. I would like to know its location and attempt to confirm the presence of these two men there.

Again, I cannot tell you what I plan to do with the information you provide, but hope that my past actions and behavior would serve to reassure you I will continue acting with honor in all I do.

Please know you are in my thoughts and prayers.

> With love and fondness,
>
> Davi

Davi clicked send and hoped the e-post would arrive undetected. His mother would be very worried about him. It had been too long since they'd had contact and she'd be relieved to get any message. He promised himself when things got better, he'd set aside extra time to spend with her. He treasured her love and devotion to him. It was something he never wanted to lose.

He wondered how Yao would receive his message. Yao knew of his heritage, and perhaps also knew by now about the warrant and his involvement with the workers. He hoped their deep friendship would supersede Yao's loyalty as an Alliance officer. Yao had always been a free thinker, more sympathetic to his own sensibilities than the strict order of the law. Either way, the e-post had been sent through public servers with special encoding. It could not be traced to his location at the WFR base. Even if it did get intercepted or their sympathies for him had been tempered, he still bore little risk of discovery.

He'd asked around about the prison after his conversation with Tela.

Many had heard the rumors of its existence, but few knew any facts. He'd concluded the only way for him to find out if his father lived would be to seek help through more official channels. He felt confident that Yao and Miri would be discreet and careful. If they decided not to help him, his inquiring of them would not raise great alarm.

He sat there for a few moments longer, before checking his inbox. *Of course, they couldn't respond this fast.* He laughed to himself. *Give them time on this, Davi. It won't be easy to uncover information.*

One of his greatest longings, ever since he'd discovered his true identity, had been to know his father. He'd never had a father and always dreamed about it. From what everyone told him about Sol, he was a great man. Davi longed to know him, and he knew Lura longed to see him again, too. At the very least, he wanted to know what had happened to him.

He said a silent prayer asking for God's blessing on both his father and his quest. When had he stopped praying to gods and started praying to the workers' God alone? He couldn't remember exactly. He'd changed so much in such a short time. He'd never have imagined it when he left Legallis for Vertullis. He headed back to his classroom for another session with the simulators.

✷✷✷

Lord Tarkanius, Lord Kray and Lord Simeon convened in the back room of a lounge near the Council's offices. Tarkanius had arranged this meeting after the revelations at the Council meeting earlier in the day.

"As you both know, disturbing facts were presented to us at the Council meeting," Tarkanius. "I thought it wise, given recent discussions, for us to have the chance to express how we feel about Miri's request for our help in light of these new revelations."

Both Simeon and Kray looked at him with uncertainty. They, like

Tarkanius, were wrestling with what to do. Everyone on the Council knew Xalivar had never been a credible witness. He would lie about his own mother if it served his political ambitions. But at the same time, having read Bordox's report after the meeting, they all knew the facts were not in question. Despite their uncertainty about Miri's motives, she'd played a major part in the deception, and it didn't bode well for the Alliance's Royal Family to be infiltrated by a worker.

"I'm sure Miri had good reasons for her decisions," Kray said, remaining loyal to Miri as expected. Tarkanius knew she above all had never liked or trusted Xalivar.

"I'm sure the reasons seemed valid to her at the time," Simeon said. "But that doesn't mean her decisions were made with the Alliance's best interests in mind. Given the facts, it would appear not."

"Being born a worker does not make him a spy," Kray said. "He may have just discovered his own heritage for all we know."

"It is possible," Tarkanius said. "His education and opportunities all came as a gift of the Alliance. I'm sure he has not forgotten. Davi is known as a man of good character, honesty and integrity. But he's also been questioning the actions of the Alliance toward workers, which, combined with his newly discovered heritage, makes him far more sympathetic to them than he might have been in the past." Tarkanius wished the circumstances were different. He'd always liked the Prince, but he had to protect the Alliance.

"Maybe he's right to question the Alliance's actions?" Kray said. "Given the news reports of late, there's much even the Council did not know and cannot approve of."

"The recent revelations are disturbing. Even the public is beginning to voice their objections," Simeon said. "But we, the Council, approved some of those actions; therefore, we will be held accountable for them as much as Xalivar and his troops."

"We must protect the Council from further negative associations and minimize the impact," Tarkanius said.

"At the cost of betraying a loyal friend?" Kray said, outraged.

"At the cost of putting aside our personal loyalties and emotions and acting with the objectivity and integrity demanded of us when we took our oaths of service," Tarkanius said. He had no intention of ignoring what he knew about Xalivar, but Miri's role could not be downplayed either. Perhaps the Royals were turning against each other. He didn't want the Council to be destroyed in the process.

"Indeed. If we maintain our integrity above all, the Council can survive the scandal and remain free to serve the best interests of the Alliance," Simeon said.

"Go to Miri and let her know that, for now, her request cannot be honored," Tarkanius said to Kray. Kray scowled. "We will make a full review and investigation of these matters and make our decision at a later time."

"If she needs anything of us, she is free to ask, and we will do what we can within the limits of our authority and the law," Simeon said. Tarkanius nodded in agreement.

"I'd trust Miri any day over Xalivar," Kray said.

"Trust is not enough this time," Simeon said.

Kray sighed, then stood and disappeared through the door.

"Do you think Lord Kray'll be okay?" Simeon asked.

"She is as torn as we are," Tarkanius said. "She's known Miri all her life. But Kray will do the right thing." Simeon nodded. Tarkanius hoped he was right.

✳✳✳

Davi stepped out of the classroom to find Joram and Uzah waiting for him with two armed security men.

"We need you to come with us," Uzah said. It was not a request.

"What's going on?" Davi asked as the security men grabbed his arms and dragged him down the corridor behind the two leaders. Neither said another word until they'd reached the command center conference room and the door had been sealed behind them.

"What's this about?" Davi demanded as Aron and Matheu joined the others in looking at him with somber stares.

"You sent an encoded transmission through Borali government channels," Matheu said, his glare ominous.

"I sent a request to my mother Miri and a friend for help locating a secret prison on Legaliss," Davi replied. "I think my father might be held there." He scanned their faces, seeing no change. "I can't very well have the High Lord Councilor intercepting that."

Aron's eyes showed palpable relief. "I knew there'd be a logical explanation." He smiled reassuringly at Davi.

"If he's telling the truth," Matheu growled.

Davi moved toward a nearby terminal. "I can show you the message."

Uzah blocked his path. "My men are decoding it now."

Davi frowned. He'd grown tired of being treated like a criminal. "If my word's not good enough, I'll gladly resign."

"If your word's not good, you won't have to," Matheu threatened.

Aron stepped forward, furious. "Enough! You have no proof to justify these accusations!"

"I warned you he couldn't be trusted," Matheu said, unfazed.

"And I assured you, he can," Aron replied, not backing down.

Using the distraction, Davi slipped past Uzah and sat at the terminal, quickly pulling up his e-account and locating the message. "Here!"

He stood and backed away from the terminal as the others hurried over to read the message on the screen. Matheu sat at the terminal and began examining the meta data. Then he closed the email and examined Davi's outbox further.

"It's just as he said," Aron said.

"So it would seem," Uzah agreed.

"Messages can be altered," Matheu insisted. "We'll wait for your men."

Aron whirled around and walked to the door, punching in a code on the lock panel. "You're free to go."

Davi examined the others' faces again. Joram and Uzah had softened but Matheu's expression remained as somber as before. Davi nodded to Aron and hurried out the door.

✵✵✵

Miri left the Library walking on air. While doing some historical research to back up her case against Xalivar, she'd stopped to check her e-posts and found a message from Davi.

At last! She couldn't believe it! She'd been so worried about him. He was okay and it took him this long to let her know? Her excitement turned to anger. He would hear about this!

She read the e-post again—something about his birth father and a prison. She knew nothing about prisons. She didn't know how to find out either. With Xalivar keeping a close watch on her, she'd started spending more and more time away from the Palace. He'd copied Yao on the message. She thought Yao might have better connections than she did at the moment.

She arrived at the café in the starport five minutes late, making her way to the back room where Kray sat waiting for her.

"Sorry I'm late. Where are the others?" She slid onto the chair opposite Kray. Kray's face gave the answer. "They're not coming?"

Kray hesitated a moment, searching for words. "There's been a complication."

"A complication?" Had they changed their minds?

"Xalivar told the Council today about Davi's heritage," Kray explained as the breath froze in Miri's throat. "An illegal adoption from workers, without his knowledge..."

"My gods! He didn't!"

Kray nodded. "He did."

Xalivar had betrayed her and Davi! "You're looking at me as if I betrayed the Alliance, Kray."

"The Council was quite shocked by his allegations," Kray said.

Did her oldest friend really believe Xalivar's lies? "You know he'd sell out our mother to get ahead," Miri said. Why would Xalivar turn on her? She'd been so careful.

Kray's face looked sad. "I know, but the Council took his remarks to heart. I'm afraid there won't be much support for you at this time."

"None of them? What about the evidence I provided of wrongdoing? The public sentiment?"

"There has been public outcry, but not enough to force the Council's hand. The Council ordered some of the actions which resulted in the tragedies you've leaked to the press. We are all at risk too, Miri," Kray said.

Miri couldn't believe it! She'd been sure they would help her. Xalivar must have discovered her plot. Why else would he betray her?

She stared out the window. "I was barren, with no husband. I wanted a son to call my own. He's a good boy; honorable, strong character—just the way I raised him."

"You don't have to explain to me, Miri, but you know how some feel about the workers...." Kray said, her voice trailing off.

"He's a worker by blood. He's Royal by upbringing. He doesn't know their life, their ways. He's more one of us than one of them," Miri said, turning back to face Kray.

"That's not how the public will see it," Kray said.

"The public is ignorant. We are the Lords, the leaders. We have to tell them what's right to think and do," Miri said, tensing with urgency.

"We cannot support you at this time. I'm sorry," Kray said. Miri read in her eyes that it pained her to say it.

Miri slid down in the chair, dismayed. Kray seemed to be searching for something to say, but remained quiet. After a couple of minutes, she slipped away, leaving Miri alone with her thoughts.

He's my son! Everything I did was for him! How could they not understand? They all had children, too. Xalivar had conned the Council yet again, and this time his con had painted her as the enemy. She pounded her fist on the table, stood, and marched out the door.

Slipping out into the main mall, she wove her way through the chattering crowds. Someone was following her. She stopped and turned around. Two LSP Soldiers walked toward her.

She turned and walked away from them as three more LSP Soldiers appeared ahead, looking straight at her. *My gods! I can't believe he's gone this far!*

She dodged down a corridor, but they moved fast to intercept her.

"I am a member of the Royal Family," she said.

"I'm afraid we've been ordered to place you under arrest," the LSP Sergeant said.

"This is ridiculous. My brother is the High Lord Councilor! I am Princess Miri Rhii."

"The order came from the High Lord Councilor," the Sergeant said as his men grabbed her arms.

He turned and led the way as they hurried her across the mall toward a nearby exit. Miri tried to hide her face from the stares. Could Xalivar have uncovered everything or did he simply suspect? What would he do with her?

The soldiers led her to a transport outside and locked her in the prisoner cell at the rear. Whatever her brother knew, she'd soon find out.

CHAPTER TEN

Miri paced back and forth in the cell, until the door slid open and Xalivar appeared. She shot him dead with a furious look as he stepped inside and the door closed behind him.

"You have no right to lock me up in a cell like this!"

"I have no right? You have been conspiring behind my back for weeks, and you want to talk about rights?" Xalivar smiled, amused.

He knows. Her heart sank. "I am a member of the Royal Family, Xalivar. Not some mere peasant!" Miri almost spat the words out.

"I am the High Lord Councilor," Xalivar scolded. "My authority extends over you as much as the rest. Leaking top-secret information to the media, conspiring behind my back to turn the Council against me, and receiving communication from a fugitive this afternoon!"

Miri's tried to hide her surprise. He always seemed to know everything. "He's my son, Xalivar."

"He's wanted by the Alliance for murder, among other charges," Xalivar said. "You told me he had not communicated with you."

"This was the first time," Miri said.

"Which I had to learn about through other channels," Xalivar chided.

His hands hung relaxed at his sides. Why was he so calm? What did he know that she didn't? "I had not seen you yet."

"Do you wish to make a confession?" Xalivar's brown eyes met hers.

Miri looked away. "You're crazy. What would father think if he was here to see me locked up like this?"

"Father is dead, and he left me in charge," Xalivar said. "Your actions are a betrayal, not just of me, but of the Alliance itself. Whatever imbalance is occurring in that head of yours, I cannot allow it to continue."

"You are a power-hungry, deceitful, evil—"

"Save your whining for your women's brunch, Miri!" Xalivar shook his head. "I have protected this Alliance for almost thirty years; done whatever it takes."

Just once she wished she could see him perspire. "I question you as a citizen of the Borali Alliance. It's all the authority I need," Miri said. Xalivar's calmness had her worried. He never handled betrayal this well. What was going on in his demented mind?

"Your loyalty to your son has clouded your judgment. Your actions have disparaged our entire family line. I cannot allow it to continue," Xalivar turned back toward the door. It slid open and he stepped through.

Miri could see Manaen's red eyes outside. "What are you going to do with me, Xalivar?"

"Send you somewhere safe," Xalivar said as the door slid shut.

Miri pounded a fist against the door as tears flowed down her face. What could she do now? She had to find a way to get a message to Davi. He would help her. He had to help her. And she had to warn him.

***

Davi and Tela moved the training course to the west side of the base, hoping to avoid further encounters with the LSP. They also installed an electronic sensor system around it to notify them of any unknown vehicles entering the area.

The trainees had made great progress on the course in the past week. Each had now completed several runs with the targeting system on. Most had landed at least one successful hit on one of the pylons. A few could hit the majority of the targets every time. Davi was impressed with both their determination and their dedication to their training. He'd heard no complaints about pushing them too hard or demanding extra hours.

Even Nila, Dru and Brie were getting the hang of things. Of course, he still had doubts they would be able to maneuver a fighter, but they'd at least know enough to take off and follow someone else home. He assigned them to the team against the base on Vertullis and let the stronger trainees take on the Legallis base and fly the longer distances.

They'd run the course three times with increasing success, when Virun and Jorek's group pulled up beside Davi and Tela.

"We're going to try the Skitters on the trails now," Jorek said. His friends mumbled their agreement.

Davi and Tela exchanged a look. Neither one knew how to stop them, yet Davi still wanted to project a sense of command. "As long as you stick to the square mile around the course," Davi insisted. They nodded and headed off.

Some of the less skilled trainees watched them go. "We want to go, too," Dru said.

"You guys need more work on the course," Davi said.

"Can't you show us stuff on the regular trails which would help us with the course?" Dru asked.

"Yeah, doing the same thing over and over is boring," Brie said. Nila and Dru groaned in agreement.

Davi looked at Tela, who shrugged. "Okay, look, we can try it for a half an hour or so, but you guys need to master the targeting on the course."

Brie, Dru and Nila exchanged high fives.

"We're going as fast as we can," Nila said.

Dru sped off toward the trails with Nila and Brie close behind. Davi and Tela raced to catch up with them.

❊❊❊

Although he would have preferred to keep the search to his own men, for fear word of his failure on the mission might spread, Bordox had called in more troops after realizing that, the sooner he succeeded the better. In the long run, success always outweighed failure.

As soon as the code came over the comm-channel, Corsi called for a rendezvous of their forces at the scout's location, and then notified Bordox, and they headed for the coordinates together.

Bordox's heart pounded faster and faster as they sped past row after row of cedars drawing closer to the rendezvous. After this, there would be no doubt who was superior. Rhii's career would be over! He'd be in prison. Bordox would have the favor of the High Lord Councilor and be awarded medals, perhaps even a promotion. Thinking about it excited him. He accelerated his Skitter, ignoring the wind beating against his face, as Corsi struggled to remain alongside.

❊❊❊

Davi and Tela followed Dru, Brie and Nila, as they weaved along a trail through the trees. The wind whistled past Davi, rustling his hair. The air was fresh and clean. He enjoyed the sensation, the blur of the trees as they passed, and their spicy smell.

Dru and Nila delighted in swapping places on either side of Brie—one zipping in front of her, the other behind. Sometimes, they cut it a little close, startling Brie, who cried out.

"Hey! Watch it!" She would shoot them scolding looks as they slid back alongside her, and then all three would break into giggles.

Ah, to be young, Davi thought. He exchanged a look with Tela, who chuckled and shook her head.

"Try not to damage the Skitters, okay?" Davi called after them. This just led to more laughter as Nila and Dru swapped places yet again.

"I don't think they're listening," Tela said, her blue eyes glistening with amusement.

"You got that idea, did you?" Davi said as she chuckled. "So much for military discipline!"

Tela laughed. "We have kept things pretty loose. We'd better start tightening things up."

The comms on the Skitters beeped as a red light on the comm panel began flashing. They exchanged a look.

"The warning beacons," Davi said.

Tela nodded. "Better call in and see what they've got."

The brush behind them rustled and they heard a noise, turning back to see four LSP soldiers slip behind them on armed Skitters. Davi and Tela exchanged looks of alarm, accelerating toward the trainees as the LSP men fired their lasers and the cedars exploded around them.

"So much for our early warning system," Tela groaned as they sped up to catch their trainees.

Hearing the explosions, Brie, Dru and Nila turned around to look as Tela and Davi pulled alongside.

"Don't slow down! Go as fast as you can. Follow me!" Tela warned them. She pulled in front and they sped up to follow her.

Davi hung back to protect the rear, dodging fire from the LSP soldiers. All around, he heard laser blasts and explosions as LSP soldiers engaged the other trainees. The smell of burning wood and leaves thickened the air as Davi flicked on his comm-channel.

"Attention trainees: do not go back to base. Lose them, and then hide until we can rendezvous."

His private channel beeped and he switched over, steering sharply to dodge another laser blast.

Tela's voice came over the headphones. "Right about now, I'm wishing we had armed Skitters, too."

Davi reached down to the side pocket and pulled out his blaster. "I'm going to try and lay down some counter fire, but my blaster won't do much against their Skitter guns."

"Can you keep them occupied while I go help the others?" Tela asked, drawing her own blaster from the side pocket of her Skitter.

Without answering, Davi turned and started firing back toward the LSP soldiers, who zigzagged to avoid his blasts. Davi slammed on the brakes, and the LSP soldiers zipped right past him, their faces registering surprise. He slipped back in behind them and began firing at their flanks.

Tela fired two blasts from her blaster, then she and the trainees sped away, as the soldiers dodged more bolts from Davi's blaster.

Davi managed to land a couple of hits on one of the Skitters, sending sparks flying, but causing more fear in the rider than damage to the machine. As the rider and his companions leaned back to inspect his Skitter, Davi ducked off onto a side trail.

In a few moments, the LSP soldiers slid back onto his tail again. Davi accelerated to full speed, zigzagging in and out between trees, jumping over rocks, diving under overhangs—keeping his target profile as small as possible. The wind buffeted him every time he emerged from the trees, forcing him to work harder to stay on the Skitter. Then he rounded a bend to find more LSP soldiers who joined the chase.

Great! Are they all after me? He hoped Tela was helping the other trainees. He was too busy to help them himself.

Around another bend, Bordox and his aide joined the chase. *Bordox. No wonder they're all after me.* Davi smiled, waving, as he dodged their fire. Outgunned, he searched his mind for a new tactic.

Bordox sped to the front of the LSP soldiers, close on Davi's tail. Davi, looked back over his shoulder as Bordox growled: "In the name of the High Lord Councilor, I order you to stop! You're under arrest!"

Davi braked and Bordox's aide wound up in front of him. Bordox remained alongside, as Davi fired several shots with his blaster at the aide, leaning close enough to Bordox to yell: "Give my uncle my regards!"

He ducked off onto another side trail as Bordox shot on past, cursing.

The other LSP soldiers followed Davi as he followed the turns of the side trail, staying just out of range of their lasers. He shifted in his seat, trying to stay comfortable but his sweaty body and uniform made that difficult.

As he shot into a clearing, he discovered Tela, Jorek, Virun, and four others waiting for them, blasters held at the ready. Davi spun his Skitter into a one hundred and eighty degree spin and slid in alongside them, aiming his blaster as the first of the LSP soldiers came into view.

Davi's group opened fire and chaos erupted. Two LSP Skitters collided as the soldiers tried to dodge the blaster fire. Another slammed into them from behind, while yet a fourth ducked to one side and crashed into a large cedar.

Davi and Tela motioned, accelerating on their Skitters onto another trail with their trainees close behind. All continued firing blasts back at the LSP men behind them.

Tela took three trainees with her and split off onto another trail as

Davi, Jorek, Virun and two others continued on the present course.

"They're after you?" Jorek yelled, sounding surprised.

Davi nodded. "I told you before; I'm on your side." A laser blast exploded near them and Davi keyed the comm-channel button. "Try and get around behind them."

Tela's voice came over the radio. "Hang on, Davi, we've got a plan."

A plan? Who'd had time to make a plan? Most of the LSP soldiers stayed behind Davi and his group.

"Make it hard for them to lock their weapons on us," Davi said, as his group zigzagged in and out of the cedars in varied patterns, never leaving more than one of them on the trail at a time. Their skills impressed him. They had made a lot of progress.

Jorek and Virun slid to a stop amidst the trees, watching several LSP soldiers zoom past, then accelerated after them, firing their lasers.

Davi heard a rebel yell over the comm-channel. "You two be careful! They outnumber us!" Davi warned.

Jorek's voice came back at him. "Best training exercise ever!"

"Don't get cocky. This is not a game."

"No problem, Captain. We can handle it," Virun said.

Davi wondered if he'd heard right. None of them had ever called him Captain before.

Bordox and his aide pulled back into the lead behind Davi, firing blasts which exploded on either side of him. Too close for comfort!

Tela and her group shot out of the forest, firing at the LSP. Two more Skitters crashed and two others were damaged. The LSP soldiers slowed down and dissolved into chaos as they attempting to avoid fire from the lasers.

Another group of trainees shot out from a group of trees and surrounded them, firing.

"When did you have time to get all this organized?" Davi said into the comm-channel, as he glanced back at Tela.

"Quick thinking is a military necessity," Tela said. "They were all issued blasters with their uniforms, so..."

Davi smiled. "You've never been more beautiful."

He braked, sliding in between Bordox and his aide. As they passed him on either side, he swung a foot out and kicked at Bordox's Skitter. Bordox struggled to regain control but flew off to one side, as Davi slipped in behind the aide and shot at his Skitter with the blaster.

Bordox pulled alongside him again, his face a fierce grimace. "You can't escape this time, Rhii. We outnumber you," he called out with his usual menacing grin.

"You're losing men fast," Davi said as Bordox reached over grabbing for his controls. Their Skitters banged into each other as Davi struggled to push him away. His sweat soaked gloves barely maintained their hold on the handlebars of the Skitter.

"I always knew you were a traitor," Bordox said.

"I always knew you were a pompous blowhard," Davi said, freeing his leg and kicking hard. Bordox frowned as he spun off to one side.

Tela zipped up, firing at Bordox as his aide and another LSP soldier slipped in behind Davi.

Bordox corrected his course and charged back toward Davi, dodging Tela's blasts.

Davi slowed, sliding upward, as Bordox's aide and the other soldier flew right underneath him. Distracted, both turned, crashing into each other as Davi dropped down to fire on them from behind.

Bordox headed straight for Davi, who rolled his Skitter, dove off and landed on his feet in the dirt. He aimed his blaster and fired at Bordox, forcing him to turn suddenly and crash his Skitter into Davi's. The impact sent Bordox flying off into the cedars. Both Skitters sputtered and smoked, amid a field of debris.

Tela turned her Skitter back and slowed down beside Davi, who hopped on behind her as the other trainees raced up beside them.

"We've got them on the run," Virun said.

"Want us to go back and finish this?" Jorek said, sounding a bit too eager.

"No, get the others and get back to the hangar," Davi said.

"At least they don't know where the base is," Tela said.

"They know enough to keep looking for us here," Davi said. "It'll be a matter of time. We have to warn everyone. The Forest won't be our refuge much longer."

Tela nodded as the group brought their Skitters to full speed and sped away, disappearing into the trees.

Davi looked back; no LSP soldiers were following them. He couldn't believe they'd gotten away. Maybe his trainees deserved more confidence than he'd had in them.

Virun and Jorek passed him, smiling and laughing and enjoying it more than they should. He didn't have time to worry about it now. He had to get back to the leaders at the base and warn them.

✳✳✳

Bordox gave up trying to dust off the dirt clinging to his sweaty uniform and looked around for his Skitter. It was a disaster, destroyed along with Rhii's. His men were scattered everywhere.

Corsi ran toward him. "Are you okay, sir?"

"Don't stop. Catch them!" Bordox's voice was full of frustration.

"It would be a little difficult at the moment," Corsi said, motioning to several crashed Skitters.

"Get the men regrouped now and go after them!" Bordox yelled. *A bunch of untrained workers against LSP troops?* Bordox couldn't believe it! How could they have embarrassed him again! Furious, he drew his blaster and fired at a nearby cedar.

"Yes, sir," Corsi nodded, but his face questioned whether it would matter.

✱✱✱

Davi entered the command center at a run. It was busier than he'd ever seen it with technicians and workers occupying every chair, fiddling with dials, adjusting wires and screens, and talking on communicators. Final preparations were underway for what lay ahead.

He found General Matheu and the other leaders in the conference room. "Our training today was interrupted by LSP troops searching the forest," Davi blurted out as he entered almost out of breath.

"So we heard," Uzah said.

"What were they looking for?" Aron asked.

"Me," Davi said. They all looked at him with surprise.

"It's true," Tela confirmed, arriving out of breath as he answered and slipping into the room.

"Why would they be looking for you?" General Matheu asked.

"I'm wanted for questioning in the murder of a guard who was beating my cousin Nila. His death was accidental, but the Council brought charges."

"Against a member of the Royal Family?" Joram said with surprise.

"One who questioned worker policies, yes," Davi said. "And I suppose I'm also wanted for betraying the Alliance." He wondered if the minds of those who'd doubted him would change now.

"It's clear your chance encounter with them during previous training was not forgotten. They must have been searching for weeks now," Aron said.

"Which means we have been discovered. We must put our plan into action right away," General Matheu said, standing and walking over to examine some charts hanging on the wall.

"You're sure you didn't lead them back to the base?" Joram asked, as he moved over to join Matheu at the charts.

Davi whirled and glared at him. "What will it take for you to trust me?"

"We just need to know if they've discovered our location," Joram responded, blanching at Davi's harsh tone.

"I've been with you for months now, training pilots, and helping you. What's it gonna take to prove myself?"

"The decoders already confirmed your story about the e-post," Aron said, putting a hand on Davi's arm.

"You have our trust now," Uzah added with a nod.

Davi glanced around at the leaders. Even General Matheu's face looked supportive. Tela smiled reassuringly.

"I didn't get a chance to tell you yet," Aron said. "I'm sorry."

"We're sorry, too," Joram added.

Davi sighed, releasing the anger, then remembered he hadn't answered Joram's question. "It won't matter if they followed me or not. The man leading them is a rival of mine from the Academy. He won't stop until he captures or kills me."

"We can't wait until we're discovered," Aron said.

"We must prepare final plans and brief our teams," Uzah said as they all nodded in agreement. Feeling guilty for being the cause of this, Davi looked away. Rushing into battle could cause extra loss of lives. He wished they had another way.

Aron noticed Davi's sullen face and put a hand on his shoulder. "It's not your fault, Davi. It was a matter of time."

Davi still felt responsible.

"Yes, our time for execution was drawing near regardless. Now we will act while we can still hope for some element of surprise," General Matheu said.

The others all looked at Davi with anxious smiles. "My trainees are ready," Davi said. "They now have actual experience in combat."

Aron laughed, patting him on the back. The others laughed too, encouraged by the thought.

"Let's commit our plans to the Lord and He will guide us," Uzah said. The others mumbled agreement bowing their heads.

✳✳✳

The Leaders met for several hours, after which Davi joined Tela at Lura's quarters for dinner. His mother had prepared beef with Gixi sauce, accompanied by fried Gixi and fresh Jax salad. The fruits added just the right sweetness to go with the beef and red wine.

As they finished the meal, Lura raised a glass in toast. "A salute to the brave men and women who will accompany you both into this battle."

Davi and Tela raised their glasses, clinking them against hers. "And to all those who support us here at home," Tela said.

"Here! Here!" Davi said, smiling, as they sipped their wine. It brought warmth to his whole body as it flowed down his throat. He wondered how long it would be until he could relax like this again.

"May God protect you and give you wisdom," Lura said.

"May God protect us all," Davi said, placing his hand over hers on the table.

She smiled and squeezed his hand. "I'm very proud of you," Lura said.

"I'm proud to be your son," Davi said.

Lura's eyes grew moist, tears forming at their corners. "I wish your father were here, he would be so proud. He fought with Aron and Joram in the revolution twenty-five years ago."

The Vertullians always referred to the Delta V incident as The Revolution. "One day we'll find him," Davi said, knowing he would give it his best.

"It's more than I could hope for," Lura said.

For a moment, he considered sharing with her what Tela had told him, but then thought better of it. False hope would end up making things worse in the long run. "I'm sure he's here in spirit," Davi said, squeezing Lura's hand again. She smiled and nodded approvingly.

"I wish my father could be here as well," Tela said. "And my mother."

"What happened to them?" Davi had wondered.

"Dad disappeared a while ago. Another one of those unanswered mysteries that we're just supposed to accept. Then Mom died in an accident two years ago." Tela refuse to make eye contact.

"So you're alone?"

Lura reached over with her other hand and placed it on top of Tela's, squeezing. "We're your family now."

Tela smiled. "I feel blessed!"

"We're all very blessed," Lura said, nodding.

They bowed their heads and prayed for the battle ahead, committing their actions and plans to God and asking for wisdom, guidance, and safety through whatever came.

Davi had difficulty accepting that the actions he and others made might lead to the deaths of friends. But he knew the higher cause always required sacrifice, and, in the end, it would be worth the losses for his people to be free again. He thought about Tela, wondering if their relationship would have a chance to flourish or if this war would mark the end of it. He brushed the thoughts away. He couldn't afford to be distracted at a time like this. He had to appreciate the time they had while hoping in the future God would provide for them, whatever it was. As their Scriptures said in the book of the prophet Jeremiah, God's plan was perfect: a future full of hope.

*** *

Davi kissed Tela goodbye moments before launch. As flight crews performed final pre-flight preparations on their shuttles, he went over and over the plan of attack.

Uzah had obtained schedules of regular fighter patrols on both Vertullis and Legallis. The fighters were kept on the ground for several hours a week for routine maintenance. The attacks were timed to coincide with one of those periods. The ground assaults on the Vertullis starport, energy shield control center and government center would be timed to coincide with the attacks at the starports.

Davi watched the first shuttle launch, carrying Tela and her team toward the starport on Legallis. He had assigned her the majority of his most experienced pilots—Virun, Jorek, and seventeen others—since her mission would require the most flight skill and involved the most possible risk of counterattack. Davi assigned Nila, Dru, Brie and sixteen others to his team. The shuttles were being flown by experienced men who had once worked for Borali citizens as private pilots. Additional shuttles would carry Uzah and his troops to their attack points.

Tela's team had to fly into the Legallis starport under the cover of an emergency landing due to engine failure. Because there would be no WFR ground assaults like those on Vertullis, Alliance ground forces posed a serious threat. The shuttle bay and fighter bay were connected by short tunnels, so that if the team moved quickly, they could get in and out without engaging troops. He and Tela had been over the layout several times with her team.

The potential for success of the WFR's ground attacks on Vertullis had been increased by recent developments. Bordox's attempt to capture him had led to reassignment of great numbers of troops to search the forest. As a result, while the worker's base might be detected during the launch of the attacks, ground forces at the starport, energy shield control center and government center would be down to skeleton crews during the time of the attacks. Davi couldn't believe their good fortune! Aron and Tela had reminded him their God was behind them and had a hand in temporal events. Davi found it easier to have confidence in a God who played such a role in human affairs.

When his shuttle landed, Davi was already on his feet beside the door. "Go!" he said as his pilots filed out, blasters held at the ready.

As he stepped on the landing platform, he could already hear ground forces engaged in other areas of the base. By launching their attacks first, the ground forces hoped to draw troops away from the launch bays around the fighters. From what Davi could see, everything was proceeding according to plan.

Mechanics met them on the ground and pointed them to the twenty fighters which they'd prepped and readied for launch. On both Vertullis and Legallis, the mechanics had disassembled key parts to make counterattacks impossible. Only the exact number of VS28s the WFR would steal remained flight-worthy.

Special shifts had been selected at each starport, and those mechanics would return with the strike teams on the shuttles to avoid execution. Since the fighters were already scheduled for maintenance, it would take the Alliance time to call in another shift, let alone determine why their fighters weren't functional. By the time they knew, Vertullis would safely be under WFR control and protected by the energy shield and stolen fighters.

Davi's pilots climbed aboard and started preflight checks. The moment the fighters launched, the mechanics would board the shuttle and follow them out. Davi would launch last.

Venetian System's Model 28 fighters were sleek and black with snub noses and three wings—two longer wings on each side, and a third shorter wing standing vertically above the fighter's four engines. Each bore their squadron insignia, and a few bore a name painted on at the pilot's indulgence. There were laser cannons on each wing as well as in the nose. The cockpit lay beneath a gray, transparent blast shield through which the pilot could monitor the area outside the cockpit.

As the first fighters prepared to launch, Davi heard explosions near the shuttle. Interrupting his preflight check, Davi turned to see a few armed troops moving into the bay.

"Get your men to the shuttle!" he shouted to the head mechanic.

Alliance ground troops wore the same gray uniforms as the officers, but were equipped with black metal helmets instead of hats. They had matching black shields and armored vests, all three designed to withstand heavy blasts from lasers. Their black boots reached almost to their knees. Well-trained and disciplined, they were intimidating to watch, let alone face in battle. They began setting up laser cannons and firing at Davi and the mechanics as soon as they entered the bay.

As fighters launched, Davi climbed down onto the landing pad and returned fire with his blaster. An entire squad of enemy troops wound their way toward the shuttle. The lead mechanic began returning fire with a blaster as well. Davi didn't stop to ask where he'd obtained it. Their co-conspirators had prepared for the worst.

As the fighters continued to take off, Davi and the mechanic laid down cover fire. The troops ducked behind machines and starcraft to avoid their laser blasts, firing back as they continued inching closer.

Several blasts hit fighters as they took off, but the damage was minimal.

To Davi's right, a fighter lifted straight into the air and around toward the oncoming soldiers. Davi heard the whirl of laser cannons revving up to full power and then spotted Dru at the controls.

"Dru, what are you doing?" He said over the comm-channel.

Dru opened fire with the VS28's laser cannons at the Alliance troops. Machines and starcraft exploded as debris flew around the bay. Enemy soldiers dove to the ground. Some were buried under falling debris. One took a hit in the arm.

Davi chuckled at the bravery and ingenuity of Dru's efforts as he turned and climbed back into his fighter. The necklace jangling against his chest reminded him what they were fighting for.

"Get the shuttle out of here," he said into his comm-channel as he lifted his own fighter and turned it to add his own lasers to Dru's barrage.

The shuttle's engines revved up as the lead mechanic dove on board. Moments after the door slid shut, the shuttle launched.

"Go, Dru, go!" Davi called into his comm-channel as he fired another round from his laser cannons.

Dru turned his fighter and flew into a launch chute. Davi followed moments later.

Most of other fighters had already headed back toward base as Davi and Dru launched with the shuttle, but four fighters closed in around them. Davi noted with surprise that two of them were flown by Brie and Nila.

"I thought I ordered you two back to base," Davi said over the comm-channel.

"Did you think we could go without knowing you and Dru were safe?" Nila's voice rang in his ear.

"Yeah. What took you guys so long?" Brie teased. The women's laughter filled the comm channel as the fighters slid into formation around the shuttle.

"Well done, team. Let's go home," Davi said, wondering how things were going for Tela.

As they flew over the city, Davi glimpsed gunfire near the starport and government center. WFR forces had begun engaging the skeleton Alliance crews left to defend them. From what Davi could see, their attack had been a success. His prayers had been answered. He hoped Tela and Uzah were being as blessed as he had been.

★★★

Moments after laser fire exploded outside the building, Zylo received an urgent SOS from the captain in charge of the defense detail at the starport. Most of the regular defense detail had been reassigned to search the forest, in the wake of Bordox's failed capture of Davi. Bordox himself had been sent back to Legallis to answer to Xalivar, while Corsi and Zylo took over leadership of the search. The captain's voice sounded terse. Zylo thought he heard laser fire behind him as well.

"The starport is under attack. I demand the return of my men," the captain said.

"Your men are on the other side of the planet," Zylo said.

"We are under attack by unknown numbers of enemy forces both inside and outside the starport!" The captain said.

"The entire government center is under fire. I have already called back troops, but they won't be here for an hour," Zylo said, not liking the captain's tone.

"An hour will be too late! I need help now!" The captain screamed.

"You'll have to do the best you can," Zylo said, breaking the connection before the captain could launch another protest. There wasn't anything Zylo could do about it anyway.

Out the window, he saw from the size of the WFR force that his own men would soon be overrun. Alliance soldiers ran around in chaos, dodging explosions as debris flew. *A worker army on Vertullis?* No one had ever imagined organized military attacks by worker armies. The explosions outside the building drew nearer and nearer. Zylo wondered what else could go wrong.

✳✳✳

Uzah led his forces in attacking the Shield Control Center—one hundred and thirty men against twenty-five Alliance soldiers and officers stationed there at the time of the attack. They fought an intense battle, before the few remaining defenders retreated behind locked doors and shielded walls.

Some of Uzah's men used the battle as cover for a sneak attack from the rear. The five guards stationed there were easily overcome, allowing WFR troops to enter the station. They exchanged fire with the defenders locked inside, but once WFR reinforcements arrived, the battle was over. To Uzah's delight, the workers now controlled the energy shield around Vertullis.

The battle for the government complex, including the offices, barracks, and starport, took longer. Although most of the Alliance troops had been out on other duties, there were still one hundred and fifty soldiers spread throughout the complex. The three hundred and fifty WFR men under his command wounded or captured large numbers of enemy soldiers, leaving only a few strongholds.

The last hold-outs surrendered after a two hours of fighting, when WFR reinforcements arrived. Uzah immediately contacted the base.

***

"Legallis approach control, I say again, identify yourself."

Tela listened as her pilot identified the shuttle for the third time. While emergency landings due to engine failure were not unheard of, the Alliance almost never allowed emergency landings by civilian craft in military areas, and the portmaster didn't seem inclined to allow this one.

"You've been cleared to land at the civilian dock on the eastside," the voice instructed for the third time.

Tela reached over the pilot's shoulder and keyed the comm-channel. "We've told you. We're losing power fast. We can barely control her as it is. We need to land now. We won't make it to the east side."

Tela heard the portmaster's sigh over the comm-channel. "Landing Bay Five-A. Do not leave your craft until given further instructions."

"Thank you!" Tela tried to disguise her relief with a cheerful tone, but they'd been delayed almost half an hour. The other attacks were already well underway.

The portmaster sent two officers to inspect the shuttle upon landing. The moment they stepped inside, Tela, Virun, and Jorek disarmed them and tied them up. However, the wait for their arrival and their capture slowed things down.

Several times during the ensuing battle, Tela wished Davi had led the assault instead of her, but because too many people knew his face on Legallis, the leadership had thought it unwise to send him there.

It took all of Tela's knowledge and training to lead her group well. First, the portmaster's men inquired why pilots were in fighters during the scheduled maintenance period, then military flight techs inquired about unscheduled launches. While Tela and the maintenance chief did their best to allay any concerns, military police came to investigate and several mechanics died in the ensuing laser battle. Five pilots also died and the shuttle suffered exterior damage from the lasers.

When the shuttle launched, it did so with half the remaining mechanics on board. The others stayed behind to provide cover fire for the launching starcraft.

Tela mourned the loss of the brave mechanics. She also pushed her team to fly back to Vertullis at top speed to warn them. It wouldn't take long for those on Legallis to figure out what had happened, even if they couldn't launch fighters to counterattack. Despite the successful capture of the fighters, the mission felt like a loss. She blamed herself and dreaded facing Davi and the other leaders with the news.

✳✳✳

When Manaen rushed into the throne room in mid-afternoon and announced the attack at the starport, the news caught Xalivar by complete surprise. Who would attack them? No one had attacked Legallis since the settlement of the planet.

As bits of information trickled in over the next two hours, Xalivar became more and more enraged. *Disabled fighters? Mutinying mechanics?* He knew right away Davi had to be involved.

He motioned to the vidscreen. "Get me the security videos from the launch bays!"

"Yes, my Lord!" Manaen typed on a terminal and the videos played.

Davi was nowhere to be seen. Trained pilots took off in the fighters. How could the workers have so many trained pilots? He ordered the few surviving mechanics interrogated as soon as possible. They would be pumped for everything they knew before being executed.

Still, Xalivar couldn't believe what he had seen. He ordered all off-duty mechanics to be called back to duty to get the fighters airworthy. Pilots would launch as soon as possible to chase down the fleeing intruders.

Later, Manaen delivered even worse news. "There were attacks on Vertullis as well, my Lord. Enemy forces captured fighters there too, leaving the rest disabled or damaged. They also captured the entire government complex, the starport, and the energy shield." Xalivar couldn't believe his ears. "Vertullis is no longer under Alliance control."

Xalivar screamed in frustration. *No! This can't be happening to me!* The fighters he'd sent after the retreating attackers had arrived after the stolen fighters had already disappeared behind the planet's energy shield. Xalivar pounded his fists into the wall.

Is there no one competent in my entire military? How could they be caught with their pants down? The Council will have me for this! I will never hear the end of it. My gods, the greatest army in the Universe defeated by a ragtag worker army?

It had to be the workers. That much seemed certain. Who else would dare attack the Lords at their capital like this? Xalivar ordered reinforcements sent from all over the system. They wouldn't get away with this. He would show them the power of the Alliance. They would not defeat him—the greatest High Lord Councilor in the history of his people.

He paced back and forth behind the throne, cursing Bordox's failure and his sister's betrayal. Had she fed intelligence information to Davi and his co-conspirators? He would have to question her again as soon as possible. Yes, all those involved would be brought to justice. They would feel the iron hand of the Alliance.

CHAPTER ELEVEN

Davi pushed the joystick forward and his VS28 fighter dove out of the cloud cover to rejoin the rest of his squadron. As he slid into the pole position, he glanced over at Tela in position off to his right. She smiled and waved.

"Imagine seeing you here," he said over the comm-channel with a smile.

He heard Tela laugh as the squadron formed up around them, doing so without the usual chatter. Davi knew they were all as tired as he was.

It had been an amazing three weeks. After their capture of fighters and takeover of the planetary shield, the WFR stayed busy skirmishing with Alliance forces. So far, the energy shield had prevented enemy reinforcements and aerial attacks, but Davi knew it would be a matter of time before the Alliance sent in star cruisers to break through the shield.

The success of the WFR's attack plan also yielded other benefits for Davi. Once the workers had control of their planet, those who had shown little interest in the Resistance signed up like wildfire. Experienced pilots from all over the system offered their services. Davi and Tela gave those who were local an immediate crash course on VS28 fighters, enabling squadrons to be in the air around the clock, thus allowing Davi and the others time to rest.

Already the constant tiredness of the past few weeks had begun to fade. Additional fighters had been requisitioned from the Vertullis starport and brought back to the base, but fighting persisted around the starport and the Alliance still had access to fighters there. Davi and Tela continued training new recruits, while additional units were trained and added to Uzah's troops as well.

At a leaders' meeting, Davi learned the WFR forces had gained enough ground to drive the remaining enemy troops into strongholds at the government center and starport. The Alliance had failed to recapture the energy shield control center but continued trying. Davi and the pilots reinforced the ground forces by air and destroyed enemy infrastructure and equipment.

His comm-channel beeped. "Squadron One, commander," he answered.

Uzah's yelling voice came through, struggling to be heard over at the explosions and laser blasts in the background. "Squadron One, we request immediate response. We have enemy forces pinned down on the east edge of the government complex. Please intercept vehicle traffic."

The Alliance had been making use of Shuttles and Floaters to launch attacks and move troops around. His pilots strafed enemy launch sites as well as ground craft.

Davi keyed the comm-channel transmit button. "Roger, Ground Leader, ETA six minutes." Davi ran down the pilots' various skill levels and successes, devising a strategy he hoped would work. It all depended on the actual positions and activities of the enemy once they arrived.

The fighters glided over the tops of the buildings at close range, staying low to confuse the radar and maintain good line of sight with the ground. Davi divided the squadron into two groups of six fighters, assigning Tela to head the second group. "You go after ground weaponry emplacements first. We'll try and take out any vehicle traffic."

"Roger," she said. They exchanged one last look before steering their craft apart as their assigned groups formed up around them. Then each group vectored off toward their target areas.

A few minutes later, the government center came into view. Two columns of large Floaters moved up parallel corridors, attempting to flank the WFR forces. Their dark blue coloring made them hard to spot through the smoke on the ground but the shiny Alliance emblems reflecting light on both sides gave them away.

"Dru and Virun, form behind me. We'll take the group to starboard. The rest of you form behind Jorek and take the group to port."

"Roger," the pilots responded in unison as they split into subsquads.

Davi smiled, remembering when Jorek and Virun had pulled him aside after the air raids on the enemy starports.

"We owe you an apology," Virun had said.

"We're sorry we gave you such a hard time," Jorek said. "It was just hard to believe we could trust you."

Since then, they'd become two of his strongest leaders.

"Go for their weapons capabilities first," Davi instructed.

"Ah come on, boss! Total destruction is much more satisfying," Jorek said over the comm-channel.

"You can destroy them after you're sure they can't fire back," Davi said, knowing that despite his enthusiasm, Jorek's focus never wavered.

"You got it," Jorek responded, not big on comm-channel protocol.

Both squads executed the plan perfectly, swooping in on the Floaters from above, strafing them with laser fire. Outside his cockpit, multiple flashes appeared followed by booming explosions as Davi's blasts disabled the front vehicle in the column. The next Floater in line swerved to avoid it, but the driver misjudged his position, running over troops fleeing the first Floater to seek cover, before crashing into the third Floater in line.

"Three down with one shot, not bad," Davi said to himself. He adjusted his targeting and fired again, this time aiming for the laser cannons on the three Floaters. He shifted in his seat as the VS28 vibrated with each blast. The cockpit started feeling stuffy as the temperature rose along with his excitement and adrenaline.

Laser bolts flashed outside his blast shield. Spotting rooftop snipers, he didn't even bother to dodge. Blasters wouldn't do much good against the VS28's shields even at close range. He circled around and watched Dru and Virun dispatch laser cannons on four more Floaters. Several more bright explosions boomed before the Floaters split up onto separate corridors in an attempt to avoid their fire.

"They're trying to keep it interesting for us, boys," Davi said over the comm-channel.

"Good. Moving targets are so much more fun," Dru responded. To Davi's amazement, Dru had become one of the better target shooters among the pilots.

Davi and three others swooped down in tight formation and fired. Laser blasts exploded around the Floaters again. Davi's and Dru's blasts hit their marks, taking out more laser cannons. Virun's missed, but he aimed again and blasted the Floater's engines, bringing it to a sudden stop.

Troops jumped clear, seeking cover as Virun chuckled over the comm-channel. "That had to hurt."

Virun's fighter rocked with an explosion and orange flashes appeared on its port wing. "What the—"

Davi looked over to spot a laser cannon zeroing in on him again from the top of a nearby building. "Laser cannon, top of the Acron Industries building. I'm on him," Davi said over the comm-channel. G-forces slammed him back against his leather seat as he put his VS28 into a steep turn and dove down, targeting the rooftop of the office complex.

Jorek's voice came over the comm-channel. "Keep your eyes out for laser cannons on the rooftops."

"How'd we miss those?" Dru wondered aloud over the comm-channel.

"Keep your eyes peeled for others. He really did some damage," Virun warned them.

Davi's targeting computer lit up as it locked on the target. Lining up visually on the guides, he strafed the rooftop. Alliance soldiers dove to each side as the laser cannon exploded. "One cannon down."

"Thanks, boss," Virun replied as Davi steered into position above Virun and to the right.

Virun's starboard wing had black burn marks from the impact and a tear in the metal. "The damage doesn't look unmanageable from here. Can you still control her?"

"I'm not out of this yet," Virun replied turning the fighter for another run.

Davi and Dru both maneuvered into formation around him. Without further chatter, knowing what to do, they took out the laser cannons on the four remaining Floaters, and then targeted their engines.

As they circled around, Davi glimpsed Jorek's squad making similar runs. In a few more minutes, the remaining Floaters had been disabled and the squadron reformed around Davi, heading to assist Tela's team. Davi brushed his clammy brow against the sleeve of his flight suit.

They arrived at the government center to find charred remains of more laser cannons and Alliance equipment. One of the barracks was smoldering. In the beginning, the WFR had hoped to preserve as much infrastructure as possible, but Alliance resistance had made it so difficult they'd decided to do what must be done and worry about it later. They could always rebuild.

"Leave anything for us?" Jorek said as they circled Tela's team.

"We were about to ask you the same question," Tela responded as she joined their formation. The rest of her team formed up behind her.

A squadron of seven Alliance VS28 fighters appeared heading straight for them with laser cannons blazing. "Heads up, here they come!" Tela called into the comm-channel.

Davi spun his fighter into a dive as two laser blasts exploded off his starboard wing. "We need to capture that starport."

"Let's knock these boys out of the sky!" Brie said over the comm-channel.

Davi chuckled. She'd come a long way from the lost teenage girl he had known in training. Davi glanced over to see one of his fighters crashing into the top of another office building, as the Squadron divided itself into pairs and began targeting the enemy fighters.

"We lost Kinny," Tela said over the comm-channel.

Davi pounded a fist into the side of his fighter. Kinny was an experienced pilot who had joined after the initial attack. "Wingmen, cover your leaders!" They didn't really need the reminder, but losing one of his pilots switched him into teacher mode again.

Tela lined up on an Alliance fighter and unleashed a burst of fire from her cannons. The enemy fighter exploded, spiraling toward the ground. Tela let off a victory yell, "One down!"

Davi lined up another in his sights, firing several sloppy blasts through its wing. It spun out of control. "Make it two."

An enemy fighter swooped in from above, firing on Dru at close range. Explosions rocked the hull of his fighter.

Smoke trailed from it, and Davi could see the damage out his blast shield. "You okay, Dru?"

Dru sounded rattled. "She's a little shaky but I can still fly her."

Davi and Tela both dove in to provide cover, blasting in unison at the enemy fighter trying to escape. It disintegrated with a bright flash.

Dru's voice rose in excitement. "He won't do that again! Thanks, guys!"

"Don't mention it," Tela said.

"Let's clean this mess up!" Jorek said.

Davi watched as the enemy fighters retreated. "They're running," Nila said.

"Jorek, take the squadron and chase them down if you can. We're escorting Dru back to base," Davi said.

"You got it, boss," Jorek said.

"Don't let them lead you too close to the starport. They might launch reinforcements," Tela warned.

"Don't worry. We'll be okay." Jorek said as the others formed around him and peeled off after the enemy fighters, leaving Tela and Davi flanking Dru.

"I don't know about the rest of you, but I'm hungry," Dru said.

Davi heard Tela's laugh over the comm-channel as he keyed the transmitter. "Let's go home." They flew in formation back toward the WFR base.

✷✷✷

Xalivar arrived at the meeting with his military leaders feeling beyond frustrated. Never had such brilliant leadership been undermined by more incredible incompetence.

General Lucius, General Pres and Admiral Dek sat around the table in the High Lord Councilor's conference room, just down the hall from the throne room. The oldest of the three, Lucius led ground operations. He'd served first under Xalivar's father and had a long and prestigious record of service, marred solely by his involvement in the Delta V disaster. He had Xalivar's sympathy.

The two junior officers were two decades younger. Pres, the sole female to rise to the top of the Alliance military hierarchy, was descended from the people who once ruled the Eastern regions of Old Earth. Her slanted eyes and yellowish skin lent darkness to her features. She coordinated air defenses, from energy shields to in-atmosphere attack forces. Of the three, Dek looked most like a soldier—his hair closely cropped, his big-boned, muscular frame emphasized by the fit of the gray uniform. He led the extra-planetary air forces.

As Xalivar paced at the head of the table, Lucius broke the silence. "We've consolidated all remaining forces on Vertullis at the government center. We are seeking to regain ground and retake the starport."

"We sent reinforcements?" Xalivar looked to Dek.

"Our men are waiting and ready," Dek responded, "but until we find a way through the energy shield, they cannot be deployed to the surface."

Xalivar whirled around, his anger rising. "What's taking so long? We designed the shield, didn't we? We need those forces on the ground!" He clenched his fists.

Dek flinched but managed to compose himself. "We designed the shields to protect against these types of invasions. Our attempts to weaken the shield with fighters and smaller craft have not been successful. We're preparing larger cruisers for a full-scale assault."

"Our forces have coordinated attacks on the surface using shuttles, Floaters, and the few VS28 starfighters not under WFR control," Pres said.

"The greatest Alliance in the galaxy is being brought to its knees by a bunch of fly-by-the-seat-of-their-pants workers?" Xalivar couldn't believe what he was hearing! Had the years of peace turned his once finely tuned military into incompetents?

"We've seen several gains in the last few days toward recapturing the shield control center," Lucius said. "We hope to regain control of it in the next two days."

"It's been three weeks already! What's taking so long?" Xalivar saw them all flinch at his screaming. "You told me we had the finest military in the galaxy!"

"Our training is top notch, my Lord, but our troops have limited experience with real warfare," Lucius said.

"Are you actually arguing, General Lucius, that years of peace have made us soft and incompetent?" Xalivar stared at him, knowing he wouldn't get an answer. Proud men like this could never admit their failures. He shook his head. "I want all cruisers in the star system recalled to attack that energy shield. All soldiers not essential to their posts are to be brought here and armed for battle. We must recapture Vertullis as soon as possible."

The three leaders nodded. "The cruisers have already been recalled," Dek said.

"We're refitting some light aircraft with better shields to allow increased attacks on enemy positions," Pres said.

"How long will this refitting take?"

"We can't send supplies through the shields either, my Lord," Pres said. "Our men have to reconnoiter and requisition required materials."

Xalivar cursed and pounded his fist on the table. "When am I going to stop hearing excuses and start seeing results?" He turned to the door as Manaen entered holding a data pad. "More bad news?" Manaen nodded.

"I expect the next time we meet to be hearing actual progress reports, instead of more excuses for delays." He grabbed the data pad out of

Manaen's hands and stormed into the corridor, as the leaders sighed and exchanged frustrated looks.

✳✳✳

Davi reported to the command center for debriefing an hour after landing. Matheu, Aron and Joram had already assembled.

"We lost a fighter today and three others were damaged. One of those was nearly shot down as well. Repairs on two of them can be done in a few days, but—"

Matheu nodded. "Casualties of war. It happens."

Davi frowned. "Dead pilots are more to me than just numbers!" His face turned red with anger as he drew close to Matheu and looked him in the eye. How could he be so callous?

Joram stepped between them. "They are to all of us. But people die in war. It's unavoidable."

Davi stepped back, trying to regain his composure. "We'll need all the fighters we can get if we hope to continue this fight. It's only a matter of time before the Alliance brings in star cruisers to blast through the energy shield."

"We have to hope we can negotiate before it happens," Aron said from a nearby chair.

"With what leverage? We are one planet against the entire system!" Davi said, sinking into a chair near Aron and wondering how they could feel so confident.

A communications panel beeped, distracting their attention a moment as a commtech ran to answer it.

"Not everyone in the system sides with the Alliance," Joram said. "They dominate by force, not by election."

"We're making gains daily," Aron said. "The Lord's Council and the citizens of the Alliance must take note of it. Pressure will be brought to bear on the High Lord Councilor. Especially in regards to the Alliance prisoners we're holding. Xalivar may not care about them but others will."

"The Alliance hasn't even used half the force available to them. If history has taught us anything, it's that they won't give up easily," Matheu said.

"The Borali Alliance hasn't fought in years," Aron said. "They quelled a few ill-thought-out worker Movements, yes. But none of those had the military organization and planning we have."

"They don't even see us as human beings," Davi said. "You can't assume their whole way of thinking will change right away."

"Not everyone in the Alliance thinks the same way. You didn't," Joram said.

Davi nodded. "My mother saw to it that I was given unique opportunities and a liberal education most in the Alliance never have. Even she doesn't think as I do."

"Most of them only remember the history of animosity between our peoples," Matheu said.

Davi couldn't believe he'd wound up on the same side in this argument with Matheu. The tension between them had eased since they'd started trusting him, but Mathew was cold and hard, unlike Davi. "It may be a long fight."

"As soon as the area around the government center is stable, we'll retrieve what's left of Kinny's fighter. Try to rebuild—" Joram said.

"It crashed into a building. There won't be much left to salvage," Davi said, cutting him off.

"We'll take what we can from it," Joram replied.

Davi nodded as Aron stood and motioned for him to follow.

"We've been looking into the information your friend at Presimion sent you about the prison," Aron said as they walked away from the others.

Hope rose inside Davi. "You've found something?"

Aron shook his head. "Information on its defenses. It's hidden underground and very well protected. Besides the fact that it's on Legallis, there's no feasible assault plan we can conceive of."

Davi's heart sank. "I have to find a way to help Miri and my father."

"Maybe something can be worked out in the negotiations," Aron said, trying to encourage him.

"We don't even know if there are going to be negotiations," Davi said, his voice rising in frustration.

"We don't know for certain Miri and your father are being held there," Aron reminded him.

Davi turned and headed toward the corridor, feeling a need to get away from military thinking for a while.

✳✳✳

As they sat around the table in Lura's quarters that night, Tela and Lura chatted happily while Davi remained quiet. He went over and over the issues he faced, searching for solutions. The battles had grown more and more risky. They'd lost fighters before, he knew that was inevitable, but knowing it didn't make him feel any less responsible. He wished he could reason with Xalivar somehow, but he'd already tried that. Besides, he would be arrested on sight. If he could only think of a way to convince him that friendship and cooperation would be far more beneficial to both sides than war. If the workers could let go of the past, after all the Lords had put them through, why couldn't the Boralians?

Noticing Davi hadn't touched his food, Lura smiled. "You're a million miles away today, son. Don't worry. Everything will work out somehow. God always has a plan." Davi didn't even look at her as she placed her hand on his atop the table.

"We lost a pilot today," Tela explained.

"Oh, Davi. I'm sure that's very hard! But it's not your fault," Lura said, trying to sound as comforting as possible. It had little effect.

"Loss is part of war, I get that," Davi said. "But I don't like it. And the longer this war drags out, the more losses we will sustain. We can ill afford them. We're already outnumbered."

"We're never outnumbered when God is on our side," Lura said with confidence.

Tela nodded, smiling. "Amen."

Davi shook his head. "I wish I had faith like you two do. The situation seems so hopeless to me."

"I once thought my husband was lost forever, but now I find I may see him again," Lura said. "There's always hope."

Davi looked at her, feeling guilty. "A heavily guarded prison on the enemy's capital planet – we have no way to reach him. We don't even know for sure he's there."

Lura pulled her hand away, shaking her head. "I refuse to believe that. I know God will find a way."

She had so much faith. Davi hated to let her down. He didn't understand her belief that God would work things out, that God cared about the little issues of human hearts, but he wanted so much for it to be true. She'd been hurt enough. He couldn't bear to be the cause of further pain.

And Tela, who had become such a blessing to him, had grown up without a father. He knew what that was like and didn't want to disappoint her either. He wished he still had the influence he'd had as the Prince; that he could hold people accountable, issue orders, garner even a modicum of the military's respect, but those days were behind him forever. He couldn't recall ever feeling so helpless or hopeless.

"Well, he'll have to because I'm out of ideas." Davi stood and disappeared into the living room.

Tela ran after him. "Can you blame her for being so hopeful?"

"I don't blame her. I just worry about her setting herself up for more pain and loss. She's already had so much." Davi sighed as he sunk onto a sofa.

"Then she knows how to deal with it," Tela said as she sat next to him. "Besides, despite your doubts, I share her faith: God cares about what happens to us and has plans for our good."

"I never knew what it was like to have a father," Davi said, turning away. "There's nothing I want more than to have him here with us."

"If it's God's will, it will happen," Tela said, placing her soft hand on his arm.

Davi turned, his eyes meeting hers. "Okay, I know you believe that, but it's not so easy for me. I can't bear to have her hoping I'll get my father back, because if it doesn't happen, it'll break her heart. I don't want to be responsible for that."

"You aren't," Tela said reassuring him. "I want my father back, too, but it's in God's hands."

"We could have lost two pilots today, maybe even three if Virun wasn't so skilled," Davi said. "I'm responsible for those people."

"They're responsible for themselves, too," Tela said. "You didn't force them to fight. They chose to. A leader can only do so much to protect his men."

"How many pilots can we afford to lose?" Davi said, pain pounding inside him.

"Loss is a part of living, and we're at war," Tela said. "I wish I had a better, happier answer for you, but I don't."

Davi nodded, turning away. "I don't want to let everyone down."

Tela put her arm around him, resting her head on his shoulder.

"You've never let me down. You're a great teacher, a great leader, and a great friend. You gave up your whole life, everything you knew because you saw an unjust situation and wanted to do the right thing. I don't know if I could ever do that."

"I did it because these are my people," Davi said. "And because once I knew the truth, I had to do what was right, no matter what it cost."

"And I admire that so much," Tela said. "I can't imagine how hard it is. The Boralians are your people, too. You lived among them twenty years. They will always be a part of you."

Davi took her hand from his shoulder and held it in his, staring into her eyes. "Are you trying to depress me?"

Tela laughed. "You know I didn't mean it like that. The best part of them is a part of you, not the worst."

"How can you be so sure? They trained me. They educated me. I never gave the workers a second thought until I ended up on Vertullis." Davi felt moved by her faith in him. "I spent years in blissful ignorance living as a prince. I heard rumors, but never cared to investigate them. I never had to."

"You didn't know the situation until you came to Vertullis," Tela said.

"I was too busy enjoying the perks of royalty, Tela," Davi said, turning his eyes away to hide his shame. "If I needed something, all I had to do was ask. The one thing I never asked for was the truth."

"And once you knew, you did what you had to. Nothing else matters."

He turned back toward her and their eyes met. The sincerity he saw there made him choke back tears. How could she see so much good in him? After a moment, he sighed, bottling his emotions. "Sometimes I feel like you only see the best in me."

"No, I see the worst too, sometimes," Tela said. "But overall, you're a good guy, so why focus on the bad stuff?"

"I thought that's what women did—find faults in their men and try to fix them," Davi said.

"Oh, I'm not done fixing you, don't worry. But it can wait until we're past this war," Tela said, smiling. They both laughed, until Davi leaned in and kissed her. She kissed back.

"You know we're not alone here, right?" He teased.

She made a face and punched him on the shoulder. "Keep being a wise guy and you can be," she said with a mock serious look.

Davi raised his hands in surrender and she laughed again. "All I know is God is in control, and if we trust Him, things will work out for the best."

Davi looked into her eyes. She really believed i. He wanted to believe it too.

She reached for his hand. "Come on. Your mother's in there alone. Let's go give her some company." He took her hand and followed her back to the dining room.

***

"As the days stretch on and our troops experience more and more defeat at the hands of the Resistance, the situation grows more and more dim," Orson Sterling said from behind a news desk at the Media Corp. bureau. "The public is starting to protest. Many wonder why we're at war with a people who have not done us harm in many generations."

Xalivar shut the vidscreen off before the man-on-the-street interviews began. He'd caught similar reports on every channel. What was wrong with these reporters, stirring up the people to treason? He could understand the average civilian's ignorance of history, but the news media consisted of people with far more education and intelligence. How could they have forgotten what the workers had done to their people? Did no one still realize these workers were not worthy of respect or even a second thought? Could people have so distanced themselves from history that they were willing to forgive the past and treat the workers as human beings?

For days, he had been listening to news reports of growing protests and outcry to "let the workers go." Just thinking about it disgusted him.

Xalivar cursed Orson Sterling and the rest of the media under his breath. He would not be the High Lord Councilor who gave in to such outcries of ignorance. He would never live it down if he did. If the workers achieved the freedom they were demanding, they would come to regret it. They could never be trusted. If left alone, they would return to their old ways. His people may have forgotten the past, but he knew the workers hadn't. No matter how nice they pretended to be, Xalivar knew what was really going on in their minds. This was a war for the future of his people, and he wasn't about to let ignorance rule the day.

The communicator beeped. He stepped to the wall and clicked the button. "Yes?"

Manaen sounded hesitant. "We are receiving calls about food shortages."

"What?" Xalivar sunk back on the throne in frustration.

"Several of the minor planets have not received their shipments from Vertullis in the past two weeks," Manaen explained.

"Shipments have only been stopped for the three weeks of fighting," Xalivar said. Transports to Regallis at the far end of the system would take over a month at their fastest speeds. Some should still be in route.

"The last transports left five days before the fighting started," Manaen said.

Xalivar smiled, feeling smug. *Aha! So someone is panicking prematurely.*

Then Manaen continued: "But those transports were for Legallis and

Tertullis. The last transports for the outer system left two weeks before they did and arrived last week."

"So why are they panicking?" Xalivar frowned. "How can they be out of food?"

"The calls were from Xanthis and Certullis," Manaen said. Both planets were in the middle of the system. "Their last shipments arrived about the time fighting started. New transports would have left a few days later."

Xalivar cursed under his breath. "Order the emergency release of stocks from the royal surplus."

"Yes, my Lord," Manaen said, hesitating.

Xalivar waited for him to speak, hearing the line still open. "What is it?"

"The Royal surplus didn't receive a shipment either. We have enough to feed Legallis for two months," Manaen said.

"By then this will all be over," Xalivar said, clicking off the communicator and returning to his ruminations. *Everyone is blowing this out of proportion, my gods! Am I the only rational one left in the Alliance?!*

✱✱✱

Davi's Squadron circled the government center, awaiting the signal to join the battle which raged below. The call had come less than an hour before. The Alliance had launched a major push to recapture the shield. Uzah's army had been engaging the enemy for the past two hours and needed air support.

As they circled the starport, Davi noticed a line of transports still sitting as they had since the fighting started almost a month before. Some of the food shipments would have begun to spoil by now. He wondered how long it would take for the Alliance to feel the pain of dwindling food supplies. Vertullis supplied eighty percent of the system's food, along with other key agricultural products. Shipments had been postponed ever since the fighting began.

As he turned his attention back to the battle, one transport took off. "Looks like the Plutonians are getting their food," Davi said over the comm-channel.

"They're gonna love that on Legallis," Tela said with a chuckle.

Since the Plutonians and their antelope were the only lifeforms capable of inhabiting the planet outside the false atmosphere of Alpha Base, they were one of the few alien species in the system with their own governor and council. These leaders reported to the Alliance, along with everyone else, but exercised a unique amount of control over local affairs. An envoy had approached the WFR the previous week, seeking to negotiate a special shipment of food. The WFR leadership knew when word got out of such a shipment, other interested parties would approach them, and such activity would only serve to increase the pressure on the Alliance and work in the WFR's favor, so the deal had been made.

As the squadron turned back toward the energy shield control center, Davi's comm-channel beeped on the combat frequency. "Squadron One, commander," he responded.

Davi heard explosions and laser fire in the background as Uzah spoke. "We have enemy fighters coming in from the south and west."

"Roger, Ground Leader, we're on our way!" Davi said, switching back to his Squadron channel. "Okay, everyone, incoming enemy fighters. Let's go occupy them." He switched to the main combat channel again. "All fighters commence attack. All fighters commence attack."

Davi switched on his targeting system and turned his shields on full, increasing speed. As the pressure pushed him against his seat, he counted several squads of Alliance fighters approaching the shield control center, probably all the fighters they still had available. This might be the chance they'd been looking for to eliminate them.

Davi keyed the comm-channel. "Okay, form up on Tela, Jorek, Virun and me. We'll take them in quadrants. Wingmen, protect your leaders. Go for attack."

The Squadron followed his instructions, splitting into groups of five each and forming on their designated leaders.

"Go in high so you can target them before they even realize we're there," Tela said.

"Won't their combat computers clue them in?" Brie asked.

"Not fast enough for them to react," Jorek said, letting out a rebel yell.

Davi chuckled as he keyed the comm-channel. "Keep your focus. Let's make this one count."

Davi's group flew in over the top of the enemy fighters, vectoring in, then letting loose with their laser cannons. Explosions battered the startled enemy fighters as they changed trajectory and began targeting Davi's squadron.

Orange and white flashes filled the corners of his eyes as Nila took a hit on her wing, struggling to keep control.

"You okay, Nila?" he asked over the comm.

"Yeah, I'm hit, but not bad," Nila said.

Dru swooped in over the top of her and blasted the enemy fighter into pieces. "One down," Dru said with a whoop.

"Thanks, Dru," Nila said, as he slid his VS28 into position to protect her. Nila closed the distance forming up behind Davi again.

Davi glanced over to see the other pilots engaged in heavy combat. "Divide. Brie and Nila stay with me. Dru, you and Zid see if you can sneak underneath them. Let's come at them from both sides."

"Roger, boss," Dru said as he took off in another direction with his wingman.

Davi circled around for another run, angling up, with Brie and Nila in tight formation. Enemy fighters tried to intercept them, but Davi's group dove down at the last second and flew up under the enemy and onto their tails.

"Line 'em up, girls," Davi said.

Brie fired first, hitting an enemy fighter with three blasts from her cannons. Nila took out one of an enemy fighter's two engines. Davi fired on the enemy leader and watched as his two blasts landed on the enemy's blast shield. Explosions rocked the fighter causing its emergency eject system to initiate. The enemy leader ejected into space and floated by Davi's blast shield, his face shocked and surprised.

Davi chuckled. "Good shooting, you two!"

"You, too, boss," Brie said.

Ahead, Davi spotted a WFR fighter twisting and turning, attempting to ditch an Alliance fighter on its tail and realized it was Tela.

Her voice came over the comm-channel moments later. "I can't lose this guy."

Davi glanced around for her wingman, but he was nowhere in sight. He accelerated, turning in her direction and targeting the enemy fighter. "On my way!"

Davi glimpsed yellow and red flashes and heard an explosion off his port wing. He glanced back. An enemy fighter dropped down onto his tail. "Brie, Nila, I need some help here."

"We see him, boss," Nila said. Two fighters tried to get behind them as he ignored his attacker and continued his trajectory toward Tela. His mind raced as he calculated moves which would allow him to blast the enemy attacking Tela and circle around to confront his own attacker. More explosions rocked his cockpit. His control panel lights blinked on and off but he still had control.

"You okay?" Nila asked as Davi slewed his fighter side to side, hoping to avoid further damages.

"Yeah. Get this guy off me." His target screen flashed and he fired instantly, sending three blasts from his cannons at the enemy fighter chasing Tela. Its starboard wing disintegrated as it spun out of control toward the ground below.

As the enemy fell away, Tela turned around, targeting the fighter tailing him. "Thanks, Davi."

Brie and Nila fired at the same time, taking out the attackers' engines and sending him diving toward the ground.

Davi heard Brie's whoop over the comm-channel. "All clear, boss."

"Way to go, ladies!" Tela called as they all turned and headed back for the battle.

Davi grimaced as a WFR fighter exploded ahead of him, but noted the enemy had few fighters left. His pilots had done their job well.

Jorek and Virun's squads headed in for another run as Dru and Zid eliminated the last fighter of the group they'd been sparring with. The Borali Alliance's air forces on Vertullis were close to elimination.

Tela's voice came over a private channel. "That was close."

Davi took a quick glance at her fighter as she pulled alongside, noting a few scorch marks on her wings but no significant damage. "For both of us," he responded. Davi ran a quick system's check. There seemed to be no major damage from the hits he took. He whispered a prayer of thanks. "Let's clean up the last of these and go home."

He led them on one last run, and in a few moments, it was all over. The enemy destroyed another WFR fighter first but each of his groups took out an enemy fighter and Tela and Virun went into fancy dives and destroyed the last two. The Alliance had no air support on Vertullis.

"Jorek and Tela, form up the Squadron and work on those ground attackers. Nila, let's take our fighters back to base and get the mechanics to look at them."

"Okay, boss," Nila said.

"Two more coming with you," Virun said as two more injured fighters slid into formation with Davi and Nila.

"Great work today, all," Davi said as he led his formation back toward home. With no air defenses and dwindling ground troops, the Alliance would now have no choice but to break through the energy shield. He comm-channeled a preliminary report back to the command center. Maybe the WFR should take the battle to the enemy.

CHAPTER TWELVE

Tarkanius watched as the Council chamber dissolved into chaos—Lords leaning or sitting on their tables, huddling around in various groups, tables buried underneath a mass of datapads and reports – far from the usual atmosphere at their official meetings. The meeting had already been one of the most boisterous in Tarkanius' memory – Lords talking over each other, ignoring those speaking from the dais, debating every aspect and nuance of the situation with Vertullis. The word "war" was heard only in whispers. No one wanted to be the one to declare it to be the truth. They all still hoped the situation would go away.

"We've already heard complaints of food shortages, on Tertullis in particular," Lord Niger said from a table near the front. "Vertullis is the most important agricultural supplier in the system. Our system cannot survive without it."

"We can cultivate new sources," Lord Obed said from across an aisle. "There are other planets with available land and decent climates for agriculture."

"Not on the same level as Vertullis," Lord Niger said. "It would take generations to develop the same level of production."

"We don't have generations," Lord Kray said. She and Simeon sat together at a table a few rows back, across the aisle from Lord Hachim.

"Well said!" Lord Hachim said as other voices arose in agreement and concern.

"We must send an envoy to discuss the cessation of hostilities with the Resistance leadership," Lord Kray said. "They need us as much as we need them. Perhaps we can find a way to coexist and share resources."

"Why would they want to share with those who have enslaved them?" Lord Obed asked in disbelief.

"Kray is right. Some kind of discussion must take place," Lord Simeon said. "A peaceful resolution is the best option for everyone."

"There can be no peace with the workers," Obed said in disgust. Loud arguments resumed, with various factions taking up stances against each other and struggling to be heard over the others. Tarkanius had had enough.

He pounded the gavel on his podium. "Please. Please. Everyone must have a chance to be heard. We all have concerns, I'm sure."

As the Lords grunted in acknowledgement and settled back into their places, the doors burst open and Xalivar affected his usual grand entrance. He strode to the front of the room and onto the dais. "Sorry, I'm late."

"We were just discussing the possibility of sending an envoy to seek a settlement with our enemy," Tarkanius said.

Xalivar stiffened and whirled toward him as if he might strike, clenching his fists. "We don't negotiate with workers!" His sounded angry, full of contempt, his fists clenching and unclenching at his sides.

"We have no choice when our planets start to run out of food," Kray said. Voices arose in agreement.

"We still have surplus in the Royal storehouses," Xalivar said. Other voices arose in support of Xalivar's resolve.

"At the rate we have been releasing it, Lord Kray is right. It will be a matter of weeks," Simeon said.

"A week or two is all we need," Xalivar said. The Lords quieted, peering at him with interest. He clenched his fists again. "A major task force is, at this very moment, assembling to attack the planet Vertullis and punch through the energy shield."

"Do you really think taking things back by force is necessary, when we haven't even attempted discussions?" Lord Hachim asked.

Xalivar whirled toward him. "Have you so little memory of our history? We have never negotiated with those workers, and I won't be the first High Lord Councilor to allow it."

"You're not the only one making decisions. The Council has a say as well," Kray said.

"We are at war," Xalivar said. "The High Lord Councilor is the de facto leader in times of war by law. There are still options I have not exhausted." Xalivar had never spoken to the Council with such disrespect. No High Lord Councilor ever had.

"We have used force in the past and still we face the workers again," Simeon said. "Perhaps the time has come for a new tactic." Several voices chimed in supporting the idea.

"I will inform you when the time has come for a new tactic," Xalivar said with bitterness. "It is my decision to make as military leader by law."

"The laws do grant the High Lord Councilor broad powers in time of war, true, but the Council is free to have input at any juncture," Tarkanius said in a scolding tone. "You are to present your assessment and allow us to question it as we see fit." Someone had to rein Xalivar in, and, as leader of the Council, the duty fell to him.

"You are questioning without all the facts. The war is far from lost," Xalivar said, fists opening and closing.

"Only skeleton forces remain on the planet. We've lost our air defenses, the starport, the shield," Hachim said in frustration. "What more facts do we need?"

"You will have all the facts, when I say you do," Xalivar said. "I don't have time for debate. I must prepare an assault plan. We have one of the greatest militaries in the known universe. Let them do what we trained them to do." He looked around the room with a cold stare, daring anyone to question him. When no one spoke, Xalivar turned and marched back the way he'd come.

Tarkanius sighed. Miri's concerns about Xalivar consolidating his powers had been even more well-founded than he had realized. The Council would have to give considerable thought to the steps to be taken in response to the Vertullian crisis. And Tarkanius would have to use all of his authority and cunning to put the High Lord Councilor back into line.

***

Davi and WFR Squadron One raced through the hole in the defense shield and continued toward the incoming Alliance Transport. Bound from Legallis for Xanthis, it carried surplus food from the Royal storehouses. The WFR had decided to intercept any transports which passed through Vertullian air space. The agricultural needs of the system were already putting pressure on the Alliance to settle the fighting, and the sooner things came to a head, the better.

Shortages were causing alarm, and the WFR had been hailed as heroes by making private deals to supply the people's needs. Several more deals were in the works, and a transport had already been sent to Tertullis. The situation had become a can't-lose proposition for the WFR. Of course, the decision to attack Alliance transports might change things, but they'd decided it would be worth the risk.

As they passed the Vertullian moon Agora, Davi led the squadron in a tight formation. Their targeting computers lit up with multiple blips.

"Okay, we've got six contacts," Davi said over the combat channel. "Must be a fighter escort. Arm shields."

"Roger, boss," Dru responded as Davi flicked on his shields, knowing all the others were doing the same.

"They're not going to make this as easy as we'd hoped," Davi said. There were five fighters, not a full squadron, but enough to make things more difficult than they had planned.

"Keeps it interesting for us," Virun said.

For a moment, Davi wished he'd reconsidered Joram's suggestion to appoint a special squadron of top pilots for the raid. Tela had argued that they all had combat experience now, and transports had limited shields and gunnery. It would be good practice for everyone. Davi had sided with Tela but now feared he might end up regretting it.

As the large Alliance 250 transport and its escorts came into visual range, Davi ran through the scenarios in his mind. It was too late to initiate any complex maneuvers. The straight on approach seemed the wisest course. He prayed his pilots were all focused. If they could see the enemy, the enemy could see them. The gray transport dwarfed their VS28s, but it moved slower and was less maneuverable.

The transport's fighter escort shifted into a combat formation, placing themselves between Davi's incoming squadron and the transport.

"Look sharp, here we go," Davi said. "Two groups, Virun's to the left."

"Squad Two: form on me," Virun said as the Squadron divided.

"Let's show these guys the same way we showed their friends on the planet," Brie said with excitement.

"Light 'em up!" Nila said, letting out a rebel yell.

Davi laughed and swooped down with Brie, Nila and two others information on the enemy fighters as Virun's group flew around to the other side.

"Focus," Davi reminded them as the targeting system flashed and he fired his cannons. "Remember, we want to disable the transport, not destroy it."

The enemy fighters started firing right after he did, even as they took evasive maneuvers to avoid his cannon blasts.

As Davi and his team focused on the fighters and transport, a Battle Cruiser and five squadrons of enemy fighters rose up from the far side of the planet, racing toward them.

"Incoming!" Dru almost shouted into the comm-channel.

"A month ago you were begging for action," Davi muttered.

"Not this much," Dru answered as Davi noted the numbers of the new arrivals on his radar. Dru had it right. They'd soon be in trouble.

"Just a few more seconds, and I'll have the Transport's engines," Virun said.

Davi spotted Virun moving in to targeting range, his wingman close behind him. "Make it quick. We're about to be outnumbered," Davi said.

He counted five enemy squadrons of fifteen fighters each. He fired off a couple more rounds at the enemy fighters protecting the transport, watching the explosions as one lost an engine and another suffered wing damage. Brie and Nila's shots missed as the fighters they were targeting dodged their fire with quick maneuvers.

Virun and his wingman fired at the transport. "It's away!" Virun said as they arched around and raced toward Davi's squad.

The transport's engines exploded with sparks and fire. At least one of them went dark.

"Let's head for home," Davi said.

The squadron formed up on him, circling over the transport and back down toward the planet.

"Watch your tails," he warned as the enemy fighters raced after them.

A fighter near the back of their formation exploded as enemy cannon fire struck its engine compartment. Another good pilot lost, another friend dead.

"Form up on Virun," Davi said, falling back to protect the rear as the Squadron reformed around Virun. "Fly evasive patterns. Don't give them anything they can lock onto."

Flashes and explosions rocked his cockpit. Davi executed a quick spin and fired back at the closest attackers, forcing them to change course to evade. Another two minutes and his Squadron would be safely beyond the shield.

"Prepare to open the shield on my mark," he comm-channeled the base and continued circling and dodging as he exchanged fire with the enemy fighters.

"Roger, Squadron One commander," Joram's voice came back at him.

Another WFR fighter turned back to engage the enemy. Davi keyed the comm. "Brie, what are you doing? We're almost home."

"Protecting my wingman," she said. She fired off a couple of shots, hitting an enemy fighter square in the wing. Orange and yellow flashes illuminated the fighter as debris separated from its wing and it spun out of control toward outer space.

"Nice shooting. Now turn around and hightail it," Davi said, firing off two more blasts from his cannons and racing after her. "Open Shield," he said, transmitting the code. He held his breath as he awaited the response.

"Open," Joram said. Davi followed his squadron through at the specified coordinates, and without a sound or any visible sign, the shield closed behind them, but not before three enemy fighters followed them through.

"We have company," Nila said as she whirled around, attempting to target one of the enemies. The rest of the Squadron turned to engage them. Enemy lasers exploded off Nila's wing.

"Watch it, Nila!" Brie warned as Nila fired, hitting an enemy fighter square in the blast shield. Smoke trailed from the fighter as the pilot dove, but the blast shield did its job and Davi watched him circle back around.

"Good shooting, Nila," Dru said, as he targeted another enemy and sent it spiraling toward the planet below with two well-timed cannon blasts.

"You, too," Nila said, angling her fighter for another shot at the enemy she'd targeted as he came back around.

"Two to go," Brie said as Nila fired again, this time hitting the enemy on the wing.

At the same moment, Brie's engine exploded behind her, an enemy soaring past as she struggled to maintain control.

Davi swooped down alongside to check on her. "You okay, Brie?"

"Yeah, blast him!" Brie said with fire in her voice.

Virun came in from above and blasted the enemy with two laser shots on each wing. The fighter spiraled out of control toward the ground. Davi heard Virun's rebel yell in the comm-channel.

"Way to go, Squadron!" Dru said.

"We almost failed the mission," Brie said.

"Any mission where we make it home is a success," Davi said as he led the Squadron back toward the base.

What had the Battle Cruiser and its escort had been up to? *They must be looking for a weakness in the energy shield.* It would be a matter of time before the Alliance launched a major attack to try and break through the shield. The WFR had better be ready.

✳✳✳

Tarkanius and three other Lords gathered in a small study off Tarkanius' office in the upper west corridor of the Council building. Except for Lord Niger, they included the same group who had met with Miri in private several months before. The topic was the same: Xalivar.

Lord Hachim had also been invited, but Tarkanius noticed, as he glanced at his chrono for the fifth time in an hour, that Hachim was running late–very late. It was not typical of him, and it had Tarkanius worried. His thoughts were interrupted by someone saying his name.

He looked up to find the others staring at him. Kray and Niger sat on opposite ends of a divan he had imported from Regallis – as nice as anything the resort planet was famous for. Simeon occupied a lounge chair with fabric of matching colors, though it was Xanthian in design.

After a moment, he realized Niger had spoken to him. "I'm sorry. I was wondering about Hachim."

The office remained warm, despite the cold air outside. For some reason, the weather was unusually frigid for this time of year, but the climate controls in his office did their job well, and you wouldn't have known it sitting inside.

"We wondered what you thought about the peace conference. Xalivar seems dead set against it, and he's right–historically, we have never negotiated," Niger said.

"But times have changed," Kray interjected. "The citizens are no longer against such negotiations. People no longer see the workers in the same way as they once did."

Tarkanius nodded. "This is true. What Xalivar always seems to forget is that we were elected to serve the people, not just our own concerns."

The others grunted in agreement.

A moment later, the door slid open and a harried Hachim hurried in, his face anxious.

"What's the matter, Hachim?" Simeon asked as soon as he saw him.

"One of my transports was intercepted by WFR fighters," Hachim said, throwing himself into a chair next to Simeon. "If it weren't for an assist by Alliance forces studying the Vertullian planetary shield, it might have been lost."

Kray put her hand on his arm. "But they're okay?"

Hachim smiled, looking at her. "The shipment is safe. The transport's engines were damaged, but they can be repaired."

Tarkanius had been running over the scenario in his mind. If the WFR were attacking their transports, it meant they were comfortable with the control they had over the planet. They also must have learned that the Boralians' food reserves were running low. Such news wouldn't be any surprise. The Vertullians were well aware of the role their planet played in the star system's ecology.

"What are the latest reports on the battles?" he asked.

"Our latest intelligence reports say Alliance resistance on Vertullis has been reduced to all but a few pockets of troops," Niger said.

Tarkanius sighed. It was like he'd suspected. "That's all the more reason for us to question Xalivar's refusal to negotiate."

"Xalivar is a stubborn fool," Kray said with contempt.

"You'd best keep such comments to yourself," Niger warned.

"He wouldn't dare spy on the Council," Hachim said.

"I wouldn't put anything past him at this point," Kray said. "Remember Miri's warnings and look what happened to her." The rest nodded, their expressions grave.

The room remained silent for several moments, as they all sat lost in thought. Tarkanius wondered if Xalivar had listening devices in his chambers. He'd always maintained a good relationship with Xalivar and found it hard to believe the High Lord Councilor would have regarded him as a threat. Then again, the mere suggestion of a peace conference had made Xalivar quite angry, and none of them had any idea what Miri's interrogators might have drawn out of her since her capture. Perhaps Xalivar knew about their private meeting.

"I think the Council has no choice but to force the conference to occur," Simeon said, breaking the silence.

"Force the conference? How?" Niger asked.

"What if we put out a press release announcing the Council has sent an envoy to arrange it?" Tarkanius said. "Once it's announced to the public, it would be very hard for Xalivar to interfere."

Simeon nodded. "We can send our own representative to ensure negotiations occur, even if Xalivar is reluctant."

"It's the High Lord Councilor's place to negotiate, according to law, even if the law's never been used," Tarkanius said, wondering how they would pull it off.

"Our representative can act as an observer and mediate if required," Kray said. They others grunted their consent. The idea became more and more appealing by the moment.

"Xalivar's not going to like it," Hachim commented. For Tarkanius, that would be a plus.

"Xalivar's not going to have a choice," Kray said. "How much longer should we wait? Until half our system's are starving and demanding peace?"

They exchanged knowing looks. That time was fast approaching.

"The Council does have the authority to arrange conferences with other governmental bodies," Niger said.

"Yes. And even though Xalivar must be the one to negotiate, if we set the agenda, he'll have little choice," Kray said. The others smiled and nodded, knowing what had to be done.

"Simeon and I will prepare the official release," Tarkanius said. "Say nothing of this meeting to anyone until we're ready. We need to hold a secret vote to approve it. Xalivar must not get wind of it before it's released." Their faces told him they all understood.

After a few moments, the others departed, leaving Tarkanius and Simeon alone.

✹✹✹

Two neat rows of reflector pads in the center of the ceiling reflected light off the white walls with a strength that would have been blinding if Miri weren't used to it by now. Except for daily trips to the sanitation room, she'd been imprisoned now for over a month—at the high security prison Centauri Two on the opposite side of Legallis from Legon.

Located on an island in the middle of a large sea with no land around for miles, it was approachable through a few select mine-free channels via water or air–its location and approach channels so secret, Miri only knew about them from discussions she'd overheard between Xalivar and others in the past. She wasn't supposed to have known the place existed until she arrived there.

She'd even grown accustomed to the bright red prison issue jumpsuit she had been forced to wear day in, day out since her arrival. A far cry from the usual wardrobe of a princess, at least it was comfortable and she didn't have to wear it out in public. It made her feel like a giant red Vertullian cherry.

As she flipped through channels on her vidscreen—her sole connection with the outside world—for the fifth time that day, she stopped at Orson Sterling's newscast.

Ah, yes, Orson. I could sure use your help about now. She used the remote to turn up the volume.

The words "Breaking Story" flashed on the screen as she heard: "The Peace Conference is scheduled to take place at the end of the week at Presimion Academy, the Borali Alliance's leading school for future military leaders. Depending, of course, on whether the leaders of the workers agree to it in their talks with the envoy sent by the Council."

What? Peace Conference?

"High Lord Councilor Xalivar has yet to comment on the idea of negotiations with the workers. But it's unprecedented in Boralian history. Perhaps since Worker's Freedom Resistance fighters today attacked an Alliance transport on its way to deliver food to Xanthis, times have changed. Most citizens of the Alliance seem unopposed to peace with the workers, and with food supplies dwindling, time is running out for military successes. Soon, it will be a matter of survival for our people. Xalivar himself is expected to lead the negotiations at the Conference."

Miri shook her head. Xalivar negotiating at a peace conference? How had anyone convinced him to do that? He would be dead set against it. The Council must have forced the issue. Xalivar would never have agreed to it on his own.

A message indicator flashed on the vidscreen—she had an e-post. She couldn't send e-posts out but could still receive them. Since he was the only person who knew her location, she knew it must be from Xalivar. She used the remote to flick over and read the message.

To Prisoner157.83A@Centaurill.emp

From HLC@Federal.emp

Hello dear sister,

I hope this finds you well. You'll be delighted to know the Council, in their infinite wisdom or ignorance, has declared a peace conference which I must attend. It won't surprise you to know I have special plans for Davi and his friends at this conference. They may soon be joining you in your lovely new home. Unless, of course, I decide to execute them on the spot.

Enjoy using your wonderful imagination to ponder what will happen to your son and his friends, my dear sister.

> Your loving brother,
>
> Xalivar

Miri couldn't believe her eyes. *Would Xalivar really openly defy the Council? Of course he would! What could they do about it after it was all over? And if he were successful at squelching the workers' Resistance in the process...?*

Alarms set off in her mind. *How can I get a message to Kray? I have to warn her! Council members must attend the Conference. Farien!* She ran to the door of the cell and hit the buzzer to call one of the guards.

Farien had arrived there two weeks before as Assistant to the Head of prison security, an assignment arranged by his father, who had several friends on the Council. The move was a slight demotion but still not the fall to disgrace he might have expected. Farien's work on Vertullis had gotten him high marks, despite his run in with Bordox, and he seemed grateful to still have an important job. Farien had always been fond of her, Miri knew, and they'd had some pleasant conversations since his arrival there. He'd told her about his encounter with Bordox, guilt ridden over his betrayal of Davi, feeling even worse because he had been more concerned about his own career than their friendship. Hearing the facts, Miri had assured him Davi wouldn't blame him. She knew it would be wrong to exploit his guilt, but people's lives were at stake. Miri would beg him to break protocol this once and send a message for her. He was loyal to Davi, and when she explained the situation, he would be sympathetic. She hoped so. If not, she would make him realize the opportunity this provided for him to make amends.

She focused, preparing herself, and checked her hair and appearance in the mirror. She needed to be at her best for this meeting. As the lock clicked, she took a deep breath and hurried over. *Gods give me strength,* she prayed as Farien entered her cell.

His face was full of concern. "I got an urgent message saying you needed to see me, Princess. Is everything okay?"

Miri smiled, wrapping her arm around his and turning on the charm. "Yes, I'm fine, but I need your help with something."

"I'll do what I can, of course," he said with a nod.

"I need you to get a message out for me," she said, pressing a folded slip of paper into his open hand.

Farien looked down at his hand a moment and sighed. "You know I'd do anything for you, but there are strict protocols here..."

"It's urgent," she pleaded, her blue eyes locking onto his. "Davi might be in danger."

Farien looked at her a moment and she held his gaze. "I wouldn't know where to send him a message these days. Besides, after the way I betrayed him, why would he trust me?"

"The message is for Lord Kray," Miri said.

"Of the High Council?" Farien looked at her, puzzled.

Miri nodded. "Xalivar is planning to betray Davi and his friends at the peace conference." She grabbed the remote off her bed and pulled the e-post up on her vidscreen. "The Council must be warned."

Farien read the e-post off the screen, his face changing as he finished.

"You've been his lifelong friend, Farien," Miri said. "He needs us now more than ever. Please help me help him."

Farien's face filled with anger as he moved toward the door. "I have to get this out right away!"

Miri smiled, running over to embrace him. "Thank you, dear Farien!"

He nodded and rapped on the door with the back of his hand.

✱✱✱

Davi listened as Aron repeated it for the third time.

"An envoy from the Alliance is seeking to arrange a peace conference."

The WFR leaders sat around the table in the command center conference room in numb silence as they pondered it.

"It's totally unprecedented," Joram said. "The Borali Alliance has never asked for peace before, let alone agreed to sit down across the table with workers."

Davi could hardly believe it himself. The Xalivar he knew would never want this. "Xalivar wouldn't agree to this unless he had no choice."

He glanced around, the room was in disarray resulting from constant use: full waste bins, discarded datacards on the floor, fingerprints on the surface of the table amidst the stain rings left by beverages.

"The announcement came from the Council, not the Palace," Uzah said. "They did, however, say the High Lord Councilor would attend."

"He has to, by law," Aron said. "It's his place to lead any negotiations. They've just never done it before."

"It's not the kind of precedent you'd expect Xalivar to set," Uzah said.

"So it's a trap?" Joram wondered.

"Of course it is!" Matheu said. "We must not allow ourselves to be easily lulled." Davi had to agree.

"I agree," Uzah said. "A trap would be very much like Xalivar." Grumbles of agreement came from others around the table. Several nodded.

"At the same time, we can't afford to ignore it," Aron said. "Not if there's even the slightest chance that they're serious."

They all paused, eyes meeting across the table. It seemed obvious Davi wasn't alone in having a hard time believing it. Still, he wanted to. Like everyone else, he wanted the fighting to end as soon as possible.

He leaned back in his chair as the eyes of the others fell on him. "He'll want me to be there," Davi said, "as a matter of personal pride." He dreaded the encounter, but knew he had to go. Xalivar would refuse to negotiate without him.

"We need you to lead the fighters. You can't be risked," Matheu said.

"We can't afford to risk any of our leadership, but we have no choice," Aron said. "Davi's right. Xalivar may well refuse to meet if he's not there."

"This war is not some personal family vendetta," Matheu said.

"Xalivar won't see it that way. To him, our Resistance and my rebellion are synonymous," Davi said.

"We can't afford to blow the conference by holding him back," Joram said.

"Agreed," said Aron. A couple of others nodded and mumbled in agreement.

"I'm not afraid to go," Davi said. "It's time I faced him. Besides, if I ever want to put the issues between Xalivar and I behind me, I'll have to face him sooner or later."

"Of course," Uzah said as he poured himself some Xanthian tea from a pitcher on the table, "the question is whether this conference will be the best place for that."

Following his lead, others began filling their glasses as well. Xanthian tea was a traditional soothant, often used at important meetings and conferences to help people relax. Davi poured his glass with a smile. He needed to relax.

"May I suggest I meet with the envoy and hear the Alliance's expectations for the conference before we make any decision?" Aron suggested.

They all sat there a moment sipping their tea. Davi could feel a rush of calm winding through his body as the tea flowed down his throat into his stomach. It had been ages since he'd had Xanthian tea—once or twice as a child, if he recalled right. He liked it better than he'd remembered.

After a moment, General Matheu nodded. "Aron and Joram will meet with the envoy and return to us. Then we can make our decision."

Davi saw from everyone's faces that they were in agreement. Matheu dismissed the meeting without further discussion, and they all hurried back to their assigned tasks.

✱✱✱

Xalivar entered his conference room in a rage. His military officials shrank back in their seats upon seeing his face. *Some warriors those are!*

He paced in a circle at the head of the table, feeling disgusted at the weakness of the Council, as they waited for him to speak. He'd known the public had become sissies, but to see the once-great Lords of the Borali Alliance reduced to sniveling fools was too much. He must step forward and lead the Alliance back to its former glory. He would do whatever it took, even if it meant declaring martial law and dissolving the government. The thought of it made him smile.

Yes. Yes! I am the leader with the courage and will it takes to restore the Alliance! And I will not quit until I do! His fists clenched at his sides.

He turned back to the table. Lucius, Pres and Dek reacted to the smile on his face with surprise.

"You've all seen the news reports, I'm sure." They nodded without speaking. "The conference will take place at Presimion Academy in four days. Lucius and I will be in attendance, along with Lord Obed and our aides. I want the fleet assembled and ready to attack upon my orders before the conference commences."

"The Council has ordered us to negotiate," Dek said.

Xalivar silenced him with a cold stare, fists clenching again. "The Borali Alliance doesn't negotiate! If the Council has forgotten it, they are no longer fit to lead our people. The Council and the people have become weak. It threatens the entire foundation of our Alliance. We must have the strength to do what must be done."

"We live to serve you, my Lord," Pres said. "But how can we go up against the Council?"

"You answer to me, not the Council. So let me worry about the Council, while you worry about obeying my orders!" Xalivar's tone and expression made it clear he would hear no arguments.

The leaders exchanged a look, then nodded.

"Of course, we will obey, my Lord," Lucius said.

"The fleet is close to being assembled," Dek said. "Everyone can be ready in time."

Xalivar smiled again, his hands relaxed and open. "Good, Admiral. I'm glad to hear it. Lord Obed will be arranging my security for the conference, in cooperation with Professor Yao Brohma of the Academy. Please make any resources you can spare available to him."

"The air forces will be at his disposal, my Lord," Pres said. "We can move several squadrons there as needed."

"I am sure two would be sufficient," Xalivar said.

"It will be done, my Lord," Pres said.

Xalivar nodded. He liked their attitudes—total compliance. The Alliance would need more people with the same attitude to regain their former glory. "Very good. General, Admiral, see to it, while General Lucius and I discuss more details of the conference."

Dek and Pres stood and saluted. "Yes, my Lord."

As they hurried out, Xalivar took a seat at the head of the table, nodding to Lucius.

"These are dark days for the Alliance, my Lord," Lucius said.

"Indeed they are," Xalivar agreed. "Let us work together to be a source of light."

Lucius nodded. "We will do what must be done, my Lord."

Xalivar pulled out a datacard and slid it across the table to Lucius. "These are the things which must be done, General."

Lucius began looking it over as Xalivar watched, anticipating the moment when his plan would finally unfold. The light from the reflector pads shone off the table with a sparkle matching the excitement inside him. All he had done before, all he had prepared for had led him to this moment. He knew the city outside carried on its daily business blissfully unaware of the pressures he faced. But his true greatness would soon be revealed.

CHAPTER THIRTEEN

T he Royal Shuttles waited at the spaceport to take them to Presimion Academy for the peace conference as Xalivar held one last meeting with his military leaders. He walked confidently into the conference room, hands extended flat at his sides and smiled. The leaders waited in nervous silence, relaxing when they saw his expression.

"So, my dear friends, is everything ready?"

Dek nodded, a confident smile on his face. "The fleet is fully assembled and ready to attack upon your order, my Lord."

"Ground forces can be deployed as soon as the shield is neutralized. They're waiting and ready to launch at your command," Pres said.

"Good, good," Xalivar sat down, leaning back in his chair at the head of the table. He could taste the victory. "General Lucius?"

"Lord Obed informs me all security arrangements for the conference are satisfactory, and I am ready to accompany you, my Lord," the General responded.

The enthusiasm in their voices matched his own excitement at the anticipated victory. *Yes, soon the* Alliance*'s greatness will be restored!* "You have all done well, my friends. The Alliance will remember and honor your loyalty and dedication. Our finest moment has arrived!" At last, some officers worthy of his confidence!

"We are honored to serve, my Lord," Lucius said. The others nodded, then all three stood and saluted him.

"We will depart at once," Xalivar said to Lucius. "I want constant reports when the battle begins," he instructed the others.

"Of course, my Lord," Pres and Dek said in unison.

Xalivar stood and they saluted again. "May the gods be with us." He turned toward the door with Lucius following right behind him.

"May the gods be with us," he heard Lucius say.

Xalivar hadn't been so invigorated in years. At last, a major victory to remind the people who their hero ought to be! Yes, he would be hailed as the hero who restored the Borali Alliance. He picked up his pace, feeling his heart pounding in his chest—Lucius' footfalls behind him keeping time with it.

Aboard the small floater on the way to the starport, Xalivar lost himself in thought. Soon the WFR leadership would be shattered. His rogue nephew would be imprisoned along with the other leaders. Morale would falter. The rest would fall apart at the Alliance's show of force. It would be a matter of hours before victory was his. Xalivar had no doubt. The best part of all was knowing none of the weaklings on the Council would have time to object. By the time they did, it would be too late. He chuckled at the thought. How they would whine and wail. He would see to their replacements after it was over. For now, let them whine. Xalivar had the upper hand.

Knowing all this would occur at his alma matter made it much sweeter. He was a distinguished alumnus already, but these events would make him a legend. For the first time in a long while, he experienced true happiness.

***

Bordox sat at the back of the shuttle behind his father, who'd instructed him to keep a low profile until the right moment. Xalivar might have objected to his presence, but Obed had been told to handle the arrangements, giving him the authority to choose his own men. Obed wanted his son to prove himself to Xalivar once and for all. He also wanted his son nearby should the opportunity arise to finally bring down his longtime rival. This scandal provided the best opportunity since the Delta V disaster to see their family returned to its proper place on the throne. Should Xalivar fail to make peace, Obed had confessed, it was sure Xalivar's family would lose the throne. Obed and his son would be front and center to save the day when that happened.

Bordox had cleaned and pressed his uniform, determined not to let his father down. He had a career to salvage, after the embarrassing failure on Vertullis. He cursed under his breath. He'd had enough of Xander Rhii getting in the way of his success. The imbecile had been doing it since the Academy and it was time Bordox turned things around on him. He would do whatever necessary to ensure his nemesis was tried for treason.

It gave him immense pleasure to know one of the last things his nemesis would see as a free man would be the wrong end of Bordox's blaster as he helped put an end to Rhii's freedom.

***

While waiting for the shuttle to depart, Davi thought over how much his life had changed in the past few months.

He'd spent the prior evening at Lura's house, having dinner with Lura, Tela, Nila, and Nila's family. While Davi relaxed, confident the peace conference would come off without a problem, everyone else

worried he would be walking into the arms of the enemy. He'd done his
best to reassure them. He had known Xalivar his whole life. His uncle had
always treated him like a son. Yes, Xalivar felt angry and betrayed by him,
but Davi couldn't believe Xalivar would ever harm him. On top of
everything else, the Council and population of the Alliance had been
pressing for peace. Xalivar knew his options were limited. He would
grouse and growl but some compromise had to be found.

Lura interrupted his thoughts by raising her glass of Talis to propose
a toast. "Here's to Captain Davi Rhii, a true hero for our people."

"Here! Here!" the others said, as they tapped their glasses to hers.

Davi tried not to blush. "I've done what was right," he said. "I
deserve no praise for it."

"You've risen well beyond the call of duty," Tela said. "We wouldn't
have the air forces we have if it weren't for you."

"I know I would have never been able to fly," Nila said.

Davi smiled. "You succeeded because of your ability, not mine." He
felt so proud of his cousin.

"You taught me everything I know," Nila said, refusing to let him off
the hook. They raised their glasses again and clanked them together.

"Your father would be very proud," Lura said. "We used to imagine
the future, as we waited for you to be born. It was so hard for us, because
we wanted a child very much but weren't sure what kind of world we'd be
bringing you into. Life as a slave was not what we wanted for you."

Davi smiled. "Soon, none of us will have to live as slaves any longer."

"Thanks to you," Tela said. Davi focused his eyes on his plate,
embarrassed. They seemed determined to give him far too much credit.
He hadn't acted alone. "You've provided the leadership we needed to
succeed. Without your knowledge and skills, we would have failed."

"All of the leaders are good men. I'm not so important," Davi said, sipping his own Talis and hoping the moment would pass.

"I wish your father could see you now," Lura said, her eyes growing misty. "You have become so much more than we could have ever imagined."

Davi stood and moved around the table toward her. "You'll see him again someday, I promise." They embraced as tears filled both of their eyes.

"From your mouth to God's ears," Lura said. "It's all I have left to hope for."

"I promise as soon as the peace conference is over, I'll find him," Davi said. For a moment, he believed it was possible.

The others wiped their eyes, fighting back tears. "Wow, Captain, you sure know how to bring people down, don't you?" Tela teased.

They all laughed. Lura smiled, wiping her eyes. "And I can't wait for Sol to meet you, too, Tela. You'll make such a fine addition to our family."

Tela smiled. "Thank you." She looked straight at Davi, who tried not to meet her eyes as he moved back to his seat.

Nila chuckled, picking up on the cue. "Yes, so did you discuss it yet? You're joining?"

Davi squirmed in his chair. "Can we try and get the war settled first?"

Everyone laughed. His aunt Rena patted his shoulder, enjoying Davi's discomfort.

"Are you saying the war is more important than me?" Tela teased. Davi blushed again. "Ah, the great military Academy graduate blushing, how wonderful. So strong you are!"

Davi pretended to punch her in the arm.

"Okay, okay, I'll stop."

Tela would be with him at the conference. Why weren't they worried about her? As he'd searched his mind for something interesting to distract them with, Lura pushed her chair back from the table and stood.

"Let us go before the Lord in prayer for the safety of our leadership and successful negotiations tomorrow," Lura said. They bowed their heads as she led them in prayer.

Slipping out of the reverie, Davi looked over at Tela, sitting next to him on the shuttle. Thankful to have her with him for this historic moment, he lifted up a silent prayer for God's protection, for Xalivar to be calm and reasonable, and for the hoped-for peace to become a reality. So much depended on this moment. *Please God, don't let us fail our people.*

Engines whirred and the shuttle accelerated, pushing him back in his seat. Tela held her breath beside him, meditating as she always did during a launch. The pressure eased as the shuttle entered its flight path. In a few hours, he would be face-to-face with the uncle he'd always adored. He hoped some of those fond memories and old feelings would make things easier as they met.

✹✹✹

Rain fell as the shuttle landed on Eleni 1, one of the largest of Legallis' moons; a soft, silvery drizzle which draped itself over everything then slowly built to a slimy, slick coating. Davi and Tela stepped out and felt the cold rain against their cheeks; Davi hoped it wasn't a portent of things to come. A familiar dark-skinned humanoid stood waiting to escort them to the conference.

"Yao! Good to see you again!" They clasped hands and then embraced.

"You look pretty good—for a rebel." Yao said as they both laughed.

Davi turned to Tela, her eyes betraying her curiosity. He introduced Yao as a professor at Presimion. "Ah, so he's the one you leaned on to get you through the Academy," Tela teased.

Yao laughed. "She has you figured out already?"

Davi smiled, and then introduced the other leaders.

Yao led them toward the cluster of buildings that composed the campus of Presimion Academy. Designed in a style befitting their age—Presimion was one of the oldest academies in the solar system—the buildings showed signs of improvement; modern touches to the windows combined with outdoor lighting and modern landscaping.

Yao led them toward a large building where a lighted sign beside the path declared: "Lord Killeen Library and Conference Center."

"The campus is quite impressive," Aron said.

"Thank you," Yao said. "We're quite proud of it. It's the oldest Academy in the system. Many fine leaders have graduated from these hallowed halls." Yao stopped in front of double-paned sliding doors. "Welcome to Lord Killeen Library, gentlemen," he said as the doors slid open.

They stepped inside into a reader's wonderland. In addition to rows of video terminals and data card storage shelves, the library also housed a large collection of Old Earth books—the kind actually printed on paper. These were housed in special shelves enclosed in see-through fiberglass-like walls to protect them from damage by the air and other impurities. They all stopped and took in the view with awe. The shelves and terminals stretched up seven stories, reachable by a series of lifts or spiral staircases designed to appear as if they floated on air. Light from large reflector pads sparkled off them like the glint of the morning suns' first rays upon a window. Combined with the ominous silence of the space surrounding them, it lent almost a fairy-tale atmosphere to the place.

"Hallowed halls, indeed," Davi mumbled, then heard it echo, amplified by the space.

Tela's eyes met Davi's. "I've never seen anything like this!" Though she spoke at almost a whisper, the natural amplification made it sound like she'd leaned very close to his ear.

"It's reputed to be one of the finest libraries in the Alliance," Yao responded.

They moved on into the conference center part of the building—a stark contrast from the library. Here white walls reflected bright light from reflector pads, contrasted only by a drab gray tile floor. The doors were inset but also white and designed to slide into the wall when opening. Other than the Pres-imion Academy crest covering most of one wall, the walls were undecorated.

They turned a corner and stopped before large double doors. Davi looked around. Given the size of the doors and the wall into which they were cut, Davi guessed a sizable space lay behind them.

"I assisted with security arrangements," Yao said. "I hope Xalivar doesn't make things too hard on you."

Davi smiled. "He won't be happy, will he?"

Yao shook his head, chuckling.

Lord Obed appeared with a cordon of LSP men, surrounding them. "I'm afraid no security men can be allowed in the chamber."

Yao frowned. "That was not agreed upon."

"Plans have changed," Obed said with a stern look.

Yao glanced at Davi, confusion rife on his face.

"Will the High Lord Councilor's security be allowed inside?" Davi asked, frowning.

"You are in Boralian space," Obed said. "Alliance forces provide all security here."

The LSP troops began searching their escorts. Aron motioned for the WFR security men to allow the search, despite their worried expressions.

The doors slid open to reveal a large, elaborately decorated chamber with a long center table surrounded by chairs. A raised balcony circled the room above their heads, with bleacher seats in many rows.

"The rest of you may enter," Obed said with a wave.

Aron nodded and stepped forward into the room. Tela and Davi watched the LSP men a moment, feeling reticent about what had happened then followed Aron and Joram into the room.

Yao entered last. "I'm sorry. This was not supposed to happen."

"Perhaps the High Lord Councilor is already up to mischief," Tela whispered.

"We'll find out soon enough," Davi said, watching as Aron and Joram took seats along the center of the table facing the door. He and Tela took the seats next to them as the few aides who'd been allowed in arranged themselves amongst the rest of the chairs.

A bar-bot appeared to take drink orders, its facial LEDs lit up in an electronic smile.

"Let me try and find out what's going on," Yao said, worried.

Davi shook his head. "You can't go up against Obed or Xalivar. Let's wait and see."

Aron nodded. "We have little choice."

"I'll be back," Yao insisted. The doors slid open and Yao disappeared into the corridor.

***

Xalivar's Royal Shuttle arrived on the opposite side of campus from where the WFR contingent had arrived. Instead of one shuttle, he came with two—the other filled with security men and aides.

As Xalivar and Lucius stepped onto the landing pad, Manaen and Lucius' aide rushed forward with rainguards to protect them from the weather. Xalivar looked around—a dreary day, indeed. Soon their mood at least would be brightened. He smiled. So far, everything had gone according to their well-thought-out plans.

As he stepped forward, he saw Lord Obed hurrying toward them with two aides, one of whom held a rainguard over Obed's head. Xalivar smiled thinking about how easy it had been to convince the Council to make Obed their representative at the peace conference.

"Everything has gone as planned, Lord Xalivar," Obed said with a smile as he stopped before them.

"They offered no argument?"

"Only your nephew and his friend seemed bothered," Obed said.

Xalivar nodded. *Of course they were.* "They are waiting in the chamber?"

Obed nodded. "Yes. And their escorts have already been sealed away in a secure location."

Xalivar chuckled. "Good, good." His hands clenched into fists and released again. "This will be a triumphant moment for us, Lord Obed. I'm pleased you can be a part of it."

"The honor is mine, Lord Xalivar," Obed said, joining them as they continued along the pathway.

Xalivar smiled. He had his most trusted people with him today. They were intensely loyal. The only one he'd questioned had been Lord Obed, but Obed had thrown his support behind Xalivar. It reassured him to have his rival nearby where Xalivar could keep an eye on him. Xalivar's grandfather had often said: "the safest place for your enemy is right beside you." It's why Xalivar had appointed Obed to head the LSP. Since the head of the LSP reported directly to the High Lord Councilor, Xalivar could keep a careful eye on him. If things went wrong somehow at the conference, Xalivar would be sure that Obed took the blame.

He glanced over at Lucius and their eyes met. Lucius nodded. The fleet was moving into position over Vertullis. Xalivar's fists clenched again. He could almost taste the sweetness of victory. He would make sure his former nephew and friends knew they had been beaten. He wanted them to taste the defeat even as it happened. It would make up in small part for the humiliations and frustrations they'd caused him over the past months. Soon, they'd have nothing but time to think about it.

***

The Alliance flagship Victory hovered in position off Jacote, Vertullis' largest moon, as Admiral Dek and General Pres stared out the bridge blast shield at the gathering fleet.

Dek smiled. He could already feel the victory that would soon be theirs. It had been a long time since he'd led a fleet into battle, and he had been much younger then. The only action he'd seen since had been during military exercises. How good it would be for his men to practice what they'd been learning. It would keep them fresh and ready, giving them greater confidence in their abilities and training.

Perhaps there would be a resurgence of reenlistments afterwards. The military had seen increased retirements and resignations over the past several years. They needed to renew the sense of pride and commitment in their forces—something a good victory would help ensure.

"Troop ships have launched and will arrive on schedule," Pres said, interrupting his thoughts.

Dek nodded. "Thank you, General. I am pleased you are here for this historic moment."

"I wouldn't miss it," Pres said, glancing at her chrono. "The negotiations should commence momentarily."

"And they will last but a few moments, I'm sure," Dek said with a grin. They both laughed at the thought of the disappointment and surprise the WFR leadership would experience.

"The planetary radar is jammed?" Pres asked.

"All the jamming ships are in position awaiting my command," Dek said with confidence.

Pres nodded. "We await your orders, Admiral."

Dek nodded, moving to the rail lining the walkway where they stood, and looked down on the bridge. "Captain, order the Century ships to begin jamming the radar."

Below them on the command deck, Captain Colson turned to nod at them, his crisp, clean uniform so tight it fit him like an outer skin. "Lieutenant, issue the order."

"Yes, sir," a Lieutenant said from a nearby comm panel. "Century craft: commence jamming at once," he said into the comm-channel, his face full of anticipation.

Captain Colson turned back to Pres and Dek, nodding.

"All ships full ahead," Dek ordered.

Colson turned to his men and repeated the order. Soon it would all be over.

✳ ✳ ✳

The WFR contingent waited around the large conference table for forty-five minutes before the doors opened and Xalivar entered. He wore the ceremonial robe he reserved for Council ceremonies and important events, walking as if he'd already won. He was accompanied by General Lucius, whom Davi had met at the Academy, as well as Lord Obed, Manaen, and other aides. They moved to the opposite side of the table and spread out—with Xalivar across the table from Davi and Aron.

Xalivar remained standing as the others sat, a smug smile on his face as his eyes met Davi's. "Well, the prodigal nephew returns. You look well. But I'm afraid I cannot say you've been making us proud, can I?"

Davi smiled. "It is good to see you again, un—" He stopped himself. *Don't call him that any more.* "High Lord Councilor."

Xalivar smiled. "Ah, so soon we forget our family, is that how it is? A bitter sting upon my heart." He slid into his seat at the table, eyes still locked onto Davi's. "And after all our efforts to raise you with honor, give you the finest things in life..." His voice trailed off and a sad look came upon his face.

Davi knew the emotions were all for show. He tried to detect something in his voice—a clue to his frame of mind—but, as usual, Xalivar stayed controlled.

Davi allowed a bit of emotion to creep into his own voice. "I am grateful for all you have done for me, uncle. I have not forgotten. I owe you a great deal."

"Ah, I see, so you call me uncle when it's convenient then," Xalivar said. Davi kept his eyes locked on Xalivar, trying not to flinch. "You did, however, turn out to be somewhat of a disappointment."

The words stung. "I'm sorry you feel that way," Davi said. "I have always tried to live by what you and mother taught me. My sole desire was to make you proud."

Xalivar laughed, his eyes sparkling with amusement. "Make me proud? By betraying the Alliance? Betraying your family? Betraying me?"

"By following my conscience, upholding my sense of honor, and serving with bravery and integrity," Davi said.

Xalivar's face changed to fury as he clenched his fists atop the table. "There can be no integrity in betrayal, Xander." He looked away, taking in the others.

"I can assure you, High Lord Councilor, your nephew has distinguished himself well by his service to us, as a pilot, an instructor, and a leader," Aron said with a smile. "You can be very proud."

Xalivar's head whirled toward Aron, locking eyes, fists clenching. "Honorable men take no pride in acts of rebellion!"

"I believe we have come to discuss the cessation of hostilities," Aron said, still smiling.

Xalivar pounded his fist onto the table. "I will decide what we do or don't discuss!" He looked away a moment, appearing to collect himself. You could have heard a pin drop as everyone waited in silent anticipation, hesitating to even breathe. Xalivar turned back toward them. "You realize, of course, I could have you executed?"

"The peace conference was arranged by the Council of Lords," Davi said as firmly as he could manage. "You are in no position to even arrest us." His eyes locked on Xalivar's.

Xalivar's stare was like a knife slicing meat. "Do not tell me about my position, Captain."

"Why was our security contingent refused entry to this conference?" Aron asked, his voice revealing the tension inside him. "It was agreed upon in the terms."

"You are in Boralian space, not locked behind your stolen energy shield," Xalivar said. "I determine the arrangements for this conference, not you."

"So this conference was a ruse to lure us here under false pretenses?" Davi said, letting his frustration show.

"Ah, now who feels betrayed?" Xalivar said with a laugh. "The Borali Alliance does not negotiate with rebels. It's a long and proud tradition. I'm sure you studied it at the Academy."

The WFR contingent stood, chairs squeaking against the floor as they scooted back from the table. "In the name of interstellar law, we demand just treatment," Aron said, more irritated than Davi had ever seen him.

"Oh, you will receive just treatment for your actions," Xalivar said with a smile, "In prison. Take them into custody."

The doors opened and Bordox entered with a squad of LSR troops, weapons held at the ready.

✳ ✳ ✳

Klaxons blared throughout the complex as controllers and technicians raced to their stations around Uzah and Matheu.

"What is it?" Uzah asked, the worry on his face matching his voice.

"The Alliance fleet just came around from the far side of Jacote," Matheu said.

Uzah's face showed immediate understanding. Jacote, the planet's largest moon, was the perfect place for a fleet to conceal itself before a surprise attack. "How many?"

"Four flagships, twenty Defenders, and thirty other craft of varying size," Matheu said, motioning to the large radar at the center of the room.

Uzah saw red blips on the screen moving toward the planet.

"Plus, whatever squadrons of fighters they can hold."

"Pilots to their fighters," Uzah said into the comm-channel on his headset. He heard the command repeated three times by the combat computer. "Our fighters won't be able to handle them all."

"They'll have to break through the shield first," Matheu said, raising his voice to be heard over the clamor around them as technicians and controllers exchanged data and checked their systems in preparation for the imminent attack.

"How long will it take them?" Uzah asked, dreading the answer.

"With a fleet that size? A matter of an hour or two, if we're lucky," Matheu said, his voice betrayed his lack of confidence—something Uzah had never seen before in the stern military man. Matheu had always been a steady source of strength among the leadership—his bitter past experiences fighting the Alliance hardening him to the realities of war.

"Ground troops are setting up the shield reinforcers at key points," a controller said from nearby.

"Good, good," Matheu said, nodding to the controller. "They will help protect the shield control center once the Alliance breaks through.

It's going to be a long night." He turned to a nearby controller who'd been motioning to them.

Uzah moved toward the communications center to his right. "Try and get a message out to our contingent at the peace conference."

"I've been trying, sir. They're jamming us," the controller said, shaking her head. *So it begins.*

✳ ✳ ✳

Dek and Pres stood together on the bridge of the Alliance flagship *Victory* as the fleet moved into full view of the planet. "The shield is coming into solid range of our cannons now, sir," a radar technician nearby said.

Dek nodded at the man and smiled to Pres. "Let the fun begin." He was enjoying himself.

Pres chuckled. "I imagine the worker rebels must be in a bit of a panic already."

Dek laughed and raised his eyebrows. "It would be fun to see their faces, wouldn't it?"

Red lights flashed and klaxons blared as the battle stations alert sounded throughout the fleet. The command center filled with commotion. Everyone hurried about their final preparations for the attack.

Dek was proud to serve a leader with the strength and clarity to do what it takes. Those kinds of leaders had been the ones he'd always admired in history. Given the track record of the Borali Alliance over the past fifty years, he'd always doubted he would serve under one. He didn't know why others in the Alliance couldn't see how lucky they were.

After this they all will see.

He watched fighters launching from nearby ships.

***

"We hoped things would be handled with honor this time," Aron said looking down at his feet with sadness.

It took Davi a moment to believe Xalivar would really betray them. He'd known Xalivar would be a tough negotiator, ruling with ruthless strength and determination. Xalivar had a reputation. But Davi had never seen this side of his uncle.

Bordox stood staring at him, his angry eyes never leaving Davi's face. *Oh yeah, you're enjoying this aren't you?*

He hadn't been surprised to see Bordox. After all, Xalivar had sent him to hunt Davi down before—one of Xalivar's favorite tricks— exploiting the weaknesses of others. Davi watched for years as Xalivar did it to Miri. Besides, Lord Obed would want to include his son in the scheme. Obed had always been the type of stern father Davi couldn't imagine growing up with. As a result, Bordox's hardness had never really surprised him. What happened next did.

"There can be no honor for traitors!" Xalivar unclenched his fists again and motioned to Davi. "Bring him with me. Take the rest of them to where we're holding the others."

The others? Does he mean our security team and aides? Davi didn't even have time to ask.

Bordox tore him out of the chair and shoved him toward the double doors. "Move, traitor!"

Davi stumbled, but managed to stay on his feet. Glancing back, Bordox's smug smile showed his old nemesis was enjoying this. "We demand treatment for prisoners of war as governed by military statute..."

Bordox cut him off by shoving him through the door. "Walk faster, Xander!" he said with a sneer.

"You will be treated as the workers you are," Xalivar said, following them into the corridor and moving ahead of Bordox. Manaen and two LSP men followed close behind.

"Where are you taking me?" Davi asked, his voice sounding stronger than he felt.

"You'll know soon enough," Xalivar said.

Manaen's comlink beeped. Davi turned and watched as Manaen listened through his earpiece. "Thank you." Manaen raced up beside Xalivar, whispering soft enough so Davi couldn't hear.

"What are you going to do with us?" Davi asked again, with more firmness.

Bordox shoved him again as they turned a corner and moved down another corridor. It seemed like an endless tunnel of white walls.

"The same thing we're doing to your friends on Vertullis at this moment," Xalivar said, stopping and turning back with a smug smile. "Destroy you."

Vertullis? What does he mean? Seeing the question in Davi's eyes, Xalivar smiled triumphantly. "It will be a matter of moments before the fleet blasts through your precious energy shield," Xalivar said as he began walking again.

A fleet? Attacking Vertullis? Of course! This would be perfect timing! Davi did his best to hide his emotions but inside his heart and mind were racing. *We have to find a way to get a message to the base.* Uzah and Matheu would do everything possible to defend the planet. He had to get free so he could help Tela and the others.

"Who is it? Admiral Dek? General Pres?"

Xalivar smiled. "Ah yes, your old instructors are indeed participating in the destruction of your resistance."

Davi's mind raced to come up with something he could use to raise Xalivar's doubts. His uncle's greatest weakness had always been his paranoia. "Well, I hope they enjoy the surprise we have waiting for them," he said, trying to sound convincing.

"Your surprises are no match for us," Bordox said with a sneer.

"All those years in secret development at the hidden base," Davi said. "We've been hoping we'd have a chance to try it." Davi grinned, certain Xalivar's curiosity would get the best of him.

Xalivar stopped and turned back to face him.

"He's bluffing," Bordox said with mock confidence, his face betraying his doubts.

Xalivar's brown eyes locked on Davi's and they stood there staring at each other a moment.

✹✹✹

Uzah and Matheu stood at the large radar in the middle of the now chaotic command center. "The energy shield control center reported they're down to thirty percent. It can't hold much longer," Uzah said.

Matheu frowned in frustration and turned to the comm station behind them. "Launch all fighters! Prepare for enemy infiltration!"

The controller nodded and repeated the command. A klaxon sounded as Uzah and Matheu turned back to the radar.

"It took less time than we expected," Uzah said.

"They designed the shield, so they know how to exploit its weaknesses," Matheu said with a shrug as they watched blips representing the fighters launching on the radar.

✹✹✹

Dek and Pres watched the attack through the bridge blast shield as a Lieutenant hurried toward them.

"Admiral, we've got two shuttles demanding clearance to land."

"Demanding clearance?" Dek frowned, his voice filled with disgust.

"Who has the audacity to make demands of my ship?"

"Lord Tarkanius and members of the Council are said to be on board, sir," the Lieutenant responded.

Dek and Pres exchanged a look. *Council members here?* Dek knew he had no choice. "Give them clearance, Lieutenant. And have them escorted here."

The Lieutenant nodded, hurrying away.

"Why would Council shuttles be out here?" Pres wondered aloud.

Dek shrugged. "I have no idea." *But this can't be good.* "Perhaps they want to see the victory first hand." He smiled as convincingly as he could.

✷✷✷

Tela paced beside the conference table, worried about Davi. *Where have they taken him?* Davi being alone right now was not a good idea. Lord Obed stood in front of the double doors, smiling. *You're loving this, aren't you?* She fought the urge to make a snide remark, as the doors burst open behind him and Yao appeared with a woman and two men in robes and a large number of armed soldiers.

"By order of the Council of Lords, you will release these people right now," the woman said to the surprised Obed.

"Lord Kray, what are you doing?" Obed demanded as two soldiers grabbed him and pushed him to the side. "Get your hands off me! I am a member of the Council!"

"By order of the Council, you are to be detained," Kray said, eyes full of confidence.

"This is an outrage!" Obed said, watching as Yao and other soldiers untied the hands of the WFR contingent.

Tela rubbed her wrists as the binders came loose. "Thank you. What's going on?"

"A slight change in roster for the peace negotiations," Yao said smiling.

A robed man stepped forward. "I am Lord Simeon of the Council of Lords. On behalf of the Council, we apologize for the way you've been treated here."

Aron smiled and nodded. "Thank you, Lord Simeon." He glanced at Tela. Things were getting very interesting indeed.

***

From the moment he saw Davi and the others in their blue WFR uniforms, Xalivar could barely hide his disgust. *Blue!* Blue represented the opposite of order–the expanse of ever changing blue skies, the blue of cresting waves, the icy tundra of Plutonis, chaos, sadness and the bitterness of Jax fruit. It seemed to him the perfect choice for worker scum. He continued staring at Davi for a moment, making a decision. "In there!"

One of the LSP men opened the door and Bordox shoved Davi through. The others followed. As the door slid shut, Xalivar heard a commotion down the corridor. "See what's going on."

One of the LSP men nodded and hurried out of the room.

Xalivar turned to Davi, whose arms were being held behind his back by Bordox. "Secret weapons? A hidden base? You think one tiny planet can defeat an entire solar system?"

"With God on our side? Yes, I do," Davi said, nodding.

Xalivar clenched his fists, glaring at him. "Your false god is no match for the Alliance, Xander!"

"We'll soon find out," Davi said without flinching. "And you can stop calling me that. My name's Davi now."

Xalivar's face grew angrier. He turned to Bordox as Manaen reacted to something in his headset. "My Lord—"

"What is it Manaen?" Xalivar said, continuing to stare at Davi.

Manaen hurried forward, whispering in Xalivar's ear.

"Lord Kray? Lord Simeon? What?"

The LSP man returned out of breath. "There are soldiers everywhere. They're headed this way."

What do they mean soldiers? Council members? Here? His enemies seemed intent on ruining his plans, but he wouldn't allow it. He cursed, looking around them for another exit but finding none. "Bring him!"

He grabbed Bordox's blaster and aimed it at the large window along one wall. The others reacted to the sound of the laser as the glass exploded, flying everywhere.

"Bring him with me! Hurry!" Xalivar handed Bordox the blaster then stepped through the window frame, kicking glass aside with his boot as Bordox shoved Davi toward it.

✱✱✱

Yao took a quick head count. Xalivar was missing, along with Bordox, Manaen, two guards and Davi. "He took him down the corridor," Tela confirmed. "We have to find him."

Yao nodded. "Lord Kray—"

Kray motioned that she'd heard. "I'm coming, too."

Yao stopped in the doorway, motioning to a Lieutenant. "I need two squads of your best men, now."

The Lieutenant nodded, hurrying out into the corridor. Yao, Kray and Tela followed.

✱✱✱

Davi breathed in the fresh clean, post-rain air as the twin suns broke through the clouds. He wondered what had happened to Tela, Yao and his friends. His uncle's cruelty wasn't important. What mattered was their safety.

Xalivar and his officers led Davi across a broad lawn past trees and shrubs, almost at a run. Davi looked back and saw soldiers lined up in formation outside the Library entrance. Xalivar saw it too and quickened his pace.

"What are we running away from? I thought all of you are on the same side?" Davi asked.

Bordox shoved him and Davi stumbled as they hurried along the pathway.

"You already know I have more enemies than friends," Xalivar said in a no-nonsense tone. "Extra precautions are always required. For your protection as well as my own."

So, Xalivar and the Council have a rift? When Xalivar had arrived and taken him into custody, Davi assumed the peace conference was a ruse. What if it wasn't? Had the WFR really succeeded?

"Where are you taking me?"

"We ask the questions, prisoner!" Bordox shoved him again.

Davi was getting tired of it. "Could you try and enjoy this a little less, Bordox?" Davi said, pulling his arm free of Bordox's grip and moving forward alongside Xalivar. "I'm talking to my uncle."

"We'll see how you refer to me, when we're safely aboard my ship," Xalivar said. Davi didn't find the tone reassuring.

Xalivar led them down a slope almost at a run, and Davi saw the Royal Shuttle waiting on a launch pad ahead.

Lord Kray appeared in front of the shuttle, and Xalivar frowned, hesitating. He stopped at the bottom of the slope, facing Kray. "Don't interfere with me, Kray!"

"By order of the Council of Lords, you are to release the prisoner at once," she said.

"The Council has no authority here," Xalivar insisted.

"We do under the act of emergency powers," Kray said as Yao and Tela appeared, blasters at the ready with two armed squads of Alliance troops. Davi couldn't help but smile.

Bordox shoved him. "Stop smiling!"

"This is a family matter, Kray. It is not the business of the Council," Xalivar said.

"He is here as a member of a WFR contingent invited by the Council," Kray countered. "He cannot be detained."

Xalivar ignored her. "Step aside, Councilor!" He shoved Kray aside as Yao pointed a blaster at him.

"High Lord Councilor, I'm going to have to ask you to halt," Yao said.

Xalivar stopped and turned, staring at him. "I outrank all of you, Captain."

"The Council's orders override yours," Yao said, unwavering.

Bordox drew his blaster and shoved it into Davi's back. "You will allow us to pass or Xander here dies!"

Yao, Tela, and the soldiers aimed their blasters at Davi and Bordox.

"Let him go," Tela demanded, looking afraid.

"Slaves give no orders here!" Bordox shouted, pushing his blaster harder into Davi's back.

Davi winced. He'd never known Bordox to be so brave—defying the Council. Then he saw Obed being led across the campus under armed guard, wondering if Bordox had seen it too.

"Lieutenant, you are violating Council orders," Kray said, in a commanding tone. "Drop your blaster now."

Bordox stared at her, glanced over his shoulder at Obed being led down a pathway across the campus from them, and then shook his head.

"I can't do it, can I, Xander?"

Behind them, the Royal Shuttle's engines whined. They all turned to see Xalivar peering out of the cockpit, the shuttle doors now closed and locked behind him. He smiled as the shuttle lifted into the air.

"I told you—" Davi kicked backwards with his right foot, shoving his elbow back at the same moment. The foot caught Bordox's knee and the elbow dug into his ribs. Bordox stumbled backward and Davi dove to the ground. "—stop calling me that!"

Bordox hesitated a moment then aimed his blaster at Davi again. Tela and Yao fired. Bordox screamed and crumpled to the ground, grabbing his wounded leg. Davi dove and grabbed the blaster away from him, so near he could smell Bordox's charred flesh.

"Nooooo!" Bordox yelled through gritted teeth.

Soldiers surrounded Bordox as Yao reach down and helped Davi to his feet. "You okay?"

Davi smiled, reaching out to grasp his friend's shoulder. "Yes, and now I owe you my life!"

Yao shrugged. "Along with the answers for most of your tests at the Academy."

They both laughed as Tela rushed over to embrace Davi. "Thank God you're okay! I was scared for you," she said.

"Me, too," Davi admitted.

Bordox struggled and two soldiers took him by the arms and led him away. "You'll regret this, Rhii! You haven't seen the last of me!"

Davi sighed and waved.

Lord Kray approached. "I'm sorry for the way you were treated."

Davi shrugged. "Nothing that won't heal, Councilor. Thank you for your help."

She smiled. "Your mother would be very proud of you."

Davi smiled, feeling sad. He wished Miri were here. "What about

Xalivar?"

Kray shrugged. "Where can he go? The Council declared emergency powers hours ago. He'll be detained soon enough. You'll be negotiating with the Council now."

Davi nodded as Tela leaned her head on his shoulder. "I have no doubt the Council will be fair."

He could hardly believe it! With the Council's help, the WFR had won. He'd never dared imagine how it would feel. His heart jumped for joy as he and Tela walked with Kray and Yao back up the slope and across the campus toward the Library again.

EPILOGUE

The starport on Vertullis bustled with activity as Davi, Tela and Lura arrived. In the two weeks since the peace conference, things had returned to normal—transports, shuttles, and starfighters launching one after another. Workers and mech-bots hustled around loading, unloading and servicing the various craft. Passengers and ticket agents bustled around them. It was almost as if the war had never happened.

The Council of Lords had agreed to all of their demands. The workers would be free and treated as regular citizens of the Borali Alliance. Shipments had resumed from Vertullis bearing agricultural products out while other products were brought in. In the next month, Aron would join the Council as a full member to represent the planet. He would take the place of Lord Obed, who, along with the entire LSP, had come under suspicion.

Xalivar and Manaen had disappeared in the Royal Shuttle. They had not landed at any of the expected ports. Rumors had it they'd refueled at Alpha Base before word of the settlement and rearranged government had reached there, but no one was certain. High Lord Councilor

Tarkanius had declared them wanted men. Though the Council had promised no sanctions at first if Xalivar relented and abided by their decisions, his flight left them outraged. It had been a sign of total disrespect and the Council would not stand for it. Xalivar's reign had been terminated, and Tarkanius had taken his place.

Davi accepted their decision not to choose him to replace Xalivar. The Council had always chosen the ruling family by election, and given what had occurred, he could understand their feeling that a change had been appropriate. Besides, he was too young to be a High Lord Councilor, and, at this point, there wasn't anything he thought he would miss about being Royal.

Davi, Lura and Tela arrived at the designated platform, as the white shuttle from the Alliance Prison Centauri Two entered the landing bay. Lura seemed more nervous than he'd ever seen her.

"You okay, Mother?"

She nodded. "It's been so long."

"I'm sure he'll be as happy to see you as you are to see him," Tela said.

Lura smiled. "I can't wait for you to meet him."

Davi turned away, feeling nervous. He couldn't believe this moment had arrived.

Aron approached and patted him on the back as the shuttle lowered onto the platform before them. "He'll be very proud of you."

"And very proud of you, too, no doubt," Davi said.

Aron shrugged. "A Lord on the Council! We never could have imagined it."

"It's well deserved," Tela said, squeezing Davi's hand.

Davi smiled, pulling her to him. "I'm proud of you both."

The shuttle's engines wound down and the door opened. The first person to step onto the platform was a young Lieutenant Davi recognized.

Farien kept his military posture, a stern expression on his face as he walked to where Davi and Tela were standing. He stopped there, examining Davi's blue uniform. "You look like a worker to me!"

Davi broke into a broad grin, and they embraced like brothers. "It's good to see you," Davi said.

"Guess you should have kept me around to keep you out of trouble," Farien said. They both laughed.

Miri stepped off the shuttle, spotting Davi and hurrying toward him. They embraced like two people who had been apart too long. "When I heard they were bringing us here, I wasn't sure what to expect. I missed you so!"

"You, too, Mother. I was worried about you," Davi said.

"They told me you're a war hero? My own son, the worker Prince," Miri said, looking him over in the way mothers inspect their children after a long absence.

"I've done what I could, Mother. Really. I'm fine."

Miri smiled, embracing him again. "It's a mother's prerogative to be sure."

Over Miri's shoulder, Davi saw Lura embrace a man on the platform a few yards away as Tela greeted someone at the foot of the ramp.

"There're some people I want you to meet." Davi and Miri said in unison. Davi laughed.

"You first," Miri said.

Davi took her hand and led her toward Tela, who was embracing a man in his mid-fifties. His features were similar to Tela's, except he was taller, with graying hair.

"Davi, I'd like you to meet my father, Telanus."

Telanus smiled and clasped Davi's hand, his grip firm. "So this is the young man I have to thank for taking care of my little girl."

"She did a pretty good job of it herself, sir," Davi said. "In fact, you might say it was more the other way around."

Miri smiled, offering her hand to Tela. "Then it is I who must thank her, I suppose."

Tela grasped Miri's hand as Davi said: "Tela, this is my mother, Miri."

"I am so honored, Princess Miri," Tela said, reacting with surprise as Miri pulled her into an embrace.

"From what I hear, soon you may be calling me Mother as well," Miri said with a wink at Davi, who blushed. Tela laughed.

Davi turned as Lura approached with a tall and thin man who looked a lot like him. His face and hands appeared hardened from manual labor, and his hair had turned gray but he walked with confidence. A familiar necklace hung around his neck.

"I never thought this day would come," Lura said, tears flowing down her cheeks. "This is your father, Sol."

Sol and Davi stood a moment, taking each other in, and then Sol grabbed Davi and pulled him into an embrace. Sol's eyes filled with tears as he spoke. "I have so dreamed of this day, my son."

"I have, too, father," Davi said, fighting back tears of his own.

"Your mother, Princess Miri, has told me so many stories the past few days," Sol said, smiling at Miri, who was wiping her own eyes. "We are so grateful for all she's done for you."

"Thank you for taking care of our baby," Lura said, voice full of emotion as she grasper Miri's hands.

As the two mothers hugged, Sol continued, "We're also grateful for all you've done, and very proud."

Davi couldn't fight the tears any longer. They poured from his eyes as he embraced Sol again. "Thank you for saving my life!" It seemed to be the one thought out of several in his mind which he could manage to form into words right then.

They took another shuttle back to the WFR base where an elaborate banquet had been prepared for them in a large cavern. The WFR leadership, pilots and other guests stood waiting for them. The banquet table contained a spread beyond imagination—every delectable delight they could have imagined. They all ate until their stomachs were ready to burst.

Everyone exchanged congratulations as they celebrated together. General Matheu even thanked Davi for his contributions and shook his hand.

Telanus, Miri and Sol stared in amazement at what the workers had built, and it touched Davi to see the three of his parents—birth and adopted—getting along so well.

Later, he and Tela slipped off to one side and cuddled, watching them.

"I can't even begin to describe this," Tela said.

Davi nodded. "Me neither. It's so hard to believe, but somehow more than anything else, this feels like victory."

Tela smiled, pulling him close and they kissed, and then strode hand in hand back to rejoin the others.

GLOSSARY

Agora – One of Vertullis' two moons.

Auto-bot – Prototype robot created to perform basic human tasks.

Barge – A smaller transport used primarily to carry loads between neighboring planets.

Boralis – The larger of two suns in the solar system.

Bots – Robots designed to perform tasks formerly assigned to humans.

Cab-bot – Bots designed to drive air taxis and interact as tour guides with passengers.

Charlis – The smaller of the solar system's two suns.

Chrono — Watch.

Council of Lords - The elected body that works with the High Lord Councilor to lead the Borali Alliance.

Courier Craft - round, silver craft designed to carry supplies and papers between planets in the solar system with light speed drives.

Daken – large, blue, predatory birds, coveted for their beautiful feathers.

E-post – messages sent over the computer, like e-mail. Usually sent via computer terminals or kiosks in public places.

Feruca – a black fruit with a thin skin and soft pulp.

Floater - a floating platform with two seats facing a control panel at the front; which moves by manipulating the air underneath to float above the ground. The largest Floaters have benches to hold as many as twenty troops — more if ten stand in the middle. Smaller models are typically designed for four or five passengers.

Gixi - a round, purple fruit grown in orchards on Vertullis and Italis with a delicious, tender pulp and sweet juice.

Gungors - six-legged brown animals with yellow manes raised for their tasty meat.

High Lord Councilor – leader of the Borali Alliance, elected by the Council of Lords. The post typically passes down through members of the same family until the Council decides new blood is required.

Iraja - Capital city of Vertullis.

Italis - Ninth planet in the solar system, home to the Lhamors.

Jax - A blue and oblong fruit with crispy pulp and a bitter taste, which becomes tart and sweeter when boiled; often used as an ingredient in salads.

Legallis - Seventh and largest planet in the solar system and capital of the Borali Alliance.

Legon – Capital city of Legallis and headquarters of the Borali Imperial government.

Lhamor - Native to the planet Italis. Lhamors have green-scaled skin and disproportionally large, orange eyes and four arms, the lower two extending from either side of their large, round stomachs, parallel to the arms which extend out of their shoulders above them.

Lords – Elected members of the Council of Lords, usually of high bloodlines from the upper echelons of Legallian society.

Mech-bot - Bots used as mechanics in starports.

Off-worlder — Person not from the same planet as a person calls home.

Plutonis – The 12th planet in the solar system, an icy world suitable only for natives and the Qiwi antelope. Also the location of the Borali Alliance's outermost post, Alpha Base.

Presimion Academy - The Borali Alliance's leading school for future military leaders located on Eleni 1, one of Legallis' largest moons.

Qiwi – Antlered creatures found solely on Plutonis, with dark brown fur and white spots lining either side of their spines. Waist high on most humans, Qiwi have four long legs ending in black hooves. Their antlers can grow up to forty centimeters out from their skulls.

Quats — Striped creatures with long tails similar to Earth's cats but larger, like Cocker Spaniels.

Regallis — Thirteenth planet in the system, habitable only because of its development as a major indoor resort.

Royal Shuttle — Smaller version of the shuttles (see description below) reserved for the Royal family and their guests.

Serve-bot — Bots used for serving patrons in bars and restaurants.

Shuttle — White personnel transport with light gray interior. The cockpit has two black chairs facing a transparent blast shield, surrounded by controls, and is separated by a bulkhead from a passenger compartment containing four rows of seats — two lining each exterior wall and two back-to-back down the center. Each has its own safety harness. Intraplanetary models operate without lightspeed capabilities, while interplanetary models are equipped with ultra-lightspeed drives

Skitter - One-man ground craft that operate on a system allowing it to fly above the planet's surface, higher than a Floater. Sleek and fast, Skitters are easy to maneuver through trees and other obstacles and are known to handle much like Imperial VS28 starfighters.

Talis - A warm beverage brewed from beans grown on Vertullis — somewhat like the old Earth beverage, coffee.

Tertullis — Eighth planet in the solar system, home to tall humanoids similar to humans except for their orangish tinted skin and purple eyes.

Transport — Larger craft used to transport supplies, food, and other loads across the solar system.

Vertullis — Sixth planet in the system and home to the humans known as workers, the only slaves in the solar system.

VS28 - sleek and black starfighters with snub noses and three wings – two longer wings out of each side, and a third shorter wing extending vertically above the fighter's four engines. Each bears its squadron's insignia, and a few bear names given them at a pilot's indulgence. They have laser cannons on each wing as well as in the nose. The cockpit lay beneath a gray, transparent blast shield through which the pilot can see the stars in space around him.

WFR (Worker's Freedom Resistance)- an organized resistance formed by workers on Vertullis to seek freedom from the Borali Alliance's rule.

Workers — Residents of Vertullis, and age-old enemies of the Legallians; they live and work as slaves for the Borali Alliance.

BIOGRAPHY

Born and raised in Central Kansas, Bryan Thomas Schmidt currently resides in El Paso, Texas with a cat and two dogs.

He has had many stories published since in magazines like *Tales Of The Talisman, Digital Dragon, Einstein's Pocket Book,* and in the anthologies *Of Fur and Fire* and *Wandering Weeds.*

His serial space opera collection *The North Star Serial* was published in May 2010. He is currently working on his first fantasy novel, *Sandman* and the sequels to *The Worker Prince. The Worker Prince* is his first published science fiction novel.

His work, agenda, blog, bibliography and other goodies can be found on his website at www.bryanthomasschmidt.net. Bryan also hosts Science Fiction and Fantasy Writer's Chat every Wednesday at 9 p.m. EST on Twitter under the hashtag #sffwrtcht.

CPSIA information can be obtained at www.ICGtesting.com
Printed in the USA
LVOW042106090112

263117LV00002B/3/P

9 780984 020904